Spare

Parts

Book One

Cover art by David Hoult
Cover layout by Erin Fong
Book design & layout by Erin Fong
Editing by Randi Beers

First published by TRR Publishing House 2022
First edition, 2022

ISBN: 978-1-7778505-1-7

aarondeck.com

Contents

Acknowledgement

This book took a lot of time and effort, but it wasn't all mine.

I would like to thank both Erin Fagen and Alexi Surrette for their medical knowledge that helped me keep things on the realistic side.

I would like to thank David Brown who's feedback was invaluable as a beta reader.

A massive thank you to Randi Beers for her phenomenal editing job, even if I still hate you for making me cut out a character almost entirely! A thank you to her husband, Danny Campbell for offering advice and answering my calls at odd times.

Thanks to David Hoult for doing an amazing job on the cover art.

And of course, the biggest thank you goes to my wife, who put up with my shit, gave a lot of advice that I didn't always immediately follow (much to my own detriment), and for all the support she's given me over the course of the five years it took to complete this project.

Part One:
The Doctor

Simon

News article from the Montreal Independent,
April 2nd, 2016

HOSPITAL HEAD HANGS UP HAT AMID CORRUPTION CONCERNS

The RCMP launches second probe into bribery allegations

By Vivian Gregs

At a press conference today, Dr. Gregory Ouellette resigned as chairman of the St. Agnes hospital. This comes amid a probe by the RCMP into an ongoing investigation of kickbacks and pay-for-play schemes in the construction of the city's new super hospital. The probe, launched by the provincial watchdog group against corruption, alleges that Dr. Ouellette took payoffs from multiple contractors to run interference on the provincial government so problems could be manufactured, ensuring the contractors in question could bill up to twice their usual fee.

Dr. Ouellette was hired 8 years ago by the province to spearhead the move of five hospitals into one, super hospital. Since then, the proposed five-hundred million dollar budget has ballooned to over a billion. Watchdog groups took an interest and pestered the RCMP until it opened their original probe. Since then, the problems for Dr. Ouellette snowballed until he tendered his resignation...

The old woman cackled wildly and lifted her bony wrists as far as the restraints would allow. She felt a feather that wasn't there tickle her face. She saw her husband Robbie, dead for the past two years, looming above her.

"Don't Robbie," she said, puckering her lips and attempting to blow some wispy hair off her forehead.

These were the patients Simon hated the most. It wasn't because they were nuts, *that* he could deal with. Low murmurs or inane chatter were one thing, but he hated when the patients were loud. He couldn't deal with *loud*. He also couldn't deal with the looks people shot his way; the silent sorries and sad smirks.

He thanked the nurse who helped him load the patient onto the stretcher. She gave him one of *those* looks and walked away. Simon tilted his head to watch her go. After a good look, he pushed the patient down the quiet, dim hallway toward the elevators. They rode the elevator down two stories with the old woman's voice rebounded around the steel box the whole time. He hoped no one was waiting when the doors opened.

No one was.

He pushed the stretcher through the eighth floor of the medical wing with the old woman yammering the whole way. She was answered more than once from the other geriatric patients that populated it; nonsense speaks to nonsense. They traversed the floor and entered a glass-enclosed connecting bridge. He hit the stainless steel button on his right and the doors opened onto the surgical wing. Right away, even in the dim moonlight, he noted how much cleaner the surgical side was. Where the medical side was dull and leaking grey, here the floors shone with a high buff, reflecting whatever light penetrated the glass. He thought of these things absently. Mostly, his mind was on what The Doctor wanted. It wasn't the first time these thoughts had surfaced, but they were always, and easily, chased away by the same image; a stubby brown envelope containing a thousand bucks. It was not in Simon's nature to dwell on things. Also, he'd rationalized that what The Doctor was doing couldn't be too bad. The patients always came back okay. Always prompt. Always with the proper paperwork. It was no skin off his teeth. He had only to schedule his breaks around these little jaunts. A small price for almost two weeks worth of pay. Still, a certain little thing would gnaw at him if he gave it a chance. Why did The Doctor always choose the ones too far gone? The Doctor didn't cure them. Some died, but most lingered long after their visits, eventually getting transferred to long-term private care facilities. No one suspected anything about what he or The Doctor were doing.

Still, it was *always* the old and the far gone.

They exited the surgical wing and walked their way up to the tunnel that led them to The Women's Pavilion, the old woman laughing maniacally for most of the trip. They encountered no one as they turned into another series of connecting hallways. Simon sighed in relief.

The entrance to the Women's Pavilion was a steep decline for a hundred meters. When they'd left the surgical wing, they'd been on the eighth floor. Because the Women's Pavilion was built higher up on the mountain, they were going to be entering it on the third floor. Simon had to use his whole body weight to keep the stretcher from careening down and crashing into the walls, something he'd thought about letting happen on multiple occasions to annoying patients.

At the bottom of the decline, Simon swung the stretcher into a short hallway on his left. It was long enough to hide the stretcher briefly, if only barely. Digging into his pockets, Simon produced a key and unlocked the set of shabby blue doors with a newish-looking lock. The doors opened onto a long, bleak tunnel bending to the right, far away. He pulled the stretcher in and slipped the doors closed. He waited in the blackness until his eyes adjusted to the sliver of light coming from the bottom of the doors. Then, he reached out and flicked on the lamp that rested on the table near him. The sudden light shot spots into his sight. He shut them and rubbed, opening them slowly. His sight centered on a stale wooden table. On it, along with the lamp, lay his stubby, brown envelope and a slip of paper.

The paper held the pick-up time. He was to return in an hour.

Placing both items in his pockets, he slipped back out into the Women's Pavilion hallway, locking the door behind him. He could hear the old woman making noise on the other side of the door and thought The Doctor had better hurry and shut her up if he didn't want to be found out. No sooner had he completed this thought then the old woman fell silent. Simon briefly pondered opening the door and finally getting a look at *who* The Doctor was. It was the weight of the envelope in his back pocket that convinced him otherwise. Instead, he listened to the stillness of the pavilion around him before returning the way he'd come. On his way back up, he checked his SpectraLink. He had no service.

When he reached the top, he turned right and headed towards the transplant ward. Being the highest pavilion on the mountain, he knew he'd get the best reception. He made his call, got back on the clock, and was given a job. He backtracked to the Surgical Pavilion and took the elevators down to the fourth floor.

Simon walked into the Emergency Department and began speaking to the first nurse he saw. She was short, had a large ass, and was currently too busy to be hit on.

"I'm too busy to find where your patient is," Lindsay told him after lending him her ear for a polite thirty seconds.

"His name is Collins. Barry or Bernie. 'B' something."

"Not mine. Check the board." She sat down, flicked open a file, and began writing. Simon watched her for a brief moment, debated continuing his flirtation, then wandered away toward the center unit.

He found the patient's name. He chatted up a P.A.B., a beneficiary attendant who wiped the patient's asses, changed their linen, and did all the unwanted jobs that didn't fall under anyone elses prerogative. The P.A.B. helped him transfer a Mr. Brandon Collins to a wheelchair. Simon rolled the patient up to the short stay unit on the ninth floor of the surgical wing. He helped place the patient into a bed that he knew had been occupied by a dead man mere hours ago, silently thankful that The Doctor hadn't asked for the body, especially knowing that the body wouldn't be coming back.

He greased the next fifteen minutes by sitting in a chair outside the surgical elevators on the eighth floor. This late at night, there was little foot traffic for him to peruse. Simon called his dispatcher and closed out the job. He asked if anything was coming up.

"Nothing scheduled, but that doesn't mean there ain't any jobs coming up."

"I know," Simon replied and ended the call.

He waited for another twenty minutes, got up, and shuffled back to the Women's Pavilion. He produced the same key and unlocked the same double blue doors. Stepping inside, he grabbed the finished paperwork off the table and inserted it into the patient's chart. Then, he pushed the same crazy old lady through the doors and set her into the alcove while he locked up. That done, he waited and listened. He heard the sound of approaching footsteps. Simon pulled out his cellphone and began a hushed argument with a pretend girlfriend, telling her he hated how clingy she'd become. The footsteps approached and passed by without a single glance in his direction. Once the echoes faded away, he began his final journey of the night back up *that* hallway.

When he reached the top, he saw a portly man pushing an empty cart save for one lone box. It was dull grey plastic with a sharp yellow biohazard logo emblazoned on the side. It struck him as odd that someone would be doing such a run during the waning hours of the night. The housekeeper, because biomedical waste collection fell under their umbrella, gave him a quiet, sharp nod as he passed. It sent a small shiver up Simon's spine. He watched the housekeeper descend the incline he'd just come up and knew where he was headed; it was the only feasible option open in his mind. Without looking back to verify, Simon continued on with his patient.

Simon's patient howled constantly on the way back up to her room. He glanced down at her once, wanting to tell her to shut the fuck up. The words dried up in his mouth when he noticed a small incision along her collarbone. It was weeping blood, and he was disgusted by both the sight of it and himself. He grabbed a sani-wipe off one of the wall containers and un-ceremoniously cleaned the runner of blood that had escaped her tightly sewn wound. Then, he pulled her johnny gown up and tightened it so no one else would see.

After returning the patient to her quarters, he made his way up to the locker room, accepting a job from dispatch along the way. He stood in front of his locker and counted to five. Hearing no one, he opened it and removed the envelope from his back pocket and brought it to his nose; he couldn't resist a taste. He tucked the envelope into the interior pocket of his coat and reluctantly closed his locker, triple check-ing the lock.

He wandered into the bathroom and checked himself out in the mirror.

A semi-handsome face looked back at him. Both the top of his skull and his jawline sported the same three-day stubble, the first bits of grey beginning to show through. A night shift always made him lapse into his scruffy look; there were fewer people to impress, after all. His work shirt, a Polo short sleeve, was a crisp white brightly contrasted against his black skin. His black work pants were well ironed. Now, even after four hours of his shift completed, the creases could still cut cardboard. His shoes matched his shirt, for he who accessorized properly was king. Only, looking down now, he noticed something amiss. Above the sole on his heel was a tiny splash of red. A drop of blood. He reached down with a bare hand, then thought better of it.

Scouring the locker room, he found a container of bleach wipes. Neglecting to put on gloves first, he pulled one out and vigorously rubbed his shoe clean with it. Try as he might, he couldn't remember anyone visibly bleeding on him. It pissed him off slightly.

This place would be great if it wasn't for all the fucking patients, he reasoned with himself. He chuckled inwardly and dropped the crumpled wipe onto the floor before walking out, in search of his next patient.

Todd

Todd was devouring a muffin with his feet up on his desk. Crumbs drifted down onto his overindulged midsection. There was a knock at the door, startling him enough to make him cough flecks of semi-chewed muffin into the air. He looked from his computer screen, littered with emails, to the door.

"Come in."

The door opened, and his new employee walked in. Average height. A little on the skinny side. A face that would get lost in a crowd. Nothing remarkable about the kid stood out, except for the fact that he looked extremely young, and he wasn't Italian. His bland features suggested to Todd that the kid was English, or somewhere from the United Kingdom. Todd just hoped the kid wasn't Scottish. He hated dealing with that accent; granted, he'd only had one *Fucking New Guy* over the past three years that'd been Scottish. If Willie was any yardstick marker, it would prove to be a challenge.

He gestured to the two worn out chairs pushed against the wall, his own groaning in protest with each movement he made. He swung his feet off the desk and stood up, brushing himself off as he did so. He extended his hand and shook the newbie's, gesturing once again to the chairs.

"I'm Todd. You must be Giles." It was a statement.

"Yes, sir."

"Ever have a job before Giles?"

Todd saw a brief look of confusion flash across the kid's face before it became impassive again. "Yes, sir. I worked for my Uncle's cleaning company for almost three years."

"Why'd you leave?" Todd asked, sitting back down.

"I'll make more money here," the kid said with a shrug.

Todd popped the rest of the muffin into his mouth, licked his fingers then grabbed the kid's uniform that was sitting atop his desk, near where his feet had been. It was peppered with pebbles of dirt that fell to the floor when he handed it to the kid.

"Go get changed, then come back to see me."

The kid nodded and left. Todd opened the bottom drawer of his desk, selected a donut, and it disappeared in two bites. He turned back to his computer, pulled up the kid's file, and was baffled that the kid was over twenty. He shrugged. Everyone looked young to him these days. He was on the wrong side of forty and felt even older. He closed the kid's file and went back to dispassionately reading his emails while he waited for the kid's return.

They went up to the seventh floor of the surgical wing together. It was long term care and therefore an easy way to introduce the kid into the system. He saw Marky at once; the tall, lanky Filipino was easy to spot. He was always hanging around the nurse's station, flapping his gums. Todd felt a pang of remorse at leaving the kid in Marky's care knowing the kid would do the majority of the work.

Some things just couldn't be helped.

"Marky, this is your trainee," Todd said as he shuffled up to the desk.

"Day one or two?" Marky asked.

"One."

"Okay. Thanks. I got it."

"I'm sure you do," Todd said, before turning on the well-worn heels of his cheap shoes and walking away.

The Doctor

The framed picture he held in his hands, taken during a particularly hot summer, was of his daughter and him. Her hands were proudly displaying a snake she'd found slithering around in their garden, while her smile showcased two missing teeth.

A raucous roar of laughter drifted up through the vents of his study. His wife was having her monthly book-club meeting in their den. This month it was some pulpy vampire novel that Yvonne, his wife's best friend, had chosen. While he thought the novels they read were of the worst variety, he was happy that their monthly meetings brought a joy to his wife that he rarely did, even after fifteen years.

Plucking a cloth off his desk, The Doctor rubbed the glass until the finger smudges were erased. Replacing the picture, he sighed, and lifted his pen jar where a key was taped to the underside. He pulled it free and bent down, inserting it into the lock. He opened the drawer and pulled out a stack of papers. The top few were blank. He put those aside and laid the stack upon his desk. On them were the notes of his private work, stacked in chronological order with the most recent being on top. He reviewed the procedure he'd done on the latest patient

Simon had brought him. Her blood work was good, better than good, actually. Along with advanced Alzheimers, she suffered from Hepatitis C. Looking at the recent tests he'd had done on the sample showed it was Hep C free. His concoction was a success. Of course, one sample did not mean that it was a sure thing, he'd have to run other tests on more blood samples, but it was a massive step in the right direction; it looked like the work he'd done on Stanley was still paying dividends, many years down the road. Granted, it wasn't the exact strain, but the base was comparable.

The Doctor reached back into the desk and produced a leather, zip-up pencil case. Inside where a multitude of blood and tissue samples. He selected the one matching the paperwork in front of him and looked at it. Something was off. He held it up to the lamp light stationed on his desk and squinted behind a set of thin framed, round glasses. He tilted the vial to a forty-five degree angle and watched the blood slide down the interior of the glass with viscous determination.

"This is not good," he said to himself. More testing would be required, but it didn't look promising. All his previous good feelings evaporated and he sighed. He picked up his wine glass and swirled it, watching as the legs spread with the same slow speed as the blood.

16

An idea was forming in the back of his mind. He put his wine down and jotted "Marangoni Effect???" at the bottom of the sheet of paper.

He went over his research for the next couple hours. He formulated theories, jotting some down, and circled the most promising ones. It was thin, but it was a start. This was how his research always went. He'd make a few advances but have to backtrack to fix whatever problems arose from his tampering with the human genome. He was getting close, though. A few more hurdles and he felt confident his life's work would come to fruition.

When he felt his brain hitting its brick wall, he packed everything away, ensuring to put the handful of blank pages on top, and then locked up. That done, he sat back and raised his near empty wine glass to the picture.

"Soon," he said with a humourless smile.

Alessia

"Do you want to rest?"

"Yes. But I should push a little further, no?"

"If you feel able to, sure. But I don't want you overexerting yourself."

"If I can live with these staples in my chest, and to not pull them out in itching madness, then I can push myself a little further."

Alessia smiled at her client. They were halfway down the hallway of the Cardiac Surgery wing. All heart patients inevitably ended up there and were separated into two silent categories by the staff; those who wanted to go home, and those who didn't. Because they were the only ward with that specialty and turnaround needed to be quick, the staff suffered many late shifts and mandatory meetings. Alessia smiled because her patient, a Mr. Gary Chenowitz, was determined to get home. He pushed himself towards independence with a grim determination few of her patients showed. She smiled because she believed in hard work and admired Mr. Chenowitz's tenacity.

She watched his legs as he took a few more steps. On the fifth, she saw the small spasm in his rectus femoris spread to the surrounding muscles. She slid the commode chair up behind him.

"Sit for a bit," she said, placing a hand gently on the small of his back and guiding him onto the chair. Her student quickly locked the wheels of the chair before gripping Mr. Chenowitz under the armpit, stabilizing the old man's descent.

She caught John's eye above Mr. Chenowitz's head and gave him a quick nod of approval.

"How'd the date go?" John asked while their client sat and caught his breath.

"It was nice."

"Nice enough for a second date?"

"Sure. But I doubt it's going anywhere," she said with a shrug.

"It takes longer than one date to get to know someone."

"I said it was *nice*. I didn't say it was *interesting*." She saw John's eyes widen briefly and felt a pang of regret for the tone she'd used.

"If you say so," John said, abashed.

The two of them shared an uncomfortable silence. Mr. Chenowitz waited for someone to speak. He found the tidbits of staff gossip more interesting than any television show he'd ever sat through. He found that since he was a patient, only a passing character in their life's story, the staff were less concerned about what they said around him; it also helped that they saw him more as a piece of furniture than a person at times. Because of this, he knew some salacious secrets.

"How's the condo search going?"

"Not as well as I'd hoped," Alessia said, reciting the line she'd practiced hundreds of times in her head. "It's tough."

To Alessia, 'tough' was an understatement. 'Tough' was too personal to tell someone like John. No. She'd keep repeating the lie for now. To him. To everyone.

"Tough?" he asked incredulously. "From what I've heard, you've got enough money put away to afford *anything* in this city."

"It's not a matter of money," she said finally. Then, she looked down at Mr. Chenowitz. "Are you ready to continue?"

"Yes, ma'am," he said, firing off a two finger salute. He stood up, and with the help of the teacher and student, finished his circuit.

An hour later, Alessia found herself at the Emerge Ambulance entrance. She sat down on the raised concrete barrier separating the sidewalk from the wild vegetation that grew on the other side. The bare beginnings of the late spring vines snaked their way up the three-meter tall rock wall. The wall was close enough that she could smell the minerals in the water that continuously leaked down it. Sitting further down the embankment was a psych patient and their escort. The escort looked bored while the patient hoovered a cigarette.

Parked along the curb was an ambulance, its putrid yellow and green shade an annoyance to her eyes. She thought about the look in John's eye when she'd told him condo shopping was tough. She was a poor liar. Condo shopping had been easy. She took her time, a whole year, and did extensive research into each piece of property. She'd found one on the ground floor of an old bricked triplex. It had been newly renovated inside with deep brown hardwood floors and all new appliances. Best of all, the area was zoned to allow clinics; she would be able to open her own home business. She'd *had* to have it.

She'd filled out the paperwork and sent an offer. They countered. She countered. They agreed, and she received a copy of the contract. With that piece of paper in hand, she'd returned home and called her parents into their den. By the time they'd arrived, she had the contract on the table, along with a manila folder. She'd practiced the upcoming situation in her head many times, always reminding herself to keep her composure but remain firm. She almost made it.

"What do you mean you bought a house?" her father asked.

"Not a house, Papa. It's an apartment condo."

"So you have no property."

"It has a small yard, but it's still property. It's still an investment."

"Why?" her mother asked.

"Because it's time."

"Time for what?" Her mother slipped a hand onto her father's thigh. He reached down and gave it a reassuring squeeze.

"It's time for me to grow up," she said as she opened the folder and spread the documents it contained upon the table. Her father took his hand from atop her mother's, slipped on his reading glasses, and began examining the papers. Her mother didn't glance down, opting instead to look at Alessia, who shifted uncomfortably a few times while her father mumbled noncommittal sentences. When he finished, he took off his glasses and closed his eyes, pinching the bridge of his nose between his index and thumb as he did so.

"Well?" her mother asked the room.

"I want to start a business for myself," she said. "I'm going to have a physio room in my condo where I'll receive patients."

"But you have a job," her mother said. "You have a *good* job. You're working with doctors, any of which could be a potential husband."

She felt her temper creeping up but stifled it. "I'm not going to leave my job right away. Starting my own clinic will take time. Probably years."

"So you're going to invite random strangers into your home, then," her mother said. Her tone was venom wrapped in a quilt of guilt. Alessia's anger jumped out.

"They will be *clients*."

"Strangers. And you're not married. Who will protect you?"

"Me, Mama. *I'll* protect me," she said, exasperated.

"You're not married," her mother repeated.

She watched her mother's fingers begin twisting her wedding band. *Right on cue. At least my hands are steady,* she thought smugly as silence settled on the room. It was her father who eventually broke it.

He opened his eyes and leaned toward his daughter, reaching out; she gave him her hand willingly enough. He cupped it with his left while his right patted it several times. Then, he gave it a gentle squeeze.

"We are a family, *figlia*. This is a major step in your life, but it's also a major step for us too. We are a family. What we do, we do together. Please, let us all sleep on it for a week or two. Have some discussion on it. You owe us that much, at least."

Suddenly, she felt ashamed. He was right. They were a family and always included each other in every decision. So, she agreed to sleep on it and discuss it over the next two weeks.

That was five days ago, and no further discussion had occurred. *It's fine*, she thought, as the sun traced its way across the ambo's fender. *I gave them time to process my decision. It'll be easier this way.* She felt that the longer they went without saying anything, the better the outcome would be, that they'd come around to her line of thinking. A snap decision would be a hard 'no,' she knew. A long, drawn-out conversation between the two would allow them to see everything in her light; that she was over thirty and it was time to start a life of her own, away from the nest.

She checked her watch and was surprised to see that she could sit in the sun a while longer. She noticed small pockets of activity around her. The open bay doors of the laundry complex, across from the ambulance entrance, were emitting a baritone buzz. She saw mammoth sacks of sheets hoisted by chains and pulleys. Close by, on the sidewalk, she listened to a pocket of people, three employees, and two family members, huffing on cigarettes and talking about the terrible loss suffered by the Alouettes. She watched as an ambulance pulled up to a stop behind the one already parked. A man got out of the passenger side. He saw Alessia sitting there, gave her a quick, soft smile while walking to the back of the ambulance. His partner, a tall, muscled woman, popped the back doors open and climbed inside. The man bent over to open the compartment close to the wheel hub. She noted that his tight pants accentuated an already extremely cute butt, if you were into that kind of thing. She watched the partners unload an elderly patient with efficient ease and little talk, a hefty bag slung over the man's shoulder.

She watched all this and let her mind float free. She thought back to her date the night before. She'd been hot, *smoking hot* was the actual phrase, and Alessia wouldn't have minded getting into her pants, but goddamn had she been dull, vapid, and a little bit racist. While Alessia had been known to jump the bones of those she'd found particularly attractive before, age had sullied that. There had to be a mental connection as well as a physical one. And so, she'd politely refused the offer to go up to her date's apartment, pointedly not noticing the seductive eyes thrown her way. It hadn't been easy as she *did* have a body to die for. She mused on the woman's curves for a bit before checking her watch. She got up, stretched, then headed back inside.

Sheela

Thank fuck she was free until next month! Sheela hated the meetings with her fuckin' court appointed shrink.

The first year was the worst. Twice a week for the first six months followed by once a week for the remaining six months. Plus a boatload of "voluntary" NA meetings. Now, the shrink meetings were bi-weekly. While she was able to admit to herself that they *did* help, it was the neurotic little woman she talked to, a Dr. Wosniack, that made her dread the meetings; *that chick had to be fuckin' mental herself if she's been working at this place for thirty years.*

During their meetings, she never approached Sheela. She was always seated behind her desk, some color of file folder in front of her. As the weeks wore into months and then surpassed the year mark, the file folders had darkened in color and bulked in thickness. Sheela felt that The Wahz was always trying to trick her into admitting something she'd never done. After every answer Sheela would give, The Wahz would flip through her file, make a subtle mark next to some sentence, give a perfunctory nod, and then ask Sheela to continue.

Sheela reached the elevator and hit the button. While she waited, she fished around in her pockets for her phone. The elevator chimed and arrived while she was digging in her purse. The doors slid shut, and it descended to another waiting patient, *sans* Sheela.

Shit, she couldn't find it. She must have left it in The Wahz's office. Shit! She turned in the direction of the office and trudged down the hallway. When she got there, some twinge of intuition made her pause, her knuckles poised a few inches away from the door. Instead of knocking, she shifted her weight to the right and peered into the window slit that ran parallel to the door. Inside, she saw The Wahz down on her knees, a container of bleach wipes in her left hand while her right clutched one and was furiously scrubbing away at the chair Sheela had been sitting in. When the chair was clean, Sheela watched The Wahz crumple up the wipe and throw it away. Sheela watched The Wahz's mouth go slack, unhinged, as it opened to enormous proportions, before she jammed her whole hand into her mouth to the wrist.

What in the fuck is that?

Sheela stepped back from the window and shivered. She searched her pockets and purse again, hoping beyond hope to find her phone. She had no such luck. Finally, with a slight tremble in her hand, she knocked and waited.

After an unbearably long time, she heard The Wahz shout through the door.

"Who is it?"

Sheela almost didn't answer. Almost.

"It's Sheela, Dr. Wosniack. I think I left my phone in your office."

She could picture The Wahz taking her quick, small steps towards the door. She could even hear the swish of her slippers on the carpet. The door opened, but not fully. The Wahz handed the phone to Sheela and looked at her. Sheela felt herself being judged, sized up, considered for a meal. She shivered again and thought she saw a flickering pull at the corners of The Wahz's lips.

Was that a smile?

"Thank you," she said with a small voice.

"Anything else?"

"No."

"Then please leave. I have another client coming soon."

Sheela turned and walked toward the elevator. She reached out to hit the button, thought of The Wahz's jaw again and opted for the stairs; a hasty retreat was always fuckin' best.

She pushed the heavy, red stairwell door open and stepped in. She clutched the railing and began descending the first flight. There were twelve steep stairs that stopped at a landing, with twelve more descending to the next level. She was halfway to the landing when the door above her closed with a loud snap. It startled Sheela, and her footing slipped; if she hadn't been holding onto the light pink-painted railing, she would have fallen the rest of the way and possibly ended up with a broken ankle or leg. As it was, she kept herself upright at the expense of having her arm overextend itself. She felt first a pull, then a slight burning in her shoulder that she knew would double by days end. Still, she considered herself fuckin' lucky. She descended to the landing and stood there for a few moments, rubbing the sore spot in her right shoulder. She looked at nothing in particular, just shifting her gaze casually over the walls.

Something caught her eye. It was on the outskirts of her peripheral vision. It looked like the wall was moving. She took a tentative step away from where she saw the movement. Then, she scanned the scant stairwell but saw nothing obvious. Nothing moved. Nothing breathed. Nothing stirred. *Probably just my adrenaline washing out,* she thought.

When Sheela felt she had herself under control, she continued down the stairs. She passed by the second floor and then the first. Twice on her descent, she caught something moving along the walls, just outside her field of vision. Every time she turned in its direction, there was nothing but the pockmarked white brick staring back at her. She continued to the basement level, where an exit door was, except, when she got there, there was no door. She stood, dumbfounded, staring at the same pock-marked white bricks. She saw movement again, only this time it was directly in front of her. The wall rippled and expanded out in the middle by a few inches. It hung there, seemingly reaching out to her before retracting. Sheela closed her eyes and shook her head. *It's just a fuckin' lin-gering drug hallucination*, she told herself. It wouldn't wash. With her eyes still closed, she heard a rumbling and felt a faint whisper of hot air push against her face. She squeezed her eyes tighter and told herself, once again, that what she heard and felt wasn't real. Again, it wouldn't wash. Struggling, she counted to twenty and opened her eyes; a trick she'd learned in her meetings.

She looked out at what was once a sta-tionary brick wall. Now, the middle of it was bulging out like a fuckin' pregnant chick ready to pop. She watched in horror as it reverted back to being a wall before expanding again with hypnotic movements. This time, however, it didn't stop. When the majority of the wall had reached the limits of its ballooning, the center

31

kept going. It pushed out in a puff of crumbling dust. The center began to form a limb, stretching out. It stalked toward her at an agonizingly slow speed, yet she was rooted to the ground, unable to comprehend, or believe, what was unfolding before her. It was only when a finger and a thumb materialized at the end of the appendage and plucked a piece of her blouse neatly between them that panic overrode her brain. She turned, wrenching free of the fingers as they ripped a soft square of fabric from her blouse, and bolted up the stairs. She reached the first landing and looked toward the door that held her salvation, except that door had disappeared too. She stood dumbstruck, not believing what her eyes told her to be true. She heard the same sounds as before and looked behind her. The wall on the landing was ballooning out. She had no doubt that another hand would be snatching at her soon. Her brain sent a signal to her legs to run, to GET THE FUCKIN' FUCK OUTTA THERE!

Sheela sprinted up the stairs and saw flickers of movement. When she reached the second-floor landing, she felt something brush against her, struggling for a tentative hold on her clothes. She heard groans of displeasure as she skirted free of everything.

Reaching the top floor, Sheela let out a gasp of defeat. Through the sweat streaked hair

32

plastered to her face, she saw that where a door should be, none was. It was the same pock-marked brick that had greeted her throughout the stairwell. She cried out and slammed her hands against the wall. She felt immediate pain radiating from her shoulder, followed by a more familiar burn of the skin being sheared away on her palms. She pounded until her hands began to go numb. She stopped as the wall began it's all too familiar outward bulge. She cried out with the force of a trapped animal accepting its fate but vowing to fight til death.

Only, she saw that it wasn't the wall bulging out, but rather a door being swung open. Silhouetted amid the door frame was The Wahz.

"What on earth are you doing?" The Wahz asked.

Sheela couldn't answer in words. She collapsed into The Wahz's arms, crying.

Todd

"Ahh, man. Come on. It's Friday. Besides, it's not even fifteen minutes past break time."

"That sounds like an awful lot of excuses," Todd told Rico. "What I'm not hearing is any remorse."

"What do you want me to say? Sorry I had to take a shit?"

"Don't play dumb. I saw you jawing at the bullshit table when I went by," Todd checked his watch for posterity, "eleven minutes ago, now."

Rico screwed up his face. "Okay, so what, I greased my break a bit. Why are you up here banging me on that? There was a couple rooks down there too."

"I'm *banging* you because you should know better. You should be setting a better example to the new guys. That's what seniority is all about, no?"

Todd saw the defiance and anger in Rico. It was plainly written across his face.

"Hussein would never do this."

"Maybe. Maybe not. But I'm docking you the fifteen minutes either way."

Todd waited for Rico to say something. To get in his face. It would do wonders for his

34

mood to bust Rico down another peg. Who knows, if Rico really pushed it, he could skip the verbal and go straight to a written warning.

"Fine," Rico said, stepping past Todd toward his cart parked at the end of the hall.

Todd watched him walk away. When he was sure Rico wouldn't say anything else, he left, taking the elevator from the tenth floor of the surgical wing to the fourth. His mood was sour because he hated working the evening shift. Hussein didn't run a tight ship and every time he tried to enforce the rules, he could feel the disdain for him dripping off the employees. Who in their right mind would choose to work until almost midnight everyday anyway? A bunch of freaks and social pariahs, Todd thought. What's more, he was doing this as a favour for Hussein, a rather large favour now that he'd gotten lip from a lot of the employees. He was going to give the business to Hussein next time they spoke.

The elevator chimed and Todd stepped out and turned toward the Emergency Department. He'd put Giles there this evening and had left the kid alone. He seemed like a good worker, and since Todd hadn't gotten a call from Bobbie, the head nurse, he assumed everything was good. Still, he wanted to show his face to ensure that they knew he was a caring and proactive supervisor.

35

He punched in the code, the double doors swung open, and Todd stepped into Emerge.

Minor care, designated for the walking wounded, was one large square with nine rooms along its exterior walls. Seven designated places along the walls throughout the hallway had stretchers placed in them, with patients occupying each. The scant cubby holes scattered about, cramped spaces with little desk space due to the overflow of medical journals and computers from the early 2000s, were for the doctors. In the middle of Minor Care was a room used to store all their equipment and bedding. Todd did the tour and took a mental note that all the garbages were empty. A checkmark for Giles.

He passed by a dimly lit corridor encased in glass on his left. From inside, Todd heard someone yelling about ants on the walls. Off to his right was the one room triage area. It too was encased in glass; a set of double sliding glass doors bookended each side. One set led into the waiting room, and the other set led to where he was standing. Inside the triage area a nurse and two paramedics were assessing a restrained patient on a stretcher. Todd saw that the patient used all the slack the restraints allowed to continuously scratch at his right leg. His head was constantly moving side to side, like he was stuck perpetually answering 'no' to any and all questions.

He suppressed a shiver and continued into the epicenter. Acute Care. There was a large wooden counter surrounding the area where nurses and doctors congregated to do research, or relax. Above eye level, many monitors shone down with the vitals for each patient.

Continuing deeper into the bowels of Emerge, he passed the three resuscitation rooms. All three doors were closed.

Around a bend and Todd ended up at the far end of Emerge. It was a dark, closed off space with ten beds. Half were in rooms with three walls and a curtain drawn across the opening. The other half, the back half, were sealed by sliding glass doors. These rooms were reserved for the dangerous isolations like tuberculosis or measles. The smell of sickness and despair hung heavy, a tangible thing.

Giles was in none of the areas so Todd backtracked, listening as he passed the three closed resus rooms. He heard movement in Resus 1. He dipped around the corner and entered it through the utility room. Giles wasn't there. The only thing there was a corpse in a zipped up body bag. This time, Todd let his shiver show. He hated being around dead people. He was about to turn away when a flicker of movement caught his eye.

Because the operating-room-like lights were on, he twisted his head in time to see the silhouettes of fingers tracing their way down the interior of the bag.

Todd tried to scream, but it caught in his throat. He waited, frozen for several seconds, for some other noise to punctuate the room, for some additional movement to capture his vision. He`d about given up hope, with palpable relief, when he saw those silhouetted fingers reach up and poke through the head of the zipper. Todd saw the index, middle, ring and pinky push through, one by one. They were all black. As black as the blindness coming, tunneling his vision, wanting to pull him down to its oblivion, if he wished to stay around and see.

He did not and beat a hasty retreat, exiting into the main hallway. He spied Giles coming out of the security office with his cart and waved to him with a hand that was steadier than he felt.

By the time Todd had reached the office, he thought that Hussein owed him a damn big favour.

The Body

The halls of the Emergency Department were quiet. Most patients, and some of the staff, were sleeping; even sickness takes breaks at midnight. The unit coordinator, head nurse, and a P.A.B., all sat behind the central desk. They were waiting for the Porters to come and collect the body for the morgue. The man, now just a body, had been trouble. He died, was resuscitated, died again, was resuscitated again, and was almost stabilized before he crashed a final time. The wife had watched from the hallway as the staff tried to bring the man around for the third time; she'd been escorted away by security when she cried out, ran into the room, and grasped her husband's leg. During and after her removal, the staff continued their fruitless labour.

An hour after she'd called, Bobbi, the head nurse, looked up from her paperwork as the two Porters approached the desk. One was a tall, handsome black man she knew by sight, but couldn't remember his name, Mario or Melvin or something. She flashed him a quick smile that withered when she saw Dennis standing next to him. He smiled down at her, his stained upper teeth making a brief appearance.

"Hi, Bobbi. What room's the goner in?" Dennis asked.

"Resus one."

"Okay. Lead the way."

Bobbi pulled the manila folder from under her notes and stood up. She handed the folder to Dennis and suppressed a shudder when their hands briefly touched.

The Porters followed her down the hall, pushing the morgue truck ahead of them. It was a stretcher with a metal casing surrounding the mattress. Wrapped around the metal was a black canvas tarp draped over it to shield the visitors from the bodies. The P.A.B. slipped off the cover while Bobbi depressed the switch and dropped the metal casings. The Porters grabbed hold of the body and hoisted it over to the cart.

"Motherfucker's heavy," Dennis complained.

"Nah. It's cause he's dead weight," his partner said, a tired tone in his voice. "He's one fifty at most. Quit your bitching and lift."

"He weighed one forty-two at time of death, so you were close," Bobbi said. The handsome Porter shot her a smile as he deposited his end of the body with ease; Dennis was breathing deeply while beads of sweat popped out on his forehead.

Bobbi closed the metal struts and pushed the pin through, locking it in place. The

P.A.B. and Porters stretched the canvas out and put it back on. Then, the Porters thanked the ER staff and wheeled the cart out of the Emergency Department and towards the elevators.

"There are so many things I'd do to her," Dennis said, scratching his crotch thoughtfully, Mario's scowl going unnoticed.

"Like she'd go for your fat ass."

"I've got something fat for her to have."

"Fat and disgusting, more like."

"Keep running your mouth, Somalia, and you'll get some too."

The elevator bell chimed as Mario raised an eyebrow, quizzically. "And you accuse me of being gay," he said without much humour. It was the same tired old routine between them.

"Hey, now. I know you'd like it. No shame in that. I'm just doing my duty. Spreading my love."

"That ain't the only thing you're spreading you skeezy bastard."

The elevator took them down to the third floor. The doors opened and Dennis exited first. He didn't notice the nurse holding a tray of four coffees; Mario almost hitting her with the stretcher when he pushed it out. She jumped back, spilling hot coffee across her hand.

"Shit. I'm sorry," Mario said before shooting Dennis a look.

"No one was hurt," Dennis said with a shrug. He missed the dirty look the nurse gave him as the doors closed. "Besides, it's a night-shift. Calm down, Somalia."

They made quite the pair, side by side. One was pale, bloated and with a face boasting burst capillaries. The other was tall and toned with a midnight complexion.

"I'm not from Somalia, you inbred hick," Mario continued, his tired tone still intact. He mentally cursed Inshan, that Trini prick of a security guard, for shouldering him with the nickname. In truth, he was a third generation Canadian, and no one in his family knew their exact ancestry; they'd been spread across all of Africa, so Somalia was as good a guess as any. It didn't matter. The nickname still sucked.

They pushed the stretcher across the concrete bridge that connected the main pavilions of St. Agnes to the neurological wing; the bridge was situated high across an access road. Technically, it was just another wing of St. Agnes, but its separate civic address gave it some perks. It ran its own staff and budget, while still being provided money from the overall hospital network.

The two Porters were heading there because the Neuro held the final stop for some patients; the up-to-date-once-upon-a-time morgue. The old St. Agnes morgue had been cleared of its previous residents and converted into basement style offices. It would be forever encased in aging brick, forever dank, forever moist, and forever windowless.

After crossing the bridge, they turned right and took the elevator down to the basement. They exited into a long grey hallway stretching away to both the left and right. To the right was the ambulance entrance, along with a bench that would no doubt be currently occupied by Xavier, their resident homeless man. The pair turned left and walked ten paces before coming to the morgue door. They pressed the buzzer and waited.

A squat man in forest green scrubs and a papery mask hanging off one ear opened the door. When he spoke, his voice was low and his words crinkled.

"Ahhh. My new dance partner. Please, bring him this way, gentlemen."

The two porters followed him into a room, squinting against the reflective light; the aide seemed to neither notice, nor care, about the gleam. They continued beyond a set of stainless steel industrial doors. Inside the little room, the light was muffled. They positioned the stretcher by the outstretched cooling board, unzipped, unlocked and unloaded.

"Thanks 'gents," the morgue attendant said, already turning his back on them and beginning the preliminary examination of the body.

Mario zipped up the canvas and re-locked the cage. Dennis left through the metal doors, pawing at his pocket for his cigarettes. Mario pushed the stretcher back into the hall-way and then cleaned it. That done, he brought it back to St. Agnes and found a quiet corner to stash it in.

Neither he, Dennis, nor the morgue at-tendant saw any movement from within the body bag.

What would they have noticed?

Corpses don't move.

Simon

1

They were sitting on bar stools. Her legs were slightly open, which he took as an inviting sign. He inched closer to her and then took a swig of his second Red Stripe. She was drunk and rambling about how she'd done terribly on her finals, and about which classes sucked. Freshmen tended to annoy Simon. Their talk was boring, and he often spent too much on their tab.

"So, like, my stupid prof calls me up in front of the class." She stopped and blew a burp out of the side of her mouth. "She says, like, if I don't stop talking she'll kick me out. Like, hello," she said, throwing her arms wide. Simon watched the beer slop over the rim of her glass. He watched it splash down across the floor, narrowly missing his shoes. "You're not teaching me anything important," she continued. "It's two days before finals. I'm not learning anything important now. My high school chemistry always told me, 'anything you read at three in the morning will not be on the test. Just sleep, and it'll be better.'" She burped again. "Or something like that."

Simon inhaled a waft of french fries and garlic as he leaned forward. Her thighs pressed inward before opening again, brushing his knee. The hand not cradling his beer dropped down and rested on her thigh. He smiled into her eyes.

"It's terrible when profs are hard asses," he said. "I had one this year that rode my ass. Bitches, all of 'em!" He finished, widened his smile until he felt like it would drip off him. She smiled back and put a hand over his, giving it a squeeze.

Simon ordered two shots, one of vodka and one of water, with a third taxed on for the bartender. The shot glasses clinked together and liquid was downed, Simon faking a grimace from his shot of water.

They talked for another half an hour and then left the bar together. He drove them to her place and took her key to unlock the front door before she snatched them back, telling him she could do it. She used the wall as support while moving towards the elevator. When the elevator arrived, she kissed him and called him David. At her door, amid a gale laughter, the keys were fumbled in the lock and dropped a few times until she eventually got the door open. She pulled him inside.

2

Simon drove into the furthest reaches of the parking lot. He found a space that was underneath an overhanging elm that cast leaves and a shadow during noon; in the early morning hours, the space was encased in darkness. He was three hours early for his shift. He parked his car and slept. His dreams, like the night sky, were black.

He awoke when his phone chimed an over-eager alarm. He shut it off and rubbed the remnants of sleep from his eyes. He opened the door and unfolded outside into the crisp morning air. He stretched, catching the few rays of the early morning sun that filtered down through the tree branches. It warmed his skin as he deepened his stretch, accompanying it with a full-bodied yawn. He went to the trunk of his car and opened the bag containing his work uniform. He changed underneath the elm and walked into work.

His first job sent him to Emerge, and it took him fifteen minutes to make it there from the Intensive Care Unit waiting room, one floor above. He spent another five minutes searching for the proper patient stretcher that sat in the hallway. He half-heartedly asked a few nurses wandering the halls if *this* patient was the proper one. He was told, multiple times, to check the chart. He did, and it seemed right. He read the name, a Mrs. Katchem, and asked the lady lying there if she was indeed who the chart said she was. She concurred and began to bitch about her breakfast being late. He solemnly nodded his condolences and mentally thought about suffocating her so he could go back to sleep. He grabbed the stretcher handles and then noticed that the patient's binder was missing. He walked over to the nursing station and found only Bobbi sitting there, hunched over a file and scribbling furiously.

"Do you have the binder on Mrs. Katchem?" he asked.

"It's on the stretcher, Simon" she responded, without looking up.

"It's not," he said.

"Well, it should be."

"It *should* be, but it ain't."

"Did you even look?" She asked briskly. Before he could answer, she waved a dismissive hand at him while the other continued to scribble. "Nevermind. I don't care. If it's not there, check the outgoing flow logs."

He turned to his left and spun the circular holder that resided on the countertop. He sifted through the names until he came up with the one he was searching for.

"Thanks," he said, his words dripping in a sarcastic drawl that was bordering on anger. "I found it. Crisis averted."

Bobbi put her pen down and looked up at him with sixteen-hour-shift eyes overflowing with fury.

"I'm *glad* you figured it out. Now if you wouldn't mind, can I get back to the task at hand, which is trying to save a patient's life?"

Simon thought of a dozen retorts but swallowed them all, settling for calling her a bitch in his head. He returned to his patient and pushed her towards the CT scan. The patient attempted to make small talk that Simon largely ignored, only interjecting a few wayward grunts of acknowledgment. She was rambling again about her breakfast being late; a problem Simon couldn't give a shit about. What he *could* give a shit about was dropping this patient off and greasing this job for an extra twenty minutes so he could go bang the Sandman.

It was not to be.

Simon showed up at the computed tomography scan and was told that he had the wrong patient.

"Excuse me?" he asked incredulously.

"Not necessary," the jovial clerk said laughing, her belly shaking with the force of it, even though Simon was sure it was the millionth time she'd told that joke this year. He swallowed the headache that was creeping beyond his eyes and threatening his temples, to little effect.

"What do you mean I have the wrong patient?"

"It's simple," she said, smiling a toothy grin up at him. "You have the wrong patient."

"Well, who am I supposed to bring?"

"I couldn't tell you. All I know is that we don't have a Mrs. Katchem getting a scan today."

"Can you check again?"

"Sure," she said. Her fingers flicked across the keyboard as she scanned the screen. She looked back up at him. "Nope. No one with that name scheduled today."

"Are you sure?" he asked again. He heard the tone of his voice and immediately cringed at how pathetic it sounded. All he wanted was sleep. All he wanted was to be away from these people. He cursed himself, not for the first nor the last time in his life, that he should have called in sick instead of trying to brave the world. "I was told to bring her here," he continued. "Can't you just slide her in now, or in thirty minutes, and then we both won't have to worry about it?"

He watched as the smile slid off her face like she was a snake shedding skin.

"No. I can't. We have a back-up of patients that have been scheduled. I'm not screwing myself, and my team, just to placate you. Find the right patient, and I'll help you. Otherwise, we've got enough work here to last a year."

He opened his mouth to say more, but once again decided to keep it shut. All his years of trolling bars had taught him when to push an issue and when not to; he was defeated and knew it.

"Where are you supposed to be going today?" he asked the patient.

"No one has told me anything. I was supposed to be getting breakfast," she crowed.

It was then that he felt his pager vibrate. He hooked his hand around it and turned it up to him. He saw the number and promptly decided to ignore it. He couldn't deal with The Doctor's shit right then.

"Sorry about that," he told Mrs. Katchem. "I'll have you back and snacking on cereal in no time." He turned his attention to the receptionist who'd seemed like she'd already forgotten him. "Thanks for your time," he said.

"Yeah," she said, not bothering to take her eyes off her computer screen. He wheeled the patient back in the direction of Emerge. En route, he called his dispatcher.

"Dispatch," Trevor said.

"It's Simon. You told me to bring a Mrs. Katchem to CT from Emerge."

"One second please," Trevor said. Simon heard the clickety-clack of a keyboard as the file for his current job was brought up. "Yep. Done?"

"No. You gave me the wrong patient. She ain't scheduled to be anywhere."

"You sure, Simon?"

"Yes, I'm fucking sure. I got told off by Bobbi in Emerge for asking questions about the patient and then told off by the bitch in reception at CT for bringing the wrong patient." He rubbed a hand across his face and waited, hearing the familiar keyboard making its music.

"Dunno, dude. That's what I've got here."

"One sec," Simon said into the phone. He pushed the stretcher against the wall in the hallway. "I'll only be a minute," he told Mrs. Katchem. She brayed a complaint, but Simon didn't care. He walked off toward an unoccupied area of the hallway.

"What the fuck?" he asked sharply. "I'm looking like an asshole in front of a lot of people. It ain't my fault. Someone on the other end fucked up."

"I understand. But you get that it's not on my end either, right? I'm given a job and have to give it out. You just happened to get said job."

"Fuck that. I don't like looking like a fool."

"I understand, but are you sure you checked."

"Check?" Simon heard his voice rising, threatening to ring out along the hallway and throughout his head. He tried to calm himself by taking a few large breaths. "Yes, I checked," he said through gritted teeth. "I checked with Bobbi, and I checked with that fat bitch that works for CT. Don't send me on a bullshit job!"

"I'm just giving you the information I get, Simon. Don't get mad at me."

"I don't have time for this," Simon said, his temper flaring. "Don't call me for garbage jobs that you don't know shit about."

"Garbage jobs?" Trevor asked. "What time did I dispatch you for this job?"

"Listen - "

"No, you listen," Trevor said, his voice remaining calm. "You wanna be pissed? I get it. The job got fucked up. But the fact of the matter is you took thirty minutes to transport a patient a couple hundred metres. If I'd have given this job to anyone else, they'd be happy. I gave it to you because I know you. It's a Friday. Don't bring your bullshit to me."

"Listen," he tried again.

"You really wanna go down this road?"

Simon felt his pager go off. He glanced down and saw that again, it was from The Doctor. *When it rains, it pours*, Simon thought.

"No. I don't," Simon said meekly, admitting defeat. "So what am I gonna do with my patient?"

"Seriously, Simon? Return her, for fuck sakes."

"You sure? Because I was supposed to bring her to CT, which you told me, so am I really supposed to return her?"

Simon heard an audible pause from Trevor and knew what it meant. He smiled when he heard Trevor come back over the phone with a simple order.

"Return her and wait until I give you something else."

Simon did as told. He placed Mrs. Katchem back in the hallway of Emerge and then dropped the binder off in the carousel of patient files while giving Bobbi a self-satisfied smirk. Then, he walked up to the Intensive Care Unit's waiting room, found himself a corner, and slept until his next call.

Simon felt his pager vibrate for the fourth time that day and once again ignored it. He was talking to Alessia. Her long, dark hair was too enticing to warrant an interruption. He wondered, and not for the first time, what that hair would feel like wrapped around his fist, sliding through his fingers, as he pulled it while fucking her from behind. He felt himself starting to get hard and wondered if she'd be able to smell the lingering scent of his previous night's hookup on him, and if so, was it turning her on?

Because of his wandering mind, he'd missed her question.

"I'm sorry. Say that again." He flashed a smile at her.

"I asked if you'd ever been to New City Gas before?"

"Nope. Where's that?"

"Downtown. By the old Forum."

"Is it a club?"

"Kind of. It's more a dance hall for EDM and drum and bass type stuff."

"Any good talent there?" he asked, brushing her body briefly with his eyes.

"Yep. It's one of the premiere spots for a lot of international DJs and a few up-and-comers."

"Oh."

He watched Alessia shift her weight to her other foot and look to her right. She was about to speak when he cut her off.

"You still living with your parents?"'

He saw her body sag slightly, like all of a sudden she remembered that gravity existed. "Yes," she said finally. "But I'm planning on buying a condo soon."

"Cool. Let me know when you've got a new place. I can take you out to celebrate."

"Sounds fun," she said. She was looking to her right again. "Anyway, I gotta go to a meeting. See you later, Simon."

He kept his back against the wall, his palms resting along the rail, and watched her walk away. His mind retreated to its previous thoughts and he smiled. It first faltered, then died completely when he lifted the pager and saw the message running across it.

"Bring me your next corpse," it read.

He felt his stomach plummet as all the air rushed out of him in a long, low woof. Goosebumps pimpled across his body as a cold shiver wracked him. He was glad the wall was propping him up. He blinked and checked the message again, not trusting his eyes. The message and the full-bodied feeling remained the same. As per protocol with The Doctor, he deleted the message.

A dead body? He's never asked for that before. What the hell does he want with a dead body?

He took a few deep breaths and focused his vision on a circle of visitors, far down the hall on his left, in deep discussion with a physician. He watched the physician shake his head, and a young man burst into tears. An elderly woman pulled the young man into a tight, consoling embrace. *The Doc's gonna get his order pretty soon,* Simon thought. He shivered again. He watched the physician offer more empty platitudes then walk away, leaving the family alone with their grief.

As he walked by, Simon saw an arm he wasn't sure was his reach out and touch the physician on the shoulder. He wheeled toward Simon, a look of naked annoyance on his face.

"What?"

"How bad is it?"

"How bad is what?" the physician snapped.

"The diagnosis. Is he - " Simon gulped down empty air and struggled to get the last word out. "Dead?"

"And why should I be giving you this information?"

"I'm a friend of the family," he said with an easy-to-emulate look of unease.

57

The physician's look softened, his face becoming infused with gentle lines. It was a stark contrast to the scrunched up face he'd been sporting mere moments ago. It dropped ten years off him.

"I'm sorry, but it's not good. There were some complications. He's in a coma now, and his vitals are diminishing. He's got a day or two. At most."

"Thanks."

Simon breathed a sigh of relief that was mistaken for grief by the physician. He gave Simon a solitary sorry before strolling away. Simon pulled out his SpectraLink and started dialing *the* extension. After three numbers, he stopped. His mind came crashing back with a sobering thought. He was standing in a hallway, surrounded by all kinds of staff, patients, and family members. This was not the proper place to discuss his worries about bringing a body down to *the* hallway.

Clipping the phone back onto his belt, he began walking towards the emergency exit at the far end of the hall. He passed by a severely balding, portly man who was stacking grey plastic biohazard boxes onto a trolley. The man looked up as Simon passed, giving him a hard stare before returning to his work with many grunts and groans. Simon had seen the guy around. Had seen him, in fact, around *that* hallway more than once. The hard, narrow-eyed look the man gave Simon unnerved him.

"Asshole," Simon said after he was beyond earshot. He reached the end of the hallway and ducked into the stairwell.

It was bland, as far as stairwells went. It was a flat white with the only bits of color coming from the accumulated dirt and dust bunnies in the corners and on the landings above and below; it was a place seldom used and oft forgotten.

He pulled his SpectraLink out but his fingers stopped, hovering above the keys. He jerked his head to the left seeing a ripple pulse through the wall. He jumped involuntarily and stared hard at the wall. It didn't move again. *God, I'm so fucking tired,* he thought and rubbed his eyes before turning his attention back to his Spectra and dialed The Doctor's extension. It was answered on the third ring.

The Doctor

Despite knowing it was a risky move, The Doctor sent Simon's pager his request opposed to the regular "Call Me" he usually sent. He'd been ignored the previous three times and wanted Simon to know the importance of the issue at hand. He didn't have to wait long for an agitated Simon to call.

He let the phone ring a few times before answering.

"Hello?"

"It's Simon. Can you talk?"

He waited for the space of three long breaths.

"Sure."

"I don't know about your last page."

"What don't you know about my last page?" he asked, keeping his voice light.

"A body?" The Doctor could hear the anger trying to bleed through Simon's tone. He suspected he was talking through his teeth. "A fucking *body*? It's a bit much, no?"

"Simon, Simon. Why the trepidation? You've brought me live patients before without a care in the world. Why does one corpse trouble you so?" He took off his glasses and pinched the bridge of his nose. This new change of heart within Simon was getting harder and harder to manage.

"Because it does. It's -" There was a momentary pause and The Doctor knew what was coming next. "It's *wrong!*"

He chose his next words carefully.

"Now, now. I've given back each patient in good health, and they've never complained. But what I need now I cannot get from someone alive. I need a corpse."

"Why don't you go to the morgue yourself? You could have your pick."

"Because I need a fresh one. Besides," he shrugged, "what we're doing isn't strictly legal, now is it?"

"And what *are* we doing?"

"Nothing that concerns you. Your knowledge starts and finishes with the transportation of the materials I need." It was a struggle, but The Doctor kept his voice calm. Simon clearly couldn't control his anger.

"Materials?" It was almost a shout, The Doctor hearing the anger seeping between his teeth. "These are fucking *people,* not just materials."

"Yes, yes, fine. But they *house* the materials I need," The Doctor said, reciting a line from his wife's last book club novel.

"Listen. I don't know how I'd even go about getting you a body, anyway. It's a two-

man job, and unless you want someone else nos-
ing around in your shit, it can't be done."

And there it was, the way The Doctor
could get what he wanted out of Simon.

"So *that's* what this is about? Fine. I'll
double your payment for this 'two-man job.'"

"But -"

The Doctor waited. When it was clear
that Simon needed just a little more of a push,
The Doctor gave it.

"Don't worry, Simon. It doesn't have to
be today, or even next week. Just get me a
corpse by the end of the month, and I'll take
care of the rest, like I always do."

With that, he hung up, not wanting to
give Simon another moment to reconsider.

Problems upon problems upon prob-
lems. He had to find a way to alleviate a few of
them before they got on top of him. His first
thought was to ditch Simon, which he knew he
was going to do in time, once his creation was
up and moving. It pained him, as he'd been using Simon for years. He'd scoured the personnel
files, gaining access by sweet-talking the HR di-
rector, saying he wanted to develop a team
around him that would do their jobs to his prescribed set of standards. That done, he went
looking for a loser. Simon had never been on the
top of the pile, but he'd heard the rumours
floating around. The guy lived with his mother,

worked a dead-end job but had illusions of grandeur, thought he was the smartest person in the room despite being quite the opposite. It was a perfect fit. He'd started by probing Simon, offering a little extra spending money for little things at first, all on the phone; one thing The Doctor made sure of was that Simon had never seen his face. After four jobs, once the hooks were in some would say, he offered Simon the first real job, for much better pay. Simon had jumped at the idea and from then, it had been an easy working relationship; however, things change over time it seems.

It couldn't be helped. He needed Simon for two more jobs and then they would be quits. The decision carried a lot of weight, a lot of history. It didn't matter. It's what would be best in the long run. He had no illusions about that.

That was one problem dealt with. It still left him with the biggest bastard on the table, which was why he'd called Simon. After seeing that the blood wasn't reacting to how he'd wanted to to his serum, he came up with a stop-gap measure. The stop-gap turned into a plan, which had turned into a solution, if he could implement it. He needed access to an entire nervous system. He needed access to an entire network of veins to transplant into his creation. He needed access to a body.

63

Alessia

News article from the *Montreal Independent*, April 23rd, 2017

WARRANT ISSUED FOR FORMER HOSPITAL HEAD DR. GREGORY OUELLETTE

Ouellette Opts Out of Canada and is On the Lamb

By Vivian Gregs

The RCMP issued an international warrant for Dr. Gregory Ouellette in the wake of findings from their two year probe. Ouellette was found to have taken kickbacks from construction conglomerate LSC to push its bid of the super hospital through. Emails from a co-conspirator reveal that Ouellette funnelled money through a shell corporation, backed by Russian banks, in Dubai.

An international task force has been assembled, but sources close to the investigation say there is a minimal chance of the province getting any money back. Minister of Foreign Affairs, Roberta Hallderon, spoke candidly at a presser.

"We have no extradition treaty with the United Arab Emirates. While we (the government) will be doing everything in our power to repatriate Mr. Ouellette, our outlook does not remain hopeful." Preliminary reports show that Ouellette left the country with more than 20 million dollars in embezzled funds, along with a vast list of co-conspirators that the federal government wishes to obtain so they can dole out lengthy prison sentences...

"You still living with your parents?"

Goddamnit. This question again? She saw Simon staring at her, stretching his lips into a smile that Alessia thought looked more predatory than charming. "Yes," she said finally. "But I'm planning on getting a condo soon."

"Cool. Let me know when you've got a new place. I can take you out to celebrate."

"Sounds fun," she told him in a dry voice, knowing she'd be dead before ever going on a date with Simon. "Anyway, I gotta go to a meeting. See you later, Simon."

She walked away, taking a squirt of hand sanitizer as she passed the dispenser, happy to disengage from the conversation. She could tolerate Simon for short bursts of time, but he set her nerves on end. She could almost see the teeth hidden behind each action and gesture.

She reached the conference room and the end of the hallway and waited outside the door; it was empty, and she didn't want to be seen as overly eager. She passed the idle time on her phone. She was deep into an article about the Dyatlov Pass incident. She was reading the details about the expedition's tents and how they'd been shredded. It was intoxicating. She was drawn in. Engrossed. Because of this, she didn't hear her supervisor, George McKinnon, approach. She only knew he was there when he said "hello," and she started, almost dropping her phone.

"Shit. I didn't see you. You almost scared me to death," she half laughed, half exclaimed.

"Sorry," he said, not looking sorry in the least. "What're you reading?"

"Well -" She thumbed through her phone, pretending to look for the article; in reality, it was an excuse to compose herself a bit. "It's about the Dyatlov Pass."

He snapped his fingers. "Ahh yes, the Russian mountain mystery. I've heard about it. What about it?"

"Oh. Well, I was reading about the different 'what-if' scenarios."

"What's your favorite theory?"

"Realistically, it was probably an avalanche."

"Boring."

She smiled and held up her finger. "But," she said, "my personal favourite is the overly large radioactive bear theory."

"I've never heard that one. Sounds pretty good. Do you think that's where bigfoot came from?"

"It has to be," she said, laughing.

He walked by her and entered the room, seating himself at the table. She followed him in.

"What's your suggestion for Mr. Coy?" he asked, placing a light blue folder and a tablet on the table, using their downtime to get straight to other business.

"I'd like to keep him one more day. He's not ready to climb stairs unassisted yet."

"Can he do the hallway?"

"Yes, but that's not the problem. He's got severe issues with descending. He gets vertigo and can't go beyond two steps without almost falling. Without someone to catch him at home, I'm afraid he'll be back here within a day."

"That bad?"

"That bad," she agreed.

"Okay. I'll see what I can do. No guarantees."

"I know."

"And school?" McKinnon asked, shifting the subject.

"It's good. I'm not taking any summer classes, but that doesn't mean I'm not sweating over my thesis."

"Which is on?"

"Maximizing care on a budget." She saw McKinnon raise an eyebrow and continued quickly. "I'm trying to put down a list of exercises that help stimulate the patient in the shortest time frame possible." She shrugged.

"A subject close to all our hearts," There was no hint of humour in his voice.

Alessia leaned forward, resting her elbows on the table. "Do you know if they've set a date for the move?"

McKinnon began working an imaginary piece of gum in his mouth. "They have," he said slowly, "but I don't know how firm it is. They're pushing for early spring of next year." His voice rose at the end, signifying it more question than statement.

"Ten months, essentially."

"Yep."

"What's the plan for us?"

"Nothing concrete yet," he said, sighing and leaning back in his chair. "But at least there's something of an outline for it."

"Only an outline?" she asked incredulously. "We've been planning the move for years!"

"It's not the planning that's the problem," McKinnon said, still working his jaw. He leaned over and matched Alessia's posture. "It's the money," he half whispered.

"I've heard rumours. I mean, we all have, but how bad is it?"

"Well, pretty much anyone who touched a dollar stole fifty cents, from the dealmakers and consultants to the construction crews and caterers."

They looked at each other and were still sharing the look when the unit head-nurse, Marjorie, and a few others, came in. Last was a face Alessia didn't recognize. She was in her late thirties, and her smoky black pantsuit was half a size too small, riding up her cuffs and exposing pudgy wrists.

Alessia greeted everyone in turn as they sat down, including the mystery woman. She was introduced as Valerie Genereux and was the head of Human Resources for the hospital. Then, the meeting began.

Mckinnon argued for Mr. Coy's continued stay, but after Marjorie cited a heart patient slated for delivery from the O.R., among two other patients from step-down, and finally the budget, Mr. Coy was placed on the discharge list. They moved through Infection Control's complaints and then set a schedule for N95 mask fitting. All this was done with complaisant boredom on the faces in the room.

"Last item is the move," the unfamiliar woman said; Valerie Genereux. She stood up, holding her tablet in one hand. There was some shuffling from the people in the room. Alessia glanced around and saw stone faces, hands and fingers outstretched, waiting to take notes. "Unfortunately," she continued, "I don't think anyone in this room has any answers to any questions our employees may ask, but we can build something based around what we know.

"No, they haven't picked a date yet, *but* they've picked a month. We're moving in April. We have a year. Obviously, we have no idea what our patient load will be at the time, but we will be shutting down the O.R. sometime during the 'Go' week." Valerie looked around the room as she spoke. "I expect worst-case contingencies from each of you within the next two months. We'll start there and work backward. Any questions?"

The room was silent for a brief span. Someone coughed while others scratched pens onto pads. The Surgical Head, a great blimp of a man named Kenneth, broke the silence.

"I was led to believe we'd be operating on half capacity starting the week before 'Go' week and gradually scaling down."

"You will, you will. We may have to close a room or two sooner, however, as we may need to prep some of the equipment sooner than expected."

Kenneth grunted. "We'll need to know soonest," he said as he scratched a line across his notepad.

"When do we get to visit the site?" Dr. Uile asked.

Valerie rapidly flicked her finger across her tablet screen. "Ahh, here it is. We're in the process of scheduling. We'll let you know when we do."

"So you want us to do all the legwork," McKinnon said, an edge creeping into his voice.

"No. It's not like that."

"Listen," he interrupted her, "no bullshit. If I have to do extra work to get the move to happen smoother, so be it. But don't lead me," he paused and waved an open palm toward half the room. "Don't lead *us* into something blind."

"Okay." Valerie nodded. Still looking down, she picked a strand of hair off the cuff of her right sleeve. She tugged and set everything

Sheela

She raised her hand and the group leader nodded at her. She stood up and felt the familiar rush of embarrassment before brushing it aside. She breathed in and recited her piece.

"Hi. My name's Sheela, and I'm an addict."

They answered back, warm and welcoming. She took another deep breath and scanned the walls of the hospital gymnasium. It was the same stale color as the previous weeks. She closed her eyes and thought back to the *other* wall; to how terrified she'd been when it had reached out for her. She exhaled, long and full. It steadied her, and she knew how to begin.

"I've been sober for almost twenty-two months and I've been doing well with it. At least, I *was* doing well with it." She looked around at the tired, the hopeful, and the bored in the room. "But now - I'm - I'm scared," she finished, her voice hitching as she spoke the final word. She heard sounds of encouragement from the group. She looked down at her hands, figuring it would be easier.

"I was never one for psychedelics," she started. "Mine was always heroin or cocaine. There's nothing better than that first rush that knocks you on your ass. Sometimes I can still

73

taste it in the back of my throat. It's always the worst fuckin' drip imaginable. Anyway. I've never been a fan of drugs that make you see things because that's terrifying to me." She chuckled, then spoke to herself, "Acid is *my* anti-drug." The circle laughed along with her. Still looking down at her hands, she continued. "Yet, not too long ago, I hallucinated. These weren't the fun hallucinations I was told about. I - I was fuckin' freaked out." It was then that she noticed a lighter had found its way between her fingers. She watched it walk along her knuckles before squeezing it between her palms. She looked up at the open room then, sliding the lighter back into her pocket with practiced ease.

"These hallucinations were intense," she said finally. "They were too realistic. I feared for my fuckin' life. At one point, and this is the hardest and weirdest thing to admit, the walls reached out and tried to grab me." She clutched at the sleeve of her flannel shirt, squeezing it hard, mimicking the wall's move-ment. "It tried to pull me in. It scared me enough that I collapsed, crying into the first pair of arms I found. I needed a hug, and thank-fully, I got one." There were more chuckles this time as she spoke the last line. Sheela knew it was a reflex action, but hated the room all the same. How could *they* know the fear and fuckin' emptiness she'd felt, running through a seemingly never-ending stairwell hell-bent on consuming her. "I guess my question is," she continued, "has anyone else ever experienced something so vivid that they almost lost their minds?"

And with that, she sat down. A chorus of "thank you for sharing" echoed around the room.

Someone raised their hand and were called upon. They didn't stand up.

"Hi. My name's James, and I'm an addict." The room answered back with their greeting, Sheela included. "You're not alone. Not everyone gets 'em, but I fucking did. I got detoxed in a jail hospital, half inna coma. I don't remember shit of the first bit, but fuck did I ever get those hallucinations. They came about a month after I got outta the hospital. I know the feeling. I know how real it seems."

James was leaning forward, looking directly at her, his steady eyes burning with empathy. He continued. "I know it's hard to get over, but you will if you have faith." He sat back in his wheelchair, his piece done.

Another hand went up and was called upon. This person too had dealt with hallucinations; her's were of the giant insect variety. Sheela saw the woman had a can of Raid stationed at her feet. She also noticed that the woman hadn't showered in a long while and sent a bit of her heart out to her. As the tale twisted along, Sheela put her ears on autopilot and scanned the room. She could tell from the faces which ones had a shared experience and which ones hadn't. There was one woman, seated almost directly across from her, that looked more disinterested than anyone else. She had long brown hair and mostly kept her nose to her telephone. Occasionally, the woman would look around, offer a solemn smile to no one in particular, then dip back to her phone. Sheela felt a bolt of anger building up and quashed it; whether the woman cared or not, she'd always been at the rare Thursday meetings that Sheela'd attended.

After the meeting ended, Sheela walked over to her sponsor, book in hand. He greeted her with a gruff hug and took her book. She watched him briefly glance at the filled out lines since his last signature. He signed his name and the date and then handed it back to her.

"I'm so glad to see you back," he said, pushing his glasses back up his nose.

"I always make it when I can," she replied.

"I get worried."

"It's nothing. I always end up at two or three during the week. It just depends on how I'm feeling the day of."

"Okay. I won't push. I see you're still going. I just get worried and then I miss you."

Sheela didn't reply. They looked at each other while Henne took a long swallow of coffee. He was about to take another one when the woman with brown hair came up to greet him.

"Hi Alessia," he said, setting his coffee down and giving her the same hug he'd given Sheela. She watched Alessia's shoulders soften in Henne's grasp. "How've you been?" he asked her.

"Good. Busy with work. I told you I took on some new students last semester. Now I get emails at all hours from them," she said, waving her phone in front of her like she was embarrassed.

"Well, stay strong. I'm glad to see you again."

"You too." Alessia held out a book that was identical to Sheela's. Henne took it, marked his name and date in it, then handed it back.

"Thanks," Alessia said, before turning around and leaving.

Henne picked his coffee up off the table, took a sip, and looked back at Sheela.

"Now why can't you be more like her?" he asked.

"Her how?" Sheela said.

"Reliable. Every Thursday she's here, sitting in the same place. We have the same brief talk after every meeting, and then she goes. It's routine. It's something that helps us get by."

"For you? Maybe. For her? Maybe. Routine ain't for me." Sheela felt the disgust bleed into her voice. "I'm working my steps. I'm doing my time. *I did my fuckin' time!* I appreciate your help and all, but don't tell me how to live my life. Ain't that what you always preach? We're all different and have different needs?"

"But we all share a commonality," he finished. He carried a hurt look on his face that further agitated Sheela.

"Whatever. You signed my book. I'm out. I'll see you next time I'm around."

"Please," he said.

Sheela walked away then, leaving the last word hanging between them. She didn't know if it had been a question, statement, or plea. She didn't care.

The stairs were empty when she took them up one flight and exited into a golden sunset. She bummed a cigarette from one of the others in the meeting then walked a little way around the corner of the building. She stood directly in the last rays of light that filtered down from above and inhaled. She closed her eyes and hitched one foot up, propping herself against the wall with her heel. She rolled up the sleeves of her sweater to allow any blip of sun to touch her arms. It was what she needed. She stayed that way until she felt the radiant warmth move across her nose and settle on her cheek. She opened her eyes and left before it could slip further away.

She walked to the nearest metro station and descended to the platform. She walked to the front most area and waited for the next eastbound train. She stood by the yellow line and stared out at nothing. She'd forgotten her working pair of headphones at her apartment, so she was left with no entertainment. Instead, she stood, staring out and trying to imagine the wall on the other side of the platform coming to life. She tried to imagine it spewing out, brick by brick, and slamming into the unsuspecting commuters. She strained to see the walls trickling water like sweat at the exuded force to become a sentient thing.

Nothing moved. Nothing happened. The walls stayed where they were.

The metro screamed by, startling her out of her trance. She careened briefly and had a terrifying, but not-so-uninviting thought of being sucked forward and down onto the rails of the metro and being chewed between the metal. She got herself under control and entered the car.

She got off eight stops later, in the heart of Hochelaga. She traversed a young, clean park, then turned left onto rue Rouen. It was still early, but the streets held fewer people than she'd have thought.

She'd just turned south after a couple of blocks when she heard a commotion and saw the scant outlines of an altercation far ahead of her. As she got closer, she realized that it was happening more or less in front of her apartment. She slowed her pace three doors away. Not because she was scared, but to allow herself more time to collect snippets of the conversation. This was, after all, not the first time she'd seen this very scene unfold. The only difference was they'd changed the actors.

"...motha fucka! I told you don't step to me ever," Red Shirt said.

"Whatchu gooooonna do?" Black Shirt asked.

Red Shirt answered with his fists. His right came looping over the top, mashing Black Shirt's lips against his teeth. Black Shirt threw both arms up in a flailing, helpless gesture. Red Shirt used his left hand to corral both flapping arms together and launched another fist at

Black Shirt's face. It connected again in a spray of blood. Black Shirt collapsed onto his back, his head cocked off in a jarring angle, so that Sheela could see the shattered nose and whites of his eyes. Red Shirt wasted no time and dropped onto his knees; one on either side of Black Shirt's torso. He grabbed Black Shirt's shirt into a bunch and began feeding him fists. Sheela heard a sick, soft grunt, then a sharp snapping sound. She'd stopped moving forward and was now inching her way back. Someone came out and shouted at Red Shirt to stop, but he was beyond hearing. He continued to pound away at Black Shirt's face with the rhythmical precision of a piston.

Sheela stumbled into someone who calmly placed her aside before running up and tackling Red Shirt. Someone else was on the stoop next to where she found herself sitting down, crying into the phone, asking the other end "to please send help. You've gotta send an ambulance." Sheela heard all and none. She could only focus on the one eye left open on Black Shirt's face. The rest of him was a ruin, but this eye had rolled back down and was look-ing off up the street. It was bulging out like it could see the future and was terrified of what was to come.

Giles

1

Giles was embattled with calls during the first few hours of his shift. He'd been given five discharges, finishing the final room at ten minutes to eight. He called Rod and told him he was taking his half-hour break for supper, almost two hours later than the scheduled time.

"Sure thing, bro. I need you to do me a favour after your supper though. Call me when you're done." Rod hung up before he could respond. Giles sighed and wandered to the cafeteria and tossed some pizza pockets into the microwave. Four and a half minutes later, he was at one of the many empty tables. He took out his phone and saw he had no reception. He thrust his arm up and out and waved his phone around, watching as the service bars lay dead. He sighed and took a bite out of his supper. His eyes widened, and he began taking in quick, deep breaths, his mouth a tight 'O'. He reluctantly chewed while the roof of his mouth sizzled.

He got up and walked a few meters away, watching the screen of his phone the whole time. Nothing changed. He paced around the cafeteria, munching on a still scalding morsel, going to each corner of the room with the results staying the same. He cursed under his breath while the silent room looked on with zero judgement.

He walked back to his seat, lay his phone on the table and opened his backpack, placing a sociology textbook for next semester's classes beside his phone. He opened it and read paragraphs he knew he'd have to re-read to retain anything. He didn't care. He had the whole summer to read ahead, and besides, he was just happy to be off his feet; they were up on the chair across the table from him, shoes off.

His half-hour break passed with unsurprising quickness. He collected his things and walked out to the open corridor. He moved down the long hallway to get to the Housekeeping office. No one was there. He used his Spectra to call Rod.

"Yo."

"It's Giles. I'm at the office."

"Shit, already bro? Wait there, ain't no one around. I'll be down in a few minutes."

"Okay."

Giles hung up and went into the storeroom. He found the always-comfortable-looking chair and plunked himself down in it. He put his feet up on the desk and pulled out his phone. He saw he had full bars and 4g.

He was shaken awake by Rod less than a half hour later. He wiped his mouth, and the back of his hand coming away wet.

"Out like a light, bro."

"I'm sorry."

"Nah, who cares. Take them z's when you can get 'em."

"Okay."

"Listen, I need your help, bro. I need you to stay for a couple hours of overtime to clean the kitchen."

"The what?" Giles rubbed his eyes, smearing a sheen of saliva on his right eyelid.

"The kitchen. One of the night guys called in sick. We gotta cover it. It'll be easy, trust me. Just do what you can. I'll leave a note saying you covered it. It'll be fine."

Giles gave Rod a queer look. His brain was still waking up, and he wasn't sure he understood the question.

"What am I covering the kitchen with?"

"What?" Rod asked. He started laughing. He swatted Giles' feet, which he barely felt. "Nah bro, you gotta *cover* the kitchen. Do the routine."

Giles took a moment to let the information process. "I have to go clean the kitchen," he said finally.

"Yea, Bro."

"I don't know the routine," he said slowly. Thickly. "Hell, I don't even know where the kitchen is."

"Oh shit, really? Whatever. I'll show you. It's easy."

"Okay."

"Cool. You ready?"

"Now?"

"Yes. Come on," Rod said. "At least you won't have to do calls anymore," he said with a shrug, turning around and walking away. Giles got up on unsteady, tingling legs and followed. They exited the add-on wooden building and hallway and turned right into the main third-floor corridor. At the end, they took the elevator up two floors. They stepped out onto a maroon tiled hallway lit by a single orange fluorescent bulb from overhead. They approached a set of doors, padlock firmly in place.

"Everyone should be gone by now," Rod said while he slipped a key from his pocket and into the padlock. It sprang open. Giles shivered at the sound of the sliding metal chain as it clanked through the door handles. Free of restraints, the doors *sighed* open a few centimeters. Rod pulled them wider and walked inside. He was immediately shrouded by shadow and disappeared within a few mere moments. Giles waited, holding the door open. Eventually he heard a click and a small section of the kitchen lit up in front of him. He walked in to check it out as more lights flickered into life.

The entirety of the kitchen, as long and large as it was, had the same muddy maroon clay tiles. In spots, they were cracked. It others, they were worn down smooth and round as far as the grouting; Giles didn't think they'd ever been re-done since the inception of the hospital.

Rod led him to the left. They walked into a caged area that reminded Giles of the way prison kitchens were portrayed in movies. There was a chain-linked fence sectioning off an area that housed industrial sized cans of crushed tomatoes, peas, and corn, among other veggies. On the other side of the room were the walk-in fridges, stark and shiny against the bland backdrop of white walls. Rod produced another key and opened the door in the fence.

"Do the floor well. That's one thing they always bitch about. Sometimes there's sugar on the floor, and that attracts ants. Not good for a kitchen, bro."

Giles nodded and followed Rod over to the refrigerators. He was worried that he would need to polish them. Instead, Rod just pointed out the various prep stations. Then, he opened one of the fridges and went in. A cold air, devoid of scent, wafted out. Giles looked in and saw all manner of bottled beverages, prepackaged sandwiches, cakes, and pies. He watched Rod reach into two different crates, producing an apple and a banana. He exited the fridge and offered the apple to Giles, who took it but didn't eat it.

"If you get hungry, one or two fruit is okay, but don't take anything to drink that's in a bottle, or anything that's a snack. They watch that shit like hawks. You still on probation?"

"Yes."

"Yeah, they'll fire your ass for sure if you get caught." He led Giles out of the room, unpeeling and munching on the banana as he did so. The apple in Giles' hand felt heavy and hot as he walked out of the pantry. He stopped and deposited it into his backpack before reaching the entrance. When they exited the room, they went left. When Rod hit the lights, Giles saw it was the food-line. Conveyor belts snaked around the room next to empty trolleys and stacks of trays.

"Pretty simple. Again, do floors and garbages. Fuck the countertops and belts, bro. It should be quick-quick." Rod pointed to a set of descending stairs nestled off in the corner. "That's their staff area. Bathrooms and locker rooms."

Giles nodded.

They exited the way they came and turned left again. They walked down a long, slender corridor that ran by the kitchen supervisory offices and opened up on the food preparation area. The light of a rising full moon filtered down through the skylight two stories above them. It glinted off the vast vats and culinary counters of stainless steel. The corridor continued, lost in the non-light at the end so it was blanketed in black, unwilling to give up details. They walked farther into the room until Rod found the light switch. Once illuminated, Giles could take in the scope of the kitchen. To his left were more vats, three rows of five, and each was a gleaming silver. He saw giant, long-handled wooden spoons sticking out from each. *My spoon is too big,* he thought and giggled. To his right, and beyond a large plastic barrier, was the food disposal area. Further down the hallway were walk-in freezers that were built into the walls. And finally, at the far end, barely illuminated by the light was the service elevator.

"Don't worry 'bout in there, bro," Rod said, pointing to the disposal area. "That's already been done. Just wash the counters in here and do the garbages, bro. And the floor. The *whole* floor," he said, pointing off towards the elevator at the far end.

"Where does that go?" Giles asked.

"It's the service one to the five floors below. Stay out of it, bro," Rod said, pointedly not looking in its direction. He turned around and started walking toward the exit. Giles followed him, looking around. He tried to take in the full scope of the kitchen but found himself unable to. He listened to their footfalls echoing off, dying amongst the inanimate objects. Neither of them spoke until they were back at the elevators and Rod had pressed the call button.

"You gotta scrub them floors good, bro. Otherwise, Mandy clocks in tomorrow and it's your ass."

"Where can I fill up my mop bucket?" Giles asked.

Rod pointed over Giles' shoulder. "Everything you need is in there."

"Okay."

"Don't forget to lock up and call out when you're done," Rod said, stepping into the elevator and leaving Giles by himself.

2

Giles decided to start with the kitchen supervisor's office, humming while he cleaned it. It was his way to keep the creeps away.

Rod had only been gone for five minutes before he felt the unease settle into him. He'd had a hard time placing it at first. He initially thought the oddity was the smell. After being given the tour, his nostrils had been alight with every conceivable scent. It was almost overwhelming if it hadn't been for the underlying blandness. It took him a while, but he finally understood what the problem was. He discovered that when all scents were mashed together in your nose, the smell of everything eventually smelled like nothing at all.

The rest of the hospital had been quiet during the nights he'd worked, but there was always a little life to it. Here, alone in the kitchen, Giles got the feeling that everything was dead. There was a flat emptiness to the entire area. It amplified the mushy rebounds of his every action. Once he'd figured it out, it had been that much more unnerving. And so, he'd started humming to fill the void that he felt circled the room.

He finished mopping the offices and closed the door behind him. He pushed his cart along the corridor in the direction of the service elevator located at the far end. As he approached, he heard a whining, grinding sound pierce above his humming. It got louder the closer he got to the elevator. He was standing by the built-in freezer when the elevator rumbled to a stop. Even knowing it was silly to do so, he tightened his grip on the mop and pre-pared to use it as a weapon, should it be necessary. He stood ten meters away and watched as first the double wooden doors were vertically shucked away, and finally as the metal gate was pulled horizontally aside.

A tall woman stepped out into the dim light, her black hair cascading over the shoulders of her lab coat. Underneath the coat was a slim fitting black dress. Slender fingers gripped a clipboard and he could swear that the nails were painted a sexy shade of red. As she neared him, Giles saw that her face was long and plain and radiated a homespun beauty. Around her neck was a simple band of fabric, fashioned after a choker style necklace. The black of it, and of her hair and dress, were in stark contrast against her pale, milky skin. As she approached, she offered up a brief, warm smile.

"Hello," she said, her voice a quiet, rough rasp.

Giles realized he was still holding tight his mop stick, as if to ward her off, and relaxed slightly. "Hi," he said.

She stopped in front of him; her blue eyes both looking through, and eating him up, in the same instance. He looked back into them, frozen in place. He couldn't believe that a woman as beautiful as this would ever talk to him willingly. He stammered for something, anything, to say.

"I was told no one would be here," he blurted, feeling immediately like a horse's ass.

She laughed, a tinny sound that clanged around the room and quickly died.

"Don't worry," she said, "I won't be long. I just need to change. Don't follow me now," she said coyly, then walked off. Giles watched her until she disappeared toward the belt room. Then, he listened to her black high-heels send back their short, clipped bursts. After the sounds faded, he was reminded of the emptiness as it crashed back in around him. He lowered his head, walked toward the service elevator, and began mopping the floor.

3

Giles walked down the staircase into the kitchen's employee lounge. The clock in the hallway told him it was twenty past three in the morning. He stretched long and broad while his mouth echoed a yawn in tandem. He was ready to go home. He did a quick spot check of the women's locker room. The garbages were fine, as were the floors. The only thing out of place was a black leather belt that lay discarded across the central bench; above was a thick water pipe, running parallel. He did the same check of the men's locker room before quickly cleaning the unisex stalls. That done, he exited the kitchen, locked up, and went down to the housekeeping office to call out.

The city of Montreal lay sleeping as he passed through it. Even though it was the middle of a gorgeous spring, few people were milling about; some hustling, some on the prowl for a taxi. Most just resembled the walking dead. Giles assumed he fit right in.

As the sun slowly slipped above the horizon, illuminating the baggy and battered eyes of those left on the streets, Giles' mind got to thinking about the woman he'd met several hours ago. He'd caught a brief glimpse of her id card when she'd spoken with him. He didn't know her name, except that it started with a 'V'. He'd been able, however, to see her job title. It'd been stenciled neatly on the paper that'd been on her clipboard. She was a Nutritionist. He *had* to find out her name. He *had* to find out more about her. By the time he'd unlocked the door to his one-bedroom abode in the Concordia ghetto, thoughts of her had infected his brain.

As the six o'clock sun penetrated the bedsheet he'd hung as a curtain, his eyes were closed while he masturbated to her. He brought himself close, soft moans escaping him, as he thought of her wrapping both hands around his neck, choking him. It wasn't until he'd taken his belt and slipped it around his neck, pulling it tight enough to feel a momentary lightheadedness, that he was able to cum.

Todd

Todd stretched back and unleashed an open-mouthed yawn as his bosses' boss rambled on about infection control and the importance of handwashing. He looked down at his tablet, pretending to take notes, wiggling his fingers at intermittent intervals, while instead being engaged in the infinite scroll through his Twitter feed. The meeting was pointless because it was the same monthly spiel they always got, just with different details. Todd thought they'd been doing better over the last couple of months; apparently, that wasn't the case. He knew how *he'd* take care of it. *Because* he knew, he didn't need to pay too close attention. Still, he kept one eye on Harris. Whenever Harris Wilson looked in his direction, Todd made sure to return the look.

"Okay. So, let's switch gears," Harris said abruptly.

Todd sat up straight, switching to the notepad setting on his tablet.

"I know you're all concerned about the move, so I figured we take the last," Harris checked his watch, "ten minutes to address it. I'll tell you what I know, then open it up for questions." Todd watched Harris look at each of them sitting around the conference table in turn. He tilted his head and raised his eyebrows in a prepared look when Harris' eyes settled on him. Harris smiled a slight smile that Todd returned.

"First off. We *are* moving next year," Harris began. "We're not sure of the date, but it'll be before autumn. *That* we're sure of. We'll need to have each employee ready with new I.D.s. Each card will be equipped with a code that will allow access throughout various regions of the hospital." Harris reached into his pocket and tossed a set of car keys on the table. Todd noticed the four intertwined silver circles catching the light. "Keys," Harris finished, "will be obsolete."

A sharp, inhaled silence fell around the room. Everyone looked at Harris expectantly while Todd resumed taking notes.

"Second. Our base of operations will be on the second level of the basement; the sub-basement." Todd heard a groan and looked up to see Harris holding up his hand. "I know, I know. No windows means less than optimal working conditions. Stay with me people. We're there because there is a large concrete 'spine,'" he said, holding up air quotes, "that connects all facets of the hospital together. The adult's and children's sections are connected down there. It's nice because we can do our business and stay out of everyone's way."

*Sub-basement is the connecting corridor. *IMPORTANT** Todd typed. He finished his note and looked up. Harris was looking back at his watch.

"Okay," Harris said, looking up at those seated around the table. "Any questions?"

Todd raised his hand, was acknowledged, and opted for a softball.

"Are we going to get new photos for our I.D.s?"

"Good question. Yes. Every employee will need a new photo. There will be a schedule up in the next few months with time frames for each department." Harris looked over towards Meredith, her hand raised. He nodded in her direction.

"Are we going to get an orientation at the new hospital?"

"Yes. Probably. We're still working on that."

"What does 'working on it' mean?"

Todd saw the look Harris was giving Meredith and shrunk a little in his seat; he wasn't the only one, he noted.

"It *means* that *we're working on it*," Harris said slowly, his tone subtle poison in a champagne glass.

After that, there weren't many other questions. The meeting wrapped up, and the managers filed out.

Meredith was waiting for Todd outside the room. They walked in tandem down the hallway. She waited until they were far enough out of earshot of the others before speaking.

"Can you believe they're harping on with this infection control shit again?"

"It could be our guys."

"It's not."

"It *could* be."

She looked at him in disbelief. "It's not, and now you're just being willfully disingenuous." Todd wasn't sure what the last word meant so he frowned instead of answering. It had its desired effect, and she continued talking. "You've seen the way some doc's and family members ignore the signs and trot into the rooms without proper protection. You used to work as a grunt before becoming a manager."

"We've got some lazy people," he said.

"Sure. I don't dispute that, but we put our best workers on the problem floors, and it's *still* a problem. That tells you something, no?"

"Well, why are you telling me? Bring it up to our higher-ups."

"I *did*. In the meeting. You just weren't paying attention."

"So. I'll say it again. Why tell me?"

She stopped and turned on him. Todd saw the anger and passion radiating from her eyes.

"I'm telling you because I want some fucking backup." Todd scoffed and realized it was a mistake, seeing her anger double. "Look," she continued, jabbing a boney finger into his meaty chest. "We gotta stand up for *our* guys. If we keep giving them shit, if we keep throwing them under the bus, they're not gonna work as hard for us. Understand?"

Todd opened his mouth to respond with words and thoughts that hadn't yet been fully formed when his Spectra rang. He gave a silent thanks to the powers above and answered his phone.

"Housekeeping. Todd speaking."

He listened as the voice on the other end complained. He gave non-committal grunts when necessary, then said he'd take care of the problem. The voice on the other end thanked him and hung up. Todd saw that Meredith was waiting patiently for him, so he feigned annoyance at the phone call and lifted his free hand. He pantomimed a blabbing mouth with it while giving Meredith an apologetic look. Then, he covered the mouthpiece and whispered directly to her. "Sorry. We'll talk later," he said and walked away. After passing around the corner, he hung up the phone.

Todd walked to an oft-forgotten area of the hospital and took the adjoining exit. The door led to an overgrown path that led to some thirty stairs. He cursed, like always, and trudged up to the top, breathing heavily by the time he reached the midway point. At the top, he checked to make sure no traffic was coming and crossed the feeder road of the parking area to the pathway that led even further up the hill. He was heading to the Sir Gregory Renton Centre for Psychiatric Care, more commonly known as "The House That Renton Built."

He arrived at the side door, dark stains now standing out on his shirt, while he sucked in the warm, humid air. He sat down at the picnic table and attempted to catch his breath.

When he was ready, Todd pushed himself up from the table and went through the side door.

He walked through the hallway, pulling out his tablet and making note of any infractions he saw: these included, but weren't limited to, minute dust bunnies in the corners, pebbles along the hallway, and shreds of toilet paper in the changing room toilet stalls. He came upon the housekeeping break room and pushed it open. It moved mere centimeters before coming to a complete stop. He looked down and checked his watch. It was twenty minutes past eleven. He knocked loudly and prepared his face to broadcast utmost annoyance. He heard a chair scrape back, *sitting down already* he thought, and footsteps approach the door.

The deadbolt was ratcheted back and the door creaked open.

He was greeted to the half-smiling face of Sean Banner.

Todd was happy to see the smile quickly sour when Sean saw who was on the other side of the door. Todd looked down at his watch for posterity's sake and feigned mild contempt.

"By my calculations, you're not on break yet. I'm going to have to dock you," he said, still looking at his watch.

"If you gotta," Sean said. "Although, if you'd go upstairs, you'd see my work is done, and now I'm waiting on calls."

Todd heard the insolence in Sean's voice and looked up at that, cocking an eyebrow in mild annoyance. "Why aren't you waiting on the floor, then?"

"Because I have a pager," Sean replied, tapping the obsolete piece of technology attached to his hip.

"This ain't the military. That's no excuse."

"Fine. Whatever. Do what you gotta do."

"You better believe I will," Todd said. "In fact, since you're so insistent, I'm gonna do more than that. You're getting a verbal warning, and you'd better believe it's going on your file."

Todd watched as Sean's brown eyes narrowed and grew a shade darker. He took an involuntary step back. His hand dipped down and grasped the Spectra clipped to his belt.

"You know," Sean said, "maybe if you gave more of a shit about the work being done than trying to bust people for greasing a break or two, you'd garner some fucking respect." Without waiting for a reply, Sean strode back into the room and sat down, putting his feet up on the table.

Todd thought about continuing the conversation but decided against it. Instead, he settled with giving Sean more than a verbal. He was going to deliver a written warning due to violent language used directly at a supervisor. *That* would set Sean's head spinning, he reasoned. Todd walked away, content with being the bigger man.

He wandered to the end of the hall, continuing to take notes. He reached the stairwell and went up, exited on the first floor, and walked out into an empty hallway. He checked around and headed right, up the ramp that ran parallel to another set of stairs, scanning the paintings that hung along the wall. He recognized all of them, on pure reflex, except one.

Someone had hung an eleventh. It depicted two men on a sidewalk. One was lying supine, bleeding profusely from every orifice while the other kneeled above him, knees spread on either side of the other's torso. The second man had a handful of shirt in one hand while the other was raised high, bunched into a fist, poised and ready to strike. Todd saw flecks of blood staining the knuckles of the kneeling man. He shivered and wondered briefly why anyone would ever paint a picture that detailed and disturbing. Something spooked him but he couldn't place it. He racked his brain, yet nothing came. He shrugged and moved on. After two floors, and many notes, he found what he was looking for; the housekeeping group leader for "The House That Renton Built". He gave Josh the business. Josh took it with a look of indifference. Mission complete, Todd headed back to the main pavilion of St. Agnes.

He completed his day in a funk, something about the new painting nagging him the rest of the way. It wasn't until he'd exited the metro and was a couple of blocks from his house that it clicked. The painting was a depiction of his neighbourhood. Upon realization, Todd drew in a sharp breath, his step hitching, as he passed by *the very spot* depicted in the painting. *Fucking Montreal liberals*, he thought as he continued on his way. *They'll let any old asshole who can fingerpaint put up whatever filth they want. Stupid psych arts programs are gonna get me stabbed someday.* He didn't like knowing that someone unhinged, who could paint something like *that*, lived close to him.

Todd didn't notice the drying stain upon the sidewalk as he subconsciously stepped over it.

.

Simon

1

He was stretched along the booth backing, an empty tupperware on the table in front of him. Mario was arguing the finer points of why the Chargers were the worst team in football to Jimmy.

"Who'd you guys draft in the first round?"

Simon watched Jimmy open his mouth to answer. Mario cut him off with the wave of a hand. "I'll save you the time. It doesn't matter because he'll be injured or holding out come week one. He's playing on a scrub ass team, so that's the best option for him anyway."

"How many rings do you got?" Jimmy asked.

"We're not talking about rings."

"How many?"

"It doesn't -"

"Zero. We both have zero, so you can't talk shit to me about shit."

"That's cause both your teams are shit," Simon said.

"Ain't no still-living-with-my-mom motherfucker got a right to talk," Jimmy shot back.

"Some of us care about our parents and want to take care of them," was Simon's retort.

It was an ever-evolving conversation that was plagued by the same insults and rebuttals; therefore, it never changed. It didn't matter. Simon was only half listening. The rest of his attention was rolling over on itself, wondering what The Doctor was doing. When he'd first been recruited, The Doctor had told him it was for some testing he'd wanted to do on blood samples. Everything had seemed on the level to Simon; he'd even convinced himself that the extra money was standard procedure for helping a pharmaceutical study. Now, he felt a subtle gnawing of his conscience. Even though he tried, he couldn't quite fool himself anymore; he suspected he was participating in something heavier than a study. He felt like he was standing on the edge of the ocean. This next job, this bringing-of-the-body, would force him to turn back or plunge in. He couldn't decide but was leaning toward the latter.

He was still mulling the possibilities over when the dinner crew began trickling into the caf. It was a smattering of employees from housekeeping, transport, and security. Many of them were lifers, smoking and joking their lives away in the system. They always had a story to tell or a gripe to air. Most of them were funny. Some of them were assholes. Overall, Simon considered them good people.

The noise level rose substantially by the time they had a full table, each person trying to talk over the others while their dinners were heated up and laid out. It was a comfortable familiarity that Simon got lost in.

"-swear to God, I'm telling Paulo to eat shit if he put me on eight floor again," Ronald said.

"What happened?" Jimmy asked.

"Fuckin' kids laughing. I heard dem."

"That ain't nothing. It's probably coming from the daycare a few floors down."

"No. Them kids all gone home."

"How do you know?" Raquel asked.

"Because," Ronald said, turning to her, "dem parents all came and went. Kids're picked up. Staff gone home. Down there, and up on my floor."

"Did you check?"

"Don't need to. I can feel dem."

"Ahh shit, here it comes again," someone from the far end blurted out. Simon couldn't tell who, but he had a feeling it was one of the security guards, probably Brandon.

"Ain't no shit. Nuh-uh. My grandmere did the vodou. I got a bit of it in my gene." He tapped his heart twice with his index finger. "I got me a bit of it in here."

"So your voodoo blood allows you to see the spirits?" Raquel asked.

"Don't get him started," the unknown person piped up again. Simon hoped Ronald would continue. Thankfully, Ronald paid no mind to the disrespectful voice.

"Yeh. It connect me to the Loa through mind and body. I sense dem. They sense me. They seek me out, to help with outstanding problem. Most time, I can do nothing. Most time, I just see and feel."

"Is there anything you can do about it? Your voodoo, I mean."

"I could work on it and hone it." Ronald took a swallow of his food. Simon saw he wanted to say more, but was hesitant. He continued slowly. "Mostly, I don't want more. More is bad." He shook his head. "To hear those kid laugh? No. Too much. I rather not."

Simon watched the tattooed muscles on Ronald's arm clench up as he held his fork.

"Come the fuck on," Harold said. "It was probably Paulo playing a joke on you. You ain't the first, and you won't be the last one he gets like that."

"Get like what?" Ronald asked.

"Listen, the first time he put me on eight, he told me about this 'urban myth,' about how the souls of the aborted kids haunted that place." Harold burped, it was low and rumbling. His rather large belly shook with the force of it. He wiped his mouth and continued. "I thought nothing of it. At first. Throughout the night, I couldn't help but feel something was around. My first scare came when some of my stuff was moved around. Not much, but a little bit."

"Spirit don't move stuff," Ronald said matter-of-factly to the table that was now listening intently to Harold's story. "Normally. It have to be strong spirit to touch our world."

"Anyway," Harold continued, "I thought someone was fucking with me. Yet, it kept happening all week. It wasn't until my fourth shift there that I heard this echo of laughter. It seemed to come out of nowhere and everywhere. I looked around, saw nothing, but the laughing persisted. It went on for some time, and after ten minutes I was freaked enough to just leave the floor. As I was bolting down the stairs, I ran into Paulo." Harold put his meaty elbows on the table and leaned toward Ronald. "He took one look at my face and couldn't contain himself. He burst into laughter and told me he'd hidden a tiny tape recorder in the vents. He'd turned it on and left."

The table, Simon included, howled with laughter. Everyone, except Ronald.

"No one was fucking with me," Ronald said, stoically. "I felt it as real as I felt The Nutritionist."

"Oh shit. That old chestnut again," Jimmy said, pointing a half-eaten chicken wing at Ronald. "You've been dining out on that story for a year now, boy."

"I saw what I saw."

"Uh-huh. You saw what you *think* you saw. *I* think your grandmere filled your head with stories."

The two men looked at each other across the table. One stare was mocking, the other cold and hard. Simon was glad to see it was Jimmy who buckled first. Everyone went back to eating, some of the air taken out of the room. Simon knew it wouldn't last long though, their little trysts never did. From the other table, behind Ronald, a timid voice spoke up.

"Who's the Nutritionist?"

Ronald turned to see who had spoken. Simon saw through narrowed eyes that it was one of the new housekeepers. He didn't recognize him and wasn't surprised, the kid looked hardly ready to shave. The newbies came and went, most forming their own groups that stayed away from theirs. Simon figured their group must seem rather intimidating and wouldn't have been wrong.

110

"It's another wives tale," Jimmy said without looking up, the words struggling for passage through a mouth full of chicken. "Only this one Mr. Reneaux swears is true."

"It is," Ronald said.

"Who is it?" the housekeeper asked, tentatively.

Ronald told him.

Much like everyone else, she'd gotten the job by having family already in the system. She'd studied at Hamlin University in the mid 80s, obtaining her bachelor's degree in food science easily, coming second in her class. She had a power stance and a demure look, her black hair cascading over her shoulders, framing her blue eyes. It accentuated a long slender neck that was oft talked about by the men, and boys, in the kitchen. She'd been working as the surgical ward nutritionist for five years when tragedy was set in motion.

During her time there, she'd fallen in love with one of the new attendings. His name was Charles Veksler. She'd first met him while doing her rounds in the intensive care unit. She was speaking with a patient, outlining their needs, and gently telling them the dangers of excess salt in their diet, when *he* entered the room. She was a cynic but couldn't help herself from falling for him in that first glance. He was taller than her, which was something not a lot of men could claim, and his short brown hair stuck up in sleep spikes despite it being the middle of the day. It did wonders to frame his face and accentuate his grey eyes.

He walked in and looked across the room at her, a puffy smile flickering across his face. Then, he turned to the patient.

Yes, she'd fallen instantly for him.

"Mr. Tillman, I'm Dr. Veksler. I'll be your physician for the next week," he said, his voice nicked with a slight accent. "I'm sorry, Ms...?" He looked at her again, and she found herself stumbling to recite her name. When he repeated it back to her, it sounded like he'd covered it in honey. He asked her to give them a minute as he wanted to speak to the patient in private.

"Not a problem, Dr. Veksler," she said, standing up. She walked out of the room, sliding the door closed behind her, and stood in the hallway while a flush crept over her; she was imagining how it would feel, him spreading that honey on her.

Over the next six months, she saw him only a handful of times throughout the hospital. He remembered her name, and the second time they met she felt a jolt run down her spine as he spoke it. That time, they'd spoken for a few minutes about a patient's plan before parting ways. Each time they met, they talked longer and longer. By the end of those six months, they'd both known bits of personal information about each other. Eight months after they'd initially met, they went on a date. They slept together that very night.

He asked her to keep their relationship from others for the time being. The hospital was its own small town, he said. He didn't want word getting around because he was afraid of the way people would look at her. He didn't want her seen as a tramp, someone who slept her way around the office, he said. She agreed. He'd made good points, she figured, but they also spent one night a week together, either at his place or hers, so she didn't mind a little bit of secrecy. To her, it added a touch of excitement to their game.

Their relationship continued like this for several months, and after each passing week, she felt herself falling deeper and deeper in love with him. She'd never thought it possible before; however, her current reality proved all her old preconceived notions false. Keeping it a secret hadn't been hard for her, nor him. Their offices were on the opposite ends of the hospital, and they rarely ran into each other in the halls. There'd been, however, one or two occasions where she'd enticed him up to her office.

And so, it came as a shock to her when one day she heard a couple of nurses in the cafeteria talking about which doctor they wanted to sleep with most in the hospital. One of the nurses mentioned Dr. Veksler and the other one giggled. The nurse mentioned that she'd already slept with him, had, in fact, fucked him the previous week. The Nutritionist thought nothing of it at first. She reasoned that one of the nurses was trying to look bigger in the eyes of the other. She was appalled when she heard the nurse mention a dimpled scar on his ass cheek. She was furious when she heard the nurse regale to the other that he'd gotten it by being poked with a knife.

She ran into Dr. Veksler later that day and asked him to join her in her office after eight in the evening, when everyone else would be gone. She said she was working late and could use a little company. He obliged.

When he showed up, she asked him if it was true. He told her it was. She broke down, crying, asking him what it all meant. He called her stupid. He said that they'd never been exclusive and she should have known. She yelled that he'd never told her that. He called her stupid again. He said it was over.

She sat at her desk long after he'd gone. After the tears had stopped, she continued looking at the wall in red-eyed anger. Eventually, she got up and walked down to the storage area. She neatly untied a length of rope that was holding a few pallets of food together and went into the employee lounge area. The place was deserted. She unfurled the rope and tied one end around the refrigerator in the corner. Then, she climbed up on an unsteady table in the middle of the room. Casting the rope up and over the large pipe that ran across the ceiling, she tied a noose and slipped her head inside. She tightened it until her breath came in rasps.

"Fuck you," she whispered to the empty room as she first rocked, and then tipped over the table. The drop wasn't high enough, and she strangled to death, yet she didn't struggle against it. She'd accepted her fate and was bound by it.

They found her body the next morning.

3

Simon felt his phone vibrate and dug it out of his pocket; one bar of service being the benefit of sitting in the corner.

Where are you? I can't reach you.

115

"Ahhh shit," he said to no one in particular. "I gotta go." The conversation at the tables continued while he collected his tupperware and stowed it in his backpack. He gave Mario a fist bump, telling him he'd see him later, and exited the cafeteria.

When he was in an area of service, he dug out his Spectra and dialed dispatch. He listened as he was given a body to recover. He shivered and forced himself to respond with the rehearsed lines he didn't know he'd be using until now.

"Okay. I'll grab Mario and tell him to help me out."

"Mario's not up," Trevor told him.

"It's fine. He owes me one," Simon rattled off.

"It's like you want, Simon. Just don't fuck the dog on this one."

"I'd never," he said.

"Bullshit."

Simon hung up then told his Spectra what he thought Trevor could do to himself. Then, he walked off toward the elevators to go collect a body for The Doctor.

4

"I thought it took two of you?"

"Normally, yeah. I gotta chauffeur it myself tonight. We're short staffed," Simon said, adding a shrug to show the nurse he was sincere. She rolled her eyes and started to leave the room. "Can you grab a P.A.B.?" Simon asked. "I'm not gonna be able to lift this on my own." He knew he could lift the body himself, it probably weighed less than one hundred and twenty pounds, but it was against protocol. He was breaking enough of them that he didn't want to add any more to his list; not if he could help it.

"No problem, Simon," the nurse said and left.

He sat down in the chair and did the infinite scroll through Snapchat while he waited. His eyes followed the videos, but his mind didn't. Now that he was here, with the body in front of him ready to go, his previous anxiety disappeared. *They're already dead. They won't mind whatever* He's *gonna do to them.* He'd moved on to perusing Facebook by the time the P.A.B. showed up. He saw it was the fat one.

"Sorry it took so long," she said as she waddled into the room. "I got caught up reloading the linen cart. Then, Selina came over and started to ask me why I was doing *that* when her patient, you know the guy in room twenty-eight, she asks me why he's not changed yet. I held up my hands and told her I was folding linen." Simon watched her move to the body as she talked, hesitate with a perplexed look, before scurrying over to a box of gloves and selecting a pair. He rolled his eyes and stood up, fishing a pair of gloves out of his pocket to put on. She came back over to the body, still prattling away as if Simon cared. He let out a low, disgusted sigh that she either didn't hear or ignored. "She tells me she asked me to do it a half hour ago. She didn't, but she wouldn't believe me if I told her -- Oof, this girl is heavy!" she exclaimed. Simon huffed out a breath of disgust again. He was doing most of the work and knew it.

They shifted the body into the bag and zipped it up. Simon listened to the subject of her monologue change to her trip to Ottawa the previous month. He wheeled the body out of the room while she followed behind.

"The canal was nice, but what I really want to do is go in the winter time so I can skate on it."

"Excuse me," Simon said, leaning on the nursing station rail. "Do you have the dead chick's paperwork?" He hooked a thumb over his shoulder, emphasizing his point.

The unit coordinator dug through some files and handed it over. Simon was glad the P.A.B. had taken the hint and walked off, probably to go disturb some other poor staff member. Collecting the file, he went back to the stretcher and pushed it to the elevator.

No one took notice of him as he made his way to the drop off spot. He had the key prepped and was inside the dank hallway, with the door locked behind him, in less than thirty seconds. He slipped the stretcher against the wall and picked up the two envelopes on the small wooden table. The first one contained his money, all in fifties. The second, and larger envelope, bore the seal of some funeral company. Attached to the exterior was a post-it note. *Deliver to Morgue,* it read. Simon followed its instructions, but not before dropping his money off in his locker.

The Doctor

News Article taken from *The Montreal Inquisitor*, May 11th, 1931

ANNETTE BENNING, RN, PLEADS GUILTY TO EIGHT COUNTS OF HOMICIDE IN THE FIRST DEGREE

City Still Shook Up by Shocking Discovery

By Reginald Surette

Annette Benning, the registered nurse who was accused of murdering eight patients over the course of a year, was brought to court in handcuffs today and plead guilty to all eight counts of first degree murder, causing an uproar from family members of the deceased; a few had to be removed from the court room.

The eight bodies were found in the underground honeycombed system of tunnels that employees of the St. Agnes hospital called "The Catacombs." The bodies, found in the same room by a maintenance man, were in multiple states of decay. Each body was missing strips of skin off their backs.

When the judge asked why she'd done it, Ms. Benning said that it was a sacrifice demanded by the demons that lived within the walls of the hospital...

Light winked off a silver tray as it flew across the room. It struck the wall with a *clang* before clattering to the floor, scaring a family of mice from the shadows. The Doctor ripped off his mask and threw it into the biomedical box in disgust where it came to rest atop an assortment of body parts and a set of bloody gloves.

On the slab in front of him was the bloody mess of the body he'd cut open and tinkered with. He gave a sigh of disgust at the sight of it. Everything he'd tried that night had been to no avail. The only saving grace was he hadn't gotten too overzealous and experimented directly with his creation.

The current problem lay in the fact that he didn't know how to keep his creation alive once it was up and moving. The current problem lay in the blood turning sour in the veins after a while. By tweaking an enzyme, The Doctor had found a way to elongate the shelflife of the bad blood; however, by careful study, he saw that he'd never fully be able to stabilize the blood for more than a month at best. Which led him to the problem of how could he constantly replace the blood within his creation. Dialysis was an idea, but it was pricey and he wouldn't be around forever to foot the bill, so that idea was out. He also didn't want people looking too hard at his creation's medical charts.

His second choice was a cheaper version of dialysis, which consisted of him stealing blood from the hospital, or getting Stanley to do it, but he had to nix that idea as well. It was not a sustainable solution because, once again, he wouldn't be around forever.

He'd finally stumbled upon a viable solution from the most unlikely of sources; his wife. It was all about vampires, except that wasn't entirely feasible. But it was a spark that had bloomed into a bonfire once he understood what he could do. Since his serum was able to repair cells at an alarming rate, he thought to add an extra vein to her forearm. Attach it just below the elbow and fuse tiny bits of old intestinal muscles along it to aid in the peristalsis. He hadn't an idea about how it could puncture another's skin, but baby steps, or so he thought.

Now, his cadaver was a mess and he was nowhere closer to a solution than he'd been hours ago. He'd tried fusing sections of vein along those that ran close to the elbow and it worked. It was when he ran the serum through the vein that the trouble happened. It melted the connection he'd made and he didn't understand why. When he injected the same serum into multiple different parts of the corpse, he saw miracles. He witnessed a heart rejuvenated, beating again. Under a microscope, he witnessed dead blood cells spark and begin knitting their ruined brothers back together. It made no *Christing* sense! That's when he'd lost his temper and flung the tray across the room and threw away his mask.

The Doctor let out a primordial roar, lifting his hands in the air and shaking them at the roof. It took less than two seconds before he felt silly and stopped, the sound dying as quickly as his actions.

Something skittered on the peripherals of The Doctor's vision. He turned in its direction in time to see a family of mice making a hellbent escape to a tiny hole in the wall, chiseled amongst the brick. He watched the family of four disappear, one by one, into the hole. *This is the farthest thing from sterile* was the first thought to roll through his mind. The second was, *who am I kidding, it's stupid to think that I could ever produce medical greatness in a dank pit such as this. How can I reanimate my creation with mice running around.*

123

The Doctor watched as the final tail disappeared through the hole. His disgruntled attitude quickly dissipated as an idea, another possible solution, made itself known. He watched the hole for any more movement while he ruminated on everything he knew about animal testing. Yes, this plan could definitely work. He just needed a few supplies, starting with some cheese.

Alessia

1

A hypnotic thumping rhythm pounded its way through her body. Lights blazed down upon the dance floor from the stage, illuminating those close to her in flashes of purple and blue and red and orange. They stuttered in strobe light fashion, blinking and winking for many seconds before changing their pattern. The lights were synced to the music which was inexplicably synced to her heart; each thump of her pulse reflected that of the music coming from the DJ. She moved every part of her body, sometimes fast, sometimes slow. Her two other friends, standing circular with her, were doing the same.

Each song rolled into the next, allowing for a total auditory experience. Alessia didn't have to listen to her friends talk about some random job problem, nor them hers. The level of the music allowed no space in her brain for thought. It was here that she was finally able to shed all of her responsibility and be free. Unlike her friends, she didn't need to split a tab of MDMA to feel release. Music was her vice.

At one point, Jeanie put her mouth against Alessia's ear and screamed, "I need a smoke!" Alessia nodded and followed her out with Max close behind.

They walked along a dark corridor peppered with people engaged in conversations. As they passed two men, one of them stepped out and tried to make awkward conversation with the women. He asked a question that was lost to Alessia, his words swallowed up by the thumping bass. Alessia could see his jaw jittering, reminding her of the old Godzilla movies that she'd watch often with friends while she was still in college. She laughed a little, and the guy must have thought it was in response to his question because he sidled closer to her. He put a hand on her shoulder and leaned in to speak, blasting her with stale beer breath.

"You're cute," he started. "Wanna come party with me and my friend later?"

"No," she answered, shrugging his hand off and leading her two friends to the exit.

The three women stepped outside. Instantly, Alessia felt the warm breeze against her exposed skin, lapping up the sweat. With her ears and heart still pulsating to a dampened beat, she felt the night air as just another extension of her euphoria.

"This DJ is fucking incredible," Max said, still half shouting.

"He's soooooo hot too," Jeanie added. "I wonder if he'd let me lick his face." The three women burst out laughing, Jeanie's coupled with some snorts. Alessia laughed until her sides hurt. When their giggles were winding down, Jeanie looked over at Max. "I'm serious, though. I bet he tastes all salty." That set them off again.

"What did those guys want?" Max asked Alessia.

"If we wanted to go party with them later."

"Did you tell him he's barking up the wrong tree?"

"Not in so many words, but yes."

"Good on you, biiiiiitch!" Jeanie exclaimed.

Now that they were outside, Alessia checked her phone and saw a text from her parents.

Will you be home soon?

She sighed and slipped her phone back into her pocket without answering.

"Your 'rents?" Max asked.

"Yeah. They're worried about me."

"They're always worried about you. Don't they know you're a good girl?" Max slipped an arm around her waist, giving her a sideways hug. Alessia returned the squeeze.

"Good girl?" Jeanie said. "Shit. You're a fucking saint compared to us. I'm blasted, and you haven't even had a drink."

"I have work tomorrow," Alessia said, some defensiveness creeping into her voice.

"You know I didn't mean it like that," Jeanie said, her voice softening. "I'm sorry, bitch. I didn't mean it like that." She puffed furiously on her cigarette, intentionally not making eye contact.

"It's fine," Alessia said. And really, to her, it was. Her sobriety never bothered her. Sure, she would still drink on occasion, but never when she had to work the next day, nor when she was driving.

"I guess that means you're out for round two then," Max said, holding out her palm with a pill laying upon it.

"Thanks, but no thanks," Alessia said.

"You *know* I'm in," Jeanie said and plucked up the pill, biting off half, and placing the rest back onto Max's palm. Max popped it deftly into her mouth.

"You girls ready?" Alessia asked. "I've got another hour or so before I have to leave."

"You know it, biiiiiitch," Jeanie said.

They went back inside.

Quietly sliding her key into the lock, she turned it over. She entered, silently removed her shoes, and walked into the kitchen. She opened the fridge and selected one of the many standing bottles of water, and walked to the living room.

"You're late," a voice rang out from the dark.

Although she expected it, Alessia was still surprised that her mother had waited up for her.

"I'm thirty-two, Mother. I think I'm a little old to have a curfew." The lamp beside her mother winked on.

"Under our house, you'll follow our rules." It was her father speaking now. She saw him sitting in his chair. "Are you high?" he asked.

"No. And I thought you'd respect me enough not to ask."

"You can't blame me," her father said. "You told us you'd be home at midnight and it's long past."

"I'm thirty-two, Father," she said again. "I think I'm a little too old to have a curfew."

"When you're living on your own, you can do as you wish. Our house, our rules."

Hearing him say it for the second time broke Alessia. She felt a wave of white-hot anger bubbling inside her, pushing at her lips, begging to be let out. She obliged.

"How am I supposed to get my own place when you won't let me move out?" she said. "I brought papers home. Bought and paid for my own condo and *you* ripped them up, *Father*." She put all the ugliness she could muster into the last word. She saw his face in the shadows cast by the lamp. It was screwed up in a grimace of painful embarrassment, but only for a moment. Then, it became a mask again, but Alessia relished the thought of making her father feel awkward. It was a little victory, and petty, but one that she would cherish for the time being.

"Nothing to say for yourself?" She asked her parents, looking at each of them in turn.

Her father took a few moments to himself before cutting her down with one line.

"We do this because we're worried that you'll relapse."

"It's been thirteen years since it happened."

"And yet we're still worried. We're not stupid, *figlia*. We know you still go clubbing. It's

130

like a dagger to our hearts, thinking that every time you go out, we might get *that* call again."

"You won't."

"How can we be sure."

"Because you have to trust me. Jesus Christ, Father! If thirteen years isn't long enough to build up some sort of trust, I don't know what more I could do."

"You just have to be patient and give us more time."

"That's what you always say. I'm sick and tired of it."

"Don't be like that, please," her mother pleaded.

"No," Alessia said. She felt all the good vibes from the night completely drained away. Now she was left with only the washed out feeling of being used up by her anger. She wanted to get out of this conversation as quickly as possible. "I *will* be like that. I'm not a child anymore, so stop basing my entire life on one stupid fucking mistake I made when I was nineteen. It's petty, and if you don't stop needling me about it, you're going to push me further away."

She saw her mother open her mouth and held up a finger to silence her. "No more. I had a wonderful night with my friends until I came home. You've taken that away. I'm going to bed because I have work tomorrow and am *responsible*. Good night."

She walked over to the stairs and went up to her room, leaving her parents sitting silent and stoic.

Sheela

News Article from the *Montreal Inquisitor*, May 20th, 1864

SAXON SNELL MAKES CEREMONIAL FIRST DIG AT NEW HOSPITAL SITE

Ribbon Cutting Ceremony Draws Thunderous Applause

By Francois Pellord

Dr. Saxon Snell was present at the groundbreaking for the new site which will house Montreal's newest medical marvel, the St. Agnes hospital. Dr. Snell, originally from England, was the lead investor on the project, vowing to bring not only a plethora of money, but the medical expertise from a lineage of famous doctors from England.

Despite the money coming from an English family, Dr. Snell vowed to use only Quebec labour, along with Quebec limestone, formed some 470 million years ago. Dr. Snell said that using the limestone would ensure a good cohesion between the two cultures...

* * *

You've gotta be fuckin' kidding me, she thought. *No wonder that place is haunted!*

Since her hallucination in the stairwell, and her admission of it during meetings, Sheela had felt overwhelmed with anxiety. In the month since, she'd spent the majority of her time either at work, or at home watching mindless television in an attempt to shut off her brain. It hadn't worked.

Finally, late one night, she'd opened her phone and went onto the wiki entry for St. Agnes hospital. She read about the MKUltra trials run there. The Institute, where she went for her meetings with The Wahz, had been given a substantial monetary donation to look the other way while the United States government experimented on patients during the nineteen sixties and seventies. Due to the lax drug laws Canada enforced, comparative to the USA anyway, they spent a great deal of time dosing patients with LSD, running sensory deprivation chambers, exercises in telepathy and, at times, torture.

Since then, she'd read as many reports and articles and passages from books that the internet would allow her. She kept seeing a book cited in almost every entry. That's why

134

she was currently reading deBodreaux's *Out of the Darkness: The Secrets Behind The LSD Trials*.

DeBordeaux had been a political dissident, rumoured to be in bed with the FLQ terrorist organization. He was arrested during the October Crisis and was one of the sixty-two persons not released. He was held in solitary confinement for a year and then deemed legally insane. He was transferred to The Institute for observation, and ultimately placed in *the* program. He was used as a guinea pig for three years and then released, under strict probationary rules and a heavy drug cocktail. He was too beaten to resist and lived in a state of semi-consciousness for fifteen years. When he finally removed the drugs from his system, he wrote and published his book, outlining everything done to him that he could remember. He was dismissed as a paranoid schizophrenic and was recommitted to The Institute. He took his life by slashing his wrists open after only three months inside. His book had recently found itself within academia and was believed to be one of the forefronts on the subject of the MKUltra trials; even if it was seen as gross exaggerations at times.

Sheela was halfway through the copy she'd found at the library, and devouring every word of it.

For weeks I was given multiple doses of LSD each day through drops placed on my tongue. I lost track of what time effectively was. I began to see the passage of time in color. At times there was a blackness that swallowed me whole. I would pass an eternity inside, my senses no longer only mine. They were split and shared with the entity of the building itself. Sometimes it whispered to me, telling me its secrets. Other times, it would occupy my sight and grant me glimpses into its past, present, and future. They achieved a sort of telepathy with me, but not in the way they'd intended.

I was shown the first stone put in place over a century and a half previous. I was shown the first time those stones tasted blood. How a large brick was sloppily placed high atop the wall, how it tumbled down, striking a worker on the head, and cracking his skull open. I was shown the splash of blood against the wall and ground and could feel the greedy excitement from those stones.

Sometimes, in the darkness of my confines, I would see what the doctors were doing out in the light; the experiments they conducted on the other patients, the notes that they took, how they felt nothing at all for us, their patients. The building showed me their lack of empathy. The building showed me that they felt it was their duty to tinker with us. The

136

building showed me that they saw it as their right.

I was also shown glimpses of things yet to pass. I saw a young woman with shockingly unnatural red hair. She was looking at a line of paintings and one of them clearly frightened her. After she'd left, the final painting melted into the wall, erased completely.

I never told my doctors, my captors, anything about these visions. In my state, I'm not sure how I was able to hoodwink them, but I did. I suspect now that the building helped me. Aside from being left in darkness, I was dosed and left in rooms with a blinding, piercing light that permeated even my eyelids, sizzled my pupils.

During the experiments where I was injected with pure LSD concentrate, they would hook electrodes to my head and record my brain waves while they asked me questions. I would answer them as best I could, and as honest as I could, without giving away what I'd been shown. They tried to trip me up at times, asking questions telepathically. Those were easy to detect. Due to the amount of drugs within my system and the sensory flooding they were giving me, I was keyed up with all my senses stretched out to their fullest. I was never fooled by their ruse.

You've gotta be fuckin' kiddin' me, Sheela thought. *No wonder that place is haunted!*

She put the book down and sat back on her couch. She rubbed her eyes and looked at the clock. It was after two in the morning. She was going to need to get to sleep soon to wake up for her seven am shift. She stretched, yawned, and then picked the book up again.

Stanley

"What time did you start today?" Jimmy asked.

"Noon," he answered, keeping his voice gruff and non-committal. "I'm done in twenty minutes."

"Lucky asshole. I'm stuck here for another four hours."

"Yep."

Stanley turned away from the door and began weighing the biomedical waste boxes. He slid the first one onto the scale, noted its weight, twenty-two kilograms, then lifted it onto an empty cart. He repeated the process with a second and third box, watching Jimmy out of the corner of his eye. He hoped Jimmy would take the hint and leave him alone. He highly doubted he'd get his wish.

"How many years you got left?" Jimmy asked.

"I can retire whenever I want," Stanley said, not losing his working rhythm, adding "you know that."

"I got six years left in this shithole. Then I'm collecting my walking papers and never looking back."

Stanley continued with his boxes while watching Jimmy pull a rather fat booger out of his nose and flick it off into a corner. Stanley wondered how clean Jimmy's hands were after lifting garbage bags all day and decided he didn't want to know. He finished weighing all the boxes while Jimmy talked incessantly, leaning against the wall and continuing to root around in his nose occasionally. Jimmy followed him as he pulled the cart into the garbage room and disposed of the boxes into the large storage fridge that resided there.

"I don't know how you can continue to do that," Jimmy said, gesturing to the final box that Stanley was hefting into the fridge. "Not at your age, anyway."

"It keeps me in shape."

"At fifty, there are easier ways to stay healthy that don't involve backbreaking labour. Doing the garbage run is hard enough, but lifting heavy-as-shit boxes all day long's a fucking bitch."

"It's not that bad."

"It's worse than bad. Don't forget the smell too. I don't know how you can stand being down here."

Stanley shrugged as he closed the fridge and returned his cart to his workroom, going around Jimmy on his way there. He replaced everything, sanitizing it as he went.

"Yeah, it'll be it for me, soon as I fill out my pensioned time."

Stanley doubted that very much, however. He had a feeling Jimmy would be working here until he died. He even figured it would be a heart attack that would take him, and he wouldn't have been wrong. But that was years away. For now, Stanley wished that Jimmy would go back to work and leave him alone. He checked his watch, then slipped his worksheet into his pocket.

"You done?"

"Yes."

"Good for you," Jimmy said. "I think I got time for one more run."

"Probably," Stanley said and headed for the stairs. He waved a hand over his shoulder and called out a goodnight to Jimmy.

He walked up one flight and headed to his boss' office. No one answered his knock, so he slipped the paper underneath the door and signed the communal ledger. Then, he went back to the elevators and took them up to the eighth floor. He walked along the corridor until it became the first floor of The Transplant Pavilion and then took a right, the floor morphing into the third floor of The Women's Pavilion. There was no one around when he got to the bottom of the ramp. He slipped his key into the lock and disappeared behind the doors.

He walked down the corridor, fading from dim white to shadow and back again each time he passed beneath the emergency lights. Coming to a junction, he took the left fork, traveling deeper into the mountain. These were old tunnels, chiseled into the rock, carved out of the stone, dripping rain runoff, growing green in places amongst the dark, slimy stone. These were long forgotten tunnels, known through myth and lore and seldom seen. The Doctor'd had the outside lock changed when he'd first started his experiments. Now, Stanley and few others had access to the catacombs from that specific door. There were other doors, but these catacombs ran deep, and they ran far.

He took two rights and then a left, and then more turns, all on a gradual decline. He came to a long straight section and continued on for three hundred meters. He pulled another key out and inserted it into a well functioning, but badly scuffed lock. He opened the door and walked in, locking it behind him.

He heard light, classical piano wafting through the plastic divider at the far end of the room. Laid out on a work table near him were: a hooded cloth jumpsuit, rubber boots, a gas mask, and heavy gloves. He stripped to his underwear and placed his watch atop his pile of clothes, the cold concrete floor making him shift even though he was wearing thick socks. He dressed and then went into the other room.

"Good. You've come," The Doctor said by way of greeting, his voice muffled through the gas mask, reminding Stanley of Darth Vader.

"Yes. Where's the body?"

"Over there." The Doctor pointed to a waist-high marble slab jutting from a stone wall. It looked like an altar from a century or more ago. Stanley could envision a chalice and candles strewn about it, with some sort of idol or relic perched in the center. For a brief moment, Stanley heard a low moaning chant wafting in through his hood. He cocked his head comically to the side but heard nothing more. He wondered what sort of Gods they'd worshipped down here.

The sacrifice on the slab was an elderly lady. She was already cut open, her chest splayed wide by a rib spreader that was caked with blood and bits of body. He peered down into the hole and saw the body was missing an organ or two; she was also missing the lower half of both legs. Beside the body was a tray with a bone saw, hammer, an array of scalpels, and scissors. Scattered around the slab were a pair of biomed boxes.

"I'm going now," The Doctor said from behind him. "I promised my wife I'd attend a fundraiser with her. You know what to do.

143

Clean up as best you can *after*, but it's not a high priority."

Stanley waved a hand over his shoulder in dismissal. It was going to be a long night, and he wanted to get started.

"Be safe," The Doctor said, and then was gone.

Stanley looked at the body for some time, wondering who she'd been, the things she'd accomplished in her life. He wondered if she'd be upset at the turn of events her body had undergone; or would she be happy that her body was helping to further science in a way that was nigh unimaginable. He didn't know precisely what The Doctor was doing down here, he wasn't paid to know, but he had his suspicions. At times, he'd been tasked with finding an assortment of body parts and organs to bring to the doctor: an arm, a skull, a few toes and fingers, and even some bags of A positive blood. Stanley didn't know the specifics but was confident The Doctor was doing something that would change the world, no matter how unorthodox it was.

He was snapped out of his thoughts by the same moaning chant he'd heard earlier. This time, he looked around the room, pulling down his hood as he did so. There was nothing. No one. The plastic frame didn't shutter against any breeze. He noted the outline of the *other* door at the far end. He assumed it was locked, but on the rare occasion he'd been left alone, he'd never tested that theory. He imagined that behind the door was where the *real* magic happened, but had accepted a long time ago that he'd never know what that magic was.

Still, he watched the door for some time and listened intently. He heard the rasp of the gasmask rubbing his slight stubble as he breathed. He heard the slow, non-rhythmic drip of water as it dropped and plopped some indeterminate distance away. He heard no moaning or chanting. Only after he'd assured himself that it'd just been his imagination did he turn around and bend to his work.

First, he selected the saw and cut off the remaining part of the right leg. That done, he cut it into four equal chunks and deposited them into one of the bins, then repeated the process on her left. Next, he moved onto the arms. Since the arms were much smaller, he cut them off at the elbow first, ditched them into the box, and then repeated the process at her shoulders. It was an easy, clean job.

He severed the head, placing it on the corner of the slab to deal with it at the end. Cutting up the torso was messy work. He reached inside her and pulled out all the remaining organs, rolling them off the slab and into the second box. Then, he went to work with the saw.

When the slab was devoid of body parts, he lifted the severed head from the corner and laid it down in front of him so the face was looking at the ceiling. He hooked the eyelids up and stared into the eyes. They were empty but filled him with an electric sense. He felt like he could see what lay beyond the veil. He licked his lips behind the mask.

He selected the hammer off the tray then looked back at the head. He grasped it in his left hand while his right raised the hammer above his head. He licked his lips again and brought it down with all the force he could muster, hitting it directly on the forehead. The sickening sounds of the splintering skull filled the room as the hammer penetrated through skin and bone. He pried it out and brought it down again and again and again. Stanley struck the head until it was pulverized into a mass of squishy flesh and blood and bone fragments. He struck the head until his arm ached and his lips were dry. He struck the head until he was hammering more marble than human remains. Dropping the hammer on the floor, he looked at the mess on the marble for a few seconds before sweeping it into a box.

He cleaned up his work-space and stacked the filled boxes in a corner. He'd deal

with them on Sunday night, when he could ensure they would get lost amongst the weekend
workload. Then, he walked through the plastic
barrier and stripped off his protective layers,
placing the jumpsuit into a bag to be incinerated
later. The rest, he hosed off before stuffing into
a tiny closet. He picked up his work clothes and
dressed, checking his watch as he strapped it
onto his wrist. He was intrigued to see it was
five minutes to midnight. It felt like he'd only
spent twenty minutes with the body, but it had
been much longer.

He walked back through the maze of
cobblestone corridors to the entrance. He used
the alcohol wipes on the table by the door before unlocking it and walking out. Squinting to
avoid temporary blindness, he made his way
back to his work-room to change into his street
clothes. After locking everything up, he stepped
out through the emergency exit door in the garbage room.

It was only as he was walking home
that he noticed how tired his body was; how
much his arms ached from their extra workout.
He kept his hooded head low and his hands in
his pockets. He didn't want to see anyone's face
on the streets. Now that the deed was complete,
he felt ashamed. He was worried that if he
looked anyone in their eyes, they would know
what he'd done. He wanted to get home as

quickly, and as anonymously, as possible. He wanted a shower. More than that, however, he wanted to get drunk.

Home was a two-bedroom apartment on the second floor of an old Victorian house in the Plateau. It wasn't overly spacious, but there was enough room for one. He entered, kicked off his shoes, and walked to the fridge. He grabbed a beer and plopped down onto his couch. He spent the very wee hours of the morning accomplishing his two goals. By the time the sun was peeking above the horizon, his head was hanging and his eyes were closed. A little spittle dribbled from one corner of his mouth as he spoke small, incoherent words to himself. They were all things he'd said before but never remembered. Eventually, he slumped over and curled his legs up underneath him, knocking over a near empty beer bottle and spilling the dregs onto the carpet. Then, he was still and silent as he slept the day away.

Todd

It was another Monday meeting and Todd was trying to keep his eyes open. His shirt was plastered to a back that was stuck to a chair. There was a fan running in the far corner, close to the head of the table, but he did not benefit from its output.

Today's subject consisted of how their budget was going to be tightened.

"Gapping will become the word of the day."

"When," someone asked. Todd didn't see who, but it sounded like Brian Holtz.

"We're going to start next month. Does everyone know what gapping is?" Mr. Charlevoix asked.

Todd didn't know what he was talking about. He wanted to ask, but didn't want to be seen as a fool. Looking at his colleagues around the table, he wore a content look. He felt anything but when no one asked for clarification. He almost put up his hand then. *Almost.*

Better to keep your mouth shut and be thought a fool than to open your mouth and remove all doubt, his father's words echoed through his brain. It settled matters. He would figure out what "gapping" was on his own. Thankfully, he didn't have to.

"Our gapping target number is eight,"
Mr. Charlevoix said. "If we're under eight sick
calls, you make due. This is your time to shine."
Mr. Charlevoix looked at each manager in turn.
Todd gave a slight nod when they locked eyes.
He hoped his nod conveyed that he'd excel at
this particular exercise. He hoped his nod con-
veyed that he was a people person.

"What happens if we get more than
eight calls?"

Todd was interested in the answer as it
was something that hadn't occurred to him. After seeing the look Mr. Charlevoix gave
Hussein, Todd was glad he hadn't been the one
to ask the question, let alone think of it. It was
the look he gave his two children when he
wanted them to know that he knew that they
knew not to do *that*.

"That's when you start with the recall
list. You fill up every vacancy after eight that
comes in, but none before." Charlevoix paused,
his eyes narrowing as he continued to stare daggers at Hussein. "You will not, however, fill up
those eight missing spots. If you're short nine,
you call one person."

Hussein didn't buckle under the weight
of the look, however. He kept his dead-eye focus on Mr. Charlevoix as he asked another
question.

"And if we don't find enough people on the recall list to cover those missing? Are we authorized to offer overtime?"

Mr. Charlevoix rolled his eyes wide for all to see. "If you deem it necessary, then yes, I'll authorize it."

Hussein made as if to say something else, but Mr. Charlevoix cut him off by raising his hand. "However," he said, "I don't think I have to remind you that every dollar spent is a dollar less in our budget, which is a dollar less at the end of the year."

Todd understood the message, and was pretty sure everyone else did too.

"Any more questions?" Mr. Charlevoix asked. No one spoke up. "I'll see you all later, then," he said. He picked up his iPad then strode out of the room.

"This is bullshit," Hussein said after Mr. Charlevoix had left.

"Maybe, but he's the boss," Todd heard Antonio say. "We can fight it, but that won't do us much good. The word hath come down from on high."

"Hussein's right," Meredith interjected. "He's holding our bonuses over our heads like a fucking guillotine."

"And I don't want to lose either my head or my money," Antonio answered.

"Fuck the money," Hussein said. "Is an extra couple grand at the end of the year worth the headache we'll have to put up with?" The room was silent. Todd kept his head down, pretending to take some last minute notes and picking non-existent lint from his pants. Hussein continued. "Do any of you really want Bobbi on your case, twenty-four seven?"

"Then don't skimp on Emerge," Paulo said. This brought a round of chuckles from the room. Todd looked up and thought he saw a flush on Hussein's face but was unsure; most of his cheeks were hidden behind a dark, coarse beard.

"If it's not her, it'll be some other head nurse," Meredith reasoned.

"Short who you gotta," Antonio said. "I think it would be wise of us if we did a rotation. We don't want to screw over the same floor every time."

"On my weekends, I'll gap on the transplant wing," Todd said. He was looking up but avoiding eye contact with any one particular individual. "I know the unit coordinator, and he's a pushover. We could probably squeeze a couple of days out of him per week if we wanted."

"Well, that's one done," Antonio said. "Who else has some suggestions?"

"Are you listening to yourselves?" Meredith said. "You're plotting how to fuck over a lot of people, how to fuck over a lot of patients, because of money. This is sick!" Todd watched her as she spoke. She was sitting up, but made no move to collect the things in front of her.

"Welcome to middle management," Antonio said. "We don't really have a choice."

"You always have a choice," she said, her voice breaking on the last word.

"Sure we do," Todd said. "We can choose between being out of a job or making an extra two G's at the end of the year. I, for one, am choosing the extra two G's."

"So you're willing to let people die just to make more money?" she asked.

"Don't be so fucking melodramatic," Antonio said. "Our people aren't that important. We don't cause people to die."

"What about the bacteria?" Hussein asked, standing up. "If we don't kill it at the base level, then it could infect others and cause complications down the line. Not to mention a metric shit-ton *more* money spent when we have to call in extras to do the high touch that you're all too fucking stupid to see needs to be done now."

"Down the line isn't our prerogative," Antonio said. "We're tasked with what we're going to do now. Today." He too stood up and was staring directly at Hussein. "Our major function is to cut down the spending. Anything above that falls upon our superiors."

"So you're going to lay the blame at their feet?" Meredith asked.

"Yes," Todd answered for Antonio. "We were told to do something, so we do it. Anything else that comes from it is not our problem."

"Seriously?" Meredith exclaimed. "You people disgust me," she said before grabbing her things and leaving the room.

"She's right, you know," Hussein said after she'd left.

"She's a bitch," Antonio said.

"I wouldn't go that far," Todd said, shifting his weight in his seat, the chair creaking uncomfortably. "How many times has she saved your ass double checking your paperwork?"

"Sure, a few times," Antonio relented, "but she's never *nice* about it." He pitched his voice up an octave. "'You know, Antonio, I wouldn't have to do this if you knew your way around spreadsheets.' Fuck her."

"You don't have to be so rude towards her," Holtz said.

"Why? She's not in the room. Are you gonna tell on me?" Antonio asked. They stared at each other across the table, Holtz dropping his gaze first. "I thought not."

"It's a moot point anyway," Todd said. "We can't do anything to change our boss' mind, so we might as well roll with it. Sitting here, complaining about Meredith won't solve the issue we're currently facing. We need to gap, so we have to figure out a way to do it clean." He paused and looked at the remaining managers. "We have to figure out a way to *all* come out on top."

"That's what we were trying to do before *he* started running his mouth," Antonio said. He jerked a thumb toward Hussein.

"Fuck you, you --"

"Guys, can you put a hold on your dick measuring contest?" Paulo said. "This isn't helping. In fact, it's hindering. So, unless you've got something productive to add, keep your mouth's shut."

No one said anything. The silence stretched out until Antonio's SpectraLink rang. He looked down to see the incoming number, told the room he had to take it and left. That ended the meeting, and the rest of the managers quietly followed him out.

Simon

Walking through the kitchen and out onto the back patio, Simon willed himself not to drop either cake. In his right hand was an ice-cream oreo cake, made by the Dairy Queen down the street. In his left was a chocolate-chip red velvet cake that his auntie had made from scratch, started a few days prior. Each cake was stenciled with his mother's name on it in blue icing. Underneath, in larger, yellow letters were the words "Happy Retirement." His mother had worked in the housekeeping department at St. Agnes for more than thirty-five years. The last thing he wanted to do was fuck up her special day.

He stepped out into the bright spring sun and was greeted to cheers from the family and friends gathered in his mother's backyard, and by extension, his. They were all faces he knew: some of them were his friends, most were co-workers, and a very small contingent were both. There were balloons and streamers tied to the sagging clothesline, some keeled over like they'd had too much to drink. The large cobble-stones encircling the waist-high above-ground pool were littered with the remnants of party poppers; the red, blue and yellow confetti standing in high contrast against the chipped pale grey of the stones.

He heard a chorus of "for she's a jolly good fellow," as he approached the cracked glass table and deposited the two cakes. He breathed a sigh of relief and wiped the beginnings of sweat from his forehead as he was clapped on the back by Mario.

"I would have asked you if you needed help, but we all know how much you like doing shit on your own," Mario said to him.

Simon gave him an awkward, sideways glance before bending down and kissing his mother, seated on a rusty metal chair, on the forehead.

"Happy retirement, Moms," Simon said.

"Thank you, love," his mother said, leaning back and stretching her face up so she could reach around and hug him around his neck. He reciprocated and then stepped back to let the flood of people envelope his mother, giving her their warmest wishes.

Simon walked over to the cooler, rubbing each forearm briefly as he went. He opened the cooler and rummaged around for a beer. After a few tries, he found a Heineken. He popped the top and looked around, surveying the party guests. Most were his mother's age; he saw them as old timers, more jealous than happy that she'd passed her time and had gotten out before them. He could tell by the way they sipped their drinks. He could tell by the way their eyes were never far from the guest of honor. They were greedy in more than the amount of ribs and beer they'd consumed. They were greedy in the way they wanted to steal the life out of his mother. She was still around. She still had her functions and was finally out of *the* system. They wanted what she had, and they wanted it all.

There were others, too. They were younger, but they lacked the look that Simon wanted. The party lacked the *t'ings* that Simon wanted.

"Got another one of those for me?" Simon heard the voice and couldn't place it. He turned to see an aging, yet well toned white man. The man had glorious salt and pepper hair that stuck up around his ears and formed a halo that dipped no lower than the top third of his occipital bone. It took him a moment, but he eventually placed a name to the face. It was the man he'd seen around the doors to The Doctor's dungeon. He collected the biomedical waste, and Simon had a feeling this man knew more than most in the hospital.

"This one's all yours, Stanley," he said, reaching in and tossing a beer in a quick, under-hand motion. Stanley not only caught it with ease, but he popped the top with one thickened thumb and took a large swallow followed by a lengthy burp.

"Sweet zombie Jesus, don't that taste good today," Stanley said. Despite himself, Simon laughed. He held up his bottle and clinked it off Stanley's before taking a swig himself.

"I didn't know you knew my Moms," Simon said, finally. He smiled over his beer at Stanley.

"Oh no? I'm not surprised. It's not like we go *way* back." Stanley took another swig of beer. They kept their eyes on each other. Simon felt a subtle cunning coming from the man across from him. All at once, he felt the urge to kick this man out of his house. All at once, he felt an urge to ensure that this man never made contact with his mother again.

Stanley continued. "I've worked with her for the past twenty years. Not *with her*, with her, mind, but we know each other."

"Enough so she invited you here," Simon said.

"Of course!" Stanley took another swallow and burped again. "Us old-timers stick together," he said. "Sometimes, you gotta stick with those that know you."

"I guess."

"Indeed. Anyway, I'm gonna go mingle. Enjoy your day. Your mother, and you, have

159

earned it." With that, Stanley strolled off into the crowd. Simon watched him go, feeling greasy and gross without having any reason to.

He stood by the beer cooler and polished off his bottle. While reaching for another, he heard someone approach. This time when he looked up, it was a more familiar, friendly face.

"Shit, man," Mario said. "You look like you've seen a ghost."

Simon took a large swig before answering. "Nah man," he began, searching for a way to regain his composure, "I just don't like seeing a party like this without any *t'ings* walking around, you know what I mean?"

"T'ings?" Mario asked, draining his beer and dropping it into the recycling bin beside the cooler. "Yeah, I guess. I appreciate you being here for your Moms though," he said, putting a reassuring hand on Simon's shoulder. "Lord knows, I didn't get to be there for mine when she was in need."

"It's not like Moms is dying today," Simon said, then quickly added, "nor any time soon."

"True."

"I appreciate it, though."

They drank their beers for a time as music and voices danced around them.

"So," Simon ventured, "you got any gigs coming up?"

"Yeah. My agent called back. I'm gonna be the tall black guy in the back of the action sequence for this new superhero movie."

"Any lines?"

"Nah, but I get to showcase my surprise face." Mario pantomimed an exaggerated scared face and they both laughed.

"So," Simon ventured, after draining his beer, "you wanna get outta here?

Mario agreed and they went to do their rounds, Simon having quickie conversations with those he liked and giving fleeting recognition to those he didn't. Twenty minutes later, they were sitting inside Mario's car, driving downtown.

They rode a while in silence until Simon felt the need to break it.

"It's super early," he said. "Where the hell are we going, anyway?"

"Shit man, I don't know. It was your idea to leave. I figured you had the spot in mind."

"How 'bout a pub?" Simon said after a few blocks had passed.

"That could work. Where to?"

"I dunno. Just park somewhere and we'll stroll the streets, find something that looks good."

Mario parked his car along Ste. Cathrine. Both men reached into their pockets

161

and found enough change to make the meter full. Then, they began their walk.

They ended up at some generic Irish pub on Crescent Street. It was pushing eight o'clock and was pleasantly full. They walked in and waited by the hostess station even though the sign said to "seat yourself." It took them a quick three minutes looking at their phones before one of the serving staff came up to them.

"Bonsoir. Vous voulez une table?"

Simon looked up and flashed her a toothy smile. She was hot, but something about her ears was off; still, Simon proceeded with his smile. "Yeah. A spot for two, please. Preferably at the bar."

"You're in luck," the hostess said, matching his smile, he saw. "Follow me."

"No doubt," Simon said after she turned and began walking away. He slapped Mario's arm and pointed toward the hostess' ass. Mario looked down then back to Simon. He nodded.

They sat at the bar, surrounded by screens filled with sports scenes and loudly talking patrons. They ordered two bottles of Heineken and two bottles of water. Mario stayed absorbed in his phone, while Simon scanned the bar for talent. Their beers clanked down in front of them and Simon handed over money for the first round.

"So, any new gigs?" Simon asked.

"Uhh, yeah. One sec," Mario said, holding up a finger. Simon scoffed, drank some beer, and went back to taking in the room. Nothing seemed to interest him. He turned back for his beer, finished it, and ordered another. He needed to talk. He needed to drink. Something about seeing Stanley at the party had set him on edge. He'd spent the entire ride faking interest in his phone while thinking back to all the times he'd seen Stanley in the hallway, close to *the* doors.

He was still buried in his own mind when he heard a surly voice to the left of him. It was asking the bartender for a pint and a shot. Simon heard the wavering tone and looked up to see a rather ordinary looking redhead. She had some good meat on her, but there were the beginnings of bags under her eyes; still, since Mario was rooted in the throngs of gig procurement, Simon had time to kill.

"What's got you all hot and bothered?" Simon asked.

The redhead gave him a scowl. "Something," she said before turning her attention back to the bartender as he poured out her order. She was watching the bartender with ravenous eyes, but not *seeing* him at all. When he set the beverages down in front of her, she laid a twenty on the bar and downed the shot before taking a healthy pull of her beer. She sat back, swallowed and took another pull, draining half the pint.

Simon's spider senses began tingling. He glanced down at her left hand and noticed she wore no ring. He was hoping for marital problems but would settle for whatever baggage she had attached. *Maybe she took the ring off before coming to the bar,* he thought. He said a silent prayer to make it so. He'd hooked up with a handful of married women before and they'd all blown his mind in bed. Still, it didn't matter to him. He hadn't gotten laid in almost a week and was jonesing.

He pointed at her glass. "Looks like you're gonna need another one of those soon. I'll buy you another round if you wanna talk about something."

She looked at him shrewdly and then back at her drink, downed the rest of it, and issued forth a colossal burp.

"Why the fuck not," she said. "I'm gonna need to get good and drunk tonight, so a couple of freebees ain't gonna hurt."

Simon looked back, saw that Mario was still fiddling with his phone, and inched his stool a smidge closer to the redhead, holding up his hand to signal he was ready to place an order.

"So what happened?" he asked casually.

She sighed, putting her face into her hands and then running them through her hair. She took some deep breaths while Simon ordered two shots and two beers from the bartender. The drinks arrived and the redhead threw back her shot without a moment's hesitation. She went back to looking at the bar and swallowed a couple times. Simon turned back to Mario and saw no help there. He was still engrossed in a wind-bag contract, probably. Simon debated pulling out his phone, but his better sense told him to stick with it. Eventually, his patience paid off.

"I've seen a lot of fucked up shit lately," the redhead said, still staring off into space.

"Fucked up, how? Care to talk about it a little bit?"

"Well," she started before clamming up. Then, she turned toward him and looked at him, *really* looked at him; he could almost see the gears grinding behind her eyes. "Well," she started again, "outside of some really weird lingering hallucinations, I - I think I saw a guy die a little bit ago." She turned back to her beer and took another considerable swallow.

Eyes widening, Simon took a long sip of his shot, giving himself time to process this information. His brain started doing backflips to find a way to turn the dark subject matter to his favour. Being around many dying people, death never phased him, but others talking about death threw him for a loop. He knew everyone dealt with it in different ways, so his brain worked double time to come up with a way to seem caring and compassionate; mostly, he was annoyed at having been thrown such a curveball toward his conquest. Finally, when nothing good came to him, he said the only words that were circling his brain.

"Wow," he said incredulously. "What makes you think they died?"

The redhead took another pull of her beer, continuing to scan the bottles behind the bar. He felt put off by her inability to make eye contact, but once again, it was another thing he'd have to roll with.

When the redhead spoke, her voice, and words, came out in a geyser. "As I was coming home from work last month I saw two guys on the sidewalk. One of them was laying on his back, bleeding from every inch of his body. The other man was standing over him with a handful of shirt and feeding him fists. There was blood everywhere. I ran up to them and tried to stop them, but the guy on top slapped me aside and continued hitting the other guy like I wasn't even there. He threw me aside like I was a piece of garbage. I told him I was going to call the cops if he didn't stop, and you know what he said to me?"

Simon opened his mouth to answer, saw that she was going to speak regardless of what he said, and settled for keeping his silence by taking another drink.

"'Fuck off, bitch.' he screamed at me."

"Did you call the cops?"

"Yes," she said, finally looking back at him. He noticed that her eyes were glossy, brimming on tears. He smiled inwardly and pulled his stool another inch closer to the redhead. He reached out and touched her arm with his left hand. He rubbed it gently up to her shoulder in a sign of compassion.

"What did they do?" he asked intently.

"I don't know. I didn't stick around." She shrugged off his hand and took another pull of her pint. "I feel so fuckin' terrible," she cried, "but what was I gonna do? He would have killed me! Besides, I didn't see any of my bitch neighbours willing to step in. They were all looking from their porches, doing nothing. Why do I have to be the one that does everything?"

The tears came then. Simon felt awkward and looked back at Mario. He was done with his contract, subtly glancing over the top of his phone. Simon thought about pulling Mario into the conversation and settled against it. He still had a chance to get this girl's number, and he didn't want Mario to come in as the third wheel.

"That's fucking crazy," he said eventually.

"Like, I've seen some shit, but that was *some shit*," the redhead said, wiping her eyes with the tiny napkin that the bartender had laid out for her previously.

"Hey, it's okay," Simon said gently. "I'm sure that everything got sorted out alright once the cops arrived."

"But it's not," the redhead blurted. "It's not alright." Simon drew back on his stool from the ferocity of her voice, crossing his hands on the bar. She continued. "He killed that guy. I'm sure of it."

"I could find out for you," he said, tracking a busboy as he went about the room. He focused on anything in the room *but* her. He felt the empty air between them, followed by a tension shift. He knew she had turned her body in his direction. It was the inviting sign he'd been waiting for. Still, he had to play out the string.

"I work in the hospital system," he said, still keeping his focus on the room.

"Wha--?"

Simon took a sip of his beer and decided to push as far as he could. Fuck it. This chick was keeping his game sharp.

"I can look into it for you. Find out if the guy survived or not. That's easy."

"How could you--?"

Simon slowly rotated his stool until he was facing the redhead. "I'm Simon," he said, offering his hand.

"Sheela," she said, extending her own.

"Sheela," he said. "Give me your number. I'll look into what happened close to your home. Address...?" He left the question hanging in the air.

Sheela told him that she lived in Hochelaga, on Dezery. She gave him her number. He typed it into his phone and clicked the call button before sliding his phone back into his pocket. When he saw her hand dip down, he thumbed cancel. He draped his right arm on the bar and leaned closer to her, hoping to draw her attention to him. It worked.

"I'll let you know," he said.

"Why are you being so nice?"

"Why not?" Simon said. "It's no skin off my teeth."

Sheela laughed. "That's a stupid fuckin' expression. It doesn't make any goddamn sense."

"How so?"

"It's 'skin off my knuckles'. Teeth don't have skin."

Simon shrugged. "Me and my friends always said it like that."

Sheela nodded with a smile and finished her beer. After that, she left, and he and Mario went on the prowl.

The Doctor

The final rat made a splatting sound as it was dropped upon the pile of already dead rodents in the biomed box. On the slab was a plethora of their tails, the tip ends cut off on all but one of them. The Doctor stripped off his gloves and dropped them too into the box. He looked at his spoils and ran through the next steps in his head, hoping that it would work.

After sterilizing his hands, he slipped on the surgical loupes over his safety goggles. That done, he snapped on another pair of gloves before picking up his suture kit, and began lacing the interiors of the tails with bits of intestines he'd gotten from a previous operation. When that was all done he took a twenty minute break to stretch and do a few circles around the room. When he felt refreshed, he resterilized his hands, put on more gloves, and placed two tails in front of him, end to end. He picked up the business portion of the electro-surgical diathermy cautery machine, placing minute pressure on the foot switch and watched the pop of electricity as the instrument came to life and began to heat up. The room began to fill up with the smell of burnt, regurgitated coffee beans covered in sawdust. Wriggling his nose behind the surgical mask, The Doctor forced the stench from his mind and continued. After a couple hours, he had a half meter long, hollowed out rat tail. After replacing all of his instruments, The Doctor took the tail to the sink and placed the open end under the running faucet. The water stayed in place, there were no leaks. Satisfied, The Doctor emptied out the water and replaced the tail on the slab.

Yes, his plan was winfally coming together.

Alessia

"Hello, Mr. Woodson. How're you doing today?"

The figure in the bed rolled over, his eyes lolling at the ceiling. He opened his mouth and a mush of words came out.

"That doesn't sound too good," Alessia said in her most jovial tone. In reality, she didn't want to be here, dealing with the incomprehensible and incontinent. She was tired from her night out dancing; she was even more tired from being kept up until three in the morning by a vivacious one night stand. Now, at a little after ten in the morning, dealing with her first patient without any students around to help her, she was debating if she'd be able to handle a full day's workload. It was never easy dealing with one of the bedridden, but she went about her business in the happiest, most professional manner she could muster.

She lifted Mr. Woodson's arms up, extending them until he made a grunt of pain, his eyes slopping around in their sockets like a lamb stuck in a barbed wire fence. Next, she moved onto his legs. She lifted them one by one, pointedly trying to ignore his struggles and doing poorly. His legs kept kicking out and slipping out from her hands. She wished for someone to help keep his legs steady, a student was the perfect solution, but made due with being annoyed and using extra force. Around the end, she pulled his leg too hard, and he made a mewling sound deep in his throat. She hoped he'd gotten the point. He didn't, and the rest of his session went about the same.

Her disposition didn't improve as the day went on, especially after she had her second meeting of the morning with her boss, McKinnon. He saw her as she was heading to lunch.

"Can we talk? I need to speak with you," he told her.

They sat down at an unoccupied table in the cafeteria. The noise of the caf was raucous and it hurt Alessia's sleep deprived skull.

"So...?" she asked, leaving the question hanging in the air.

McKinnon took a bite of his sandwich, chewed thoughtfully, and swallowed before speaking.

"I've got some bad news for you."

"That's no surprise. What is it?"

"You're not going to be getting any students for a while."

Alessia put her fork down, still loaded with stir-fry. "What do you mean, 'I'm not going to be getting any students for a while?'"

"You know about the cuts going around?"

"Everyone knows about the cuts." Then it dawned on her. "We're getting cut, like completely? Like, no new people coming in?"

McKinnon looked down at his sandwich and took another bite. Eventually, he looked up, and for that Alessia felt her already enormous amount of respect for the man grow even more.

"Yes, but not completely. They're going to terminate all but five students."

Alessia gave a disheartened sigh. "Why wasn't it brought up today? They told me I wouldn't have anyone for the rest of the week, but why try to hide it from us for the foreseeable future?"

"Because the less everyone knows, the less the public knows. I'm only telling you this because I respect you. You're my best employee and deserve the truth, no matter how shitty it is." He rubbed a hand through his salt and pepper hair and then blurted forth a mound of words. "I'm sorry. I went to bat for us. I tried. I got stonewalled. The budget is dry. We're essentially dead in the water until we move to the new hospital."

Alessia knew it was bad but didn't know it was *that* bad. "What makes them so willing to open the purse strings after the move?"

"For one, most of the reserve budget is in place for paying for the move." Alessia opened her mouth, but McKinnon raised a hand, asking her to keep silent. "Second, they're trying to save money *and* face until then. They know they can't start the new hospital off on the wrong foot, so they'll bend over backwards to keep everything kosher once it opens, but not before. They don't want to have that kind of black-eye on their profile. Not after everything else that's gone down."

"So, you're telling me because I'm a good employee?"

"That, and I want you to be prepared. I'm giving you this as an aside, but also, so you're not overworked. You're going to have to manage your tasks with this knowledge; a knowledge that won't become widespread for another month or two. I'm telling you this so you can plan ahead. Don't worry about any shit that comes down the pipe. I'll have your back on that." McKinnon caught and held her eyes. "That's a one hundred percent promise. I guarantee it."

She sat back in her chair, trying to allow her brain to process the information. She could survive the rest of the week fine, she only had one more working day left, but it was the following week that worried her, and the weeks after that. She knew they were getting a few heart transplant patients early next week, and they were always the most work, especially because they tended to be older and less willing to do the work without someone there helping them, twenty-four seven. She dreaded what was coming up.

Alessia spent the rest of her day in a haze of gloom. She tried not to let her remaining patients sense her annoyance but knew she didn't do a good job; it didn't help that she pushed her patients harder than they'd wanted to go. She was trying to clean her slate before the next week hit her with all its force. She did her best but knew it wasn't going to be enough.

There was one bright spot to her afternoon, however.

She was on her way to her next patient's room, a Ms. Wisconsin, when she saw a large group wheeling a stretcher into the cardiac ward. It was a heart transplant and it was on her list, so she was happy to note that the attending surgeon was Dr. Veksler. He had the best bed-side manner, but more than that, he never treated his staff like shit. He looked over at her and offered up a curt nod that she returned. She'd be lying if she said she wasn't touched by it.

While she was walking down the hall with her patient, Ms. Wisconsin slipped and fell. On instinct, she reached out and clutched her patient's arm a little too hard and the force of Ms. Wisconsin's falling pulled Alessia's arm in an awkward way. She kept her mouth clenched shut and cried out low enough that no one heard; however, that meant no one noticed and came to her aid, or so she thought.

As Alessia was struggling to help her patient up, she saw an arm reach down and gently take Ms. Wisconsin around the waist. Together, they helped her up into a seated position on the commode chair.

"Thank you so much," she said, looking up and seeing who came to her aid once her patient was comfortable.

"Nothing to it." Dr. Veksler said. "Need some help with your patient?"

"Oh, I couldn't. It's not your responsibility."

"I don't mind. As long as I only have to push *this*, I should be good, no?" he said, holding on to the back of the chair. He smiled at her, and she smiled back.

There was a silence while Ms. Wisconsin caught her breath and energy. Alessia noted how Dr. Veksler bent over and looked at the patient with a shrewd eye. He took the stethoscope from around his neck and placed it on her chest. He pulled a triangular rubber hammer from a pocket and tapped Ms. Wisconsin underneath the knee. The leg lifted immediately. Veksler closed his eyes, asked the patient to take a deep breath, and Alessia marveled at the care he was showing.

"I hope you're not too overworked," Veksler said without looking up.

"No," she said, laughing at the absurdity of the question. "I'm not. Thanks for asking." She watched him breath heavy and neatly tuck his instruments away. "How is she?"

"She'll live. Will you?" Alessia felt that she kept her face under control, but something must have given her away because Veksler waved a quick hand in her direction.

"Sorry for asking."

Before Alessia could answer, Veksler bent down and spoke with the patient.

"Are you ready to continue?" he asked, putting a hand on her shoulder and squeezing it with zero force. Ms. Wisconsin looked up and nodded with bright eyes.

Alessia helped the patient to her feet. They began the laborious walk down the hallway.

"So, how are *you*, Alessia?" Veksler asked. Her reaction must have shown on her face because Veksler chuckled to himself. "I make it a priority to know my team," was all he said.

179

"I'm good," she said, not giving any conviction to the lie. She sighed and started again. "No. I'm sorry. Nothing's good."

"Why not?"

She took in a large breath and then let it out in a machine-gun rattle.

"I'm getting hit with work. I'm getting more patients than I can handle, yet I'm asked to turn them around in record time. I'm doing the best I can, but they're fucking me. Oh shit. Sorry. I didn't mean to say 'shit' and 'fuck'. Shit. I said it again."

Veksler laughed before she could continue.

"Don't ever apologize to me. You're doing a hell of a job. You're helping these folks get to where they need to go. Isn't that right, Ms. Wisconsin," he said, placing a grandfatherly hand on the patient's shoulder.

Alessia watched the patient nod, looking at Veksler with elderly lust.

They walked the patient down the hallway in silence.

"So," Veksler asked while they were maneuvering the patient in front of the nursing station. "What's your plan of action?"

"The same as all heart transplants," Alessia said without thinking. "Why? Is there something special I should know?"

"No. No. She's just a regular patient. I'm sorry," he said, looking over at her with eyes that were no longer a dead grey. "We're working together, so I always do my diligence."

"I'm going to exercise their extremities first, and as soon as they're able, I'll start working on their core," Alessia said. She wanted to say more, the words on the edge of her tongue, but said nothing.

"Just do your best. It's all I ask," Veksler said.

The doctor and the physiotherapist walked the patient back to her room in comfortable silence. They put the woman to bed and Alessia checked her vitals while Dr. Veksler put the commode chair into the bathroom.

"Thank you for everything," Alessia said, and before she could stop herself, she added, "your daughter would be proud."

"Thank you. That means a lot to me," Veksler said automatically. "I'll see you tomorrow with our new patient." He walked out of the room before Alessia could give him a nod of acknowledgement.

Sheela

The sidewalk outside her apartment still showed the faded remnants of a stain. Footsteps and the sun had been the only things at work to erase the blood during an unusually dry spring. Sheela wondered why nobody ever hosed it away when it was still fresh. She looked around and saw the patchy grass and sprouting weeds upon the lawns as she walked. Some had tiny, wrought iron fences surrounding them, but most were open to the sidewalk. One in three miniscule yards had a hose. Shit, how could she give her neighbours grief when she didn't own a hose of her own?

Still, even the sight of the grotesque splotch was less sickening today because Simon had texted her a week ago. He'd said that one guy had been discharged from the I.C.U. a while ago, while the other was out on bail. And even if the beaten-to-a-pulp man had died, it's not like that would have been the first time she'd seen someone die. Fuck no. But this one was different. She was out of *that* life and didn't expect *it* would have followed her this far, to within spitting distance of her home; that's something they'd never told her about in the meetings. Sure, some of your past shit would come back to either haunt you, or straight up pop up into your real life and scream, "Here I am. Deal with me!" But not death. Not it finding her this close to her new life. And yet, that wasn't the worst part.

The worst was this "almost" death had flattened her with a jarring sense of deja vu. She knew, one hundred percent, that she'd seen that scene before. She *knew!* You don't fuckin' forget that kind of thing. She only wished she knew where she'd witnessed it before. Her brain was drawing a blank on that score.

Regardless, nothing could dampen her mood today. She was off to her final meeting with The Wahz. This one would pay for all. She'd more than likely continue with the NA meetings because they held a certain therapeutic sway over her. With those, she could also come and go as she pleased. No one asked questions, except for Henne, and even then, he never pushed *too* hard. The Wahz always had questions from those piercing, beady fuckin' eyes of hers. No thank you. She was out. She was done.

She rode the metro with a smile, not minding when she was shunted aside by some rude soon-to-be students. She skipped the bus and decided to walk up the hill to The Institute. The early morning air filled up her lungs. She took as much of it as she could. It helped her center herself.

And so, she *was* centered when she pushed her way through the front doors of The Institute. She made her way to the Wahz's office and sat down in the chair in the hallway, waiting. At precisely eight-thirty am, the Wahz opened her door, looked up and down the hallway before spotting Sheela, directly in front of her.

"Oh good. You're here," The Wahz said. "Please, come in."

Sheela got up and followed her into the room.

"As you may or may not be aware, today is our last meeting," The Wahz said, once they were both seated.

"I'm aware."

"I won't bore you with things you don't want to hear. I feel our sessions have been productive, and I'm proud of all the work you've put into yourself, and I wish that you continue doing so." The Wahz said it with a pleasant enough voice, but to Sheela, it sounded like she was reading off a teleprompter. No doubt this was a speech she had memorized for such patients that were in *her* situation.

"I will. Thank you. I know I said these meetings were bullshit sometimes, but they weren't. They've helped."

"I know." The Wahz said this as a thin smile crept across her lips; they parted enough

184

to show the thick chiclet teeth she hid behind them. The interior of her lips were very pale, Sheela noted.

Sheela opened her mouth to speak but was cut off.

"How have your last two weeks been? Did you experience any triggers? Is the blood stain finally gone from in front of your place?"

She looked at the lady across the desk. She couldn't remember telling The Wahz anything about *that* attack, although it wouldn't surprise her if The Wahz knew. She'd had a couple of rough meetings around the end. She'd been scared of a slip back, caused by the hallucinations in the stairwell, and had spoken rapid fire and uncomfortably during the meetings afterward. She could have said anything. It was only natural for The Wahz to look out for her, even if Sheela felt it was a complete bullshit act. Despite all that, Sheela was determined to allow nothing to dampen her day.

"I don't really notice it anymore. Like, I know it's there, but I never *really* think about it."

"And when you do think about it?"

"It's not that big a deal, honestly. Half the time I think it's an old puke stain." Sheela faked a laugh and scratched her thigh. *Old habits,* she thought, and forced herself to stop.

"Okay."

She watched The Wahz lick the tip of her pencil and scribble something in.

"Look," Sheela said, sitting forward in her chair. "You know I'm off, haven't been on in years." As she said this, she reached into the back pocket of her Salvation Army jeans and pulled out a book. It was filled with dates and signatures. She laid it on the desk, gently, in front of her.

She waited, hoping The Wahz would get the point.

"I've got a job," she continued, "and I'm living on my own; have been for eighteen months." She kept her voice at a casual cadence, like she was reading the news. "At the beginning, I didn't want to do fuckin' *anything.* Now," she shrugged her shoulders, "I do. I feel good. I *feel* good," she said again. "I'm not fuckin' cured, I know that, but I *want* to fight."

The Wahz scratched down some more notes before licking her fingers and turning the page. She sat back and Sheela mirrored her movements.

"I also want to stop coming here. No offense, but I'd do whatever it takes to stop coming here." Sheela said, gesturing around her. She meant *this* office. She meant *this* building. The Wahz nodded and folded her notepad closed.

"You've shown good judgement and commitment," The Wahz said, holding out a business card between two knuckles. It seemed to have materialized out of thin air when Sheela blinked. She hesitated at first, because she already had the number monogrammed on the card committed to memory, being given the same card two years ago. Knowing that it would look bad if she didn't take it, she reached out. She flipped it over and read a new number, scrawled hastily in blue ink, on the back. She looked up, the surprise plain upon her face.

"It's my out-of-office number. If you need help at any time, please, call me."

The look Sheela got was full of earnest sorrow. It was also filled with quiet hope.

Sheela tucked it into her wallet. "Thank you," she said. She got up to go. The Wahz stood up too, opening a folder and holding out a document. Sheela signed it before The Wahz added her own.

Sheela opened the door and stepped out.

"Door closed," The Wahz said from behind her desk.

The latch clicked, and Sheela walked down to the elevator. Each step, like always, got lighter. She was gliding by the time she pressed the button. She briefly considered the stairs, but one look at the door dissuaded her.

She went down to the first floor and took the handicap ramp. At the bottom of the ramp was a small lobby with that asshole Patrick at security, it *was* a Tuesday, and then the door. After the door, it was fuckin' freedom. Midway down the ramp was the row of ten, *eleven?*, paintings. The third to last one was crooked, so, feeling in grand humour, Sheela stopped and attempted to straighten it. She couldn't because it was too high. She stepped back to look at the wall and see if she could find better purchase.

Her vision was drawn to the final picture on her left. It was odd for two reasons. It was a person, *A! Fuckin'! Person!,* tied to a slab. Their mid-section was chopped open, revealing a black and red chasm filled with organs and meat. Sheela had seen gross things before; maybe not as detailed as chopped open bodies, but it hadn't been no fuckin' painting what she'd seen. This one cut deeper because there was something missing about the body. What was missing was its skin, which lay dangling on hooks six feet above the slab. It was stretched out into an almost translucent sheet. Almost.

Sheela looked at the painting then quickly turned her eyes back towards the exit. She'd read about this place and knew those sicko Christian shitheads liked to fuck with people. She figured the newly added piece was an experiment. She dismissed it from her mind as she walked through the lobby and out the exit, making sure to give Patrick the finger on her way by.

Alessia

Her eyes began to get itchy and sore after she'd been staring at the computer screen for two hours. Two hours after that her eyes were red from rubbing, and Alessia thought they'd begin bleeding soon if she had to look at a computer screen any longer. She snapped her laptop shut and got up to stretch, her mouth echoing her movements with a tremendous yawn. She walked out of her room and moved toward the kitchen where she heard her mother puttering around. She passed her father in the sunken den. He was stretched out along the couch, a laptop resting on his slight paunch. He looked up, raising a quizzical eyebrow at his daughter as she passed.

"How's it going?"

"Long. Really long."

"Finished?"

"For the day, yes."

"How much work do you have left?"

Alessia thought about all the untouched files that waited for her on her flash drive. She'd cleared out maybe a third of them today, so that left a conservative estimate of about twelve hours worth of work. Not for the first time, she cursed John under her breath.

She'd gotten the bad news that her student, along with virtually everyone else, had been cut because of the lack of budget. John, like all the other students, had been called individually in front of the board and had to go through an interview. If he'd been evaluated on his work ethic and his bedside manner, he would have passed in spades. It was his shoddy paperwork that had done him in; *more non-existent than shoddy*, Alessia thought when she'd first been handed all his files. There were mounds of missing information. She'd spent an extra few hours after her shift ended on the previous day combing through patient files and jotting down some particulars. Then, she'd uploaded all the information to a file and brought it home with her so she could spend her weekend fixing all the problems John had left for her. What made matters worse was she'd gotten a very stern talking to from HR. She was told, on top of losing her student, that her teaching ability was being revoked for the time being. She'd been negligent in her duties by not double checking John's work. She was told she'd have a letter in her file and would be on administrative probation for the next three months, which meant they were going to watch her intently. Despite having no one to blame but herself, she currently harboured an extreme resentment towards John. Sure, she should have continued to double check his work, but after the first two weeks, it had been excellent. Every instance afterward, when she'd slyly asked him a question or two, he'd always had a quick and accurate answer.

After her meeting with HR, she'd sought out McKinnon. They commiserate over a cup of coffee, George buying, obviously. He tried to keep her spirits up, telling her that if she ever got a chance to peruse his file, she'd see not less than five letters of disapproval scattered amongst all the good.

"Sometimes, they just need to make an example of someone. Word will trickle down, and they'll have immaculate paperwork for the next couple months."

"But my file," she protested. "I had a clean record until now. Almost ten years of hard, honest work, and I'm getting *done* like this?"

"HR views the world in black and white," George said calmly, silently chewing air. "More often than not, it works. Sometimes, someone gets thrown under the bus. Don't take it to heart. It was just your turn."

"My *turn?* It boils down to it being my *turn?*"

"Did you stay vigilant and check on his work?" George asked, looking at her over the rim of his cup as he took a sip.

That stung. Alessia knew he was right, but having it so bluntly stated, by someone she looked up to, hurt more than the black mark in her file ever would. George saw the look on her face and pushed on quickly.

"Listen. I know you're an amazing employee. You care about the patients, having only the best intentions for them. You do your work well, and it shows. You were never in danger of getting more than a slap on the wrist. I wouldn't allow them to do more to my best employee."

Alessia couldn't help but smile at the sincerity and respect the man across the table was giving her.

"What you have to understand though, is now we're playing for keeps; we will be until we've moved into the super hospital. And even then, I expect it to keep up for another two years while our budget plays catch-up with our debt.

"What I mean is, you, me, and everyone we know is under the microscope, and will be for a bit. They were looking for an example to be made, and it just happened to be your turn."

"That's not exactly the most comforting thing," she said.

"Maybe not, but it's the truth. Just keep doing what you're doing and you'll be fine."

And so, here she was, working from home on her weekend off, struggling to play catch up.

She sighed, not trying to hide her displeasure from her father.

"A lot," she said.

"I'm sure you'll conquer it," her father said, looking back down at his laptop. "Nothing in life comes easy, you know."

Alessia moved into the open kitchen, heading straight for the fridge. She pulled out the fixings for a sandwich and laid them on the green and black marble-top counter. As she did so, her mother sidled up and began preparing the sandwich for her. Alessia knew better than to protest and sat down on one of the stools that circled the kitchen's island.

Neither of them spoke. Instead, they both shuffled nervously through the silence that had encapsulated them like a shroud. It stretched out, punctuated only by the knife chomping down on the cutting board as her mother cut the crusts off the sandwich.

The plate was slid in front of Alessia, a ham and cheese sandwich with a mound of potato chips.

"Thanks, Mama," Alessia said.

Her mother waved a hand and went back to puttering about. Alessia chomped down on her sandwich and watched as her mother cleaned an immaculate stove. When the sandwich, and stove were done, Alessia munched chips while her mother swept invisible crumbs from the floor and then passed a barely-wet mop.

She watched and waited for her mother to say something, *anything*. She was sufficiently annoyed by the work placed on her that she would've welcomed a blow-up, hoping it would alleviate the irritation she felt. Her mother, perhaps sensing her tone and thoughts, said nothing. She finished up the cursory mopping, pushed invisible dust bunnies into a dustpan, and replaced everything, walking out of the kitchen and into her bedroom. The door was shut with quiet gentleness.

Alessia went to the den and sat on the chair opposite her father.

"What's Mama's problem?" she asked with a gentle sigh.

Her father closed his laptop and sat up. He rubbed his eyes and watched her watching him.

"She's just worried. I am too." He paused and took in a deep breath, holding it. After releasing it, he spoke in a hurried voice. "She thinks you hate her. I wish you'd go and speak with her, expel that notion of hers. It would go a long way to getting her to calm down and begin to feel better."

What about me? You're the ones who are making this so difficult. Why should I do the apologizing when it's my feelings, my future, that's being hurt and possibly ruined? She knew she could say no such thing. She felt some anger towards her parents, but mostly she felt sorrow. She was keeping a rather large secret from them; something that would ruin her relationship with her mother and, quite possibly, her father too. She wanted to be out from under their roof before dropping that particular bombshell on them. So, she held her tongue as best she could.

Still, she felt she had to say something.

"I understand she's worried, Papa, but I'm going to have to leave home someday. I'd rather it be sooner rather than later. I cannot stay here my whole life."

"We know. It's just, you're our only child, and your mother and I only want to keep you safe. It's dangerous living on your own. There are monsters that will try and...," he paused briefly, searching for the right word, "...and *take* anything and everything from you."

"There's no such thing as monsters, Papa," she said.

"I don't mean literally," he said, giving her a look she'd last gotten when she'd been twelve. She rolled her eyes.

"I know. You don't have to worry, though." She held up a hand when he opened his mouth. "I know you will, but I'm strong and I have a good job. I can take care of myself financially as well as physically if I have to."

They looked at each other again, a tentative silence filling the room. She was the one to break it.

"But, I will go speak with Mama. I'll be kind."

With that, she got up and walked to her parent's room. She knocked softly on the door and asked if she could come in. She heard a murmur from behind the wood, so she opened the door and went in.

Simon

"So, tell me more about yourself," she said.

"Not much to tell, really," Simon said, taking a sip of a half-full glass of wine. "I work to get money. I use the money to party with my friends. You know, the usual Montreal life-style."

"And what do you *do* exactly, for fun?" She was running a hand through her red hair. Simon saw that it was blonde at the roots and wondered briefly why she dyed it. He preferred blondes.

Simon gave her a wan smile. "A little of this, a little of that, you know. What about yourself?" He regretted having to ask the question, but he needed to string her along a little bit longer.

"Well, I'm kinda all over the place these days." He gave her a look and she hastily continued. "I went through a book phase where I was a voracious reader, then a movie phase. Really, any kind of media has been my thing as of late. I find it keeps the boredom at bay while keeping my mind occupied, so I don't slip back into old habits."

Simon nodded as the busboy showed up and left their table, carrying their dirty dishes away with him. Simon took a sip of his water and looked across the table at his date. She'd told Simon she was in her mid-twenties when they'd first met, but in this low light, she looked more mid-thirties. Still, she wasn't terrible to look at. Despite spending her formative years strung out on drugs, you'd never know it to look at her. She had meat on her in all the right places that concerned Simon and, more importantly, she'd been giving him a stare he understood how to manipulate. This time, however, he was going to have to manipulate her in another way; getting her into bed was the last thing on his mind.

She'd contacted him on his burner phone shortly after he'd gotten a call from The Doctor. He'd been told his services were requested for one final job and that his payout would be hefty. When he heard his task, he was mortified. When he heard what his payment was, he was flabbergasted. A thousand scenarios had bloomed in his mind, and each one was canceled through common sense. He'd told The Doctor he would think about it and spent many a long night doing just that. Then, after he'd texted Sheela about the man in the I.C.U., they'd stayed in contact. He found out little bits of information about her, such as she had no parents, siblings, nor close friends. Her only connection to others were some coworkers that she disliked. She mostly stuck close to home. That's when he'd had an epiphany. A plan presented itself with an almost audible click. And so, he'd asked her on a date, which was where he currently sat, making talk of the small and medium variety. She'd made comments throughout the night, trying to steer the conversation into the more personal, but he'd deftly sidestepped them. He didn't want to know too much about her; it would make his upcoming task all the more difficult. Still, bits and pieces of her history had slipped out from behind the veil, and he had to keep reminding himself that she was a job, not a person.

"So, what do you want to do next?" She asked him.

"There are many things I can think of," he said at once and felt his phone vibrate in his pocket. He pulled it out, looked down and shut off the alarm he'd previously set. He furrowed his brow and texted The Doctor that he was en route. He looked up and offered her his most apologetic smile. "I'm sorry," he said. "Normally I hate using my phone on a date, but this is kind of important."

"Oh, don't feel bad," Sheela said. "Do what you have to. I'll just run to the bathroom."

"Alright. I'll pay the bill, and then we can get outta here, go find another way to amuse ourselves." Simon winked at her.

She beamed briefly at him before getting up and leaving the table. Simon waited until she'd turned the corner to put away his phone. He got up, paid the bill, and waited for Sheela by the hostess's station. He chatted with the hostess while continuously staring down the front of her dress. It was a good view. Eventually, Sheela came back and they left. They walked to his car, parked a few blocks away from the restaurant. At one point during their walk, with the moon peeking between the highrises littered around them and illuminating their faces, he stopped and pulled her aside. He placed a hand under her chin and lifted her face to his before descending and placing his lips upon hers. Their kiss was deep and passionate. It ignited some seldom felt fireworks in the belly and loins of Sheela. She was being kissed with a determination that stripped her mind bare and made her heart float. Essentially, the kiss was like a long overdue embrace of heroin. Had Simon known, he would have been proud.

When they were beside his car, Simon dropped the noose.

"Listen, Sheela. I hate to ruin this date, but I've gotta stop by work for five minutes." He fished into his pocket and held up his phone. "It was my boss that texted me earlier. He lost my vacation form. Normally I'd deal with it when I go to work on Monday, but today is the last day to submit them, and--" he looked at her sheepishly, "--I've got a trip planned and don't wanna get fucked over. I hope you understand," he finished, flashing her the most sincere smile he could muster.

"Oh, that's no problem. I don't mind making a stopover," she said, running a hand up his inner thigh. He felt himself go hard instantly and struggled to banish it. No use. "That is," she continued, "unless you want to end our date now so you can take care of it."

"No. I like you. I like spending time with you." *Oh, you're such an asshole. How do you lie to her so easily? Do you even have any idea what* He's *going to do to her?* "I'd like to continue this date. I just have to make a quick stop. You're more than welcome to come with me." *You're leading her to her death, you know that right? Why else would* He *make such a request?* "I could give you your own *private* tour, if you want." *You're condemning yourself to hell! You're condemning her to--"*

Simon silenced his thoughts with ten thousand locks, one for each dollar he was to be paid. He saw her give him a bashful smile.

"I like you too," she said. "I'll come with you, as long as it won't take too long." Sheela bit her bottom lip, her eyes catching the sliver of moon hanging in the sky. He saw lust and need dancing in them.

They drove to the hospital, her hand resting close to Simon's lap the entire trip.

Simon led her through a side entrance and then skirted down some seldom used hallways. With each new corridor, he'd glance up and around casually, pointing out different paintings or offices to Sheela; in truth, he was ensuring no cameras were present.

They made their winding way to the ramp and descended.

"They sure stick you guys outta the way," Sheela commented when they'd reached the bottom and turned left into the little alcove.

"Yeah, we were added on almost as an afterthought. They were struggling for space at the time," Simon said, shrugging. "The view's crap, but it's cool in the summer." He produced a key and slid it into the lock. He turned the handle and opened the door. He felt Sheela's grip tighten on his hand as we led her in. For a brief second she resisted his pull, and then she was over the threshold and the door closed behind them.

Simon turned to see a figure lumber out of the shadows and drape a rag across Sheela's face. Her grip clamped down on his hand for a few seconds before going limp. Simon slipped his arms around her waist while another pair of hands held the cloth over her face for another few moments. Then, those hands grabbed her under the shoulders and helped lower Sheela's unconscious body to the floor.

"Can't damage the goods. The Doctor would be pissed," the voice came from above. When Simon looked up, he saw it was Stanley.

He wasn't surprised.

Stanley

He came out of a side room, pulling an old gurney. Positioning it beside the body of the unconscious woman, he bent down, slipping his hands once again under her armpits. He hoisted and began struggling to get her onto the gurney, laying her head and shoulders onto its cold metal surface. He steadied the woman with one hand while the other found firm purchase around her waist. A sheen of sweat broke out on his body while he shifted more of her dead weight onto the metal. He cursed himself for sending Simon away, money tucked politely away into his pocket, as hastily as he had, but there'd been something about his look that Stanley hadn't liked. It looked as if, for the first time, it'd fully dawned on Simon what they'd been doing in this disused portion of the hospital; and that if Simon had seen, or done, more, he'd have run to the nearest person of authority and confessed. Stanley couldn't have that. The Doctor couldn't have that. So, Stanley had sent him away and felt comfortable in that notion, although, for the next little while he'd have Simon under his thumb. As a safety precaution.

Stanley rolled the gurney down the dark corridor with its leaky walls. While the stagnant water deposited a smell of mould, it kept the dust at bay, and he'd since gotten used to the scent.

He took turns he knew by heart, not really paying attention to where he was going, but rather trusting his feet. He thought about inconsequential things: what movie he would watch later, what he planned to do on the weekend. He whistled briefly but couldn't quite find a tune. He stopped, and heard the last three notes resound around him. They produced an eerie, hollow sound that he didn't much care for.

He came to the door and placed the gurney by the wall. Then, he rapped smartly on the wood. He waited and watched the girl, trying to spy any movement, his fingers fingering the rag in his pocket. She was still motionless when the door opened.

Like always, The Doctor was dressed in a large lab coat with a latex apron draped over it. His gloves were a sleek black that went up to his elbows. He wore a bandana on his head, keeping his hair hidden. His face was covered by an orange operating mask with a see-through face shield. The only thing visible to Stanley was The Doctor's murky grey eyes.

"Yes, Stanley?"

"I've got your patient." Stanley dropped his voice to a near whisper. "*The live one.*" He saw The Doctor's eyes brighten at once and could see the formation of a smile outlined in the mask.

"Excellent," The Doctor said, clapping his hands together once, eliciting a wet *schlock* sound that reverberated away. "Please, do bring her in. I've been waiting."

Stanley pulled the gurney inside. They went through the first room, parted the plastic strips, and entered the back room, the one Stanley thought of as the *Experimental Surgery Room*.

"Over there, please," The Doctor said, pointing to the stone slab off to the side.

Stanley wheeled the gurney over and noticed eight chains hanging from the ceiling. Attached at the end of each chain was a sharp fish hook about 2mm in diameter.

The Doctor came over, bringing with him an I.V. pole and a heart-rate monitor. Hung from the pole were two bags of saline and two bags of blood.

"Help me slide her onto the table, please," The Doctor said with giddy delight.

They moved her with gentle precision.

"That's everything for tonight, Stanley. I'll need your disposal service in three nights time. Does that work for you?"

Stanley conferred with the tiny calendar in his head and said he'd be there. The

Doctor thanked him again and then ushered him out to the corridor.

Stanley walked back the way he came. He thought about trying his hand at whistling again, but settled on listening to the dripping water instead.

The Doctor

Obituary taken from The *Westmount Observer*, June 14th, 2011

It is with deep sadness that we announce the passing of Alex Emelia Scheherazade Veksler. After a years long battle, she succumbed to leukemia while surrounded by friends and family. She is survived by her parents, Charles and Claudia Veksler.

Born in Montreal, on Sept. 30, 1990, Alex started gymnastics at the age of four. When she was 11, she won the gold medal in the under-15 provincial gymnastics tournament. Despite contracting leukemia in her 14th year, she was enrolled in the honours program at Marconi High School, landing in the top one percentile of her age group. From there, she went on to study microbiology at Hamlin University with plans to enter into the medical field eventually...

The Doctor stepped into his operating room and immediately went to work. He spared no time for personal reflection. That would come later, while he waited for the woman to regain consciousness.

First, he stripped the woman and strapped her down, ensuring there would be no escape. Once hands and feet and midsection and head were bound tight, but not *too* tight, he set about preparing his instruments. He did this with the efficiency of a conductor placing their musicians. The scalpel, his violin for this *particular* concerto, was at the forefront of the tray on his left. A special scraper, one he'd invented himself after much trial and error, was positioned behind it. He thought of it as his brass section; it would be doing the heavy lifting, after all.

He arranged everything to his satisfaction and only then did he put on a rotation of music. Bach, Brahms, Chopin. He pulled a chair up to the table and picked up his baton, a hypodermic needle filled with ketamine. He waited for the woman to stir so he could finally begin the second movement of his symphony.

The Doctor thought back to what led him here. He didn't try to convince himself that what he was doing was necessary. He believed it was, just as he believed that all scientific ventures must take risks when approaching a wall they wished to circumvent. What he did wouldn't be considered good. *Good* was such a relative term anyway. What the doctors had done in the concentration camps had been despicable, but they'd also advanced medical science leaps and bounds faster than their counterparts, and everyone now benefited from those atrocities. He knew he'd be looked at as a monster. He didn't care. He'd kept meticulous notes on his experiments. He wanted them to be published when he was ready. People *would* study it and follow up; they'd be too curious not to.

He was destined to be both founding father and martyr to reanimation, no matter the cost. It would be a long road, and he knew the final outcome. It didn't bother him. There was more than just his life on the line.

He was curious as to what the brain would retain and what it could be taught; would it act on pure instinct, or would the prevalent memories take hold. It was an exciting time.

This was the precipice.

He was mildly amused at how nervous he felt, but wasn't surprised. After his first year of slicing open patients, he'd lost the pre-surgery jitters because he'd learned to see those under his knife as nothing more than a lump of cells that needed fixing. This time it was different. This time it was important. This time was for his daughter. Now that he was *this* close, yes, he was nervous.

With no one in the room, he let out a triumphant roar. He'd already brought life to his daughter a few days ago. He'd quickly shut it down and waited. He'd done this five more times since, each time leaving her awake for longer increments. He knew it could be completed, and more importantly, he knew how to recharge her batteries. All that was left was to dress her and then begin his teaching and observation.

At one point, some hours after being brought in, the woman stirred. Twenty minutes after that, she was looking around the room with hooded eyes. The Doctor knew those eyes were taking in everything and nothing. Her brain was still scrambled, and her thoughts were fuzzy. Her fear would come soon, but for now, it was thankfully absent. She opened her mouth and smacked her lips. The sound was drier than a snapping strand of hay.

"Water," she croaked out, and then The Doctor was there, bending a straw down and placing it between her lips. She drank half the cup greedily before The Doctor took it away.

"Don't want to be getting sick," he said.

"Where am I?" she asked, slow realization dawning in her eyes as she tried individually to move her limbs.

"Where you are doesn't matter," The Doctor said calmly. "I just wanted you awake so that I could thank you for the sacrifice you're about to make on behalf of medical science."

The Doctor saw fear bloom on her face. She opened her mouth to scream, and The Doctor placed a rag into it. He did it with the care a young parent uses when wiping the bloody knees of their child. She tried to spit out the cloth, twisting her head as far as the restraints would allow, which wasn't much. He saw the fear gallop across every inch of her body as he held up the hypodermic needle. As she was naked, he could see all the veins and tendons stretch out until they looked ready to rip from her skin. He admired her tenacity, however fruitless it was.

"I'm sorry," he said in fake sincerity, "but I can't put you into a coma. I can't have you dying on me. This," he said, wiggling the needle in time with the woman's movements, "will make you completely numb so you won't feel a thing."

He brought the needle up, swabbed the injection site, then blasted her off. At once, her muscles sagged, all the fight evaporating from them. Then, he picked up his scalpel and moved to her feet. He looked at her unfocused eyes one last time. A tear trickled down her cheek.

"Now, let's get you out of this beautiful skin of yours," he said, bending to his task.

Part Two:
The Hospital

The Dream

1

The grease on his fingers picked up the low light in the bar, giving them a perfunctory shine. It diminished as he licked them clean before taking a swallow of beer, then, he picked his hamburger up again. As he bit in, juice ran from the rare patty and dribbled down his chin and fingers, coating them again. He took a few more bites before wiping his chin, licking his fingers, and taking another sip of beer. He was only halfway listening to what Jack was talking about; like all hospital employees enjoying a beer after work, Jack was bitching about his job. Todd didn't care. He'd gotten it enough times from his colleagues and underlings over the past few months that he didn't want to waste his off hours rehashing the same tired bullshit.

"How's Zelda doing, anyway?" he asked, hoping to change their conversation to something pleasant.

"She's good," Jack said before taking a sip of beer.

"Glad to hear it."

Todd took another bite and washed it down. He saw the pensive look from earlier return to Jack's face. It furrowed his brow, and although it could have just been the heat, he could swear that he saw beads of sweat pop out on his friend's face. He knew Jack was one to guard his emotions, and just getting the call on a Wednesday afternoon was telling enough; they usually only went out on Fridays for a *cinq-a-sept*. Today, however, Jack had called him with a nervous tick in his voice, asking him to join him for a beer. He didn't explicitly state that he needed to talk but didn't have to. The phone call was evidence enough for Todd.

And so, that was how Todd found himself at *Bar Des Pins* on a rather sunny, and muggy, Wednesday evening. The bar was a shithole that only the habitual drunk would find enticing. It was close to the hospital but attracted only a scarce portion of *that* crowd. It was dimly lit by bulbs hanging amongst green rectangular shades with beer sponsors etched upon them. There was a pool table that was playable, but only if you knew how to navigate the subtle bumps and curves that populated it. Todd was not the best pool player, but he'd hustled some money out of the odd med student that wandered in and wanted to play a game or three.

After finishing his burger, and then his beer in one long swallow, Todd burped. He noticed Jack's beer was verging on empty and called the bartender over and ordered another round. When the mugs were deposited in front of them, and the bartender had left to lean against the wall and watch the sports highlights for the umpteenth time, Todd turned to Jack.

"So, what is it you wanted to talk about?" his tone even while he spoke.

Jack took a long slug of beer, clearly wrestling with whatever was on his mind. Then, he spoke without turning to look at Todd.

"Have you ever been haunted before?"

The question was so absurd that Todd almost burst out laughing. Despite Jack saying earlier that his relationship was going well, Todd still thought the reason he'd been called out was to discuss a problem of the marital variety. Now, he was faced with a question of another sort. He chuckled inwardly before responding.

"Nope. Can't say that I have, Jacky-boy."

"Are you sure? How long have you been working at the hospital?"

"'Bout twenty years, give or take a few months."

"And you've never felt, or *seen,* anything out of the ordinary?"

"Nope. Can't say that I have," he repeated, and immediately felt a nagging inside his mind. *Are you sure about that?* the voice asked. *Are you sure you can declare* that *with a straight face?* The memory of the dead, black fingers poking through the body bag ran through his mind and he suppressed a shiver.

He shook his head, clearing the half-remembered horror that he'd felt.

"What?" Jack asked him, looking at him intently.

"Nothing. Just saying that nope, I've never been haunted before." He took a sip of beer, then asked pensively. "Why? Have you?"

"Yes," Jack said with no shame in his voice. "It's why I called you out tonight."

Todd was about to say something, either a cheap comfort or a joke, he didn't know, when he was spared an answer, because Jack began to tell his story.

2

Jack was working an overtime evening shift at the Chest Institute. It was supposed to be his day off, but because Zelda was off visiting her father and wouldn't be home until well after dark, he'd accepted the shift and left a note for his wife. The Chest Institute was a self-sufficient building with the residents staying for the remainder of their lives. Because of this, Jack's tasks were minimal, and he'd had a lot of downtime.

The night shift nurses had come in shortly before eight and the day shifters had departed. He spoke with nurse Michelle briefly about what she wanted programmed in for the following day before she left. She advised him to leave a message for the funeral service as she believed one of their "clients" wouldn't make it through the night.

Now, as nine-thirty approached, so did Jack's last half-hour break. He'd spent the majority of his shift mindlessly surfing the internet on his phone. His eyes were heavy, so he decided to take a nap. He descended the eight flights of stairs and entered the basement. To his right, down a slight ways, were a few closed offices. The only door on his left, at the end of the hallway, was the morgue. He had no interest in that direction. He turned right, followed by another quick right, and was walked by a set of elevators and a solitary chair. At the end of this little hallway was a break room, fitted with a fridge, microwave, couch, and a few chairs.

He punched in the code and entered.

Despite the outside summer heat, the break room was cool and dark. He went over to the couch at the back of the room and lay down, his eyes singing their relief when he closed them. It wasn't long before he began to drift into a fitful sleep.

His dreams took him down to a hazy place where he was still at work. Everything was grey and the sound of laughing surrounded him. It would come from all directions and no direction at once. He glanced around the large, cornerless room that he was in and could see nothing. He felt a dull sense of fear, but that was all. Everything in this room seemed muted and drained of life. Then, he heard the laughter increase from behind him. It grew at a steady pace, flying towards him on beating wings that lay just under the sounds of voice. Jack tried to turn, but before he could manage it, was struck on the back of the head with something fleshy and wet.

He awoke terrified and didn't know why. Already the dream had taken on a hazy blur of incompleteness that even then was fading fast. He knew vague details, but no specifics. He tried to raise his hands to rub his eyes, but they wouldn't move. He tried to wiggle his toes but only got the same numb result. That's when he became nervous. He tried moving his head and found that he could, albeit only a little. The rest of his body, no dice. *Sleep paralysis* the rational part of his mind reasoned with him. *Okay,* he thought back, *that's good. I can deal with that. As long as it doesn't last too long.* He wanted to be free and clear of the room before the dream had a chance to resurface.

As he was still trying to get his limbs to move, he heard the handle of the breakroom door twist and then saw a caravan of humans enter. There were two P.A.B.s that he knew and a nurse. They entered in a gale of laughter and conversation. The two P.A.B.s walked to adjacent chairs and sat down. The nurse made a beeline for the couch that Jack was stretched out upon.

"Move your legs, Jesus dude. Some of us want to sit down," the nurse said, staring down at his immovable body with hidden laughter behind her eyes.

"I can't," he said at once, looking up at her as much as he could. "I think I've got sleep paralysis. I can't move anything except my mouth and eyes."

The nurse scoffed at him. "That's an old wives tale. There is nothing in any medical textbook about it. Stop being a bitch and move so I can sit down," she said.

"I *can't*," Jack said again, continuing to watch her. Something about her was out of place. In this small facility, she should have

221

been familiar, but wasn't. He watched as the skin around her face rippled softly before forming back into place. He strained his eyes up and out to look at the two P.A.B.s. When he looked at them, he saw the same thing. Their faces wavered and swam in an undulating pattern before fully forming. It made Jack want to scream.

He almost *did* scream when he felt a shift in gravity. The nurse, standing over him, had grabbed his legs and tossed them unceremoniously onto the ground. She sat down in the vacant area on the couch and returned to her conversation with the two P.A.B.s.

"What the fuck?" Jack said.

"Don't be a bitch about it," the nurse said without turning toward him.

Jack felt the pull of gravity then, slowly dragging the rest of his body towards the ground where his feet, and legs, now rested. He also felt a tug of terror in his heart. He didn't understand why until the momentum of his shift in gravity pulled his entire body to the ground.

Jack landed with a smack as his cheek planted itself upon the floor. He heard laughter above him but was unable to move his head to see who it had issued from. It didn't matter. It swirled around him, like his previous dream, and rebounded off the walls, like it was coming from everywhere and nowhere.

The shock of the hit had given him a blurry, black vision. As it cleared, he realized that he was seeing black because he was staring underneath the couch. The blackness was like a fog that swirled and moved in eddies of distortion. Jack's heartbeat kicked up a notch as he thought he saw something upon the very edge of that darkness; something that was struggling to make its way to him. He watched, incredulously, as the swirling mass began to take shape. He saw the outlines of human hands forming far off. These hands inched their way forward, searching for purchase on the flat, grey ground. Apparently, they'd found some, because as the seconds stretched out, Jack was able to make out the shape of arms and then a head that followed the ever-searching hands. He saw hands that were adorned with gnarled knuckles. At the ends of each, as they came into focus, were fingernails that were painted a dry, coppery red. Jack did not doubt they were coated in blood.

Jack opened his mouth and screamed then, uttering forth something that was more animal than human. He felt dust enter his mouth, making his tongue feel fat, but continued to scream all the same. He watched as the thing fully materialized out of the dark; a creeping, crawling figure with the face of a woman that was half melted off. Portions of her skull showed through the translucent skin that

223

draped the right side of her face. The left side was covered in blood. Jack screamed louder as the nightmare wiggled and fought her way closer to him from under the couch. His screams were met by another burst of high, shrill laughter. He tried to look around at them, to beg and plead with lambs eyes, but all Jack managed to do was make the cords in his neck stand out. He was still unable to move.

Feeling in Jack's extremities arrived too late. He felt his hand fuzz back from numb as one of the grotesque woman's hands closed around it. She dug her fingers into his skin, causing a soft, searing sensation that built up in its intensity over the seconds as she grasped him. He felt a burning sensation across his palm where her thumb dug in, as hard and cold as steel. Then, he felt a violent tug as she began to pull him under the couch.

This time, his scream morphed into one of words, instead of the unintelligible sounds they'd been before.

"SOMEBODY FUCKING HELP ME!" he cried. It was met with a chorus of sadistic laughter. He knew two things in that instant. There would be no help from those above him, and that he was still dreaming. The second realization gave him no solace. Instead, he continued to scream as he was pulled underneath the couch. He continued to scream as the flesh dripping woman pulled her face up to his. He continued to scream as she opened her mouth, showing teeth that wished to gash and chew and pull the skin away from his face. He continued to scream as she pulled herself within kissing distance and he could see down the dark entrance that was her throat; it was like looking into the void to hell. He continued to scream as she pulled his cheek into her mouth and took her first bite. He felt a searing, burning pain and then...

3

"...I woke up," Jack said, not looking at Todd. He took a shaky sip of beer and then continued. "When I woke up, for real this time, I was overcome with sleep paralysis. I couldn't move my arms, nor my legs, and I was doubly scared." As if to emphasize this point, Jack finished off his beer in one long swallow. Todd, without waiting, held up two fingers, signaling to the bartender. Despite himself, he asked a question.

"What happened next?"

"What happened next?" Jack threw his head back and laughed long and loud. By the time he was done, wiping the tears that had escaped his eyes, the bartender had placed two

225

new frosty mugs in front of them. "It's obvious, isn't it?"

"I don't follow," Todd said, dumbfounded. It was only then that he realized he was sitting on the edge of his seat, in danger of falling off.

"Nothing," Jack said, coughing out a tiny laugh. "Nothing at all. I regained the sense in my limbs less than thirty seconds after waking up."

"Oh," Todd said, his voice sounding oddly defeated to his ears.

"I'll tell you this, though," Jack said, straight-laced and suddenly sober. "While I was waiting to regain the use of my arms and legs, I heard the door handle turn a few times. It was like someone was trying to get in but didn't know the code. Like they didn't understand how a door worked."

Todd made a non-committal noise and took a swig of his beer.

"I got the fuck out of there *tout-de-suite*, as soon as I was able," Jack said. "In fact, I don't ever think I'll go back." Todd watched Jack take a sip of beer and then almost spit the next words out in a mist of foam and alcohol. "Fuck! That! Shit!"

"That's a helluva dream," Todd said, wanting to break the sudden silence that threatened to fall.

226

"It was more than that."

"How so?"

Jack let go of his grip on his beer. He laid his hand flat upon the bar, palm facing up. Todd looked down at it and saw something that made his testicles slink up inside his body. Emblazoned on Jack's palm, like the world's worst tattoo, was a thumbprint blacker than a midnight shadow. He drew in a sharp breath and let it out in a soft exhale of "what-the-fuck."

"Yep," Jack said with a level voice. "I've washed my hands probably a hundred times since then and it won't fade. I tell you again. *I'm never going back!*"

"I'll drink to that," Todd said without any good humour. They clinked glasses and continued drinking. In fact, they drank for a while. They drank until the bar was close to closing. They talked a lot about things that had come and gone, and things that could be in their future.

The Abortion Clinic

When Pat came into work that evening, he was assigned the eighth floor of The Women's Pavilion.

"But I got seniority, man," he said, pleading with Hussein.

"That you do. And?"

"Put one of the rooks on the floor is what I'm saying. You know that's a heavy floor."

"I do, and I want it done right. That's why I put you there."

"Ahh man, this is some bullshit."

"You think it's bullshit that I think you're one of the best workers?" Hussein asked in a steady tone. He watched as a bashful red crept up and over Pat's face. "That's why I'm asking you to do me this favour."

Pat looked back at Hussein and the blush receded, knowing he couldn't say no now, but still wanting too. He liked Hussein, as he'd always gone to bat for him if Pat had needed anything, but it *was* a Friday evening. He wanted something easy to finish off the week and it wasn't looking that way. Hussein could sense Pat's reluctance and decided to sweeten the pot a little more.

"If you get everything done, and I mean done well, you can leave at ten. You don't even have to skip your breaks if you don't want."

That was the ticket and Hussein knew it as soon as he saw the way that Pat's eyes flared.

Pat took his stock and slowly made his way to the floor. He knew he had an hour or two to kill while the offices were vacated and the last few patients were shuttled out of the recovery section of the O.R. He spied Mario outside the elevators and made random small talk with him. They discussed weekend plans with Mario telling him he had a gig as an extra for one of those superhero movies being filmed in the city. They'd moved on to giving each other shit about their respective favourite football teams when Mario got a call and left.

Pat continued on his way, descending the ramp towards The Women's Pavilion. When he reached the bottom he stopped, as something caught the corner of his eye. He turned in time to see a set of doors off to his left click shut. *That's odd. I've never seen anyone go in there before. I wonder where it goes,* he thought. He suspected it was some maintenance worker, going deep underground to a tunnel built into the rock of the mountain that housed the hospital. *Gone looking for some ancient rusty pipe that needs fixing*, he mused.

He continued on to the elevators and rode up. It was forty-five minutes into his shift, but already the floor had a deserted quality to it. Many of the offices were locked and vacant for the weekend. There was only one patient left in the recovery room, and she was being politely ushered through the final steps of her process by a vastly overweight nurse. Pat had a hard time understanding how someone so overweight could work in any capacity as a healthcare professional. Disgusted, he turned around and went to his closet. It was one of the bigger, and better, housekeeping closets that populated the hospital. It was square and had a comfortable plush chair and a side table with a lamp. Pat pulled a box of toilet paper in front of the chair and sat down, putting his feet up on it. *One could almost be comfortable here,* he thought.

He spent the next thirty minutes idly scrolling through his phone before deciding that he wanted to leave earlier rather than later. He set his stuff up and went to work, starting with the offices. He'd finished the majority of them by the time his supper break came around.

He joined his colleagues in the cafeteria and was immediately asked what floor he was on. He told them.

"Man, fuck that floor," Thomas said, eliciting a few nods from those at the table.

"Yeah, I'm not a big fan of it either. It's a lot of work," Pat said morosely.

"Yep. I wouldn't go up there again for all the money in the world," Thomas said.

"Why not?"

"Oh shit. Here it comes," someone at the far end of the table said, and a few of those seated laughed. Thomas looked in their direction with a stern face, but that only made them smile and laugh more. He turned his attention back to Pat.

"It's haunted," he said.

"I don't believe that," Pat said.

Thomas' face grew stern. "I don't care if you do or don't. I'm just giving you the truth of the matter." He spread his hands out on the table, as if to say, take what you will from it.

"It ain't haunted," the same voice from earlier. It was the fat Porter, Dennis. "I think you got goofed on by Paulo."

"*No,* I didn't," Thomas said.

"*Yes,* you did. It's an old trick he's been playing on you gullible shitheads for years. He takes a recording of children laughing and plays it through the venting system. There's an easy way to access it from one of the offices."

"I didn't say I heard laughter. *In fact,* I didn't say anything about it, just that it was haunted."

231

"Fuck," Dennis said. "You and that voodoo loving Haitian, Ronald, would make a great couple. Bunch of ghost believing faggots."

An unaccustomed quiet fell over the table as the two old-timers stared each other down. Before it could get too intrusive, Pat spoke.

"Hey. Does anyone know where the doors at the bottom of the decline in The Women's Pavilion lead?"

A few pairs of eyes looked at him. Pat thought he saw one of the black porters, Simon, jump a little at the question.

"It's an old corridor that was used to connect The Women and Transplant wards before we had the bridges," George, the Greek, said. "If you go far enough along it, it runs into the catacombs."

"It *ran* into the catacombs," Thomas corrected. "Years ago, one of the walls caved in and made the tunnel impassable. Since then, it's been locked and barred and off limits."

"Oh," Pat said. He saw Simon slump even further in his seat.

"I hear it's haunted by monsters and demons that'll eat you up," Dennis said, snorting with laughter before the final words were out of his mouth. No one paid him any attention, except for Simon, who glanced at him before averting his eyes.

232

"What are the catacombs?" another housekeeper asked. It took Pat a few seconds to place him. He was one of the rooks. His name was Guy or Guile or something like that.

"They're an old set of tunnels that run under the hospital and beyond," Thomas said. "Why they were originally built, I have no idea. Now, they're used for storage of anything and everything."

"I was down there a couple months ago," a person from the laundry department that Pat didn't recognize said. "I found a back way in through the basement by the dentistry department. You know where the old cargo elevator is?"

There were a few nods from around the table.

"Anyway, I went down there, but not too far. It was dark and cut into the stone of the mountain. Super creepy, right? There wasn't much of anything, but I did see a room filled with a bunch of old toilets, and another where someone had painted 'Nuclear Storage' on the wall. It looked legit too because there were a bunch of barrels just lying around and stuff."

"We have a nuclear medicine department," Thomas said. "So it makes sense they'd want to store everything down there."

"Sure, sure," the laundry guy said. "Still, I got the fuck outta there when I saw these big old mutated looking rats gnawing on shit that could have been bones or something else."

"Damn," Pat whispered.

"Haunted or not, I don't think I'll ever go back down there again."

Pat's mind flooded with the images of rats, massive and mutated from years of eating whatever waste had trickled out from those barrels.

"I don't blame you," he said.

Their dinner break ended, and Pat made his way back to his floor to continue where he'd left off. He powered his way through the majority of his work. He skipped his second break, wanting to finish early.

It was then that things started to get weird.

He was in the middle of his final operating room for the night. He'd already sterilized the walls and equipment that was within his reach; all that was left was the floor. He walked out of the operating room and into the clean room when he thought he saw the far door clicking closed. Before it did, he heard the soft whisper of laughter leaking through the dwindling crack. He felt the hair prickling on the back of his neck, arms, and legs despite being weighed down by the heavy jumpsuit he was wearing. He turned to look behind him, suddenly sure that something was standing there, ready to slip some cold, dead hands around his neck and choke the life from him, and heard the shuffling against his ears. *I'm just hearing things because of the hood. That must be it,* his mind urged at him.

"Sure, sure," he said aloud to the empty room.

He collected his mop and wrung it out. He went back into the main operating room and began passing it along the floor, strands of hair trailing it like the tail of a comet. He made it to the operating table and put his mop down against the wall. He unlocked the wheels and pushed it out of the way. Underneath was a rather large, and crusted over, smear of blood. It was oddly misshapen and he stood, transfixed, looking at it for a moment or two. He was trying to figure out what it was a picture of. Eventually, it snapped into his mind and he shuddered.

He noticed the oval shape of it first. It wasn't perfect, the topmost part of it was streaked up and away, fading even as it left the main dimensions of the splotch, but it *was* an oval. Once he saw that, the rest clicked into place. The eyes were wide and round with a little red speck of pupil within each one. The nose was pudgy and the mouth was a smear filled with either laughter or a scream. The blood stain resembled the face of a child; his brother's face. His brother, who had died before reaching his first birthday. The stroller had been hit by a drunk driver and mangled both mother and child.

Man, this night just can't get any fucking weirder, he thought.

That's when the laughter started.

He knew at once that it wasn't some sound muffled and distorted by his hood. It was too clear for that. It was high pitched and piercing like a summer's glee. He looked around frantically and saw he was alone in the closed room. He looked up to the vent, remembering the earlier conversation in the cafeteria. It *sounded* like it was coming from the vent, but with the hood on, he couldn't tell. He shucked it off and strained his ears. Far away and behind him, in the direction of the door, he heard the stamp of running feet on tile and trailing laughter. Eventually, it faded away to nothing. He stayed still, stretching his ears out, willing them to pick up any trace of sound.

He was alone.

"Fuck that," he whispered under his breath and quickly mopped the remainder of the room. He left the table in its new position and stepped out to his cart, shedding his jumpsuit and mask in the clean room.

He exited into the hallway, peered left, and then right. He had a snakey suspicion that he wasn't alone, but he couldn't see anything down either end of the fat, bland hallway. He checked his watch and saw it was quarter past ten and dumped the cart in the housekeeping closet. For only the second time in his life, he neglected to clean it out and put everything away.

He wanted out, and he wanted out bad.

He walked to the elevator on instinct and heard it arrive. The doors slid open with a *scrrrreeee*.

No one got on.

No one got off.

Pat was close to the staircase and froze. He heard the doors slide shut on their rusty runners. Then, they *scrrrreeeed* open again. Silence followed for what seemed an eternity.

Nothing moved in an eon. Nothing stirred.

Pat heard the doors begin to close and looked around with mounting anxiety. Still, there was nothing. He was standing by the staircase door and button hooked into it. He took the stairs three at a time and exited on the third floor. He popped out the door and almost screamed when he looked left and the haggard face of some patient looked back at him.

She was taking slow, shuffling steps towards him. One hand was planted against the wall to steady herself. If it weren't for the hospital johnny, he would have sworn the lady was shithouse hammered. She looked to be in her thirties, but it'd been a hard three decades if he was any judge. Her skin was taught, lines crisscrossing her face like ancient mine shafts. Pat scolded himself for being such a pussy and made a small move towards her, the words *Est-ce que vous avez besoin d'aide* poised on his lips. They dried up in his mouth and he swallowed them like desert dust when he saw her eyes. They were deep blue and vacant when he first saw them. As he made his small move, they lolled in their sockets. The eyes faded into a dead, soulless stare and focused on him.

All good Samaritan thoughts evaporated in Pat's mind, and he turned away from her. As he did, he saw one hand stretch out, like it was pawing, grabbing, reaching for him. His eyes saw the pale pink scar that ran around the outline of those hands and arms. It wasn't a series of scars but rather one long connected one. His eyes saw, but his mind disbelieved. Instead, he quickly turned away from her, muttered an incomprehensible 'sorry' and began briskly walking towards the incline.

When Pat got to the top, he turned left and saw Stanley, the Biomed guy, coming up the

238

hallway toward him. They passed each other and Pat mumbled a 'Hussein said I could leave early. Bye.' He didn't care if Stanley believed him or not. He had to get out of there. He made for the elevators but once again took the stairs down from the eighth floor to the first floor of the surgical wing.

He walked out the main entrance fifteen seconds later, a walk that generally took him at least a minute, and went to his car. He exited the parking lot and called Hussein on the road.

"I'm done and leaving,' he said briskly.

"Okay. Thanks again."

"No problem. Just..." he gulped. "Just don't ever put me up there again."

"Too much work?"

"Something like that."

"Alright. Have a good night."

Pat sped home and stopped at a gas station to buy a fifteen pack of beer. He decided that tonight was a good night to play video games and get blasted.

That's precisely what he did.

The Feeding

1

Stanley saw Pat come around the corner and drop his head to examine the floor, walking briskly past, mentioning something about being allowed to leave early, and continue on without looking up.

Good. The less he sees, the better, Stanley thought as he pushed his cart with two Biomed boxes in the direction Pat had come.

Stanley reached the bottom of the incline and was about to turn left when he saw what had given Pat such trepidation.

Far off and lumbering along the hallway was The Doctor's creation. She was using one hand to prop herself up upon the wall while she made a steady shuffle forward. Stanley stared at her for a moment before turning his cart towards the doors and then unlocking them. That done, he pulled it in and was greeted by The Doctor as he materialized out of the dark corridor.

"Hello, Stanley. I was just wondering about you. You brought what I asked for?"

It was an odd question because The Doctor had only ever questioned Stanley at the beginning of their working relationship.

Stanley had been inflicted with a necrotic disease more than a decade and a half ago. He'd taken his meager paycheck, saved up for years, and went on the most remote jungle safari that he could find. It'd been a wonderful, brilliant, eye-opening experience until a peculiar animal had bitten him. That animal had transferred a deadly strain of bacteria into his system. It was fine at first, as the disease had laid dormant in his body for close to ten years. Eventually, it had surfaced. Being a veteran, even then, of the hospital system, Stanley had called up every favour owed to him as his skin first began to turn a pale grey, then black, and then to rot off. Nothing came of it, however, and every new physician he'd talked to had essentially condemned him to death, using pretty, digestible words. It was only when he was on his deathbed that a certain someone had approached him and offered him a rare, unsanctioned treatment. All this doctor was asking for in return was loyalty. Although this figure spoke in ten cent words, Stanley understood him at once. *Your life for your loyalty.* It was an agreement that Stanley made without hesitation.

He'd been wheeled into some dirty, underground cellar and when he woke up, five days later, he still had his life. It was not hard to give up his loyalty and dignity and soul after that. In fact, Stanley had purposefully forgotten The Doctor's name many years ago. He felt that even to *think* his name would be a betrayal; something that could be pulled from him in his darkest hour. So now, it was simply "The Doctor," and that was all anyone would ever get from him.

Stanley looked at The Doctor. He nodded, knowing no words were necessary.

"Good. Excellent," The Doctor said, clapping his hands together like an excited child. He lifted off the top of the first box and beheld the bags of blood that lay inside. "AB positive?"

Stanley nodded again.

"And the second box?"

"All that you asked for."

"Excellent. Thank you."

Stanley beamed with unabashed pride, even while he watched The Doctor dig through the second box. He saw the smile widening upon The Doctor's face as he inspected each new treat Stanley had brought. Along with the blood in the first box, the second contained organs he'd scrounged up that hadn't yet touched a drop of formaldehyde. While watching The

Doctor dig through his prize, Stanley heard a faint noise coming from the door. He turned around and saw nothing there, yet the noise continued. After a few brief seconds, Stanley was able to place it. It was the sound of finger-nails on the door. He listened to the sound as it ratcheted up in intensity, and his subconscious immediately registered it for what it was. Those sounds were becoming more anxious. More hungry. The creature on the other side of the door could smell the blood and organs he'd brought. He took an involuntary step back as the creature rocked against the door, using more force than it had previously shown. The doors shuddered, but showed no signs of giving in. Stanley was surprisingly grateful for this fact.

The noise of the doors creaking brought The Doctor out of his trance, and he looked toward them for the first time.

"Ahh, my daughter is back," He said with that same childish glee. "I think she can smell the goodies you've brought her. Open the door and let her in, please," The Doctor said, looking at Stanley, who gulped and tried to keep his face blank.

He walked towards the doors, knowing they couldn't burst open at any minute, but not completely trusting them. His hand reached out and grasped the knob, turning it ever so slowly, ready to jump back if the thing on the other side should happen to burst through with blood lust in its eyes.

The door swung open, and the creature, *the woman*, came shuffling through. He stood frozen as he looked into it's, *her*, dead eyes. She reached out and grasped his arm. Immediately, he felt the heat and strength of it, *her*, in that grip. He looked down to the tendons and veins laced along her arm, seeing something that froze more than just his movements; he saw something that froze him down to his very bones.

One of the veins split open and a tentacle no thicker than a rat's tail squirmed out, the tip of it like a needle, and he watched as it began to slither from her arm onto his. It wrapped itself twice around his forearm before the tip stood up like a cobra emerging from a snake charmer's basket, hanging in the air, poised and ready to strike. Stanley was transfixed and knew that something bad was about to happen. He heard, rather than saw, The Doctor's hand clamp down on the creature's, *her*, shoulder.

"None of that now," he heard The Doctor whisper. "We've got food enough for you. I don't need you feeding on my friends."

Despite the terror coursing through him, Stanley smiled inwardly at The Doctor's casual way of calling him a friend.

He watched as the tentacle dipped towards his arm, as if debating that he would make a better meal than the second-hand parts; a better, *fresher* meal. Then, it slackened and unraveled off his arm. It slid neatly back into the creature's arm. The wound, gaping like a dead, red eye only moments ago, folded in on itself and closed, leaving only the barest of marks on her skin where it'd come out.

"That's good, that's good," The Doctor continued to whisper as he shut and locked the door, keeping one hand on the creature's shoulder. "Now, I need you to come with me before you can feed."

Stanley saw her twist under The Doctor's grip, but the hand bore down harder on it's, *her*, shoulder.

"None of that," he said, more firmly this time. "Come with me."

He led the creature a little way down the hallway where a wheelchair waited. He seated her in it and began to push. "Please, follow me, Stanley," he called without looking back.

Stanley stayed like a statue. His mind wanted a second to process what had just happened. After a few moments, he was able to convince himself that he needn't worry. The Doctor was watching out for him. The Doctor always would. Stanley had proved himself a valuable commodity and would continue to do so. He was safe.

With that thought reverberating in his mind, he took hold of his cart and followed The Doctor.

2

Once Stanley had placed his cart in the corner of the room, and The Doctor had pushed the chair against the slab that served as an operating table at times, Stanley was dismissed. He took one final glance back as the creature sat in front of the marble slab, like it was eagerly awaiting supper, which he supposed it was.

The Doctor watched him go before lifting the top off the second box. The smell, he knew, was intoxicating for her. He quickly snatched the heart on top. It was the freshest one he'd found upon first inspection. He moved over and dropped it in front of her. It made a wet *splatting* sound as it hit the stone; it still held a lot of juice. Her trembling hand reached out and grasped it. Then, that long, thin tentacle made an appearance again. It roped itself around the heart twice and then punctured it with the needle end.

The Doctor watched as his experiment, his creation, *his daughter,* fed. Pulsating lumps began moving up the vein. It didn't take long for her to desiccate the heart. By then, however, the doctor had placed another organ, a kidney, down. Before she removed the tentacle, The Doctor watched with naked fascination as those pulsating lumps reversed direction, putting her bad blood back into the heart. It ballooned back up to its regular size.

In the end, it took five organs and a bag of blood to satiate her hunger; this last he watched disappear at a robust rate.

"All done, sweety?" he cooed.

She looked up at him and he saw a dark intelligence broiling behind the vacant look. She was slowly getting healthy. With infinite care, he took her forearm in his hands and turned it over. He noticed the hint of a scar, like it was a year or two old. Already he could see that the mixture of enzymes he'd chosen were working. He knew Simon must have wondered why The Doctor sometimes took what looked like the sickest and weakest patients in the hospital, but each one of them had held something special within themselves. A little of this mixed with a little of that and a significant load of tinkering had led The Doctor to something incredible. And now, the lingering, fading scar was proof that it had worked; that she was even

247

alive and conscious in the first place was all the proof The Doctor needed.

She would only need him for a couple of more weeks now, he knew. After that, she'd be able to exist on her own. This next phase thrilled The Doctor. He wanted to see if she could co-exist with those around her without them becoming suspicious. This next phase would be her true Turing test.

The Doctor stood up, placing his hands into her armpits for stability.

"Come with me," he said and guided her up like a spotter. "It's time for you to get some rest."

He led her to the back room, the one no one else had been permitted entry. Initially, it had housed a rather extensive operating room set-up. Since the birth of his daughter, he'd moved everything further down the hall, into another locked room, and had converted this one into a workroom/bedroom of sorts. There was a bed pressed against the side wall. It wasn't much, but the mattress was serviceable. Scattered along the back wall was an assortment of machines and supplies, a bookshelf, and a cluttered metal table: a stack of paper, a microscope with corresponding slides, a few medical texts, and a box of gloves sat upon it. The drawers of the desk held all the little things he needed to perform his experiments. All was cast in shadow from the Coleman lantern standing on a stool beside the door.

He led his daughter over to the bed and then went to grab an IV pole and a bag of saline. He tucked her in and drew out a needle. He pulled her arm out and was about to tap for a vein when the skin parted and her tentacle popped out.

"No," he said firmly. "I have to put this into you a specific way. The salt, directly into your heart, will cause it to begin firing double time and you'll suffer cardiac arrest, or worse. It all amounts to the same thing in the end, however. You will die. So put that away and let me do what's necessary." He watched the tentacle retract and the hole close up.

"Good. Thank you."

He inserted the needle and immediately saw the skin aggressively close around the hole. As long as it didn't clog the tip, The Doctor wasn't concerned. Even still, he had a feeling that the stock of saline bags would soon go unneeded and unused. He wondered about her other hunger, though. Would it grow? Would it be sustainable? How would she manage it on her own? He stepped back and out of the room, extinguishing the light as he went.

He dumped the used organs and bag of blood into a Biomed box. All except the heart. That he placed into a plastic ziplock bag. He slipped the bag into his briefcase and brought it home with him. He figured to do his mini autopsy with it in the following days, but when he finally pulled out the bag and examined the heart, an autopsy was useless. The bag contained mostly black liquid. In the center were the deflated remnants of the heart. It had melted from the inside out.

The Counselor

He knew she was dead, could see it in Keith's eyes. When you got past the hustle and the jive, when you got straight down to it, he *knew* she was dead. He knew, but hadn't come to accept it yet. That was the hardest part, even though it was Henne's job to help Keith come to terms with this fact of life; it was his job to help a lot of people come to terms with a lot of things.

"It gets so surreal sometimes," Keith continued. He was looking out into the room and keeping good eye contact; it was one of the things that Henne stressed to his groups. *Despite how ashamed you are, or how pitiful you feel, you must engage good eye contact with others. Let them see your remorse or pain or whatever else you're feeling. And you, in turn, will see how they feel. Everyone has lived some sort of traumatic experience, so don't be afraid of yours. Use it as a common bond between yourselves.*

"So surreal," he repeated. "Her toothbrush is still next to mine. I know I should throw it away, but, *what if?*"

"She'll be a zombie and brushing her teeth will be the last thing on her mind," Terry said. This elicited a few chuckles from around the room, along with a less than pleased look from Keith.

"I *know* she's not coming back," Keith said, irritation prickling his voice. "But I can't help the way I feel about it."

"Careful with that line of thinking," an elderly woman said from across the room. Her name was Eileen, and her husband was ten years in the ground. "It's all too easy to fall into the 'I can't help it' trap. You'll start with pure intentions, but soon it's your crutch. Once your grief becomes where your personality starts and ends because *you can't help the way you feel,* you've lost your way."

Henne was not surprised to hear this coming from Eileen. She'd been a ball of grief when she first started coming to the group sessions. She'd spent a year in the dark throws of pity but pulled herself out a piece at a time. Now, she accepted all with a grim pragmatism and spoke without fear of contempt from others.

No one said anything. Keith, who had been looking into her eyes when she began talking, was now inspecting his hands, as if they may hold the magic to break the spell of his grief. The silence filled the room like air into a balloon, expanding it and pushing it to the point of popping. It was Henne who broke the silence, as was his job.

"They say time heals all wounds, but I don't believe it. Time doesn't heal anything, but it does make the pain we feel bearable. It's distance that heals those wounds, not time. Distance through experience. Distance through the many miles of life that still await you. Time is a form of distance, but time can be used to brood and pine." Henne saw a few of them stirring, looks ranging from mild annoyance to one instance of bubbling anger. Still, he persisted. "Take time if you must, but don't rely on it."

He looked down at his watch, pretending to take in the time. There was still ten minutes left in their sessions, but he'd already decided to let school out early.

"Before we break for the evening, does anyone have anything they want to say?"

No one did, so he dismissed them.

Henne watched them file out through the main doors of the chapel and into the hospital's inner workings. He thought it was a little crude that their weekly meetings were held in the one place where a few of their loved ones had died. He did work there, however, so the chapel was free. That won out over most else. After the last person left, he collected the twelve chairs and stored them in the back room.

While he kept his hands busy, his mind reached out again to the recurring thought he'd been having for the past few weeks. She was dead. He knew it, yet couldn't believe it. He'd been a counselor for over fifteen years. He'd spoken to people from all walks of life who dealt with one type of addiction or another, and he felt that in the past five years, he'd gotten very good at judging who would crawl through the shit and come out clean on the other end, and who would not. Sheela had been one of those he'd pegged as making it through. She hadn't looked like much when she came to her first meeting, the court-mandated ones never did, but she'd held on with a grim determination. She'd truly wanted to get well, for reasons pure or not didn't matter, and she'd dealt with her shit and come to terms with it. She'd been willing to open up and face the demons she'd kept hidden. It took guts and Henne had been proud of her. And then, a few weeks ago, she'd stopped coming. He'd been worried when, after her third missed meeting, he'd called her home and gotten no answer. He tried once or twice a day for the next few days, getting the same result every time.

Once he'd put everything away, he knew what he had to do.

The next day, he hopped on a bus and took a trip down to her neighbourhood. He stood on her porch and waited while his heavy knocking floated away in the humid air. He knocked again and called out her name. She was gone. He knew it before an elderly lady stuck her head out of the window of her second-floor apartment and hollered down at him to quit the racket before he woke the dead.

"I'm sorry, miss. I'm looking for the woman that lives here. Her name is Sheela."

"She ain't been around fo' awhile. Prolly couldn't pay the rent and skipped out like I seen 'em do time an' again. Not really the best clientele in these parts."

"Are you sure?" he asked, his heart already sunk.

"Sure as can be."

Henne sighed. "Thank you," he said and descended the short three steps to the sidewalk. He stood there, sweating, and thought about what he could do. He supposed he could call the police, maybe file a missing persons report, but what if she really did skip town ahead of some kind of trouble? A run-in with the cops could push her all the way back. But, if she was dead, as she almost certainly was, she deserved justice. He pulled his phone out of his pocket and began looking for the local PD's number. Despite having to call the line multiple times when group members became violent, he'd never memorized it. He found it and was ready to press send when a better idea came to him. He supposed there were a couple more places he could look before giving up and putting the search in the hands of more capable profession-als. He slipped his phone back into his pocket, the number undialed. He had a few visits to make back at the hospital.

He walked to the bus stop under a sil-ver studded sky. Clouds covered the sun, yet he wasn't given reprieve. It was early summer, and the humidity was a pounding force, soaking his shirt to his skin before he'd made it to the stop.

Half a block away, he heard a chuffing from behind him. He turned and saw a bus, *his bus*, bumping and shunting its way up the street. He put on a little speed and joined the three-long line as the bus pulled up to the cor-ner. Ahead of him, in the line, were two old ladies, one rather fat, and a hard case middle-aged man. A tiny bite of memory attempted to surface about the man but dissolved before fully forming; *I must know him from group,* he thought. He glanced to his left and saw only a single seat free as he dug into his trouser pocket and produced his card.

He boarded, scanned his pass, and then walked down the aisle towards the back. He stumbled as the bus made its stuttering start and years of rock climbing took over. He reached out and grasped the railing without thinking and his eyes shifted downward, to avoid bags and legs, while he re-established his footing. He happened to notice Hardcase taking up the previously empty seat. Their eyes locked for the barest of moments. Hardcase's eyes registered distaste, for Henne's clothes, for Henne's satchel, for Henne's whole being, before moving on without a trace of recognition. Henne, however, was struck by a powerful *deja vu*.

He walked to the back of the bus and stood, shaking, rattling, and rolling as it passed over the potholes and cracks along its journey. He was able to follow the bus' movements easily with his body because his mind was far away. He was looking, but only out of the corner of his eye, at Hardcase. Something about him rang a bell. It wasn't just his clothes, nor his posture, nor the contempt he held for the fat, old woman as she looked down and seemed to plead with him with her posture. Something about this man struck Henne. He watched him and searched his brain as passengers departed at the next stop; the fat, old woman sitting down in a recently vacated seat with a *plop* and sigh of disgust.

He traced his mind back through all the group members he'd had while more passengers filed on and off. He went back to his University days, and still he could not remember having a man such as Hardcase sitting around a circle. It annoyed him because he took pride in knowing, and watching out for, his flock. The fact that a character such as *him* could elude Henne's memory was a trifle troubling to him.

It wasn't until Hardcase's stop that Henne connected the dots.

The man hit the button, requesting the next stop, and stood up. As he got to his feet, his left arm thrust up to grab the bar above his head to steady himself. His right arm came up, half-cocked, and was a fist for a split second before he lay it by his side. *That's it! That's the ticket!*, Henne's mind yelled at him, as Hardcase stepped out onto the sidewalk.

Henne had worked for St. Agnes Hospital, in one form or another, for close to twenty-five years. There were a lot of problems, and a lot of wasteful spending, but one thing Henne couldn't fault them for was the artwork. Every year they were allocated a million dollars from their budget to procure *something*. He'd seen it come and go. Some exhibitions, *"Instruments of the eighteen-hundreds"* were downright beautiful. Others, such as the *"La Vie de Muerte"* were not. But none had shocked him, nor laid a curtain upon his soul, like *"Une Promenade du Montreal"* had.

He remembered the ten pieces that had adorned the hallway in the entranceway of The House That Renton Built. They'd been laid slightly askew and slightly out of reach on the wall above the wheel-chair access ramp. Only, what Henne was remembering was eleven pictures above that particular access ramp. Eleven portraits of city life drawn in red and black and grey as the city slowly gave way to progress. Eleven themed, framed, painted portraits of urban life; except, the last had been more than urban life.

It had been urban death.

The final painting had shown a man being bludgeoned and beaten to a pulp. The caustic scratched lines of the bludgeoner had been hyper-detailed. They'd shown the face of the Hardcase as he beat some unsuspecting citizen to death.

Henne's mind connected, shivered, and his body followed suit. He *knew!*

He rode the bus the rest of the way in a silent and grim satisfaction. He'd set out with a riddle unanswered and solved it.

Eventually, the bus stopped and Henne got off. He watched it stutter away before turning his attention toward the rising brick building in front of him.

He had three stops he wanted to make and began with making his way into the main building to speak with someone he'd seen often, and always on time. He located the physiotherapist's main office, and after a little enquiring, found where Alessia was working that day. He went up to her floor and saw her walking with a patient. He walked towards her and got within ten feet before she looked up. A nervous scowl dropped briefly upon her face before being erased. He knew what she was thinking. It was bad news that he was here, bringing their personal business into her professional one, but, he assured her once he spoke with her, it was urgent. He asked her to meet him in the cafeteria when she had a moment. It was important enough that he could wait a few hours if necessary. She told him it wouldn't be, and that she'd see him down there in fifteen minutes time.

She was as good as her word. Fifteen minutes later, they were seated at a table in the far corner, sipping coffee.

"I'm sorry to impose myself upon you like this," Henne started, "it's just, I have a bad feeling, and I think you may be able to help me."

"What's this about?"

"Do you remember Sheela? From group? Had dyed red hair the past few months? She hasn't been around in a while. It's not like her and I'm worried."

"No. I haven't seen her."

"Are you sure? I know she comes here for one-on-one sessions, and I figured maybe you'd seen her wandering the halls or something." He lifted an eyebrow at that, hoping against hope that this wouldn't be a dead end.

"I'm sorry. I haven't."

There was a slight pause in her sentence. It lasted for less than a second, but Henne, his ears fine-tuned to listen to those pauses over the years, for it was the pauses that sometimes told you more about someone than the words that passed between their lips, heard it. He knew that even if she hadn't consciously *seen* Sheela, she'd marked her in the past few weeks. It lightened his heart.

"Are you sure?" he asked one last time. He knew what her answer would be, but had to ask all the same.

"Yes. I'm sure."

They talked of inconsequential things after that with Alessia continually sneaking peeks at her watch.

"Listen," Alessia said as a way of apology and Henne waved it off. "I don't have that long for this break."

"You gotta do you. I'm just happy you've got a stable life and are keeping it as such."

"Sure. Okay. Thanks for the coffee," Alessia said before getting up and walking away. Henne finished his coffee with a glad heart and walked with a lighter step as he trudged up the hill towards his other place of business. He had to meet Dr. Wosniack and talk to her about her patient.

He found the doctor sitting at her desk, her door slightly ajar; it shifted inward as his knuckles made contact. The doctor's gaze jolted upward toward the interruption and she was on her feet in an instant, edging her back into the corner of the room that was half bookshelf, half window. Henne saw one of her hands dip to her desk, now concealing something in her palm. He noted the half-opened letter on her desk. He didn't fault her, as you didn't work in this place without getting a little jumpy from time to time. He stifled a laugh watching her retreat because he didn't look like your typical down-and-out; quite the contrary with his crew-cut and valise, but who could tell these days.

"Who are you?" she blurted out sharply, startling the smile of his face.

"I work here, Dr. Wosniack," he said at once.

"I don't know you. What are you doing in my office? I'm going to call security." Her words came out in the fast spit of a tobacco auctioneer. Instead of explaining, Henne held up his ID card that was strapped to a lanyard hung around his neck. He held it up like a talisman, hoping to ward off the evil that she felt was emanating from him. It had a portion of the desired effect. Her body tension softened while she drew her eyes to slits and looked at him shrewdly, the hard edge simmering below her words.

"What do you want, Mr...?"

"Henne. Just Henne. I came to talk with you about a patient you've had."

"I don't discuss anything private about my patients. *You* work here and should know that."

"I just need some answers," he said.

"I told you, I don't discuss anything private about my patients."

Henne shook his head and realized that he'd have to be clinical to get anything from this woman. He watched her wring her hands and then bring the left one up halfway to her mouth before dropping it into her right. She wrung them again. Her eyes darted around the room, first left, then right, then back left again. It took him a moment to place it, but she was counting. *This chick's as crazy as her patients,* rang through his head. Once that thought had surfaced, he found himself knowing how to deal with her. The devil you know, after all.

"I'm sorry. Can we start again?" he asked, flashing her a smile that felt plastic on his face. He hauled out a folder from his satchel and laid it upon her desk. He watched her scurry forward to peak at the name written across the top of it.

"You and I share a patient, and I'm concerned about her. I understand that you cannot give out the personal information you've talked about, but that's not what I'm asking. I just need to know if she's doing alright."

"Why wouldn't she be?" Wosniack snapped back at him.

"I don't know," he said slowly. "She hasn't shown up to group for the past few weeks, and I'm worried that something might have gone wrong. Maybe she had to flee the city."

"How would I know?"

Henne sighed. He wasn't going to get anything of consequence out of the woman yet had to try.

"Did she mention anything at all? Was there someone after her? Have you seen her at all over the past few weeks? I understand that your mandated sessions were slated to end a month or so ago, but has she reached out since then?"

"No. She hasn't. And she wouldn't. She wanted to be free and clear of me, of the system, and of this place as soon as she could." Henne felt his heart sink with each word the doctor said. "It seems to me," Wosniack continued, with an edge of delight in her voice, "that once she was done with *you*, she got as far away as she could."

"I don't believe that."

"Believe's got nothing to do with it," Wosniack said dryly. "I don't feed my patients fantasies, and I won't feed you one either. She's left her old life behind and is trying to get as far away as possible from it, now that it's been allowed to end."

Henne opened his mouth, then closed it. What could he say to this woman? His time with Sheela had been spent in the company of multiple others. They'd never had a chance to really *get down to business,* as he was wont to say in his few one-on-one meetings. Sure, Sheela had opened up now and then, but mostly it'd been something superficial; something that was on the outside that she wasn't afraid to show. He had a feeling, and he'd prodded her a few times in that direction, that there was something unsettled within her; that she'd been reluctant to speak about it only seemed to provide further proof to him.

Wosniack's declaration stuck him like a slap in the face. Sheela had played him, made a fool of him, acting like she needed his help and would depend on him for some time, all the while knowing that she was going to jump ship at the first chance when she was finally in the clear. He felt an anger, which had always been slow to begin with, curling up in his belly like a ball of molten lead. Not wanting to let it expand any farther, he closed his eyes, sighed, and thought of his wife and child; it was the quickest way to snuff out his anger.

Henne opened his eyes and looked across the room at Wosniack, who was holding his folder out to him, a sad smile on her face.

"I'm sorry," she said. "It's always the ones we think we can help the most that destroy our hearts."

Henne returned the smile and collected his folder, feeling guilty of the thoughts he'd had against Wosniack. Sure, she was a little frayed around the edges, who in *their* profession wasn't, but she'd spoken bluntly to him when he'd needed it. She clearly shared his feelings of remorse that one of their flock had gotten away.

"Thanks," he said, putting the folder back into his satchel before walking to the door. Halfway there, a question appeared on his lips. He turned back and saw Wosniack's left hand drop back to her side, like it had been reaching up to her mouth again.

"If you *do* happen to be in touch with her, could you please let her know that Henne would like to speak with her?"

"Alright," Wosniack said, "but it's doubtful I'll speak with her. She's dead and gone, and you know it."

Henne did a double-take. "Excuse me?!"

"I said, she's fled and gone, and you know it."

He looked at her across the room, her eyes not showing the sorrow they'd held mere moments ago. They were blank. He searched them for an answer and after a span gave up. What this woman knew or didn't know he'd never find out.

"I'm sorry to bother you," he said sheepishly. "Thank you for your time."

She gave him a perfunctory nod.

"Please close the door on your way out," she said.

Henne left and made his way down to the first floor. He'd struck out on two dead ends and was disheartened, but after the rude awakening of Wosniack's facts of life felt he had to play out the string, just in case. He called her parole officer and asked after her whereabouts, knowing it was a dead end. If her service was over and she'd decided to cut and run, he'd never find her unless she turned up dead.

Henne lumbered his way along the corridor and stopped beside the ten paintings that hung on the wall. This time, they were all donated from the University of Concordia's first-year photography class. *If these are the best young minds have to offer, I feel bad for the arts,*

Henne thought. They were mostly mosaics of outdoor fluff: flowers, a field of corn, a crumbling red brick wall in some shit-hole outskirts county of the city. He looked at them all, counting them as he went, and then went back and counted again. There were only ten. Why was he so sure that he'd seen Hardcase's face on an eleventh then? He thought it might be because of the different sizes of the exhibits, but when he asked the passing security guard if it'd always been *only* ten photos or pictures, the security guard said yes. They never did more because the spacing of the artworks would be off, due to the proximity of the doors.

Henne shook his head and left the building, all-of-a-sudden the urge for a drink overtaking him. He wasn't a teetotaler by any stretch, but normally he only drank on special occasions. And so, at three in the afternoon, Henne found himself in a bar with a pint of beer and a shot of whiskey in front of him. He stayed there long, nursing both glasses, thinking his thoughts. About Wosniack. About the Hardcase and his family. About Sheela. He wished her well and sent his heart out to her, hoping that some good vibes couldn't hinder, and may well help.

Those vibes never reached Sheela, as we all know. She died with her skin peeled off.

The Nutritionist

1

Giles awoke with a mouth feeling like it was stuffed with shit and cotton while his telephone blathered on beside him. He breathed in, felt little give in his airway, and switched to his nostrils. They were immediately hit with the funk of potted plants and pungent perfume. He knew that perfume, and knew it well. It took his booze-addled mind a few seconds to place it. He was with *her*.

He opened his eyes to a ceiling that was showing the best part of the sun drifting by, despite him not knowing it. The ringing phone chimed in time with his pounding head. He heard a muffled grunt, a low-key fart, and then some rustling as *she* turned over, edging *her* way to the farthest reaches of the bed in hopes of escaping his ringing phone.

Reaching out with a lead hand, he grasped his phone and proceeded to drop it on his chest. It *thunked* down and the brief jolt of pain woke him up more. He glanced at the number and saw that it was unlisted, meaning only one thing. He considered ignoring it, but his booze brain was quick to thwart that idea. *I dunno how much money you spent last night, but it was a ton. You're gonna need all the shifts you can get to pay for it.* He answered his phone and was offered an evening shift. He accepted.

With a buzzed mind, Giles tried to piece together the events of the previous night. He'd been out at Korova with a couple of friends, even though he hadn't wanted to be there. He'd been content drinking his night away at home since his roommate had left for a last minute camping trip up north for the weekend. He'd told his friends no, that he was too tired to go out, but when they'd shown up at his apartment with an abundance of beer around eight in the evening, he'd let them in and things had spiraled from there. They'd proceeded to get drunk as lords before wandering over to rue St. Laurent to get up to as much debauchery that some university kids could find on a Friday. They'd bar hopped until finding a few empty stools at Korova. Giles had just ordered his second "Big Boy" of Trembley when he noticed that *she* was there. She was cutting up the dance floor wearing a black dress that hugged tight to her ass and breasts. She wiggled and weaved within her group of friends and Giles immediately got hard, thinking about all the times she'd moved like that when the two of them had been naked, exploring each other's bodies, and facilitating each other in orgasms that Giles judged hadn't been felt by more than ten percent of the world population. He felt a wave of shame and sadness sweep over him as his brain registered it as something that *had* happened, but would never happen again. He resigned himself to continuing his heavy drinking adventure and did his best to keep his back to her.

She'd seen him earlier in the night, however, and was making a point to make him furiously jealous with her body. Because he'd turned his back to her, her movements and gyrating and jiving had little effect on him. She saw this and only tried harder. She ignored the *You're so fucking sexy's*, the *My cock is so rock hard right now's* and even the wandering hands that found their way to her ass. She heard and felt them all but paid them no mind. Maybe later she'd do something about these advances, but right then, she'd only wanted Giles to notice her. And so, when he hadn't turned around and acknowledged her in even the barest of glances, she decided to take a more bold approach. She left a cascade of blue balls on the dance floor and made her way to the bar, butting in between Giles and a random neighbour on his left.

She wiggled into the confined space between the two stools and almost lay across the bar, propping her tits up on it as she did. It gave

Giles, who did a double take when she stopped moving, a fantastic view of her cleavage. She looked over at him and displayed a face that was surprise hinted with a sense of remorse.

"Hi," she said.

"Hi," he replied, his eyes shooting a glance down the front of her dress. The erection that had previously vacated the premises came back.

"What're you doing here?" she asked casually, the drunken slur in her voice currently hidden.

"I'm with friends."

"Which ones?"

Giles threw a thumb over his right shoulder, indicating those sitting beside him. She looked and gave a brief wave before turning her attention back to him.

"Listen," she started. She hesitated, like she was searching for the right words to use. "I'm -- I'm sorry how things turned out between us."

Giles took a swig of his beer, buying some time to find the right way to answer her. He settled for simple instead.

"Are you?"

She shifted again, almost folding in on herself and Giles felt a momentary pang of anger at himself. Surely he'd said the wrong thing.

"I am," she said, looking him in the eye. It was hard, with her breasts on display like that, but somehow he managed to keep contact. "It's just, we're young, Giles, and I wanna sow my wild oats. I wanna see what's out there for me in the world. We moved too fast, and it scared me."

"It scared me too, Krystal. I feel like I can't help myself around you."

She eyed him coolly as one of her hands came off the bar and reached down between his legs, feeling his erection before squeezing it. "I see what you mean," she said.

He heard himself groan and hated himself for it. It'd taken time, but he'd come a long way back from the previous spell she'd put him under. Now, one grab of his dick and he was already putty in her hands. He knew it. She knew it. His two friends sitting beside him, watching the scene unfold with exasperated looks on their faces knew it. One stroke, one grab of his "magic wand" and he was back under her spell.

She bit her lip, still maintaining eye contact with him.

"Maybe there's something not so broken about us after all," she said and turned to leave. Before she'd gotten two steps, she turned back to him, a look of pure seduction and wanting and need and greed all over her face.

"Will you come?" she asked

God help him, he did.

He remembered the basics but not the details of their encounter the night before. He checked the time, saw he still had better than three hours to make it to work, and then rolled over, draping an arm over her naked torso. She snorted in her sleep and brushed it away.

He lay that way for the next ten minutes, hoping she would wake up. When she didn't, and his headache began to reach stunning proportions, he got up and used the bathroom, not trying to be silent as he moved across the room. He returned to her room and saw that she'd shifted positions, now lying where he once was, taking up the majority of the bed. He thought about crawling back in but dismissed the idea. Instead, he collected his clothes, dressed, and walked to her front door. He opened it and left. Standing out in the hallway, his headache abated a bit but his stomach did a sour loop in his belly. He sat down with his back against the door, waiting for the wave of nausea to pass. He fought against it and won, but knew he might not win the next bout. He immediately regretted leaving her place so quick, but knew he couldn't have waited around for her to wake up; it would have looked too desperate.

He forced himself back to his feet and took the most miserable metro ride of his life back to his apartment. Once there, he took a shower and felt a little better. That done, he opened his fridge and dug out some leftover pizza and beer from the night before and thought about what the previous night's experience would mean; three slices of pizza and two cans of beer later, he still had no idea. The only thing he'd decided was that he should text her and see how she felt about the whole thing. He texted her and immediately felt a bit better, knowing that whether it was the smart choice or the dumb one, at least it had been made. That done, he took a quick nap and then got ready and went to work.

2

Giles was given the kitchen/cafeteria routine. It was an easy one, being a Sunday and all, and Giles was glad for this fact. If he'd been given calls, he would have gone home and damn the consequences. As it turns out, maybe that would have been for the best. He spent the first few hours of his shift feeling miserable and mostly miming the work that had to be done. He did a perfunctory check on the cafeteria and showed his face in the kitchen, mostly pushing garbages down so they didn't look like they were about to overflow. He gave up all guise of work and retreated to a housekeeping closet when *she* texted him.

He was nervous, unsure how she'd respond to his heartfelt text, but hoping for something similar. It was the polar opposite:

Hey Giles.

Last night was a mistake. i think u and i both know it. i dunno what came over me when i saw u at the bar, and against my better judgement, i took u home with me. i think this should be a one time only thing. Like we fucked one last time to get each other out of our systems. i'm sorry for conveying the wrong message but i was drunk AF so please don't hold it against me. Youre a sweet guy but i think its best we move on. i think its best if U move on. Please dont text me again. im going to delete ur number and all contact off social mediaz. Sorry.

Love Krystal.

Giles read the message again, sure that he'd gotten it wrong the first time. Midway through the second reading, the words became blurry and he was dumbfounded. He wiped his eyes and was astonished to find that he was crying. Once the knowledge was known, however, he closed his phone, put his head in his hands and wept.

He took his supper break in the housekeeping closet, eating his food with a grim determination and not really tasting the final slices of his leftover pizza. When his break was up, he did a quick garbage run in the cafeteria and then back to the kitchen to do the bulk of his work. He didn't want to, in fact, he just wanted to pass the remaining four hours of his shift locked away, feeling sorry for both his heartbreak and hangover, but knew he couldn't. As a head nurse in the Emerge once told him, "People were counting on him."

He arrived in the kitchen as the last few humans were finishing their menial tasks. He passed by the kitchen supervisor's office and stuck his head in the door.

"Hello," he said.

The supervisor looked up from the scattered forms on her desk with a startle, her hand jumping up, wanting to clutch at her heart, but stopping before it could get that high. She looked at him shrewdly before noticing his blue shirt and pants. Then, her look softened and she smiled slightly.

"Hello," she said.

"My name is Giles, and I'm cleaning your kitchen tonight."

"I know. I saw you up here earlier."

"Have you? Okay." He paused while he looked at her. Even on her best of days, she would never have passed for the woman he met the first time he worked in the kitchen. She had the same color hair, and seemed the right height even though she was sitting down, but that's where the comparisons ended.

"May I help you?" she asked, pulling him out of his thoughts.

"Oh. Yes. I - uhh - just wanted to know if there was anything special you wanted me to take care of tonight?"

Her eyes widened momentarily, and then a broad smile overcame her face. "Actually, you could," she said. She slapped her hands on her knees. It was light and easy and the sound didn't echo. "If you could pay some extra attention to the employee locker rooms, it would be greatly appreciated."

"Yeah. Okay."

"It'd be a nice treat for them when they come in tomorrow. To see their area spick and span would be good for them," she continued, as if not hearing him. "Yes, I think that's just the ticket."

Giles nodded. "Anything else?"

"No, no." She hesitated, then added, "Thank you, Giles." She bent back to making markings on her papers, dismissing him.

Giles started his cleaning in the large, main cooking area. Beginning at the far end, near the walk-in freezers, he mopped the floor while listening to the echoing footfalls of the few remaining employees. They milled about a bit, and by the time Giles made his way to the pots, he assumed he was alone.

The first time he heard the thumping from inside the walk-in freezer, he dismissed it as the cart washer taking the back exit out. The second time, he stopped mopping to listen, *really* listen, and heard the soft *thunk* three times behind him. He turned, but nothing was there. He lay his mop against the wall and walked over the freshly cleaned floor to where the three walk-in freezers were, worried that someone was trapped inside.

Someone had left the lights on in the first one, and as Giles peered in through the tiny, rectangular window, all he saw were slabs of meat hung up on hooks. He debated turning off the light but didn't.

The second freezer's light was also on and held more of the same. He turned toward the third one as three pounding thumps came from that direction. He jumped a little and then turned around, glad no one was watching him.

He peered inside the third freezer. There was no light on inside. *If someone was stuck in there, surely they would have the light on*, he thought, puzzled. His hand reached out and had just grasped the handle when a black hand hit the glass. He jumped back, nearly pissing himself. The hand pulled away. *What in the fuck was that?!?*, his mind screamed at him. He

279

saw his hand involuntarily grasp the handle and begin pulling.

No. No! NO! Bad. Fucking. Idea. Too late. He opened the door and was greeted by the sweet smell of decay for a brief second before the overpowering smell of cold meat overwhelmed his senses.

He held the door open, one hand ready to shut it at a moment's notice, and gazed inside.

"Hello," he called out. "Is anyone in here?"

No answer came back. He let go of the door and eased himself forward. He stood on the threshold while his right hand searched blindly for the light switch on the wall. He found it, flicked it up, and was basked in golden light.

The freezer was just like the others, albeit with a smear of blood on the floor underneath the nearest piece of hanging meat. He waited, taking in large breaths of the cool, stale smelling air. After counting to ten, he turned out the light and shut the door.

Just nerves, he thought to himself. And on the heels of that, *The nerve of* her. *For fuck sakes.*

He struggled and pushed *her* out of his mind. He didn't want to start crying again, regardless if people were present or not. He succeeded, albeit barely. He went back to his work and had made it all the way into the offices before he heard the rapid three *thunks* again. He pointedly ignored it, concentrating on his work instead.

The next time Giles checked his watch, it was almost ten-thirty. He made his way down to the employee locker rooms. He'd promised to do a good job, and he would, for his remaining hour. He cleaned the women's locker room first. He placed a chair upon the wooden table that stood in the middle of the room, and reached up to run a dust rag over the jutting pipe high above the room. Particles of dust floated down and made him sneeze three times in quick succession. He rubbed his face on his forearm before continuing his work. Then, he swept and mopped the floor and cleaned the bathroom to a shine. He stepped back and gave himself a brief moment to admire his work. He was satisfied and knew that the kitchen supervisor would be too. He walked over to the men's locker room and repeated the process. Midway through cleaning the bathroom, he heard a series of soft clicks. He paused in his work and cocked his head to the side, trying to identify the sound. As it approached in a wave of sound, he was able to place it. It was someone walking around in the kitchen, advancing in his direction, in a pair of high heels. Immediately, he thought that Krystal had somehow come to find him, to tell him that she regretted everything she'd said in her earlier text. The majority of his brain knew that it was false hope, but part of him couldn't help wishing it was true.

Giles listened as the footsteps continued to increase in volume and then made a turn towards him. He heard them descend the short staircase and begin their journey down the back corridor that connected the two locker rooms to the main kitchen area. Giles held his breath as the footsteps grew to what seemed like monstrous levels as the clicks echoed around the short, brick hallway. He heard them stop, but not outside the men's locker room. Giles heard the squeak of the hinges as a door opened. Silence followed, and he allowed himself to breathe again. It took the span of five breaths before the hinges squeaked again. The footsteps started up once more, but only for a brief moment. They stopped outside of the men's locker room door. He had a sudden vision of a frost-bitten black hand curling around the edge of the door as it opened. He whimpered, knowing he was trapped for whatever monster lay outside, waiting to come in.

The door, less noisy than the previous one, opened a crack, then an inch, then fully. Standing there, silhouetted inside the frame, was the strikingly beautiful woman Giles had seen the first time he'd worked in the kitchen. She smiled when she saw him standing close to the back of the room, thunderstruck, with a dumb look on his face.

"Hi," she said. "I thought I heard someone down here."

Giles relaxed and opened his mouth to say something, his cheek dancing, then caught a flash of who, and what, she really was. He saw a blue, bloated head atop a severely skewed neck. A purple and black bruise snuck out from underneath the remnants of a rope that was noosed around her neck. He snapped his mouth shut, feeling ridiculously like a fish, and blinked in sudden, startled surprise. When he looked back at her, all the gruesome details of his imagination were gone. She was just a woman.

"Not the talkative type, are you?" she asked.

"Sorry. You scared me."

She laughed. It was hollow and scratchy. She stretched a hand up to rub at her throat, her face gently taking on a pained expression. "I guess I did. It looks like you've seen a ghost." The expression evaporated into a wry smile.

"You scared me," Giles repeated.

"It looks nice," she said, looking around the room. "Thank you for taking the time to do it. I know they'll appreciate it tomorrow."

"It was no problem."

"What's your name?"

"Giles."

"Hello Giles, I'm Vero." She walked into the room, holding out her hand. Giles came forward and shook it. It was cold and clammy. His hands too were damp because he was sweating, despite the chill he felt in the air.

"What're you doing here so late?" he heard himself ask.

"I was just finishing up some last minute tasks. I was on my way out when I thought I heard something, so I came back to check it out." Her smile persisted. "Can't have rats running around when no one's home."

"I guess."

"You know, you're rather cute," Vero said, taking her hand back and running it through her hair. "Do you have a girlfriend, Giles?" The way she said his name sent a shiver through him. It was sexy yet sharp as a guillotine.

"I used to. I guess I don't anymore." He looked into her eyes as he spoke; he found it impossible not to. They were black, inviting pools that begged him to let go and plunge in. He felt his mind slip a notch and he allowed himself to dip a toe, just a toe, inside that pool. He found it warm and inviting.

"So what's the use of a cute, young man being down? You are free to explore all sorts of things." She lowered the lids of her eyes, hooding them. He felt himself slip a little farther inside those pools. "I can show you all kinds of things," she whispered to him. "Things that will blow your mind." She dropped her hand and snaked it underneath her dress and up her thigh, pulling the dress up as she did so. "Things no one can *ever* show you." Giles was hypnotized, following her hand as it reached her panties and pulled them aside, exposing herself to him. "Things that you'd never experience in this world, or this lifetime. Ever." Giles saw her place two fingers on her cleft and apply pressure. He took a halting step toward her and fell to his knees. With his face that close, he could smell the tang of her. It was pungent and sweet and mossy.

"Come," she whispered, using her free hand to pull his head to her. He timidly opened his mouth to taste her. She lifted a leg and placed it on the chair. She removed her hand from her cleft as his tongue came in contact with it. With his eyes closed, he plunged his tongue into her. He didn't even mind when she slipped a belt onto his neck and pulled it tight. It burned, but in a good way. With his eyes closed and his thoughts occupied, it was easy for him to miss the way her eyes rolled up to whites, like a Great White biting into its prey. It wasn't until his breath was fully cut off and he was hoisted in the air, his legs dangling, that his brain registered something was amiss. And even then, it was a slight thing. He kicked once at the end of his life and then his body was still.

His mind followed The Nutritionist down whatever hole to hell she'd chosen for him.

They found his body the next morning.

The Man Behind The Curtain

Milt Hoffman sat on the edge of his bed. He was flexing his left leg with the help of his physical therapist, Alessia. Her hands were soft, almost fuzzy, as they held his calf. He knew that feeling was because of the drugs, but he didn't mind. He was high-as-an-apple-pie-in-the-sky. Such an elegant feeling, if he did say so himself. He'd never taken anything harder than aspirin in his life until five days ago. He'd been up on a ladder, cleaning out the gutters of his house, when he'd suffered what the doctor later told him was a mild heart attack. To Milt, there hadn't been anything mild about it. He'd forgotten he was on a ladder and clutched at his chest, gasping for air. He'd fallen onto the soft grass beneath him. Because he landed on the grass, and not over his driveway, he was spared the worst of injuries. He'd sprained both legs, but nothing was broken. His wife, doing dishes by the kitchen window, had looked up to see him sprawled upon the grass, wiggling about. She'd immediately thought he'd broken his neck, which was a fair assessment due to the height of his fall. She called 911, and a few minutes later, as the pain in Milt's chest had all but abated, an ambulance arrived.

And so, here he sat, pleasantly stoned while an attractive woman who wasn't his wife held his leg.

"How does that feel, Mr. Hoffman?" she asked.

"It's okay. It hurts a little, but I don't know if it's because I'm on the mend or just the drugs."

She laughed. "Probably both," she said.

She moved her hands onto his other leg and began the same series of stretches. Milt watched her for a few brief moments before turning his attention elsewhere. He looked up at the muted television and saw the talking heads trying to explain away the day's newest tragedy; nothing good there.

A flutter of movement drew his eyes to the curtain that was behind Alessia. The window was open, and a slight breeze was sauntering in. He watched the curtain swirl in random patterns as it danced with the breeze. He smiled. Alessia looked up and saw it and smiled back. He was still watching the curtain when he saw something that made his smile falter. Below the curtain was a set of bony feet bookended by a robe. He rubbed his eyes, trying to clear them, unsure if what he was seeing was really there.

"Is it hurting?" Alessia asked.

"What? No. No. Everything's all fuzzy, so no pain. I just thought I saw something."

"What was it?"

He looked and saw the feet weren't there anymore. "Nothing," he said.

"If you say so. Feel up to any walking today, Mr. Hoffman?"

He was surprised to find that he *did* want to go for a walk, if only to clear his head a little.

"Sure. I'll push as much as I can today," he said, and meant it.

They got up, and with the use of a walker, made it all the way down the hallway. He had to allow himself to be pushed back to his room on the commode chair, however.

"You did good," Alessia told him twice on their ride back. He knew it was the truth, only yesterday he hadn't been able to make it halfway down the hallway, but was still disappointed with himself. He wanted to be out of his room a little longer; even a millisecond longer would have been better, he felt. As they neared his room, a dull, fuzzy fear crept up his back with thick fingers. They were numb, and couldn't grip him *too* hard on account of the drugs, but they were there.

Immediately upon entering the room, Milt's eyes darted to the curtain. It was still

289

moving perceptively, but thankfully, there were no feet underneath. With the help of Alessia, Milt was positioned back in his bed, propped up so he could better watch the talking heads on the television.

He lay that way awhile, watching boring television while enjoying the effects of the drugs coursing through his system. It was a calm, quiet time. His wife wasn't expected to visit until six that evening, after she finished her shift at work. She'd wanted to spend another day with him, but Milt had held stern, telling her that it was only a 'mild' heart attack, and he would do well with a day of rest. She'd relented and went back to work, although how much work she'd actually gotten done today was anybody's guess.

And so, he was still in a drugged out daze, courtesy of a nurse who'd given him another dose around four-thirty in the afternoon, when he saw the feet again. They were in the same place as before; unmoving behind the curtain. He briefly thought of ringing the nurse, telling them he needed help, telling them something, but a voice spoke up inside his head.

Don't. There's nothing to worry about.

He stopped his hand from reaching out for the call button. It took effort, but not as much as he would have believed a few hours ago. He dropped his arm to his side and looked back toward the curtain. The breeze outside was still kicking up enough to make the curtain flutter in all but one place. Boney fingers held the outskirts of the curtain. The polished white of them went up and disappeared into a cloak that was more blue than black, but only a little. The sleeve of the cloak bent at the elbow around the corner of the curtain. It was all he could see.

Not Yet, a voice spoke up in Milt's mind. *Soon. But Not Yet.*

"Soon what?!" Milt heard himself blurt. His roommate stirred not in the least. He was off in the land of nod, sleeping an Ativan laced sleep.

Soon, the voice repeated. Milt watched the fingers curl harder around the curtain before releasing it, as the hand and cloak disappeared behind it. Milt watched the bony feet below first grow transparent, and then cease to be altogether. Milt promptly peed himself and lay that way until his wife showed up.

She took one look at him, one *smell* of him, and demanded of Milt to tell her about the conditions they were forcing him into. He told her it wasn't their fault, that he never rang them. She tried to yell at him, took one look at his complexion, and thought better of herself. She went out to the nursing station, but instead of yelling, as she'd originally planned, she told them she was going to change her husband.

They asked if she needed help, and she declined, saying she could handle it.

With Milt freshly changed and smelling like powder, Gretta sat with her husband as they watched t.v. together. After changing him, she'd pulled her chair beside his bed so she could hold his hand. When supper came, she watched him dump two spoonfuls of soup onto his johnny before getting closer to him and feeding him herself. It was an arduous task, as he drooled the majority of his soup on the front of him, but eventually, it was done. He thanked her and even gave her a perfunctory kiss on the lips, straining forward to do so. It lifted her spirits, and if she'd have known it was the last kiss he'd ever give her, she would have made it last a season. They spoke a little as the minutes pushed on into hours. She mentioned that she was cold, that they should close the window, but he wouldn't have any of it.

"I need it open. It's -- " He almost said *It keeps the curtain moving so I don't have to think about it,* but bit his tongue at the last minute. "It's nice to have a breeze," he finished reluctantly. She argued that it was cold, he said that it wasn't. They breached the outer field of an argument and wavered there. They looked at each other across thirty years of marriage and old arguments welled up inside Milt. He opened his mouth to say something, but they were saved the inevitable when a nurse came in to administer more pain meds. He slipped under and stayed that way until Gretta left a few hours later, kissing his brow sweetly.

Milt awoke alone, in a dark room. The window was still open, and a cool breeze still walked across the room. It curdled the sweat that had broken out upon his skin. His first glance was towards the curtain. He saw the toes and the hand along the edges of it. He felt the fear come back, expanded by the darkness encompassing his room. He looked around and saw his roommate still in the deep sleep of drug. He turned back to the curtain and saw the feet closer to the edge; they had shimmied over to the left while he wasn't looking. Milt pried his eyes off the ground and walked them up the edge of the curtain. The hand was now completely lost in the sleeve. He scanned his vision higher until he saw a head. Milt could only see half, but what he saw gave his heart a lurch; it began beating fast and threatened to *throw another rod* as he fought against it, trying to cool it off. If the thing behind the curtain wanted to kill him, he reasoned, it would have already done so without fuss or muss.

He looked back at the head. One dead eye stared out at him. One half of a grin that was covered in teeth and was all skull smiled at him. It tittered, the sound falling empty and hollow amongst the two humans in the room.

Milt thrust his hands out, palms up in a begging gesture. "If not now, then when?" he blurted, offering himself up as a fake sacrifice, trying to keep his voice steadier than he felt.

Soon, the voice thundered in his head and tittered. He was thrust back against his pillow, eyes straining. They began to grow heavy as he felt a strong urge to sleep and fought it. Milt knew if he closed his eyes now he'd be dead, that the thing behind the curtain, *that the grim reaper behind the curtain,* would devour him. So, he fought and waited.

An eternity in ten minutes passed. The figure behind the curtain moved not one iota. He wondered again if it was something his mind had made up in its drug-addled condition, but somehow, he didn't think so. It looked too real. It felt too real. It smelled too real; his nose had picked up a small scent of decay and bleached bones. He opened his mouth to speak again when a flicker of light off to his left caught his eye. He turned toward the door to see a figure standing stark and silhouetted against the dull hall light. He couldn't make out many features on the person, but he noted the scrubs and saw the long hair. It was a female nurse, he reckoned.

She walked over to his bed and looked down at him. This close, he saw that she was once-upon-a-time pretty, but the late night shifts and, what he assumed, a hard life had taken their toll on her. She was pale, and lines stood out across her face, like she was twenty-five going on sixty. He saw her eyes dart to the curtain and then back at him. He followed where her gaze went and knew, even before seeing and confirming it, that the apparition would be gone. It was.

"Hello - Mr. Hoffman," she said with a voice that reminded him of the creature behind the curtain's laugh. "How are you feeling - this evening?"

"I feel odd," he said, and it wasn't a lie.

"Any pain?"

Milt searched his body over and felt a multitude of twinges of pain throughout his legs.

"No," he lied. "I feel fine. I don't think I'll need a dose tonight after all."

He saw a look of something flash across her face. It could have been anger, but he thought the look fell into the camp of disgust more than anything else. He wondered briefly if these nurses and doctors had quotas to hook patients on drugs, then pushed the thought aside. He knew the oath that all medical professionals

295

took, so he couldn't fathom them pushing something unnecessary on him.

"Well, that's good," the nurse told him. She looked down at his arm, where a tube was attached. She reached out and grasped it with a deft touch that was cold and froze his sweat even more than previous. She made a *tisk tisk* gesture with her mouth, clucking her tongue against the side of her cheek. It was loud and jarring in the silence of his sleeping roommate.

"Whoever did this needs to be - fired," she said matter-of-factly. She pulled his arm closer to her with none of the softness with which she'd previously used. Milt looked at her as she rotated it with a brute grace "I'm gonna have to - change this." She looked at him without out a hint of care in her face. "If you - don't mind, that is."

Milt said he didn't mind. He had a feeling that her asking him was just a formality, and that she'd go about changing his pick-line whether he voiced an objection or not.

"I'm sorry if - this hurts," his nurse told him without any remorse in her voice. She went to the counter and collected a few sterile alcohol swabs. She came back to him and swabbed the insertion point before unceremoniously ripping out the line. Milt yelped as it was pulled, feeling his skin extend to the point of ripping before finally letting go of the foreign object. A few droplets of blood welled up from the wound and Milt could have sworn, before he was beyond the point of doing anything but dying, that the nurse had briefly licked her lips when the red specks caught her eye.

She tightened her grip on his arm almost to the point of pain. Milt's eyes flashed wide, and he opened his mouth to say something but froze. He watched a tentacle snake itself out of her arm and wrap itself around his. It was soft and cool to the touch. He watched as the tiny tip of the tentacle wound its way down his arm and slide across the crook of his elbow. He saw it lift and then pause as it poised itself above the skin before plunging in. He was hit with an immediate sting that faded to a euphoria. He saw the tentacle within his skin. He saw the bumps along the line as his blood was being pulled from him into her. He felt his lifeline slipping. *This is what's meant to be,* he thought each time a portion of him exited his body. In his final moments, he tried to argue with himself that he was doing everything he could, but knew it was a lie. He lay back, accepted the truth pulsing through him, and gave himself up to her.

Part Three:
The Nurse

Todd

It was dubbed an "Emergency Meeting," yet they'd waited three weeks after the suicide of Giles to call it. Mr. Charlevoix was standing up at the head of the large, rectangular table. It was late in the day so his top button was undone and his tie was askew. The HR representative was leaning against the wall, arms crossed, close to the door.

"You all know why you're here," he started off. "I want everyone to feel comfortable here. I called this meeting so we could discuss the incident. I want everyone present to speak their mind if they have something to say. I know it was a tough thing that happened, and I feel bad about it, but I'd like you all to know that there was really nothing anyone could have done to avoid this catastrophe."

Mr. Charlevoix looked around the room, holding eye contact with each manager present for the prerequisite amount of time. Todd thought he could almost see the HR rep nodding each time Mr. Charlevoix moved on.

"Would anyone like to speak?" he asked, still scanning the room.

It was Brian Holtz, of course it was, who was the first to speak.

"I think you're mistaken if you think that there was nothing we could have done," he said plainly. "In fact, I think what happened underlines a growing problem with not just our department, but the entire health care system."

"Which is?" Charlevoix asked, his stare radiating needles.

"The mental health of our workers, obviously." Holtz held Charlevoix's gaze, not giving him an inch. "How many people have taken some sort of stress leave this year?"

Charlevoix bristled. "I don't have that information on hand."

"That's too bad because I think it's likely to be a lot. I know a manager or two that has utilized it."

An uncomfortable silence blanketed the room. Someone coughed, weight was shifted in chairs, fingers were drummed underneath the table. When no one spoke up, Holtz continued.

"I don't have the numbers either, but since taking over a managerial position ten years ago, I've noticed a steady uptick in the amount of workers who go out on stress leave, or sick leave, when there's no physical malade present. Let me ask you another question, Mr. Charlevoix. Who is in charge of speaking to our employees about their mental health issues?"

300

This time, Charlevoix perked up. Todd knew he'd been speaking to their resident counselor before the meeting; everyone had seen her coming out of his office earlier that day.

"Dr. Duncan," he said immediately.

"Sure, she's who we send people to if we warrant it necessary, or if they ask. But who's the front-line for us? Which one of us is trained to spot the beginning symptoms or behaviours that led to the death of Mr. O'Conner? Because it sure as shit ain't me."

Once again, an oppressive silence came down like a curtain.

Holtz rolled along. "We need to work on our ability to note and track this shit from the beginning. It's the only way we're going to be able to succeed in keeping our workforce at near full capacity, while also avoiding disasters like the one that befell us *three* weeks ago."

"What do you suggest then?" Todd asked. He rubbed the bridge of his nose with his thumb and index finger. This meeting wasn't going the way he thought it was going to go. He'd wanted people to speak nicely about the deceased and decide that it wasn't their fault that he'd killed himself; that no one would have been able to see it coming under any circumstance. Now, Holtz and his boss were heading towards a confrontation that he wanted to nip in the bud. If it continued in this vein, he knew someone would pipe up, either Holtz or that bitch Meredith, that Giles had been his charge and that he was at fault for not spotting the unstoppable sooner.

"You seem to have all these ideas," he continued, "so why don't you enlighten us on what we could do?" He saw Holtz open his mouth and held up a finger. "While you're at it, why don't you explain where this extra money and time is going to come from."

Todd chanced a glance at Mr. Charlevoix, but only out of the corner of his eye. He saw the shadow of a smile on his lips. He knew he'd struck a good chord with his boss and relished that feeling.

"We need *training*," Holtz said. Todd saw his eyes had the glossy look of someone on the verge of tears. "Have Dr. Duncan give us a couple of day courses about the early problem signs. What are the triggers? What are the borderline behaviours? What are the red flags?" Todd opened his mouth and saw that Holtz stuck up a retaliatory finger. He closed his mouth and coloured, thinking that Holtz was going to regret doing that in front of the boss.

"As for the time, well, we're all going to have to *make* time. They're *our* employees, and we need to do right by them." Todd looked around and saw Meredith and Hussein nodding their heads in tandem. "As for the money,"

Holtz continued, "we need to find it *now*. We'll save it in the long run with our employees working a year without needing personal time, instead of spending money out of our asses on overtime."

"Unfortunately, we don't have the money today. Maybe in a few months, but definitely not today." Mr. Charlevoix said.

"*Fuck* in a few months," Holtz nearly yelled. "We need the money now. Unless *you're* telling us straight up that our employees are expendable. Is *that* what you're saying?" Holtz asked.

There were a few gasps around the room. The HR rep took this as her opportunity to jump in.

"It's a good idea, Mr. Holtz, and something that we're going to look into. I'd like to speak with you privately afterward if I may."

Holtz didn't say anything, settling for a curt nod.

"Okay. I understand this is a difficult time for most of you. I'd like to keep this as civil as possible," Mr. Charlevoix said. "Does anyone else want to speak?"

General conversation followed. Most people spoke in platitudes that Todd was more comfortable with, welcoming the shift in conversation. He echoed their sympathies when he felt moved to speak, but couldn't help adding another dig at Holtz, however, hoping to show off for his boss.

"No offense to Mr. Holtz, but I don't think there's anything we *could've* done," he said, after extolling the virtues of Giles as a worker. Holtz frowned at him, but he pretended not to notice. "How many times do we read about some celebrity killing themselves and everyone's like 'We never saw it coming?' You can't put a face on depression. I'm sorry, but it's a fact. I don't think there's anything we could've done for Mr. O'Conner, and I don't think we should feel bad about the terrible choice he made."

Todd saw the HR rep and Mr. Charlevoix nod along with his statements. He stopped speaking and sat back, content to quit while he was ahead; an easy lesson he'd learned long ago.

The meeting broke up shortly afterward. Todd's fingers tapped absently on the dark screen of his tablet while the others departed. Todd sat up when he felt a tap on his shoulder. He forced himself to look up casually and saw that Mr. Charlevoix was standing directly to the right of him.

"Hello, sir," he said, flashing his biggest, toothiest smile.

"I was wondering if I could have a minute of your time," Mr. Charlevoix said. "In my office."

"Not a problem, sir. Right now?"

"No time like the present."

Todd issued a small laugh that he hoped didn't sound as forced as it did to his ears. He stood and followed his boss out of the conference room. They walked down the hallway, not quite abreast; Todd stayed a few inches to the left and behind Mr. Charlevoix. They walked towards the elevator, the clicks of their heels the only sound shared between them. Todd spent the walk inspecting the minute bits of dirt lodged under his fingernails. They got into the elevator and took it down to the third floor, heading toward their offices.

They took the unvarnished stairs down to the lower level of their building. It was a wooden shack built on as an afterthought to the stone castle, boxed in by the main pavilions.

Charlevoix unlocked his door and walked in, Todd following. The room was small. Charlevoix's desk was stuffed up against the wall, but he still had to turn sideways to sneak behind it. He took his seat while Todd remained standing. When given his cue, Todd sat in the metal chair opposite his boss. He shifted his weight a few times, then resigned himself to being uncomfortable. Looking across the desk at

305

each other, Todd was determined not to say the first word. He'd been summoned, and it was rude to impose, so, he waited.

"You seem like a good man," Mr. Charlevoix said after a lengthy pause. "A good, *company* man."

Todd smiled. He couldn't help it. He nodded but felt it wasn't enough.

"Yes, sir. I like to think of myself as a company man."

"Good. That's good." Mr. Charlevoix leaned back in his chair and put his feet up on his desk, the chair creaking the whole way. He cast his gaze at the ceiling and plucked a pencil off his desk, twirling it around the middle finger of his right hand. When he next spoke, he had the air of someone deep in thought, like he'd just come across the answer to life's most significant problem.

"You know, I think you could be a *great* company man." He looked at Todd, shrugging with lazy, nonchalant movement. "That is, if that's what you *want*."

Todd corrected the slouch that had crept up on him. This *was* what he wanted, and to hear it put some openly, so boldly, both shocked and delighted him. Suddenly, he knew this was his chance to make some headway in the department and what would be asked of him. Choosing his words carefully, wanting it to be his boss' ask, he spoke.

"I would like that very much."

"Excellent news. In fact, maybe you could help me out with something."

"Maybe I could. What is it that you need help with?" Todd asked slowly.

"Well, it's a delicate matter. I'm hoping that I can trust you to be discreet about this."

"Certainly, sir." Todd mimed zipping his lips shut.

Mr. Charlevoix laughed and Todd joined him, straining to make it genuine.

"That's a good one," Mr. Charlevoix said, repeating Todd's pantomime. "I'll have to remember that. Zip! Zip!" He wiped his dry eyes and continued. "Seriously though, I need an ear on the ground within the managerial department." He took his feet off his desk and leaned across it, becoming every bit the boss that commanded attention and respect. "Someone is costing this department a lot of money."

"What do you mean?"

"Someone's been ordering stock after being given explicit instructions not to do so. I know who it is, but I don't know how they're going about doing it. I have an idea, but nothing concrete. Nor do I have any proof."

"Who do you suspect?"

"You know, that's something you'll find out for yourself if you're as smart as I think you are."

Todd opened his mouth to speak but saw Mr. Charlevoix hold up a finger.

"I know, I know. You're thinking that if I tell you, it'll make your job easier. While this is undeniably true, it would also colour your perception of the task at hand. What if I'm wrong? Then you'll have spent a lot of time for nothing, following the wrong person."

Todd had watched enough Law & Order to know what he should say next.

"You want fresh eyes and ears on it. I understand."

"Exactly. That's the ticket. Now, do you think you can do this task and be," he drew his fingers across his lips.

"Yes, sir. Not a problem."

Mr. Charlevoix sat back. "Good. Now, if you'll excuse me, I've got some emails to respond to."

"Okay, sir. Have a good day."

Todd got up and left the office, shutting the door behind him without being told.

Simon

The rearview mirror was vibrating as Simon looked into it before checking his blind spot and changing lanes. Safely done, he reached down and increased the volume. He looked over at Mario, grinning.

"Sounds good, doesn't it?" He almost had to shout to be heard, *almost;* the knob not yet a third of the way up.

They drove that way for some time, the music blasting with their arms dangling out of open windows. They were cruising around the city, no particular place in mind. The sun was casting early shadows, meaning sunset wasn't far behind. Simon was not looking forward to another bitter winter. He'd recently purchased a warm, and expensive, coat and a nice pair of boots that matched. They'd been necessities, and why not splurge a little since he *was* in funds. The stereo, however, was his vanity item. His cars were always bottom shelf, and he didn't mind. What mattered was if you could blow panties off with the bass.

So, he'd upgraded. Why not? He came by the money honestly, so he was allowed to spend a little on himself. He'd saved the bulk of the cash in a duffle bag that he kept in the closet of his room. He saved it for when his mother would need a mobile chair to get up to the second floor. He saved it for when his mother would need bedside care. He saved it to supplement her pension when she was stretched thin to tearing. He would see to it that she died with dignity and comfort in her own home. It was more than he could say for many of those he shuffled around the hospital.

They were currently cruising through the plateau, seeing what sights there were to see, smelling what scents there were to smell. University had been in session for less than a week and the neighbourhood, and its surrounding areas, was teeming with the last remnants of life of the season. Traffic was backed up on St. Laurent due to a street sale on Mont-Royal. Simon didn't mind. He could sit idly in his car all day, watching the t'ings walk by, if that was what was required of him. He sensed Mario was happy doing the same. They talked of sports and small things, mostly content to stay quiet and enjoy the view.

They reached the Mile End and meandered their way along no particular path until the chill of the departing sun told them it was time to pick a destination.

They settled on going over to Oscar's house for pre-drinks before deciding where the night should take them. Oscar, a co-worker, lived close enough to the downtown core that parking was a nightmare for Simon. They arrived twenty minutes after they said they would.

Oscar greeted them at the door and ushered them into an apartment that had booming music and a sticky floor. Mario was called over by a group of porters and housekeepers while Simon scanned the room. There was only one girl there he didn't know, so he marked her and went to mix himself a drink. There was the standard fare, so he made a rum and coke to sip on. Then, he went in search of the one unfamiliar face in the crowd. He found her talking with a housekeeper by the stereo, both with a slight sway in time to the music. Walking over, he caught her eye. She smiled shyly at him and then went back to looking at her friend, or so Simon assumed. Either way, it wouldn't stop him.

"Hey," he said when he got beside them.

"Hey," they both replied in unison. He smiled at them. They had a deep connection, he was sure, but it wasn't anything he hadn't encountered before.

"What brings you two here?" he asked both of them, while looking only at the girl.

"We got invited by a friend," the guy said.

"Which friend?" Simon asked, still not looking at him. He kept his eyes as playful as possible and saw her shift subconsciously to a more open posture toward him.

"Been friends with Oscar since way back," the guy said.

"What's your name?"

"Mike Shorton."

Simon turned at the mention of the name. "Oh shit, you're him!" he exclaimed.

"I'm who?" Mike asked with a look of surprise mingled with skepticism.

"Oscar told me he was looking for you, like two minutes ago."

"What's he want?"

"Dunno man. He didn't tell me. Go ask him."

"You sure?"

"Yeah, man," Simon said. "That's what he told me. Oscar said, 'If you see Mike, send him over.'"

Mike eyed him suspiciously before walking off in the direction of Oscar. Simon turned toward the girl, not wanting to waste any time.

"Hey, so are you two together?"

"Straight to the point, aren't you," she said with a wan smile.

Simon took a sip of his drink, looking at her seductively over his glass.

"Well, Oscar didn't actually wanna see Mike, so I don't have much time to get to know you."

"Is that how it is, then?"

Simon let out a non-committal grunt, accompanied by a shrug of shoulders.

"So, are you?"

"No. We're just friends."

Simon brightened substantially. "Is that so? Well, I should get your number so I can take you out some time."

"What's wrong with getting to know me right here? Right now?"

"We could, but if your friend comes back, I don't think he's gonna be too happy with me for moving in on his girl."

"I'm not his girl," she said playfully.

"From the way he was looking at you, that's not how he sees it."

"How he sees things and how they really are are two completely different things," she said, running a hand through her hair.

"Is that so?"

"Those are the facts of life that he doesn't seem to understand. What can I say?"

"You can say you'll give me your number. How's that for starters?"

"You don't even know my name."

"Well, you can add that into my phone along with your number," Simon said, holding out his phone. She smiled and took it, quickly punching in her number. She handed it back and he immediately pressed the call button, taking note of her name as he did so. It rang once before she reached into her pocket, extracted her phone, and hung-up.

"Wow. You're not a very trusting soul, are you?"

"What can I say? I've been burned before by girls far less prettier than you. I just wanted to make sure."

"Is that it?"

"Uh-huh. So, what do you do, Debbie?"

"I like to pick up mysterious people at parties. Speaking of which, why don't you tell me your name so I can close the file on *this* mystery."

"I'm Simon." He held out his hand, and she shook it. "It's a pleasure to meet you, Debbie."

"And you. As for what I do, I'm a police officer in training."

Simon held up his hands in mock surrender. "Don't shoot me, please."

"Don't be an asshole. Put your hands down," she said amidst a chuckle. "I wouldn't use my gun on you, but my handcuffs could be another story."

"Is that how it is, then?"

"Wouldn't you like to know."

"Maybe I'll call you later this week, and we can find out."

"Maybe."

"Well then, Debbie. I'll leave you to that thought and text you later."

"You do that."

Simon flashed her a final smile before wandering off to find Mario amongst the crowd. He was easy to find, being both the tallest and blackest person there. He was currently in conversation with a group of Porters and a nurse or two that Simon recognized by face, but not name. They were in the middle of talking shop and regaling each other with the rumours they'd heard over the last few months.

"...you'd have to be stupid to think that place isn't haunted," Jose was saying, as Simon sidled up to the group.

"Haunted how?" Mario asked.

"I dunno. Just in general, you know. No place that is a home to misery and depravity like that for centuries gets away unscathed."

"So, you don't know specifics," Simon said.

"I do," Ronald said. "It happen to me beaucoup-de-fois."

"Not more of your voodoo shit," someone said. Ronald ignored the remark and continued to scan the group with his gaze.

"I work overnight and sleep in the break room one night, huh? I listen to my music while I sleep, but something woke me. I didn't hear music. I look down, my phone still locked. I enter my passcode and the background picture change. No longer my daughters, but a man. An old man with long white hair and blue, blue eyes. They stare at me. They stare into my soul. Behind the man was the wall of that room. Too much. I leave and never go back to that room at night."

"That's fucked up," one of the nurses whistled under his breath. "Do you still have the picture?"

"No. I delete it right away. I didn't like looking at it. At *him*."

The group looked at him, not fully believing his tale. Before anyone could voice their disbelief, the other nurses spoke up. Simon recognized her from the cardiac care unit.

"I haven't seen anything like that happen, but some weird stuff has been going on as of late." She looked at the other nurse, who nodded his head, either as an urging to continue or a gesture of solidarity Simon didn't know.

"What kind of stuff?" Mario asked.

"Well, I don't know if I can say. It's not the kind of thing the bosses would look too kindly on if word about it got around."

"I'm sure it's been spread around already," Mario assured her. "Besides, if anyone asks, we can always use the trusty fall back of 'I heard.' It means everything and nothing at the same time."

"Still..."

Ronald reached out and gently took her wrist. She took a startled step back but didn't try to pull free. His eyes blazed at her from across the circle as he spoke.

"There be some bad shit going down, huh? I can feel it. I can taste it. Please. Tell us so we can be prepare."

She held his gaze and spoke directly to him while the entire circle felt the weight of her words.

"I don't think it's what you're worried about, but there have been two strange deaths with patients over the last little bit."

"Are we doing this?" Greg, the other nurse, asked, his voice wracked by turbulence.

"Why not? It's bound to come out. Besides, if this is as bad as we're worried about, it wouldn't hurt to have more people prepared for the possible storm and quarantine that could be coming down the pipe."

"Wait, wait, wait. What fucking quarantine?" Simon blurted. "We're talking about ghosts and tall tales and all of a sudden we've got - we've got -"

317

"A potential pandemic," Mario finished.

"It's not a pandemic," Greg said sharply. He sighed. "Truth is, we don't know *what* it is, or what's causing it. We were told to be on alert and watch everything. To triple check our work, and our colleague's work."

"For what?"

Britt looked at Greg. "Go on. You might as well tell them now. The cat's already out of the fucking bag," he said.

"People are melting," Britt said.

The group erupted in a barrage of curses and expletives. Ronald crossed himself while Jose and Mario took a half-step away from Britt.

"What do you mean people are fucking melting?" Simon heard himself ask.

"Just that. Two patients were fine one day, and the next, when we did morning rounds, they began bleeding from their cavities. The first guy was in a coma, so he didn't feel anything as his vitals tanked in under ten minutes. The second guy, well, he was awake and was screaming about how it felt like worms were crawling under his skin and burrowing into his organs. How could he feel his organs? We tried everything, but he screamed for a good twenty minutes while a steady flow of black blood exited his body. He was *sweating* blood by the end."

"It was a painful death," Greg interjected.

Britt snapped a look at Greg, who held up his hands in a defensive gesture. She turned back to the crowd that had grown by a person or two. "They did the autopsy and then had a very closed door M and M conference. Since I'd had the second guy as a patient the night before, I was asked to give a deposition. They took my statement but didn't ask me any questions, which I found odd. Then, they ushered me out and never gave me an official reason as to what happened."

"Then how do you know he melted?" Mario asked.

"I spoke with Bob, the assistant head nurse on the floor. He felt that since I'd been in contact with the patient, I had a right to know what went down, and if there were any countermeasures I could take to protect myself from a shared fate. Turns out I'm fine because the patient wasn't killed by anything viral or bacterial. His innards just liquified."

"That's so fucking gross," Jose said.

"Tell me about it," Britt continued. "The thing is, they liquified over a short period of time. Like, in the twenty minutes it took from

319

when he started screaming to when he eventually gave up the ghost. It's crazy to hear, and even crazier to witness, but he was fine one moment, then the next..." Britt snapped her fingers, "...it was like all his organs were taken out, blended together, and then slipped back inside without anyone seeing it happen."

The group fell silent. Some shuffled their feet, while others took large swigs of their drinks. Simon stood stoic, looking ahead with a blank stare on his face, fully realizing the scenario.

After several people drained their glasses and beer cans, Simon spoke.

"So, no one has any idea as to what's happening?"

"Nothing official," Greg said. "I imagine there are a bunch of half-assed theories floating around, but no one is going to give them any credence until there is some evidence backing them up."

"The prevailing theory is it's either a mutation caused by a certain drug that only shows up in a handful of people, or witchcraft," Britt said, looking directly at Ronald as she spoke the last word.

"That's fucking disturbing," Mario said. "That's two in a month that've succumbed to the same thing. That sounds like it's a contagion or... fuck, something. I don't know."

"It's really not that many because my bosses checked around after the first instance. There has been nothing like it ever recorded since we began *taking* records," Britt said, her tone hushed. "So two people in the entirety of the recorded human race constitutes a barely handful, in my opinion anyway."

"It still won't make me sleep better to-night," Mario mumbled.

Slowly, the conversation moved on to other things. Simon didn't partake, however. He was still concerned about the news the nurses were spouting. The spark that started tiny was now blooming into a bright, white star. Despite telling himself it was impossible, he knew who was responsible for those two deaths. More so, he knew two of the accomplices for those deaths; Stanley, and himself. He felt his balls shrivel up inside him as a cold front permeated him. He had to make a call. He bummed a smoke and excused himself out onto the back balcony that fed directly off Oscar's master bedroom. He knew no one would be there, so he'd be afforded some privacy. He pulled out his phone and dialed the number from memory.

Simon was greeted to a mechanical voice telling him that the number he wished to reach had been disconnected. He hung up and re-dialed, hoping he'd made a mistake. No such luck. He lit his cigarette and breathed in the noxious fumes, coughing out an exhale.

He finished his smoke and pitched the butt over the edge. He felt lightheaded and a little nauseated, but it was better than feeling the sinking feeling within him. When he got back inside, he decided he was going to get blindingly drunk and proceeded to do a rather good job of it.

He woke up the next morning with a thunderstorm of a hangover raging through his body. He remembered hearing more talk of what had happened at the hospital over the past month or so, and that had forced him to finish his drinks in quick succession. He remembered getting silly and almost telling some girl he'd met at the party, Denise? Delilah?, his involvement with The Doctor when asked about the rumours. Almost spilling his story made him more ashamed, which led to more liquor. After that, there was a supermassive black hole where his memory ought to have been.

He shuffled around his house, still in his boxers, and made his way down to the kitchen. It was after eleven, and he knew his mother would be out for the day. He looked outside and saw his car in the driveway. He rubbed a hand over his face and felt a fresh wave of guilt stab him. Had he driven home last night? He didn't know. He hoped not, but he had a sickening feeling he was hoping against reality. He got himself a large glass of water and choked it down with two aspirin. Then, he went to the couch and collapsed upon it. He opened the television and shuffled through Netflix, settling on some stupid cartoon show. He was still lying there when his mother came back five hours later.

Alessia

She was asleep and in total darkness. She heard the beeping of a heart-rate monitor somewhere off in the distance. She felt cold spots dotting her body. She smelled antiseptic and industrial food. She opened her eyes and saw her parents looking down at her. On their faces were a mix of anxiety, relief, and disappointment. She opened her mouth to ask them what happened, but as she did so she felt cotton filling her it, instantly soaking up all the moisture. A dry cough escaped her instead of words. She lifted a weak, trembling hand and reached into her mouth. She pulled a wad of cotton out, dropped it, and went back for more. She pulled out handful after handful but was not able to empty her mouth. It seemed to her that the cotton filled her mouth faster than she could pull it out. Her parents continued to look down at her, stone-faced with judgement. She began choking then. Her hands went up and began clawing at her throat. She felt the cotton descending, clogging up, and cutting off her airway. She squeezed her eyes shut, feeling on the verge of dying. She felt the cotton become abrasive and scratch its way down her throat --

Alessia opened her eyes and saw a bright light shining down. I guess they're right about following the light, flashed through her mind before the light was blocked out by a silhouette. The figure was holding onto a tube and began forcing it down her throat. She tried to raise her hands but found them bound to a bed by restraints. She bunched her hands into fists as the tube was pushed further down. She gagged twice, tasting bitter bile on the back of her tongue. She watched the figure push the never-ending tube further into her mouth. She felt it breach her stomach and settle there. The figure grabbed the end of the tube and set a funnel into it. He held out his hand and a roll of duct tape was dropped into it. The figure unwound a generous portion of it and taped the funnel to the hose. The figure tossed the roll of tape aside and hollered out for charcoal. The language he spoke resembled tuba more than English, French, or Italian, yet Alessia understood everything. She watched as a large cement bucket materialized in the figure's hands. He balanced it on one finger like a spinning basketball while the other hand grasped the end of the funnel to hold it steady. He upended the bucket and dumped the contents into the funnel. Alessia watched as chunk after chunk of jet-black charcoal careened into the funnel and down the tube. She felt them rush down into her stomach and heard them clinking together as they landed on top of each other.

She felt her stomach expand as more charcoal was forced into it. She knew immediately that she was going to vomit. It began building up, leaking through the cracks in the charcoal, bubbling up her throat, pushing past the tube and filling the crevasses along the way. She opened her mouth wider to let it out --

A pill was placed on her tongue. She asked what it was but didn't really care. She just wanted something. The music was pumping, the crowd was jumping, the lights were a techno-color blur of ecstasy; and so was the pill. Her friends, Jeanie and Max, were already flying. They'd both dropped in the taxi on the way to the club and were constantly assuring Alessia that they had the good stuff, that it would knock her socks off. She tasted a bitterness on her tongue as the pill began to dissolve instantaneously. As always, it gave her a quick jolt, knowing that the countdown was on. She held it there for another few seconds, teasing herself, before swallowing it with a swig of water. She felt the pill run down to her stomach and settle. Her eyes widened. Her pupils dilated. The drug hit and the bass dropped. The crowd was energized, but Alessia was above and beyond. She felt every beat, thump, pound of the music thrusting through her. Her legs began shucking and tucking, her arms jiving and thriving. She reached out to the sky, feeling higher than any airplane that ever soared. She felt confidence and heat coursing through her body. The heat increased throughout, starting in her heart and radiating. She shed her satin camisole and continued dancing with her friends in only her bra and a pair of daisy dukes. The heat continued. She began sweating profusely and took a swig of water. It turned to steam on her tongue and evaporated away before she had a chance to swallow it. She felt her heart, already raging like a locomotive, pick up more speed, thumping double-time in her chest compared to the techno blasting out of the speakers. A feeling of extreme fear materialized within her. She took another sip of water with the same result. She thought about getting rid of more clothing and looked down at her body as it lay collapsed on the floor. She felt an immediate state of euphoria; all her problems washed away in an instant. Her friends quickly rushed to her side as she floated higher, watching as they frantically tried to get a reaction from her. They shook her and screamed. She wanted to tell them that it didn't matter, that life was fine and dandy, but death was even better; life was hard and painful, death was not. She couldn't tell them, however, so she just watched with a feeling of fascination. She floated higher, now level with the overhead beams that stretched across the ceiling of the venue before going through them. As she did so, everything went black --

Alessia opened her eyes to a street lamp shining its dull light in through her bedroom window. Her heart was a frantic machine within her body, her skin a tapestry of goosebumps. She lay still, letting her body and mind come fully out of the dream. She felt tears slip down her cheeks and wasn't surprised. It was a reoccurring dream that was too close to home, always leaving her feeling sick, shaken, and ashamed. She hated that she still held these feelings even though her overdose was more than ten years in her past. Never one for being an abuser of drugs, she'd just been unlucky with a bad pill that had changed her life drastically. She knew why her parents fussed over her, but it made her angry, even pissed at times. She'd gone to drug counseling, and continued to do so yet they continued to watch her every move. She'd taken the *opportunity* to go back to school, get a degree in physiotherapy, a good job, and still they watched her every move. They were happy for her career change, but mostly because they thought it would give her a chance to get engaged and marry a doctor. It irked her.

She lay in bed replaying the nightmare against what she could remember from reality, tossing and turning the whole time. Eventually, she gave up trying to get back to sleep and got up, dressing in a pair of pajama pants and a light shirt, and went to her desk to study for her eventual thesis defense. She knew all the material by heart, so reviewing it was always a surefire way to get her to fall asleep. Not this morning. She was slowly slogging her way through the paper when she heard the sound of her parent's alarm go off. Two sets of footsteps went plodding in two different directions. One disappeared into the master bathroom while the other went to the kitchen to start a pot of coffee.

Alessia stayed silent in her room. She didn't want to see her parents yet. She was afraid of what their expressions would be. She could imagine all too well their stone-faced judgement, especially her mother's; she never made an attempt to hide her displeasure, unlike her father. It's why she loved him more, which was something she'd never admit to another living soul. So, she continued staring at pages without soaking up the information, biding her time until her alarm went off. When it did, she went out to get some breakfast.

She'd been worried for nothing. Despite feeling the lingering effects of her dream, her parents were not the disappointed monoliths waiting to judge her as they'd been in her dream, and in reality those many years ago.

They made small talk about the news while her mother cooked her eggs with a side of bacon and hashbrowns, everything a body needs, her mother was fond of telling her. Still, she ate quickly and left the house early.

Once at work, Alessia secluded herself in an unused therapy office, logged into the system, and played the game of catch-up on her paperwork, leaving the door open. She mused, briefly, that the writer of *The Never-Ending Story* could have gotten a lot more play out of an office worker and their paperwork than a flying dog creature.

A million clicked boxes later, there was a soft rapping on the door. She gave a small start and turned around to see George McKinnon standing there, a mix of amusement and concern on his face.

"Sorry. I didn't mean to scare you," he said softly.

"It's no problem," she said. "I'm just a little jumpy this morning."

"Oh yeah? How come?"

She debated on telling a lie, but only briefly. She and McKinnon had a good relationship that went beyond just being mere co-workers. She felt that she could trust him, and because of that, she opted to tell him the truth.

"I had a nightmare last night that I just haven't been able to shake all morning."

"Oooh, do tell. Did all your teeth fall out? Were you haunted by the ghosts of paperwork past?" He pointed at the computer screen as he said the last.

She knew he was trying to cheer her up, and she loved him for it, but knew today it wouldn't work.

"Nothing like that." She sighed. It was long and heavy, like she was trying to shed herself of its mental weight. "It had to do with what happened to me before."

All at once, the amusement disappeared from McKinnon's face and concern dominated it.

"Shit, Allie. I'm sorry."

She saw him struggling, like he wanted to say more. He didn't, and she was grateful for it.

"Don't worry about it. It was a long time ago. The dream was just very vivid and it always sours my mood for the day."

"So it's a recurring thing?"

"Yes and no. I do dream of it, but not often and it's never the same dream. But the context and emotions attached to it are."

"Did you ever think about going to a counselor? Maybe you're suffering from a mild form of PTSD."

"I am not suffering from PTSD. It was a one-time occurence where the drug I took was spiked with something harsh, and it caused me to O.D.," she said matter-of-factly.

Mckinnon worked his jaw, chewing his invisible gum, already knowing about Alessia's past. She tried to think of a way to change the subject and couldn't, her mind blank. All she wanted to do was forget about her dream, but her conversation with McKinnon was dragging her further down into its grasp.

"Well... do you want to talk about it?"

"Not really," she said honestly. "I'm over it. Like I said, it was years ago. If you don't mind though," she said, gesturing toward the computer, "I'd like to just forget it and go back to finishing this."

"Sure," Mckinnon said, pulling back and slinking away. He tossed a look back over his shoulder that Alessia missed. He was worried about her. He knew she'd been working extra hard the last month or so because of their cuts. It was starting to show around her edges. Underneath her eyes were dark and more puffy. Her usual sunny demeanour was sliding into the land of peevish. He didn't like it, but didn't know what else to do. He knew she took the health of her patients to heart and cared for their well-being almost a little too much. She was being run ragged, and despite being her boss, he couldn't do anything to help her. And now, she seemed to be losing sleep over old things. He vowed to himself that he'd watch her a little more carefully in the coming months; he wanted to curb any potential breakdowns that may be lurking in her near future.

Alessia stared blankly at her computer, faking work, while trying to avoid what her brain wanted to replay over and over again with zero success.

It wasn't until early afternoon that something made her forget all her problems.

She'd finished up with her second to last patient, a Mrs. Christie, and stepped out into the hallway when she saw her. The woman in question was tall with flowing chestnut hair that was almost a carbon copy of Alessia's. She was dressed in scrubs that didn't do much to accentuate her chest, but her thighs rubbed together. As she passed by, Alessia took a peek at the back end and was not disappointed in the way the scrubs hugged her butt. The woman passing her seemed out of a dream, and not one of the clean variety, either. She watched the new nurse stop outside the room where she'd just finished up with Mrs. Christie, an eighty-two-year-old smoker that'd gotten a by-pass and didn't seem to be responding well to any physiotherapy; the fact that she wasn't trying, and seemed content to stay in hospital, wasn't lost on Alessia.

She found it weird that a nurse would be going into the room at such a time. There was nothing on Mrs. Christie's schedule until an hour or so later, so she caught up with the nurse.

"Excuse me," she said. When the nurse didn't turn, Alessia reached out and tapped her on the shoulder. The nurse turned and a look of disgust flashed across her face before vanishing and being replaced by a look of forced calm.

"Are you going in to see Mrs. Christie?" Alessia asked.

The nurse stared blankly at her for a second or two, reminding Alessia of a robot, before nodding once.

"Yes. I'm going in to see Mrs. Christie," she said, her voice monotonous and mono-chrome.

"What's this about? She's not due for any tests."

Again, there was a look of dissociation and blankness, like the nurse was taking in her words and processing them.

"She is now," the nurse said simply before walking into the room.

Alessia followed, a perplexed look on her face. She watched the nurse lean down and speak to Mrs. Christie.

"Hello - Mrs. Christie. I've been told by - Dr. Veksler that you need a new - PICC line and IV," the new nurse said haltingly.

Mrs. Christie's eyes looked up and saw the nurse; seeing, but not seeing her. Her eyes glazed over with a look that Alessia didn't like. Mrs. Christie opened her mouth and a mewling sound came out. She lifted her arm. The nurse grasped it and pulled it up.

Alessia reached out and tapped on the nurse's shoulder again. The nurse whirled on her, a flash of anger and annoyance prevalent on her face before being wiped away, replaced by that blank look again.

"What?"

"I'm sorry, it's just that Mrs. Christie isn't scheduled for anything of the sort," she said quickly. "I don't have anything of that nature in my notes."

"That's none of my concern," the nurse said. "If you want - clarification - go speak with - Dr. Veksler. He's in charge. - He told me what to do."

Alessia opened her mouth to say more but was suddenly taken in by the new nurse's eyes. They were a lovely swirling pool of deep blue. They were beautiful. They were stunning. They were vaguely familiar. Alessia felt herself being sucked into them, and a brief struggle occurred within her; her will against an intruding force. Alessia lost.

She found herself nodding, wanting to do anything to appease the strange invading force within her brain. She opened her mouth and heard words she never felt spoken come out.

"Yeah. Okay. Sure. I'll ask Dr. Veksler." Alessia said the words, but her brain told her she had no intention of doing such a thing. Her only intentions were to leave the room. The nurse nodded once, sharply, and then turned back to the old lady stretched out on the bed, still holding the outstretched arm in her hands. Before turning around to leave, Alessia saw the nurse softly petting the skin along the inner forearm.

Alessia shuffled towards the door, each slow step softly shaking the intruding spirit in her mind. When she reached the doorway, she felt an involuntary jerk and turned back. She saw the nurse gently cradling the forearm of Mrs. Christie. Snaking out of the nurse's forearm was a slick, black and red thin tentacle that wound its way down the arm of the other woman, wrapping it tight. Pricked into the less than meaty portion of Mrs. Christie's forearm was the other end of the tentacle. Alessia watched as lumps of liquid pulsed up through the tentacle and entered the new nurse's body. She felt her paralysis begin to break. She shook her head, trying to shatter it.

The nurse turned on her with another quick snap of the head. Alessia recoiled. She meant to cry out in terror but stopped cold when those piercing eyes once again took her in. All the rage and disgust was extinguished within her. She felt a veil of calm descend over her. She watched, transfixed, as the nurse opened her mouth and spoke.

"This is none of your concern," she said, her voice still monotonous and monochrome.

"Okay," Alessia said dreamily. "It's none of my concern."

"Good. Leave me to my work."

"Okay."

The nurse turned away and went back to feeding on the patient. Alessia entered the hallway and took a few jagged, quick steps before she regained her original gait. By the time she'd gotten to the nursing station, she'd forgotten most of what had happened in the room. The only thing from the encounter that stayed with Alessia was the feeling of a forgotten word on the tip of her tongue.

It stayed with her for the rest of the day.

Stanley

1

Stanley was masturbating furiously when the screen went dark. He grunted a curse and reached down on the chair and picked up another five dollar bill. He was close now and wouldn't need more money than that. Once the bill was deposited into the slot, the screen became transparent again. He was greeted to the woman, down on all fours, back-end toward him, stuffing a dildo into her vagina and another into her anus. He watched her hips begin to buck as she dropped her head to the ground, turning it to the right. He caught a glimpse of her face and almost lost his erection when she appeared to lock eyes with him. She had a look of resigned fate, of unabashed sadness, and for one moment Stanley was sure that she could see what lay in his soul, attempting to connect with him; to tell him that she understood and that all *wouldn't* be alright. He would have lost it if she didn't then twist her head so her mouth was buried in the carpet, trying to stifle her scream as an orgasm shook her. Stanley resumed his rhythm and finished after a quick ten tugs, spraying his spunk upon the screen.

He hoisted up his pants and made a per-functory effort to clean up after himself, using the box of wipes he kept in his backpack. That done, he slunk out of the booth, out the back-door, and onto the late afternoon streets, feeling both ashamed and sated.

It was a release he'd needed after hear-ing the news and rumours floating around the hospital. Some said there was a contagious dis-ease going around that led to a gruesome, painful death; others speculated that some or-ganization had paid a healthy bribe to experiment on patients without their consent, ala the LSD trials in the sixties. The more pious individuals believed that there was a demon roaming the halls and that it would continue killing indiscriminately until they found a way to exorcise it.

Stanley thought the third group had it closest to the mark.

Hearing all the rumours, and *knowing* the truth of the matter, made him feel powerful. He had knowledge over those that had looked down upon him for so long. It was a knowledge that he would never lord over anyone, but it made him feel good all the same. And so, when the build-up got to be too much, like it had this day, he found his release in another form of a power trip. His release, however, always left him drained and feeling closer to the edge than not. He always felt disgusted with himself after expelling his load across the window separating him from the object of his desire. He knew someone would have to clean it up and didn't envy them; after all, he'd had to clean up his fair share of unsightly messes in his career as a janitor. But that wasn't what was troubling him this time. No. It was the booth girl's face that made him feel uneasy and on edge. He didn't like seeing their faces. Every time he did, he felt like they could see him behind the mirror and immediately know his secrets. It was the same way with his other business. He never had to see faces, to have first-hand knowledge of the victims; it was all hearsay. When he did get up close and personal with The Doctor's creation, it was always because he'd brought another load of spare parts. It was easier that way.

He made his way back to his bachelor apartment to grab some sleep. He had to return to the hospital later that evening to take care of some business for The Doctor. He wasn't sure if it was going to be a late night or not, so he didn't want to take any chances, but had a feeling it would be the latter. He was batting clean-up tonight.

Nine o'clock found Stanley using his key, unlocking the door to the catacombs that led to his *special* workspace. Before locking the door behind him, he reached out and flipped the switch on the table lamp. His eyes adjusted to the dimness before he continued down the corridor. He didn't need the light, he knew his route by heart now, but he felt that it couldn't hurt to always be prepared.

He was halfway to his destination when he noticed something disconcerting, almost missing it in the dim glow cast by the emergency lights. Hunkering down on his heels to inspect the stain, Stanley saw that it was black blood; the splash pattern and lack of trail made him think that it had been vomited out. He ran a finger over it and bits flaked off, sticking to him. He pulled his finger up to his mouth and ran his tongue across it, tasting only a hint of copper. The majority tasted like stale death. There was another flavour hidden behind that that his palate couldn't determine. He ignored it for the time being and concentrated on what to do next. He knew The Doctor would need an update, but felt it was too early to do so. If there was something wrong with His creation, then informing The Doctor now, without having all the facts, would change little. He decided to push on to the room to check on Her. If She was sick, or dead, an extra few minutes wouldn't change that.

Keeping his eyes open, Stanley made his way down to the room. He saw no more dried pools of blood, but did notice grooves in the moss that covered the walls, like She'd been using them as a way of keeping herself upright. He frowned and continued on. He neared the door and from a distance could make out another puddle of dried, black blood. His frown deepened as he walked over to it and used the toe of his boot to scuff it away. As the flakes wafted up, he caught a stronger scent of death; moreover, it didn't dissipate once he scuffed away the dried blood.

He opened the outer door and waited, listening for any movement as the groan of the hinges faded away. There was nothing. Stanley had a sinking feeling as to what that meant and was not surprised to see Her laid across the marble slab when he parted the plastic divider and stepped into the back room. She turned Her head when She heard him, a pained expression plastered on Her face. Stanley could see the effort it took and shuddered. Immediately, he pulled out his phone to dial The Doctor but got no signal. He cursed under his breath and made a move to the exit, thinking about where the closest place he could get reception was when he heard a moan come from Her. He snapped his head back and saw Her stretching an arm out in his direction. She opened Her mouth again and a mushy sound came out, semi-forming the noise for "help."

"I'm going to. Well, not me," he stammered. "I'm going to get someone to help you."

She opened Her mouth and issued out another mushy sound that could have resembled "No. Stay."

He opened his mouth to tell Her no, that staying would be more detrimental for Her than leaving, but felt the words dry up in his throat. He saw the pain behind Her eyes, even from far across the room. He felt drawn toward Her and took two quick steps in Her direction. She stretched Her hand out further, straining to reach him, Her fingers extended, resembling something more alien than human. He shifted his gaze from Her hand to Her eyes. They were swirls of pain and anxiety and he felt their call. He felt their need. He advanced a few more steps, then stopped cold. Out of the corner of his eye he caught movement from Her outstretched arm. He thought it was Her fingers wriggling, the spell She held him under momentarily breaking long enough that he saw that it wasn't Her fingers. The skin on Her arm had parted and a tiny tentacle was protruding. It wagged in his direction, beckoning him over. He stumbled back and saw Her tentacle reach out even farther. It coiled a few feet beyond Her outstretched hand and made a quick grab for him but he was already out of reach. His butt connected with the plastic and he uttered a tiny yelp, surprising himself.

"I -- I -- I'm gonna go get you some help," he stammered again while continuing to back up. He reached the door, eyes still locked on her, and frantically searched for the knob with a blind hand. After a few seconds, he found it. He tried to twist it but it slipped in his sweaty palm. He was successful on his second attempt.

He bolted out into the hallway and pulled the door shut hard enough to make it rattle in its frame. He reached into his pocket and produced the key. He thought about how close to disaster he'd come and a massive shiver enveloped his body. He dropped the key and it bounced off the floor and disappeared underneath the door. His heart, already at a breakneck pace, sped up like a jackhammer, threatening to drive through his chest. He dropped to his knees in a panic and tried to jam his fingers underneath the door. They connected with the wood and the fingernail of his middle finger peeled back and broke off. He barely felt the throbbing pain that exploded up his nerves because he'd heard a slipping shift from far away on the other side of the door, which was followed by a wet, meaty thump. He envisioned Her hitting the ground and beginning Her slow, laborious crawl toward the door. He felt pain flare up and pushed it away, concentrating on stuffing his fingers underneath the door to retrieve the key. The sounds behind the door advanced and icy panic flooded his veins. The pace of his search became frantic, the fingers on his right hand probing for a key but finding only air. He heard the thump of a hand hitting the concrete, much closer than he'd thought possible. His panic doubled, and so did his efforts. His fingers struck something cold and he yelped. When the object didn't latch on, he closed his fingers around the key. Then, he felt something thin tickle the back of his hand, immediately knowing what it was. He yanked his hand back, raking the top of it along the bottom of the door, but keeping the key in his grasp.

Once the key was in sight, he closed his hand around it and stood, his knees pistoning upward, popping like firecrackers. He slammed the key home and twisted it over as he heard a pawing at the door. The door was firmly locked, but he watched in horror, breath catching in his throat, as the knob twisted with what little give it had. He said a little prayer of thanks to The Doctor for making it a key only door, and not one of those cheap ones that could be popped open from the inside.

Stanley listened to his heart hammering away in his chest and took big breaths, trying to calm himself down. He took two steps away from the door and felt better. When he had himself under some guise of control, and he was positive that the door couldn't, and wouldn't, be opened from the inside, he retraced his steps back through the corridor until he had a signal.

He called The Doctor.

The Doctor

1

He hung up the phone, placed his elbows on his desk, and leaned into his hands. His thoughts were treading water, threatening to drown him. Things had gone smoothly with his daughter until now and this was a significant setback. It was the only *major* setback but extremely frustrating. He felt all the work he'd done in the last twenty years on the verge of slipping away. And so, he buried his face in his hands and thought about all the possible causes, and solutions, to his current problem. He knew he was going to have to go down into the catacombs and see her, to figure out what was ailing her, but also knew he had time. There was no point showing up half-cocked and making a mistake in a heated, emotional state.

The Doctor sat in that position, like a statue, for the better part of fifteen minutes. He ran through every possible scenario in his head and kept coming back to the same answer. It was enough. With a large sigh, he lifted his head and stared at the overhead lights which reflected briefly on the trail of old tears from ten minutes ago.

He stepped out of his office and made his way down to the sitting parlor. It was a sunken den of sorts that was filled with two light grey, high back chairs. They were situated beside the two openings that led into the den; one from the kitchen, the other from the entranceway. Pushed back against the wall was a couch that matched the chairs in style and colour. All three pieces of furniture were standing on a plush white, wall-to-wall carpet. There was a dark, mahogany coffee table in the middle of the room and a large cabinet pushed up against one wall. It was filled with high class, high tension booze; most of which was scotch and brandy.

The Doctor's wife was splayed on the couch, a picture album laid across her legs, and he knew what pictures populated *that* particular album. He also knew what was causing the glazed over look in his wife's eyes; he'd prescribed the drugs after all.

He walked over to her and planted a kiss on her forehead. She looked up with doe eyes, glassy and large. She mumbled something mushy.

"I know, love. This day is hard on me too."

His wife's mouth quivered, and he saw fresh tears threatening in her eyes. He wiped his hand over his face, took a large breath, and gave her his bad news.

"I have to go to work, my love."

He saw the pleading look plastered on her face and felt his heart sink. He took her hand in his and tried to give her some of his warmth, knowing he was picking the worst time to leave her, but it couldn't be helped; knowing that what he was doing was more important than both their griefs combined. He wanted to tell her, but couldn't. She was in no state to understand what he'd be telling her. He wondered briefly why he hadn't told her before, especially now that his daughter was functioning, albeit, not without some kinks. And currently, he was looking at one nasty kink.

"I know, I know," he said with calm compassion. "It's something that cannot be put off, however. I'll be home as soon as I can."

She nodded and sniffed back a tear or two. He brushed back the few fallen strands of hair that had attached themselves to her forehead and then kissed it again. She turned her face up and he kissed her heartily on the lips.

He took his leave then and made his way to the hospital to see his sick and dying daughter.

The Doctor met Stanley, who was smoking a cigarette, halfway down the corridor. After hearing Stanley's voice on the phone, he'd been worried. More worrisome had been the details Stanley regaled to him. Any remaining hope The Doctor had was quickly dashed when he saw the cheesy complexion of Stanley's face.

He resisted the urge to immediately run into the room and check on her. Instead, he walked by Stanley and beckoned him along. Stanley didn't move. The Doctor felt his nerves trying to break out and scream. Instead, he stopped and turned around, looking directly at Stanley.

"Are you coming?"

Stanley took a massive, final drag of his cigarette and crushed it underneath his boot. He took another deep breath and looked back at The Doctor.

"No."

"What do you mean 'no'?"

"What I said. No."

"Why not?"

The Doctor watched as Stanley swallowed a large lump in his throat and knew what he was going to say.

"She tried to kill me." Stanley paused, opened his mouth, shut it, and took a long breath. "She tried to eat me."

Stanley looked down at his feet, and The Doctor felt ashamed. He didn't want her to kill those that helped him, but he was willing to sacrifice anyone, and anything, to complete his mission. He took a few tentative steps towards Stanley.

"I understand. Walk with me to the outer door and tell me everything. Leave no detail out." As he spoke, he looked toward Stanley and held his eyes there, waiting for Stanley to look up and meet his gaze. Stanley did. The Doctor saw the reluctance splayed across his face, mixed with a hint of adoration. The look said that Stanley was ready to do what *he* needed; a little push was all that was required.

The Doctor opened his mouth and lied.

"Remember when you told me, 'My life for you?' Well, it's my turn to speak those words."

"No," Stanley said. He shifted his eyes down to his shoes again and leaned against the wall. The Doctor shook his head, eyes wide, being taken utterly by surprise. How dare Stanley say no, after all he'd *done* for him. He fought to keep the anger from his voice and succeeded.

"What do you mean 'no?'" he said for the second time.

Stanley fumbled in his pocket for his cigarettes. He withdrew his pack with a shaky hand and stuffed one into his mouth. It took him two tries to light it. He took a tentative drag and chuffed out smoke in a massive gout.

"I mean, don't say those words." Stanley took another drag. "Those are *my* words. They're words *I* said to *you*. You don't owe me anything."

The Doctor was touched, his anger evaporating. He knew how Stanley felt, but to hear it in such blunt, bold terms tugged his heartstrings. He felt bad for lying. Almost.

"Okay. But now you know how I feel. Will you come?"

Stanley prematurely finished his cigarette and pushed himself off the wall.

"I'll tell you, but it ain't pretty."

They walked down to the outer door, Stanley behind The Doctor on his left, talking the whole way. They stalled outside of the door while Stanley finished off his tale, now telling the full story. He looked down with quick eyes and The Doctor's followed them, taking note of the dried blood on the underside of the door.

The Doctor listened while straining his ears to hear if *she* was still active on the other side. He heard nothing. He reached into his pocket and produced his key, the dull light winking off it. He inserted the key and turned it with deliberate, slow speed. The tumbler caught, turned, and released. He pushed the door open a crack and took half a step back, the door groaning with the movement. The Doctor felt Stanley tense while involuntarily reacting the same. Nothing came out. Two breaths exhaled as one as The Doctor stepped forward and laid his hand against the door. He pushed it open, and still, nothing came out. Nothing stirred. He felt Stanley's gaze upon his back and walked into the room, undeterred from the tingling fear prickling the back of his neck. He saw a little splash of blood upon the plastic curtains and furrowed his brow.

He heard shuffling behind him, knowing full well what was happening. He walked over to the plastic and waited until he heard the door shut behind him and the flick of the switch, shutting off the emergency lights in the catacombs corridors; all standard procedure.

"Double-lock it, please," he said. "We can't take any chances."

He heard the bolt being pushed into place as he waited, his heart hammering in his chest. He took a series of large breaths to steady himself for what he'd find beyond the threshold. He assumed that she would be dead, or close to her death rattle. He was worried that if she was dead, or did die, then his reanimation technique would not work again on twice dead flesh.

When he felt he had himself under sufficient control, he parted the plastic and walked in, beckoning Stanley to follow.

She looked over as the pair of men stepped through. She was sprawled atop the marble slab on her back in a slipshod fashion, one leg dangling over the edge and her arms a tangle. The Doctor saw the same sick, pleading look in her eyes that he'd seen in his wife's earlier that evening. He approached her cautiously, betting on her not attacking him, but not wanting to take any chances. He stopped when he was a foot or so outside of her reach. She stretched out one arm, curling her fingers inward in a come-hither gesture. He stood, frozen, as the skin parted on her forearm and a limp tentacle came out, seemingly tasting the air, before slithering back in. After viewing these weak movements, The Doctor knew he was safe.

He stepped forward, and her hand immediately tried to grab at his thigh. He brushed it away and made cooing noises. It worked, as she pulled her arm back to herself. He leaned over her, pulling out his penlight as he did so.

"I need you to lie back and be still. I'm going to shine a light in your eyes."

She obeyed him as he checked her pupils. He found nothing out of the ordinary. He wasn't surprised. He wiped a hand across his face, closing his eyes as he did so. He was worried that he'd have to perform exploratory surgery, and soon, but he wanted a moment to stop and think about what the problem could possibly be. He'd noted the bloody vomit on his way in, and he'd noted the way she moved; not with her typical smooth grace, but with halting, jerky movements. A thought came to him then; it was a long shot, but he was in too deep and had to play out the string given to him.

With his head still down, clutching the bridge of his nose, The Doctor spoke.

"Have you been vaccinated?"

Stanley

He heard the question and paused while taking half a step forward. The Doctor had been quiet for some time, and since he was shielding Stanley's view of Her, he'd been worried that maybe She'd entranced him, or worse, had latched on to The Doctor and was currently sucking out His essence. He didn't think She'd do that to Her creator, but he had his reservations about *that*.

He thought for a moment about what he'd been vaccinated for, but more importantly, why The Doctor would pose such a question to him now. He'd been around Her since Her inception, so if he was at risk, it would have already struck. He must have taken too long in his thought process because before he could answer, he heard the tone of irritation bleed into The Doctor's question.

"Have you been vaccinated for tetanus and malaria?"

Stanley had both; being a member of the hospital staff *did* have its perks. Still, he was hesitant. While he knew he owed his life to The Doctor, he was afraid that the time had come where The Doctor was going to call it in. Another part of his mind, the more rational part, spoke up then. It asked him why The Doctor would want to kill him. He'd been an integral part of the process, and The Doctor would be hard pressed to find someone else as trustworthy as he was. His irrational mind spoke up again, screaming on top of the other part. It told him, with conviction, that The Doctor wanted to shut him up. To ensure that his tale would never be told. But, Stanley just couldn't bring himself to believe that, no matter how hard that piece of his mind wanted to convince him. And so, his conclusion was the most practical; The Doctor needed his help to get Her correct, and Stanley still owed him service and his life.

Stanley walked over to where The Doctor stood, telling him that, Yes, he'd been vaccinated for both malaria and tetanus.

"That's excellent news," The Doctor purred. He turned around, and Stanley saw something in his face that made him falter, his knees turning inexplicably weak. There was a look of profound sadness etched onto a backdrop of determination. The Doctor held out his hand, and Stanley saw a minute shake pulse through it. It almost broke his heart.

He went forward.

"I need you to strap her in," The Doctor said. As Stanley made to do that, The Doctor left the room. By the time Stanley finished, The Doctor had returned. He carried with him a tray. On it lay a scalpel, two Petri dishes, alcohol, some swabs and quite a few strips of gauze. He placed it on the table next to Stanley.

"Where?" Stanley asked, knowing what was wanted of him.

"High up on the left thigh, as close to her pelvis as you can get, and then another on her calf."

Stanley nodded and began removing Her pants. He pulled them down to Her ankles before realizing She was shackled in. He figured pants down was just as efficient as pants off, so he began prepping the place where he would cut. The Doctor stood over Her head, gently stroking Her hair and murmuring calming words.

Stanley slipped on a pair of medical gloves and swabbed Her thigh. He looked up at The Doctor, who gave him a nod. He picked up the scalpel and hovered it an inch above the prepared area. He looked up again and saw The Doctor give him another curt, irritated nod.

Stanley leaned down and conducted his business. She thrashed and tried to pull away from him as the scalpel slipped through Her skin. He watched black blood bubble to the surface, seeping out around the edges of the cut. He pulled the scalpel out so as not to cut too much away.

"Don't prolong it, Stanley. Do it!" The Doctor said as He continued to stroke Her hair.

Stanley went back to his job and slowly cut away a swath of skin as the muscles jumped and jostled under the blade. When he had the small rectangle piece severed, he placed it on the petri dish on the rolling table next to him. He turned back to the wound and set the strips of gauze onto it. The first one turned black almost instantly, so Stanley placed the others on top of it. He put pressure on the wound and held it there for nearly a minute. When he took his hands away, only a few splotches of blood showed on the uppermost one. The Doctor kept stroking Her hair as Stanley stripped off the used gauze and dropped them into the Biomed box beside him. He grabbed more strips of gauze and placed them on the wound, winding tape around Her leg to keep them in place. That done, he went down to Her calf and repeated the process, checking once with The Doctor to ensure he was cutting in the right spot. Once the bandages were in place and taped on, he pulled up Her pants gently, thinking that it helped Her regain some dignity.

The Doctor bent down and kissed Her on the forehead, then placed his hand over the spot.

"You did good, sweetie. Your part is over. We're going to make you better again."

The Doctor left Her and walked over to the locked back room, picking up the Petri dishes on his way by. He pulled a key out of his pocket and unlocked the room. He turned back toward Stanley.

"Can you wait around for me please, Stanley?"

"Yes, of course," Stanley said, thinking, *Anything. My life for you.*

The Doctor

He left Stanley alone in the room with his daughter while he went into the back room. He deposited the Petri dishes on the metal desk along the back wall. He preferred the luxurious mahogany desk he had at home, any desk made of wood really, but knew that it would rot away given the conditions of his secret workspace. It was also metal for cleaning purposes, easily erasing any traces of himself should someone happen upon this spot and break in. On the table was a microscope with a smattering of slides positioned beside it, along with two containers of bleach wipes. There was a stack of plain white paper held down by a weight. The top twenty pages were blank. Underneath those were his ongoing notes about his current work. He never left a page there for too long, always taking them home so any potential snoops couldn't track his progress. It made him nervous, however, leaving portions of his life's work here, but sometimes it couldn't be helped.

He opened a drawer and brought out a pair of tweezers and a bottle of alcohol. He dipped the tweezers into the alcohol and plucked the first specimen off the Petri dish, it was the strip from her thigh, and laid it on the slide. He placed the slide underneath the microscope and bent over to have a look. Everything was normal, at least for his daughter. He saw the cells moving around at a rapid rate. They were knitting themselves along the ends of the ragged strip, trying to repair the damage done.

The Doctor pushed the slide away and repeated the process with the second piece of flesh. He was gravely concerned with what he saw. Once again, he saw the cells working hard to knit themselves back together, which would have been fine if they were regular cells. They were not. They were cancer cells.

The tibia he'd gotten from a terminal patient. When he'd taken a smattering of cells from it and applied his special enzymes, they'd killed off all the cancerous cells, so he thought he'd be safe putting the bone into his daughter. Now, he saw that it wasn't the case. *It must have to do with the sheer volume of cancerous cells within the bone itself,* he thought. It was disheartening. It was worrying. It was aggravating.

He pushed himself away from the microscope and leaned back in the chair, disgusted. He closed his eyes and tried to think of a solution. He quickly nixed the idea of chemotherapy and radiation. She was a medical miracle, and he didn't want to risk altering her DNA or anything else he'd done to make her function. It was too much risk for something he wasn't even sure would fix the problem. He thought about what his next logical course could be. He wondered if he could maybe make a serum that would boost her already fast immunity and healing, but he quit that idea too. Her cancer was running rampant through her leg, bolstered by her healing ability. What had worked so well in allowing her to be born was now working against her at an alarming rate.

His next thought was giving her a transplant, which seemed the most viable. He was worried about the timeline on that, however. She was fading fast, and it would take a while for him to find a match. He chuckled to himself, knowing that any leg would be feasible due to what was inside of her, but the point still stood. It would take time to get a leg even if he tasked both Simon and Stanley on it. It was *the* long-term solution, but he needed something to mend her in the short-term.

The Doctor opened his eyes, an idea bursting behind them. He had his short-term solution standing in the next room. He'd saved Stanley with something similar, pumping a concoction into his veins that had allowed him to continue living a productive life. What was it Stanley always said? "My life for you." The Doctor knew it was time to call in that favour.

The Doctor didn't move, however, wanting to be sure this was the only solution.

He didn't want to waste the valuable commodity that was Stanley, who'd helped him tremendously, but knew there was only one way that Stanley could help him now, and in the most critical way possible. In his mind, that settled it.

The Doctor pushed himself to his feet and walked to the door. He unlocked it, opened it, and saw Stanley standing as far across the room from his daughter as he could, smoking a cigarette. The Doctor had to suppress a haunting chuckle. It was like Stanley had clued into The Doctor's plan before he had.

"It's okay, Stanley, she won't bite." This time he did chuckle. He couldn't help it. The situation was just so damn absurd.

Stanley breathed out a large chuff of smoke but couldn't look at The Doctor, preferring instead to inspect his shoes. The Doctor walked over to him and placed a hand on his shoulder, causing Stanley to look up. The Doctor saw the pleading in Stanley's eyes and felt a twinge upon his heart. He grasped Stanley and pulled him in, embracing him in a large hug. He felt reluctance in Stanley's body at first. It slowly slid away as The Doctor felt arms come up and embrace him. It was gentle at first, but as The Doctor held on longer, Stanley's grasp tightened like a death clutch, which is precisely what it was.

They separated but didn't break contact. The Doctor held Stanley at arm's length, hands on his shoulders. He did this so he could look him intensely in the eyes, trying to betray what he really wanted from Stanley. He thought it worked because when Stanley spoke, The Doctor heard the words he wanted to hear.

"What do you need from me?"

"Well, it's pretty simple, actually. I need you to help me prep the patient for an amputation." As he said the words, The Doctor heard movement behind him. He turned his head and saw that his daughter had turned her head to look at them. He dismissed it for the time being and turned his attention back to Stanley, sending out psionic thoughts for her not to worry, that he was going to get her fed.

"Is it her leg?"

"Yes."

"What should I do?"

"Cut her pants off and sterilize her lower leg. Mark it off an inch above the knee."

The Doctor walked over to the large, metal cabinet off in the corner and opened it, pulling out some bottles of isotropic alcohol and a bottle of iodine. He rummaged around further and pulled out a few tattered rags. "Don't worry about being too exact," The Doctor said over his shoulder. "We just have to cut somewhere above the knee to counteract the cancer crawling through her body."

"Okay," Stanley said, walking over to her, picking up a pair of scissors, and snipping off her scrubs; she was subdued, not trying to attack nor squirm, The Doctor noticed. He felt that maybe, *just maybe*, his thoughts had gotten through to her.

The Doctor went back to his office to arrange all the needed tools on a cart he neglected to sterilize. He wheeled it out of his office to where Stanley stood, marking off a dotted line halfway up her thigh.

"Can you please tighten her wrist restraints, Stanley?" he asked, parking the cart by her feet.

When Stanley knelt and undid the restraint holding her left wrist, The Doctor made his move. Despite his advanced age, he slid deftly and looped his arms underneath Stanley's armpits. He interlocked his hands behind Stanley's head, holding him in a full nelson. Stanley began struggling instantly, trying to buck his head back and give The Doctor a bloody, or broken, nose while simultaneously trying to piston himself from a squat into a standing position. The Doctor was ready for both moves and forced Stanley's head forward while bearing down on him with all his weight.

For added measure, he ground his knee into the small of Stanley's back to aid in his control.

Stanley opened his mouth to say something, or to cry out, The Doctor didn't know. When he felt the workings of Stanley's throat and jaw, he pushed down on the back of the head, forcing it forward and closing off the airway. Stanley's struggles subsided, and The Doctor loosened his grip slightly before speaking.

"Now," he said, making eye contact with his daughter.

She reacted immediately. Her left arm, now free, stretched out and began reaching for Stanley, who attempted to thrash his head back and forth again. The Doctor tightened his hold and pushed Stanley's upper torso forward in a straining lean. His daughter's fingers reached out and found Stanley's face. Her thumb slipped between his lips and pushed against his left cheek. Her middle finger wormed its way into the right corner of his mouth. Stanley tried, and failed, to clamp his lips down tight. She wiggled her middle finger in far enough to open up space for her index finger. Once she forced the index finger in, her two remaining fingers had free roam. The Doctor watched the cheeks of Stanley puff out in undulation as she forced her way further into his mouth. With all her fingers inserted, Stanley's mouth was pried open. From his vantage point, The Doctor saw the tendons inflating and popping along the top of her hand. He heard a garbled sound coming from Stanley, like he was screaming through a mouth full of mashed potatoes.

A smell of burning flesh and bile permeated the room. Stanley began to shake violently, causing The Doctor to increase the pressure he bore down with. A mix of thick reddish-brown liquid poured from Stanley's mouth. It ran down his daughter's arm to the elbow until it dripped onto the floor. Stanley's feet began to beat a staccato against the hard concrete while she drove her hand further into his mouth, melting more of him.

The Doctor saw the back of her hand pulsing as she took the life essence within Stanley unto herself. He noted the change in her disposition as it happened; she went from being ashy and dead on the bed to regaining colour and propping herself up on her left elbow. She stared at Stanley with a sickening, grateful look.

It wasn't long before she tried to get into a sitting position. The Doctor witnessed the attempt to move before she realized she was tethered to the marble bed. She looked up at The Doctor and he released his hold on Stanley. He walked over to her legs to free them and was amazed at the strength she had. She held Stanley with one hand while he danced his dance of death. He freed her legs and she swung them over the edge of the slab, putting her feet on the ground. The Doctor released her right wrist and she reached over, cupping Stanley's chin and placing him gently on the floor; one hand in his mouth the whole time while the veins resembled an ocean in turmoil. The Doctor was touched by her compassion.

His daughter knelt over the body and worked her hand further into Stanley's throat, his face sagging more as each second passed. The Doctor watched as the gorge of Stanley began rippling in peristalsis as her tentacle worked its way down to his stomach. He saw Stanley's midsection bulge out underneath his shirt. He could only imagine as to what was happening inside while Stanley's face continued to grow slack and melt away like candle wax. The Doctor wrinkled his nose at the fetid air that continued to infect the room. It became viscous, yet he refused to leave for some fresher air. This was the first time that he got to see his daughter work in real time, and he wasn't about to waste the opportunity. His mind was buzzing with notes and tallies that he kept silently repeating. He was looking intently for a way to save her from the cancer that he was sure had metastasized.

He watched his daughter work for ten more minutes until Stanley had wasted away into practically nothing; his body now a gaunt skeleton in a puddle of clothing.

When he was sure that his daughter was finished feeding, he went to his back room. He stayed there, scribbling away on his papers, jotting down everything he could remember. He added his thoughts on top of his observations and then spent time trying to work out the problem as to how to save her.

By the time he finished it was only a few hours until dawn. He stepped out of his office and saw his daughter fast asleep on the slab. The emaciated body of Stanley lay where she'd left it. He went over and picked the body up, marveling at its lightness. While Stanley hadn't been fat, he'd been stout, and now The Doctor guessed his weight at less than seventy pounds. He took the body over to the stretcher he kept stashed away in one corner. He laid Stanley down carefully and covered him with a sheet. He would deal with the corpse later; it was dried out, and he doubted it would decompose much before he'd had the time to take care of it.

He went to the plastic barrier and pushed it aside, sparing a final concerned glance at his daughter. He watched her take a few long, slow breaths and sent his heart out to her. Then, he went out to the corridor, locked the door, and made his way back to the main pavilions, his flashlight beam and thoughts his only company.

Simon

1

"You guys don't have *any* idea." Simon burped. "Legit. It happened."

"I'm callin' bullshit," Mario yelled. His voice carried briefly above the noise and clash of the club. Mario had one arm wrapped around a girl who was wiggling, her hips smoothly shifting along Mario's palm.

"No bullshit!" Simon answered, taking a sip of his bottle of Red Stripe, the crowd around him drinking as well. "If you'd shut the fuck up, maybe I could finish my story," he said.

Mario turned his head toward the woman on his arm. He raised an eyebrow and she responded in kind.

"Alright. Lay it on us," he said, flashing a smile at Simon, while his hand slid down, *smooooooth*, to grasp the girl's butt. Mario gave a little squeeze and she uttered a tiny laugh.

"I can't," he said.

"Bullshit, you can't. Whadda you say?' Mario cried, turning toward the woman once again.

"Yeah!" she interjected. "Spill your guts, Sean!"

"Simon."

"Whatever! Spill it. You were juss talking about it."

He opened his mouth, ready to give it all away when he burped again which turned into a hiccup halfway through. Mario and the girl laughed fit to split as he convulsed. The girl pounded her hand on the sticky table, glasses of drinks long past jumping at the force; Mario took no notice. He reached over and slapped Simon across the back.

"Don't be a pussy."

Simon thought for a moment and made his decision.

"I'm working extra for a doctor," he yelled.

"Oh yeah?"

"Yeah," he said, swallowing a lump, buying time, waiting for a dip in the song to allow his voice to traverse the space. "I am."

"Oh yeah? That's crazy!"

"He's made me do some shit."

"Oh yeah?"

"Are you even listening?"

"Yeah, yeah, man. I am. I wanted you to tell me the fuckin' story, didn't I?"

"Alright, alright, calm down. I will." Simon sipped his drink again, buying more time while his mind spun out, thinking about where he should begin. He didn't want to tell Mario *everything,* but he wanted to tell him *something, anything* to make Mario envious to his status. He didn't know why, but felt it a necessity.

"This doctor has me bringing patients down to him so he can perform experiments on 'em and shit," Simon said at last.

Mario's hand stopped mid butt squeeze, his mouth falling open.

"What do you mean 'experiments?'"

"I dunno," Simon shrugged. He took a swig of beer, only to find it empty. He raised his hand, signalling a waitress over. She came and took their orders, a round of beers and tequila. When the waitress walked away, Simon looked over at Mario.

"I dunno what he was doing, man. Experiments is all I know. I bring 'em down, and he does shit to 'em. After that, I pick 'em up like nothin's happened."

"That's kind of messed up, man."

Simon thought for a moment about how he wanted to phrase the next few sentences. He didn't want to sound too brash, he just wanted to be cool. Fuck Mario for making him feel small in what should have been his tallest moment.

Eventually, he said, "I know, but it's not like he does anything too bad to 'em. They're always returned in the same state I drop 'em off in."

374

Mario leaned forward so Simon could hear him over the pulsating music.

"It doesn't matter, Simon." He flicked Simon on the forehead with a finger. "He's abusing the patients and that ain't cool."

"What if he's helping them?"

"Helping them how?" Mario almost yelled, incredulous. "If he was helping them, he'd be doing it in a clinic or on a fucking floor."

"Maybe it's just unorthodox. Maybe he doesn't want anyone to know what he's doing 'cause it could compromise his research?"

Simon saw Mario's look, scoping him out like he was a small child.

"Do you really believe that?" Mario asked.

Simon did, in fact, believe that. It was what The Doctor had told him, almost verbatim. Simon hadn't asked too many questions, but The Doctor had given up some small details with reluctance. Simon assumed it was to assuage any fears he may have had with their deal, and he would have been right.

"I do."

Mario sighed, focusing both eyes on Simon. The girl, grown bored with their conversation, was talking to one of her girlfriends that had wandered over to their table. Mario didn't seem to notice.

"I don't *think* you're *thinking* too hard about this," Mario said.

"Whaddya mean?"

"You're being blinded by money."

"I axed him about it, an he told me everything was on the level." Simon heard the edge to his voice, hated himself for it but not being able to help it.

"Then why haven't you said anything to anyone?"

Simon felt the defiance building up in him; more than that, he felt annoyance at Mario questioning his actions, especially since Mario knew his situation. They'd grown up together, hell, his mom had gotten Mario *his fucking job*! *The audacity of that prick!* He wanted to strangle his friend. "Because he pays me well, and that helps me and my Moms," he said, a finality in his voice.

Simon was happy to see a look of hurt pass over Mario's face. He smugly took a sip of his new beer to hide his grin. Mario sighed and put his free hand on Simon's thigh, leaning forward as he did so.

"I want you to listen to me, and to listen well."

Simon saw the sincerity in Mario's face and leaned to within kissing distance.

"I applaud you for what you're doing for your Moms, but it ain't gonna help her if you, or this doctor, get busted and you in jail facing massive fucking time."

"I ain't gonna help her sittin' on my ass n'ither. Not wit the bullshit pay we get at dis garbage job," Simon said hotly, feeling drunken anger trying to boil up. He hated being questioned about what was best for his family. He never expected Mario to agree with him a hundred percent, but having Mario directly question, and let's not lie to ourselves here, insult the decisions that he was making, well, it didn't sit straight with him. He knew Mario came from money. *He* didn't know what it was like to struggle, forking over the majority of your paycheck to keep you and your mother's head above water.

They looked at each other across sips of drinks, Simon determined not to speak first, lest his anger get the better of him.

"Look, I'm sorry. I know you gotta do what you gotta do. But, I think it's wrong, and that's all I'll say about it." Mario reached out to touch Simon but changed his mind midway through the movement. He pulled it back, rested his hand on his left knee instead. "I just want you to be careful. Don't get greedy."

Simon saw the look in Mario's eyes and the underlying meaning behind it. *Don't jeopardize your soul*, they said. *Don't get caught*, they said.

Simon decided that if Mario was going to drop it, he would too, although he was still pissed off.

"I get it," Simon said, looking down at his bottle, which he found was surprisingly empty. "I'll be smarr 'bout it," he mumbled. What he didn't add was that he knew the arrangement was off.

They ordered more drinks and turned their talk back to trivialities, Simon's memory of the rest of the night bordered with a hazy hue.

2

Simon awoke the next morning with a head that felt three sizes too big. The contents of his stomach, two half-digested pieces of pepperoni pizza and a boatload of beer, sloshed around. Light beamed in from a slit in one of his curtains and lit directly on his eyes. He checked his phone, pulling it from under his pillow, and saw that it was shortly past ten in the morning. He groaned, rolling over so his back was to the window. He shut his eyes and tried to will himself back to sleep. He squeezed himself into a ball and tried to ignore the ugly sensations cascading through his body. His brain ran through the conversations he'd had with Mario the previous night. He grimaced at the perceived notion of how badly he'd kowtowed for Mario, pulling himself deeper into a ball; mostly, however, his brain kept pulling his thoughts to the way Mario's eyes pleaded at the end, asking him to watch his soul. *Had* he been doing all this for his Moms and him? *Was* he doing it for righteous reasons? In the late morning light, it was harder to convince himself that all his motivations were pure. He balled his silk sheets under his chin and tried to quiet the voices.

When that didn't work, he reached under his pillow and produced his phone. The hand of the analogue clock display had advanced less than a quarter of the circle. He replaced the phone and pulled the sheets around him, cocooning himself once again. He tried to force himself back to sleep, knowing it was a lost cause. His mind peeled back and began to replay each patient he'd taken to The Doctor. He was trying to ease his drunken mind into showing him that he'd made proper decisions, that all patients had come back fully functioning and festively alive; outside of the one body Simon had delivered and been paid for. That wasn't the case. He couldn't shake the thought of what might have happened to the patients. Sure, they'd been in goodish conditions when he'd brought them back, but most of the people he'd delivered to The Doctor had been really far gone. He had doubts that they even knew what had happened to them. That thought was the precursor to the simple, bald fact that The Doctor could have done any number of shady things to the people who wouldn't remember anything, let alone have the functionality to tell anyone about it. Suddenly, on the heels of that thought, coming in hot and heavy, was the memory of blood on his shoes. The spot wasn't much, nothing more than a smidge really, but it came back sharp and clear. He remembered with stark disgust how he'd *been* disgusted and had cleaned his shoes off with a cavalier attitude. He tried to remember which patient he'd taken down to The Doctor but couldn't recall. Try as he might, their face was distorted by a blot of blood. He felt his stomach roll over. It was then that his brain screamed at him a single name. Sheela. He'd completely forgotten about her. The thought slapped him hard and he knew that he was going to puke, something that he hated more than anything.

Simon bolted up and out of bed, sprinting towards the bathroom. He barely made it before all the liquid and gruel in his belly came up on the express elevator from hell and splashed into the toilet, careening off the convex, rebounding, and wetting his face. He was convinced it was blood, despite looking at the mess that lay in the toilet. He frantically wiped at his face with a hand, suddenly sure it was not just blood, but *their* blood. When he felt the wetness along his hand, his gorge reacted again and he threw up the remaining contents of his stomach. Then, he gagged and threw up some stomach lining for good measure.

With that done, and Simon was sure that nothing else would be forthcoming, he stood up and went to the sink to rinse his face off. He brushed his teeth before heading back to his bed.

He curled up, wrapped in the safe space of his silk sheets, and tried to sleep. Once again, it was a fruitless endeavor; while his belly was sated, his mind was anything but.

Todd

1

Todd sat back in his easy chair and wiped his hand down his big cheek, thinking about how good fortune, any fortune, came in threes; today, his second had come in the form of a phone call. He leaned back further and closed his eyes, replaying the previous conversation, not quite believing it.

It had started innocent enough.

It was a weekend afternoon and he'd been lounging in his lazy boy. Half his attention was loosely following the movie his wife had put on, and then promptly fallen asleep to, along with both children, while the other half had been focused on the infinite scroll of his phone.

He almost dropped the phone when it began to vibrate.

He looked down and didn't recognize the number. He thumbed green and brought the phone to his face.

"Hello," he answered tentatively.

"Hello. Am I speaking with Todd Scatalon?"

Todd cringed. It *was* his fucking cell phone.

"Yes, I am he," he answered.

"Good. Good. My name is Thomas Veksler, and I have a proposition for you."

"I'm glad you thought of me." Todd took a breath. "Forgive me for being curt," another breath, "but I have no idea who you are, sir." He added the sir almost as an afterthought; much like his mother taught him, he always erred on the side of polite when opportunity *could* be knocking.

Todd heard a light, low chuckle on the other end.

"I'm sorry if I didn't properly introduce myself. I work at the hospital with you. Well, not *with* you, but we occupy the same space and time."

There was a pause, and Todd felt a tickle of recognition. A myriad of faces swam through his mind; something about the last name. It was a trigger, and he was intrigued. More importantly, he was beginning to think that the caller was legit. It wasn't some scam job or some horseshit telemarketer.

"You work at the hospital?" he asked, his voice a fifth above normal.

There was joy in the voice answering him; Todd could swear he heard the sound of hands clapping once, sharply, in the background. "Yes. That's exactly it. Well done."

"What do you do there?"

"That's an interesting question, but it's not why I called." The voice was even. Calm. "I'm more looking forward to what you can do for me."

Todd began to make a noise before being cut-off.

"You'll be well compensated, of course. I wouldn't want to bother you for no gain of your own."

It was magic to Todd's ears. After years of sucking up, he'd found two rabbis in as many months. He held the phone out in one hand while the other pumped silently.

He brought the phone back to his face.

"What did you have in mind?" he asked, lowering his voice so he wouldn't wake his wife and kids.

"A healthy amount of money for only a tiny service here and there," came the answer.

Visions of him holding large canvas sacks with dollar signs embroidered on them danced through his head; that this was the standard caricature of villains didn't cross his mind.

"Well," Todd started, feigning worry in his voice, not wanting to seem too eager, "I guess my next question is, what services did you have in mind?"

"I need some biomedical waste pick-ups that are not on your scheduled routes," the voice said.

A shallow wave of relief washed over Todd. What was being asked wasn't anything that he couldn't accommodate; however, he knew he wouldn't be receiving this phone call if everything was above board. A million questions flitted in his mind. The foremost was, why was he cryptically called instead of being approached face-to-face? Surely there were unasked favours, and if so, what would they be? The voice on the other end, whom Todd was ninety-nine percent sure was a doctor, had whispered of great treasure.

It was in the words he *hadn't* said.

It was in the price Todd would have to pay.

Todd heard the tiny waver in his voice as he asked if there was anything else that might be required. The voice on the other end sighed with the force of a collapsing star.

"Well, I'm performing some rather delicate experiments that are time sensitive. Sometimes I need help procuring certain," there was a pause, "materials that are otherwise not always easy, nor legal, to acquire."

And there it was. Todd felt his testicles shrink at the words. He *knew* there had to have been a caveat, yet he wasn't *not* happy about knowing it.

He took a breath, and before he could speak, was cut off.

"I want to reiterate that it's *mostly* for Biomed collection."

"So, what would these other activities consist of?" Todd asked, knowing he was fishing. A light laugh greeted his request.

"Perhaps we can take our lunch together sometime this week."

"Yes, I'd like that," Todd said, nodding along to himself.

"Excellent," the voice said, "I'm happy to hear it. I know a nice little coffee shop that's around the corner from our business."

Todd listened to the time and place. He agreed, and the phone call was over.

2

Todd sat in a corner booth in a cafe that was adorned with wood paneling and kitsch decorations. His wife would have said it was shabby-chic; the colour scheme was easy light blues and soft creams. It reminded Todd of deck chairs perched at the end of a dock, overlooking a large body of water.

Todd checked his watch as his latte arrived, missing the server's dirty look, and saw that he still had ten minutes to wait. He nursed the coffee and scanned his phone, looking up every time the chime above the door dinged.

Five minutes after the appointed time, Veksler walked in. Todd waved at him and the man nodded and came over, carrying a manila envelope. As he approached, Todd took in the man's increasingly familiar appearance. He had military style salt and pepper hair with a close-cropped grey beard. He wore an open-throated polo shirt underneath a tight fitting sweater vest that did little to hide the slight paunch he carried. Below the vest were dark slacks and immaculate dress shoes. The outfit was not lost on Todd.

Once Veksler took his seat and deposited the envelope on the table, Todd recognized him immediately, although the missing stethoscope had thrown him for a loop. They sat in silence as the server came over and took Veksler's order; coffee, black. Todd asked for the same thing with a glass of water on the side.

"So, you're a doctor," Todd said.

Veksler nodded.

"It makes sense," Todd continued. "No one else would really be asking for Biomed

387

pick-up unless they were in your position. *Especially* the manner in which you asked," he said. He spoke the last sentence almost as an afterthought. Todd made sure he was looking slightly above Veksler's shoulder, trying to keep his voice calm and his demeanour aloof when he felt anything but. He let his eyes lazily wander back down to Veksler's face and saw an impassive mask.

"Clever deduction," Veksler said. Todd caught a shift in Veksler's posture. They locked gazes, and Todd was suddenly glad to be sitting down because he felt the muscles in his legs go limp. The eyes across from his were piercing and intense, Todd's wide and sheepish. He bore up under the look as long as he could but averted his eyes first, casting them up towards the analog clock above the coffee bar. He saw the server coming over to their table carrying their drinks and was glad for the momentary distraction. She placed their mugs on the table in front of them.

When she was gone, Todd wrapped his hands around the mug like they were cold and leaned over it, blowing at the steam that was curling up around his face. When he spoke, his voice was soft, barely carrying over to Veksler's ears above the background noise.

"So - uh - what is it that - uh - you need me to do for you?"

Veksler took a sip of his coffee, wincing from the heat of it, Todd guessed. He answered the question with a question, which in Todd's estimation, wasn't an answer at all.

"How much do you know about me?

Todd took a sip of coffee to buy some time and think about it, but succeeded only in burning the roof of his mouth. He took a long drink of water while he thought about the question and realized it was pointless as he didn't know anything about Veksler at all.

"In all honesty, I don't know anything about you."

Veksler's eyes narrowed. "Not many do."

Todd felt a chill course through his body, accompanying the loose legs that hadn't gone away. He watched as Veksler sat back, folding his hands on the table in front of him, and gave him a grave gaze.

"I asked you that to prove a point. I keep my work, how does your English expression go, 'close to the chest?' I say this so you know I'm serious, and you do not take lightly what I'm going to tell, and potentially, show you."

Despite the fear and anxiety that Todd felt surging through him, he couldn't lie to himself that he was extremely intrigued.

"I'm listening," he heard himself croak. "Sir," he added quickly, to show the respect he felt.

"I need someone, a partner you could say, to help me procure certain things that aren't always legal, and even if they were, would be viewed very poorly by your contemporaries. I need someone, a partner, to gather these things because oft times I don't have the availability to get what I need. This is because I perform certain experiments that, while life-saving, would be frowned upon by the medical community."

Todd's eyes flashed wide and his mouth dropped open. He could not believe his fortune. Part of him was thinking about how much money he'd be able to milk out of Veksler now that he knew his secret. But that part was dwarfed by the more practical side. Veksler had just confided something *huge!* in him. Todd was pretty sure Veksler was looking for a confidant. He assumed that Veksler wouldn't be letting this much slip if he didn't need a right-hand man. Todd swallowed so his salivation would not be noticed.

"How many others would I be working with?"

A flash of sadness peppered Veksler's face. When Todd blinked, it was gone.

"There is just you," Veksler said with a level voice.

So, either he doesn't want me to know about them, or he's shut them up. For good, Todd thought.

With a voice more steady that he felt, Todd heard himself ask, "What kind of experiments have you done?"

Veksler looked hesitant to answer, so Todd nodded his head slightly while holding up an index finger. "I ask because if you're doing some Nazi-type stuff, I'm out. If you're doing something somewhat on the level, then we may have a deal."

He watched as Veksler gave him a stone stare, all the good-natured humour sapped out of his face; it was not a look that Todd held up well under. He looked down into his ever-dwindling coffee. He heard Veksler's voice, steeped in controlled anger.

"I do not do what you say. I would *never* do this. I'm striving to make this world a better place, not fuck it all up."

"I'm sorry. No offense meant," Todd said. "I just wanted to know where you stood on the whole thing." He sighed and looked up, telling himself he *wouldn't* look away this time. "I just meant that I'm not gonna follow you on something that's dangerous and disgusting."

Veksler's face softened. "It's forgiven." He took a breath. "No, I do not do any Nazi experiments, nor anything they would approve of. I'm simply a man trying to advance the medical field by any *proper* means necessary." Todd noticed that Veksler kept his voice calm, despite the minute flickering of the muscles in his right cheek.

"Is that a record of your work?" Todd asked, nodding towards the manila envelope that was lying dormant and almost forgotten on the table between them.

"Yes," Veksler said. "Take it. Please."

Todd's hand reached out and snapped up the folder. He slid it into the briefcase he'd set beside him earlier. Veksler stretched out and took a large drink of coffee. Todd felt the mood and decided to end the meeting.

"Okay. Well. I'll be in touch after reading this." He shuffled out from the table and grasped the briefcase in one pudgy, sweaty hand. He looked down and saw Veksler casually leaning back, taking another sip of his coffee. He struggled, looking for additional words, not wanting to leave with *those* as his last. "I - uh - look forward to speaking with you soon."

Todd looked back as he neared the door and saw Veksler still sitting back, but this time his hands were laced behind his head, like he was deep in thought. Todd wondered what exactly was going on in the old doctor's head.

Alessia

1

It was a rare, slow morning for Alessia but was something she saw as becoming more frequent as they slowed down the operating rooms as the moving date came closer. She only had five patients to tend to for the day, the majority of whom were on their final day or two. She only had one patient of major concern that would require extensive work, but she didn't mind. With her current free time, she was catching up on paperwork.

She felt pain in her left hand and looked down. There was a nasty red lump forming on the middle finger. She dropped her pen and shook it out, trying to get some feeling back into it. Once the thousand needles came and departed, she checked her phone and saw that she still had better than fifteen minutes before having to go over to The Women's Pavilion for her next client. She rubbed her eyes and looked back down at the paperwork strewn in front of her. All the previous words she'd written swam around the page, producing a hypnotic quality that she found oddly familiar. She continued looking down at the words, growing more and more spaced out over time. She was retreating into the recesses of her brain, trying to unlock the mystery of where she'd had this feeling before.

Her phone alarm began jangling, pulling her out of her reverie. She shut it off, amazed at how the final fifteen minutes had slipped by when the previous hour had stretched out for an eternity.

Alessia got up and slipped her paperwork into the locked filing cabinet below her desk and then pocketed the key. She stepped out of her office on the eighth floor and began the long walk towards The Women's Pavilion. She'd made it to the ramp and was about to descend when she saw two people at the bottom. There was a man with two legs and a woman with only one. Despite the distance, she thought they both looked oddly familiar.

With her face screwed up in a scrutinizing look, she began the descent. When she was halfway down when the man looked up and back and beckoned to her. He was older and had the look of someone who greatly cared for the person at his side. The woman with him looked withered and on the verge of death, leaning hard against the left side of the hallway for support.

"Excuse me, Miss," the man said, raising his voice. "You're a physiotherapist here, yes?"

Alessia stared at him, and slow recognition dawned on her face. It was Dr. Veksler and her caution evaporated in an instant.

"Yes, I am Dr. Veksler," she said, scurrying down to him, a wide smile on her face.

"Excellent. Hello Alessia," he said. He made a notion of clapping his hands but couldn't because they were braced around the female patient with him as she leaned against the left wall for support. "As you can see," he said with a slight nod to the woman he was with, "I'm in need of your help."

Alessia's instincts kicked in. She hurried forward and grasped the woman placing her arm around the waist while keeping her shoulder notched in the woman's armpit.

"I see you don't have a commode chair with you. Why not?"

"I'm sorry," Veksler said, a chuckle hiding behind his words. "I don't have one with me, but there is one close by."

"Where?"

"Just inside the alcove ahead. I saw it as we passed."

"Can you get it, please?"

Veksler left his patient with Alessia and went down the final few feet of the decline and disappeared behind the curve.

Alessia felt the woman try to turn in her direction.

"No, no. Stay facing forward. You don't want to twist too much and overexert yourself." Alessia spoke with soothing words, not wanting to upset the patient.

Despite this, the patient still tried to turn toward her. Alessia kept her grip tight but found herself losing the fight to restrain the patient. Despite the look of being extraordinarily fragile and about to be snapped in half by a semi-stiff breeze, Alessia felt an absurd amount of strength radiating from her.

The patient turned fully toward Alessia, and she had a moment of extreme anxiety due to recognizing who the patient was. She remembered her ass first and how snug it had looked in a pair of scrubs. That thought was chased away by a sudden sinking feeling that she'd been manipulated by her in some way. She had a vague notion of seeing something horrible happening to the patient the nurse was with. The thought was too grotesque for her to comprehend, and when she felt the reality of it trying to peek around the veil, she immediately pushed it away.

She tried to look away, subconsciously knowing what was coming next, but felt strong hands upon her face, slowly turning it towards that of the patient.

One look into the patient's eyes was all it took. Alessia was thoroughly entranced and her face became slack, the animation draining away in a blink. Her mind swirled away into a blank slate, waiting and willing to be formed at the will of those gripping eyes. Had she been in her right mind, she might have noticed The Doctor coming up beside her, a useless rag in his left hand. His right hand was creeping up to her shoulder but stopped when he saw the look that his daughter was giving Alessia.

But, Alessia saw none of this. The last thing she heard before tumbling into darkness was, "Good girl."

2

When Alessia regained full control of her mind, she found herself unable to move. Her eyes came to focus on a dingy ceiling that was covered in cobwebs and completely unfamiliar to her. She tried to lift her arm to her face to give it a rub and found that she couldn't. She tried to turn her head to see what was obstructing it and found that along with each of her limbs, she was unable to. Panic began building within her and she tried to choke it down. Her mind ran back to how she got to where she was and felt it snap shut when she couldn't remember her exact movements. She heard her mind screaming out that it was impossible and shut that part out immediately. She didn't want to think about it, because the momentary glance she'd gotten disturbed her.

She remembered being in the hallway, walking towards The Women's Pavilion during the daylight hours, but then everything went blank. Her fear first bloomed, thinking that she'd taken, or been spiked with, some kind of drug. On the heels of that was that her parents were going to be pissed, but more importantly, extremely disappointed in her. She pushed those thoughts away because she knew it couldn't be true; she hadn't ingested anything harder than booze for over a decade. No, she was facing the reality that she was missing a large portion of her memory for an inexplicable reason. She remembered a one-legged woman with a doctor in the hallway but nothing else.

Alessia tried tugging at her restraints again but found them as taught as before. Feeling the chafing against her wrist, and the burning that accompanied it, she felt the panic she'd been keeping at bay roar up inside of her. It was real. She screamed out then, crying out into the somberly lit room for anyone that might be walking by to help her. She exhausted her voice but kept screaming until the only noises escaping her were squeaks and deflated air horn sounds. That's when reality really sank in. She was tied down in some dank dungeon with any sort of horror lying in wait for her. She shivered, as much from fear as from the chill on her near naked body.

She found out what that horror was ten minutes later.

She'd come to terms with her situation, but despite the burning she felt along her ankles and wrists she was methodically worrying them back and forth, looking for any give within her restraints. She vowed that no matter what came, she wasn't going to go quietly; she would fight tooth and nail with whatever effort she held within her until she was dead. If her captors didn't intend to kill her, then she'd give them hell as soon as she was free.

While wincing at the pain of the leather rubbing against raw skin, she heard a door open. She rolled her eyes as far as they would go in the direction of the noise. It was only then that she saw, or at the very least registered, an IV pole with a bag of blood and a bag of saline solution attached to it. Upon seeing the pole, her arm sent signals to her brain that there was a needle placed somewhere in her arm. She wondered briefly if that had been the cause of her memory loss, but squashed it, wanting to keep her attention focused on the person that was entering the room.

She heard the squeak of metal wheels rolling across uneven ground and strained her eyes in that direction, feeling like they were going to bust out of their sockets. She didn't see anything as the sound of squeaky wheels cranking over stopped just shy of her position.

All her good sense left her then, and she began attempting to jerk her head in that direction but to no avail. Her hands flapped at the wrists, balling themselves into fists and relaxing, repeating the action in spastic movements. She tried to kick out with her legs as well, but all that would happen was her feet would jerk up, bending almost comically, before kicking back down; she was twitching and jerking with maximum effort to minimal response. It was like she was having the world's most restrictive seizure. Eventually, she gave up.

"Hello. Is anybody there?" she croaked out.

No answer came back. The silence was more chilling than any response would have been. At least, if words came back to her, she'd be able to discern certain things about the individual, or individuals, holding her hostage. As such, her hoarse, dry voice ricocheted once around the room and died.

"Whoever you are, I won't say anything. Please just let me go," she said, not expecting an answer, but feeling she had to try.

There was a shuffling of feet off to her left and she decided to try once more, knowing that it would probably do no good.

"I beg of you," she said, forcing as much emotion into her dead vocal cords as she could muster, "I don't want to die."

She heard a soft chuckle come from somewhere outside her field of vision. It froze her blood and sent cold ball bearings rolling around in her stomach. She knew in that moment that she was going to die, no ifs, ands, or buts.

Alessia lay still then, hoping to show an air of pacificity. She wanted her kidnapper to get close enough to grab so that she could pinch their throat shut. If she *was* going to die in this disgusting, gross locale, then she'd do her best to murder the motherfucker too.

She heard footsteps approach and finally, *finally,* caught sight of the human that had captured her.

A green, surgical cap was the first thing that broke her field of vision. It was followed up by a pair of bushy, white eyebrows. Underneath the eyebrows were a pair of piercing grey eyes. She thought that she might still be drugged, but could have sworn she recognized them; it wasn't the eyes, but rather the compassion she saw in them that was familiar. A surgical mask obscured the bottom of his face. Upon seeing the preparation that he'd done, her mind let go. She howled out unintelligibly and began thrashing against her restraints, only to further chafe her already raw skin. She bucked her head back and forth within the little leeway she had until she felt slick, cold, clinical rubber gloved hand press against her forehead, forcing her to be steady.

That was her final breaking point. With the feel of that hand pressed upon her head, her bladder let go. She felt a sudden wave of embarrassment flood through her as her urine soaked her underwear and trickled onto the slab, ending up as a puddle on the floor.

"We'll have to get someone to clean *that* up, yes?" the man above her said. He sounded neither angry nor agitated. Instead, his voice resembled that of a parent dealing with a sad child who had made a mess on their carpet.

With the urine still wet on her leg, she felt herself dwindle, not believing it possible given the situation she'd found herself in. Sensing her discomfort, the man above her began petting her head, making soft, soothing noises. It did not comfort her. It disgusted her. She tried to move her head out of the path of his hand. She failed. He felt the movement and uttered a sad chuckle.

"Alright then," he said quietly. "We'll get down to business then, yes?"

The man left her point of view and she heard him rummaging around on the table he'd wheeled out. She heard him pick something up, and then he was back in her field of vision. He brandished a large needle above her, her eyes widening at the sight of it. She didn't know if he meant to scare her with it, or what the purpose was, but she refused to beg and cry out. Not again. She'd already pissed herself and didn't want to degrade herself anymore by blubbering, apparent it would be of little use.

"This is a local anesthesia. I can't risk giving you a general, as you've already been under once and I'm not sure how to judge the dosage. Sorry."

The voice was vaguely familiar, but she couldn't place it.

He disappeared again, and before she could wonder what was going to happen, she felt a sharp sting high up on her left thigh. She heard him walk away. She lay perfectly still, feeling her leg first go fuzzy, and then disappear altogether. She tried to wiggle it and felt nothing. She tried to raise it with what little leverage the restraints allowed and felt nothing. She knew he'd not been bluffing, but she'd had to check all the same.

He came back some indeterminate amount of time later. To Alessia, it felt like he'd been gone for less than a minute, but she knew that couldn't be true. She'd heard about time stretching like taffy when the cocktail of fear and adrenaline took over the body. She would have welcomed it as she knew something grisly this way comes. Instead, she'd been cheated from a long waiting period. In the blink of an eye, he was back and ready to do whatever ghoulish thing he'd planned.

She heard him stop by her leg, only viewing the top of his scrub cap, and saw him lean over to do something, presumably with her leg. Then, she heard him lift something off the table and go back to his previous position. She felt nothing as he bent over and hummed to himself as he went about his work. She felt a slight burning sensation that seemed far away and unconcerning to her body but played heavy on her mind. She kept her composure until the room began to fill with the smell of blood; *her* blood. She felt a whimper fall from her lips, despite her insistence that she would not give him the satisfaction.

"Almost done, yes?" she heard from somewhere below as the burning morphed to a dull cooking. She saw the cap as he stood up. It disappeared as he went back to the tray and dropped his used instrument. It clanged heavy upon the metal and then she heard him select another one. The next sound she heard chilled her blood and forced more urine from her. It was the high pitched whine of a saw. It spun for perhaps three seconds and then was shut off. Then, he, and his tool, were filling her vision.

"I'm almost done now," he told her, a sick sense of good humour in his voice. "I'm sorry for what is going to happen, but you must understand that what I do, I do out of love." He sighed. "What I do, I do out of necessity to help my patient. My daughter. You of all people should be able to understand that."

"What are you going to do?" she croaked out.

"Just a little surgery. Don't worry. It's almost done."

With that, he disappeared and she heard the saw spin up once again. She clamped her mouth shut while her chin trembled. The saw continued its high-powered whine for a mere second before the oscillations of it slowed. She wondered what it meant, and then knew. A vibration, starting from the ghost of her leg, worked its way up her body; her whole being hummed with the feel of it. She felt it in her arms and hands and spine and skull. She heard a grunt and felt a pressure on her lower extremity as a curl of grey smoke wafted up from beyond her vision. She inhaled through her mouth and tasted dust and marrow. The pressure on her ghost of a leg increased while the room became hazy with shards of skin, muscle, and bone. Then, she heard a loud crack, like a tree branch threatening to give way under an enormous amount of weight. The crack was followed by a deafening snap.

She passed out.

Simon

1

He checked his phone for the hundredth time that day; still nothing. For the last few weeks, he'd been on his phone more than when he was chasing pussy. He felt like a loser, hanging on the whim of a person that wouldn't text back, yet here he was. He closed his phone and stuffed it back into his pocket, knowing he was going to feel phantom vibrations in a few minutes and recheck it. He wasn't sure why he cared so much, at least not in his conscious mind. He wanted to believe that it was because his source of extra income had dried up, but it wouldn't quite wash. It was Mario, *fucking Mario,* that wouldn't leave his mind. The drunken talk they had had had wormed its way into his mind and wouldn't leave.

His SpectraLink vibrated, and he instinctively reached into his pocket where he'd just stashed his cellphone. He scolded himself and pulled up his Spectra. It was a job. He had to take a patient from the E.R. and bring her to The Women's Pavilion.

He arrived in the E.R. and couldn't find his patient. He searched the boards and came up empty. He turned around and scanned the room for the unit coordinator. No such luck. All he saw was a bunch of nurses and doctors with zero smiles and bags under their eyes. Still, he asked the three people nearest him and was given either the cold shoulder or non-committal responses. So, he turned to the lazy Susan that held patient folders, spun through the files, yet still couldn't find the patient's name. He debated walking through the halls and asking every patient he saw if they were the woman he was looking for, but knew it was a bullshit plan. Then, he saw Bobbi and knew she'd be the one to direct him to his charge.

"Hey Bobbi," he said, waving at her. He saw a brief look of disgust pass over her face before it morphed into the more placid one he was accustomed to. As she walked over to him, he leaned against the counter top, laying an arm across it, and slouched.

"What's up," she asked, then immediately added, "Who're you looking for?"

"You," he said casually. He saw the look Bobbi gave and immediately regretted his joke. He saw the dark circles underneath her eyes, her rumpled clothes, and the way single strands of hair were escaping her bun. He knew he'd picked the wrong time to try and get cute.

"I don't have time for your games, Simon. I'm working a double tonight, and we've already had two addicts tear this place up, along with a criminal that assaulted a few of our staff. Say what you want and then fuck off."

He looked at her, swallowed, and then saw a semblance of humanity leak into her face. "Sorry," she said finally. He could tell that she didn't mean it.

"I'm looking for a Ms. Gettleman. I'm her chauffeur, he said sheepishly.

"No one here by that name," Bobbi said immediately.

"Shit," Simon said. "I was told she was here." He slapped his forehead comically with his hand and then added, "I think my dispatcher fucked up."

"Clearly," she responded dryly.

He tried to think of a cute direction to steer the conversation but failed. He took a final glance into her tired eyes and spoke.

"Okay. They probably fucked up the name, but do you have any patients slated to go to the fifth floor of The Women's Pavilion?"

Without hesitation Bobbi spoke. "Yes. Ms. Waddlelan. She's in sub-acute 7."

"Thanks." Simon turned to leave, *wanting* to leave, but had to look back at Bobbi and ask the next question despite not wanting to.

"Anyone down there ready for me?"

"How in the fuck should I know, Si-mon? Why don't you go down there and check for yourself?"

"Sorry. Sorry. I just thought I should know what I was walking into," he said.

He turned away from her and began walking toward the sub-acute section. He passed druggies and sickness and wannabe sickos en route. Some called or cried out to him while most just looked at him with pleading eyes, wishing for him to take them away.

He shrugged them all off.

He found his charge and stood around for ten minutes while waiting for a P.A.B. to help him. He scrolled through his phone, wait-ing for that phone call or text from The Doctor. It never came.

He wheeled his patient out of the E.R. and took her to the elevator. It chimed, and he went in, meeting Dennis.

"What's up, Africa?" Dennis asked in his usual slow drawl.

"Nothing, man," Simon mumbled.

"What's that? I couldn't quite hear you, boy."

The words were meant to sting, but Si-mon ignored them.

"Where you taking the broad?"

Ms. Waddlelan craned her neck back to see who had spoken. Simon saw a sour look on

411

her face and then couldn't help but respond to Dennis.

"Man, fuck you," he blurted. "Just cause she's a woman, don't make her a broad. Why don't you show some goddamn respect."

Dennis didn't flinch at the anger oozing from Simon's voice. He just continued to chew on a soggy toothpick and regard him with callous eyes.

"Who pissed in your Cheerios this morning," he asked as he butted his way by Simon, walking out of the elevator as it stopped on the seventh floor.

"You did," Simon said, and as the doors closed, adding, "motherfucker."

He looked down and saw his charge looking up at him.

"Sorry, ma'am. He brings out the worst in me."

"Don't apologise to me," she said at once. "He seems like an asshole."

At once, the tension Simon felt building inside of him dissipated. He laughed aloud, and the woman followed suit. He wheeled her out of the elevator towards The Women's Pavilion as tears streamed down both their cheeks. He didn't know why it was so funny, just that it was. His laughter cut off as he rounded the bend and came to the descending ramp that led from

the main to The Women's. He re-adjusted himself and took her down slowly, something he'd
never done before. He heard his keys jangling
as they hit his backside and slowed his progress
even more. The closer they got to *the* door, the
louder his keys seemed to cry out. Eventually,
he was wheeling her down at nothing short of a
crawl. Normally, it was a free fall frenzy, almost
a game, where the porters bragged about how
far they were able to let the stretchers slide before pulling up the break and gliding the patient
to safety. This afternoon, that wasn't the case.

He brought her up to the fifth floor, en-
gaging in small talk the whole way. He placed
her in her room and passed her file off to the
nurse, feeling lighter to be rid of her. He knew
why. It was the keys that were heavy upon him
today. He plucked them off his belt loop and
tossed them in the air continually, catching
them as they fell back to earth. Even while waiting for the elevator, he knew what he had to do.

He rode the elevator down, tapping his
keys nervously against his hip as it ticked off
the two floors. No one was on the other side to
greet him, as he assumed there wouldn't be.

He turned right and began walking
back to the incline, knowing, but dreading,
what he was going to do next. He'd neglected to
call in the job done, knowing that since he'd accepted and completed the job in record time for

him, he'd have at least fifteen minutes before he was missed again. He assumed it would be enough time.

Simon walked to the incline and instead of continuing up, took a right into the little alcove, wiggling the correct key between his fingers. *Are we going to do this?* his mind asked him. It was the voice of Mario that answered. *Of course you are. You owe it to yourself, and to those you've condemned.*

Hating himself and cursing Mario, Simon slid the key into the lock.

2

The hallway was pitch black. Simon was used to having a light close to him, illuminating the ins and outs of the entranceway. He stumbled on a stone he never knew existed and went to one knee, skinning it. He winced, and as he went to put a hand on it felt his cellphone in his pocket. He pulled it out and saw no new messages or missed calls; he wasn't surprised.

He turned on the flashlight app and squinted until his eyes were adjusted to the glare bouncing off the wet, stone walls. He saw a long tunnel stretching out before him and started down it.

3

Simon stepped gingerly along the greasy, green cobblestones that peppered the hallway. He was lost. He heard the leaking of water around him as it dribbled down upon the cold stone that surrounded him. He knew he was somewhere underneath the bowels of the hospital, but had no idea where. He'd followed the indentations of footsteps and wheel ruts for as long as he could until he hit a tri-fork and the marks had suddenly stopped. He stared at each entrance, debating which one to take, when his phone died. Simon was plunged into almost complete darkness. Immediately, he spread out his arms like some unseen attackers were going to rush him, flailing them frantically in a vain attempt to fend them off. When no such attack came, he stopped moving, although his heart kept on its run-away pace. He took deliberate deep breaths to slow it so he could hear all the noise around him. Nothing stirred, nothing moved.

Except something did stir. He heard a sound off in the distance. It came from his right, or so he thought, but in the swallowing darkness, direction had no meaning. He decided against all self-preservation that he would follow where that sound came from, everything else be damned. He reached out, found the wall, and continued his way along.

At one point Simon noticed that he could see a tiny bar of light off in the distance, along the ground. He marked that as a point of reference and walked toward it. He stopped outside a door and with a sweaty palm grasped the knob. He twisted it delicately and tried to open it. It was barred somehow. He waited outside, straining his ears to hear any movement from beyond the door. Eventually, he did hear a sound. It was a soft moan. It shook him for he knew that sound. That moan. It was a patient in pain. It was a drugged up human in *excruciating* pain.

He forced the door so a miniscule crack appeared, then pressed his face against it. He could see nothing, yet heard a human again muttering in pain. He checked behind him once, twice, three times, and then began trying to force the door open with his shoulder. It held, but he could feel the give in it, waiting for him to apply more pressure.

He heard muffled crying from within and stopped. He'd come this far and *knew* that he should continue but could only stare dumbfounded at the door. Beyond was what he'd come to do; beyond was what he'd come to stop The Doctor from doing, yet he couldn't move. He heard the whimper, he heard the cry, but his blood froze. *If she can't defend herself, what chance do I have?* blasted through his mind. He knew he was being a pussy. He knew he was being chicken shit. He urged his body to move, but it wouldn't respond. He had no idea how long he would have been that way if he wouldn't have heard the voice beyond the door. A muffled moan of pain escaped through the door and he thought he recognized the voice.

Simon turned the knob, twisting it with slick hands, and felt it slipping each time he tried. He grasped both hands together, but the knob continued to yield nothing.

"Fuck," he yelled. "I'm coming. Don't worry."

He threw a shoulder against the door and it rattled in its frame. He let go and went back to the edge of the corridor. He charged forward, throwing his shoulder with all his might at the door as he approached. It shuddered on its frame. He repeated the process three times before giving up. The door was either exceptionally well built, or had been bolted from the inside.

Simon had an idea which one it was.

He retreated down the dank, dark hallway until he could find a lump of a brick that was loose upon the ground. He pried it up, ignoring the sensation as the skin on his pinkie peeled back as he did so. He knew someone was in need of help beyond the door and he'd do everything he could to help them.

That's when he heard the blood-curdling scream.

He ran at the door, brick in hand, aimed solely at where he thought the mechanism would be, forcing all of his weight behind it. He rammed it once. Twice. Three times.

On the fourth time, the door blew in.

Alessia

Alessia awoke with no previous memory. She twisted her head and found she could not move it. She lifted her arms and found they could not move. She lifted her legs and found they could not move.

She shivered as she looked up at the ceiling, the only thing her restraints would allow her to see, and pondered her fate. Slowly, it came back to her. She was trapped. She was held captive in a dank, dark, disgusting underground sewer and nothing was going to save her. She had no idea what the freak was trying to do to her, but she knew he was a doctor, she'd seen him with her own eyes. She was going to die unless she got herself out of this situation.

Once again, she took stock of her body.

Her head couldn't move. It was restrained.

Her arms couldn't move. They were restrained.

One leg couldn't move. It was restrained.

One leg was fuzzy.

She concentrated on the fuzzy leg, willing it to shift, lift, or pivot. Anything. After five minutes, she smiled.

She felt triumph as she lifted her left leg in the air. She had a portion of her free. That son-of-a-bitch had forgotten about it. She'd make him pay. She was deciding on how such a thing could be accomplished when she pulled her leg close and noticed the stub of her thigh bucking towards her; there was no lower limb attached. She screamed then, but it was less the full-bodied bellow she'd thought it would be and more like the wheezing end of a balloon with the air gently being squeezed out. Her memory came blazing back with vivid ferocity. She greyed out thinking about it but reached down within herself, not allowing herself to lose consciousness for a third time.

To accomplish that, she focused on the hate she felt brewing in her belly. She let it grow until it became a part of her blood, coursing through her veins. Immediately, she began to feel warmer, like the emotion was a tangible thing. She let it crawl and infect every part of her; it didn't take long. It surged through her, and she felt a rush as it slammed into her brain with such velocity that she had a momentary thought that she could break the binds that held her. She flexed the muscles in her arms, feeling the restraints snap outward. She pulled at them and felt a smidge more give than before, and never mind the burning sensation that encircled her wrists. Hope added itself to the mixture within her.

She watched the light flicker incessantly above her. After a while, it seemed to her that it was pulsing in time with each pull at the restraints. She soon became tired however, feeling like her life force was slowly draining out; for all she knew, it could have been. Not being able to see if the wound in her leg was properly dressed nagged on her mind. She felt herself growing weaker with each pull and soon gave up the effort.

A whimper escaped her. Once the first one came out, the others that had been locked behind her grim determination spewed forth. She began blubbering. Her body shook with the force of them, bucking against the restraints that held her. She felt a slick sensation encompass her wrists and ankle. Added to that was a fire that had built up in her joints. Even if she did manage to break out, she'd be in no condition to choke the life out of the doctor that had done this to her.

Instead of tapering off, the tears and shakes increased in intensity. She pounded the slab with whatever give was available to her. Each appendage made soft, fleshy, thumping sounds against the marble. The reverberations made their way around the room and echoed back to her. She felt hope spring within her but quashed it. It was a false hope, she knew, and didn't want it to dig its clutches in. She needed to keep a clear, clean head to get herself out of the mess she was in.

That thought helped steel her, knowing she could only rely on herself to get out of her situation. She lay still, deciding that conserving her strength was the proper way to go, although a final cry escaped her lips. She felt her whole body relax as the air escaped her, pushing her into a state of tranquility. Mostly, she was tired. She felt a sense of euphoria wash over her. Despite all her early inner talks, she felt that her time had come. She was strapped down, short a leg, and let's not beat around the bush, in a shit situation. She stopped lying to herself then. There was no situation, barring help, that she was going to have a leg up in.

She resigned herself to at least trying to die well when she heard a voice yelling from far off on her left. At first, her mind didn't want to register it. She felt false hope was more the conclusion; however, her brain wouldn't let this one go. Whatever noise it had been, her brain screamed at her that it was words spoken from off her map. It *wasn't* too good to be true.

Her brain picked up what her ears missed the first time. A voice had said, "Fuck. I'm coming. Don't worry."

She latched onto that, and it became her mantra for the next few minutes. It culminated and was screaming through her mind, and she'd just gotten back to the *Fuck* when something pounded against the door. She started, the restraints digging further into her raw wrists. The pounding came again and again and again and again. Now, she knew. It was clear that someone was on the other side, trying to get in.

Her heart leaped in her chest as she felt rescue was almost certain. She opened her mouth, willing every ounce of energy to settle in her voice, and screamed with everything she had left.

The Doctor

He mopped up the blood on the table and floor with pads, smearing it more than collecting it, then stuffed the pads into the Biomed box beside him. It had been touch and go, but he'd finally managed to suture the arteries in her left leg. After that, he'd used a cheap, Home Depot blowtorch to cauterize the wound on Alessia.

He put the leg on ice, knowing that he'd be attaching it to his daughter in not too long. Alessia was still passed out, from pain or shock he didn't know, nor particularly care. He felt bad for visiting this horror upon her, but it couldn't be helped. He'd been desperate for anyone, spending the better part of an hour walking his daughter up and down the same portion of hallway, waiting for a single occupant to come by. He'd lucked out when he saw Alessia, using her profession as a means to get her close. His luck held after she'd dropped into a trance and no one else came by. He'd stood behind her as his daughter walked Alessia back through the maze and into his work chamber. The Doctor had helped his daughter lay Alessia down on the slab. He commanded her to make Alessia go deep into the trance, ensuring that she'd forget all and be immobile for long after he'd restrained her, and his daughter complied. He'd needed time to make his preparations without interruptions or annoyances.

Once again, his luck held and Alessia remained under while he prepared everything. He'd explained to his daughter what he needed for her to do while he dealt with Alessia.

Once again, his daughter complied.

Now that the operation on Alessia was complete, and she was patched up, he went into the back room, pulling the tray with the freshly severed leg on it with him. He saw his daughter lying on the table, an IV already protruding from her arm; the pole contained multiple bags of blood and saline. He wheeled the cart to the table, explaining once more to her what he was going to do and how he hoped this would cure her of her affliction.

Once everything was how he wanted, he bent to his mission.

2

He looked up from his notes when he heard a noise from the other room and glanced over at his daughter upon the table. She was breathing heavily, highly sedated, but awake. He watched her silently flex her leg, trying out the mobility with her new limb. The noise hadn't come from her, no. What he'd heard was a whimper.

He ignored it and went back to his notes, being almost finished with them. He was at the critical stage now and wanted to allow his brain to finish its train of thought while it was still running rampant. He knew, along with the medical marvels he'd already achieved, that if this current experiment worked he'd be looking at a Nobel Prize at a minimum. He finished off his notes with a broad smile on his face.

He looked up thirty minutes later when he placed the final period on the page. Alessia was crying in the other room. Once again, he felt bad for what he'd done, but not *too* bad; he would do the same thing again, if needed. He smiled until he heard a faint shout coming from far off, knowing it wasn't from Alessia.

These shouts had come with more force than he judged Alessia capable.

These shouts were masculine.

These shouts were from a familiar voice.

He felt all the hairs along his body spark up with tension. He held his breath, hoping that maybe Simon wouldn't hear anything and go away but *knowing* Simon had heard Alessia and was going to get in.

He stood up and strode over to his daughter. He leaned down and began whispering what he needed her to do. He was mid-way through his instructions when he heard a loud noise emanating from the outer door; it couldn't be denied anymore. Veksler spat out the rest of his instructions in rapid succession, tripping over his words a few times. When it was done, he heard a tremendous crash and imagined the wood on the outer door splintering around the deadbolt. He cursed himself for not making the door metal and to hell with the attention it would have attracted. *Oh well, it can't be helped now*, he thought. He could only react to the situation presented to him. He felt that things could still play out in his favour, despite the inevitability of it getting bloody.

He helped his daughter to her feet, ready to steady her with his weight if she tottered. She didn't. He watched her take a few ginger steps. He watched as her eyes narrowed, and she focused on the door leading to the other room. He felt something slimy slither around his wrist. He looked down with a jerk and saw that her tentacle was looking for a place to feed while her eyes were far away, envisioning what tasty morsel was on the other side of the door. Gently, he pulled his arm out of her grasp and placed his hands on her cheeks, turning her face toward him. He heard Simon's voice from the other room, sounding rather calm all things considered, and ignored it. He knew it would take Simon a few minutes to free Alessia, so he wasn't in a rush.

He looked into his daughter's eyes and saw she was trying to hypnotize him. *Silly girl, it won't work with me*; he'd guarded himself against such an attack.

He'd broached the subject delicately with Dr. Rhodina. She hadn't laughed. She'd directed him to a fringe psychologist that would either a) have the answers he was looking for, or b) direct him in the proper direction. She'd warned him about being cautious in his discussion of the matter with other professionals as an off-hand remark. He'd laughed to show her he wasn't offended.

Option A had paid off in spades.

And so, he let his daughter stare *into* him and *through* him. While never even half succumbing to her charms, he felt himself get sleepy; he felt himself fall back into his brain. It was pleasant, but he used his training and pulled himself back to the now. He perked his ears up and heard muffled movements from the other room. He was done wasting time. He had to put her on the move.

The Doctor looked at his daughter and spoke.

"Can you do it? Will you do it?"

She looked at him with her cold, far away gaze. He didn't know if she would answer him until she nodded her head once.

"Good girl. Go feed," he said and let go of her, stepping back into the shadows against the wall. He watched her lumber up to the door and open it. He could see Simon and Alessia shambling toward the plastic barrier, the effort on Simon's face palpable. Then, she stepped through, and the door closed.

Amid the sounds of struggle and scuffle and screams, he went over to his desk and gathered his papers, stuffing them down into a backpack, he'd deal with their condition and do the necessary re-writes later, when possible.

Once everything was stowed away, he went to a bookshelf and pulled it out, revealing a tunnel behind. He turned back to the door when he heard Simon scream, "Get the fuck outta here! I'll take care of this," and his heart went out to all three of them in the other room, although his wallet was on his daughter. Then, he stepped into the hallway and used the ring attached to the bookshelf and pulled it back into place. He reached along the wall, found his hanging flashlight, and flicked it on.

He walked away, leaving the three of them to whatever fate had decided.

Confrontation

1

The door shuddered in its frame as Simon slammed against it with the brick. He kept it level with the locking mechanism and after three good run-ups, he felt that he was close to breaking in.

"I'm coming. Hold on just a few more seconds," he yelled through the door. He backed up, eyeballing the height of the lock, and sprinted towards it as fast as he could. He connected with it on two points of contact, his right shoulder and his left hand that held the brick. The lock snapped with violent force and the door burst open, slamming against the wall and rebounding back at him, catching him off guard and almost knocking him over.

His eyes scanned the room with quick, sharp movements. He saw the hanging plastic curtains and darted through them into the back room. He saw Alessia strapped down on a marble slab and immediately went to her, casting the brick aside into the corner as he did so. Stopping a few feet from her, the horror of her situation bloomed in his brain with slow recognition. He saw the restraints binding her to the

431

slab of marble. He saw her wrists bloodied and raw from the chaffing of her struggles. He saw the remnants of blood on the floor; it looked to be a fantastic amount. He followed the dried smear up the slab to where Alessia lay and cocked his head sideways, like a dog confused by a magic trick. Something was amiss with her, and it took a long moment for his brain to register what his eyes were seeing. One of her legs was wagging above the slab, whether in excitement or relief he couldn't tell. Then he saw what was off-putting, and his heart sank; she was missing her leg from just above the knee, the fleshy, ragged stump flailing about. It was pink and raw and grotesque. He felt tears spring out in his eyes while a thick ball of sick bubbled in his stomach. He turned away, a hitching in his gorge. He wrestled with it and won. Still, he had to spit to clear his mouth and head.

Simon went over to Alessia. She looked up at him, pleading with her eyes. She opened her mouth and was barely able to croak out a "Thank you."

"Don't try to speak. I'm gonna get you out of here," he said.

He bent to his work, releasing the restraint on her head first before working his way down her body. When he'd released the strap holding her across the waist, she put her hands on the slab and tried to push herself up into a sitting position. Simon slipped an arm around her midsection and put a hand on her chest to stop her progress.

"No, no, no, no, no," he said softly. "Stay on your back. Let me detach you first, and then I'll help you up."

She tried to push back against him, dead set on getting off that *fucking* marble slab. She wanted to tell him that she'd been down there for far too long, that the last thing in the world she wanted was to lie back down. She opened her mouth to tell him, and a mushy sound was all she was capable of.

"Nooooooeyeeeeeeddddddouuuuuuuu-waaaaneeeewwww."

"Uh huh," Simon said, not understanding one damn iota of what she'd tried to say. "Just stay there while I finish what I gotta do," he said with as gentle a voice as he could muster considering the circumstance. He felt an unbelievable amount of force coming from her, so he gave up trying to get her back down. Instead, he held her steady until he felt that she wouldn't tumble over. That done, he went to work undoing the final restraint that held her right leg before putting a hand around her waist to help stabilize her. If she'd been able to talk properly, she would have told him it wasn't necessary. Despite the blood loss and impromptu surgery she'd just received, her body was pumping fear, adrenaline, and hate in equal parts; enough to make her feel like she could burst through the walls like the Kool-Aid man. Still, she couldn't deny the warm feeling of having helping hands holding her. While not needed physically, it did a lot for her emotional and mental state.

While Simon held her, Alessia swung her leg and a half over the edge, immediately feeling light headed. She leaned over with Simon still holding her and threw up onto the floor. Simon let go of her and stepped back, her puke splattering upon the dirty floor, mixing in with the blood and dirt and dust but missing his shoes.

When Alessia looked back at him, his small smile was gone, replaced with a look of utter concern.

"You okay?"

She nodded, trying to save her voice from any unnecessary strain. Simon reached down and pulled out the two I.V. lines that were stuck in her left arm. He saw a grimace of pain tug at her mouth.

"Sorry," he said, meaning it. "You ready to get the fuck outta here?"

She nodded again and shimmied to the edge of the slab. She dropped her hips to place her right foot onto the floor. She leaned a little weight on it, testing it. Her body said it would hold. She felt Simon slip around to her left and put an arm around her waist.

"Okay. On my count. Ready? One. Two. *Three.*"

They lifted, and suddenly Alessia was swaying on her foot. They moved forward one step, and Alessia had a thought blast through her head. *Huh. I must have dreamed he cut it off. I can feel the stone floor underneath my feet.* She was about to smile when she dropped a foot before Simon caught her weight. He grunted, and she jerked her head in that direction, catching the strain standing out in his face. She apologized with her eyes and shifted her weight back to her right foot.

Once they were stable, Simon spoke.

"Alright. We're gonna have to cou--"

A door was thrown open ahead of them. Dim light flitted through, obscuring the silhouette of the person that stood within. Simon made as if to move towards the person, but Alessia gripped him hard around the shoulder. She didn't think the figure standing in the doorway was a victim. She had a feeling, and it turned out to be right. The figure stepped into the room and shut the door behind them. Simon's vision became blurry as the force of the closing door stirred up a layer of dust. Alessia could make out some of the details on the figure because she'd squinted her eyes as the door closed. Some far away part of her brain recognized the colour of the clothes and knew it was the woman she'd last seen before being whisked away to lie on a slab to have her fucking leg hacked off. The fear and anger boiling through her blood morphed to rage, and she began tugging on Simon's shirt, pointing in the direction of the figure.

Simon looked in that direction but couldn't see anything. He dug the knuckles of his index finger in one eye to clear the darkness he saw. It half worked, spots exploding in his vision, and he was afforded the sight to see an outline and vague colour. While he'd been doing that, the figure had advanced a few steps. It was a woman, Simon could now make out. She was almost within grabbing distance and Simon lurched back, pulling Alessia with him. He thought that the figure could use some help, but his brain told him that to support the weight of two women would crush him. As the two of them stumbled back, the figure closed the gap.

The woman reached out and grabbed hold of Simon's left arm with surprising speed and force. He looked up with startled eyes and began to speak but stopped, his mouth hanging agape. Alessia saw what was happening and her brain snapped into place. *She's trying to hypnotize him*, it yelled out at her. She reacted without thinking, using all the force she could muster by bending forward and slinging a right hook. She connected on the shoulder with a muffled *thwap*, deadened by the clothes the woman was wearing. It didn't matter. The force of the punch threw the woman off enough for Simon to snap out of his reverie. He looked around, lost for a second, before registering the arm of the woman still gripping him. He saw a smooth tentacle coming from a split in the woman's forearm. It had wound its way around him and was picking him in a probing measure, looking for something it wanted to connect with.

That was it for Simon. He let go of Alessia, who tumbled to the ground, and slapped his hand on the woman's shoulder in an open palm. He tried to push her back, but she didn't budge. He felt fingers dig deeper into his flesh. He felt the poking and prodding of a needle as it walked its way along his skin, searching for the proper place to punctuate his outer layer.

"What the fuck?!?" he exclaimed.

The woman standing opposite him paid no mind to what he was doing and went along with her business.

Simon was saved from being drained when the leg of Alessia kicked out and struck the woman in the thigh, causing her to bow forward and loosen her grip for the slightest of seconds. It was all Simon needed. He doubled his efforts and pushed the woman back, causing her to land on her butt but pulling him forward in the process; her tentacle was *still* wrapped around his arm.

The two tumbled to the ground and became a ball of appendages in search of purchase for anything that would give them the upper hand. She reached up with a hand and cupped it around the back of Simon's head, pulling him closer to her face. When they were within kissing distance, she opened her mouth wide, exposing the gaping black hole that was her throat. Simon's eyes widened as he saw another tentacle, slimy and slithering, approach his face. It shot out of her mouth and opened up like a second mouth and connected with his face, covering his eyes, nose, and mouth. He screamed, or tried to, and then snapped his mouth shut as he felt an ancillary tentacle begin probing his face, looking for a hole. He had no idea what to do about his nose, or God forbid his eyes if it chose to dive in through the sockets, so he began blowing his breath with violent force out of his nostrils.

Simon felt the sticky end of the tentacle looking for an opening before it was jerked back with such force that the tentacle holding his face popped off with a thick, echoey *plop*. He looked around wildly and saw Alessia's leg kicking out, striking the woman with ferocious force. Two more kicks and the tentacle wrapped around his arm slithered free and he was no longer attached to her. He turned to Alessia then and yelled at her, as much a prompt as it was a way for him to save his soul he later thought, when he had time to think.

"Get the fuck outta here! I'll take care of this." His heart took a jump as he saw her roll onto her belly and begin crawling away. To Simon, she looked like an infantryman that he'd seen in war movies past trying to escape a shoot-out by laying belly flat while going for cover. He allowed himself a brief respite. *I saved her. At least I did that much.* Then, he turned his full attention to the creature at hand. Either he was going to kill it, he knew this now, there was no escaping such destiny, or he would die trying. It was a small pittance to make up for what he'd done, but it was a pittance he found himself willing to pay.

Simon turned to her with a determination in his eyes. The two combatants looked at each other, each ready to battle to the death as was required. Simon slipped his left hand around her throat and raised his right, poised to punch her lights out. He brought his right fist down with the force of a locomotive and felt it hit concrete. He felt the crunch as two of his fingers snapped along the knuckles as they rammed into the floor. He screamed at the pain and released the hold on her throat. She snapped up into a sitting position, throwing him off her and onto the floor where he lay, sprawled spread eagle on his back. His head connected with the ground and he saw stars. He watched as she pounced on him, both knees planted on either side of his torso; they began to dig in, looking for vital organs to squeeze for punishment. Much like earlier, but now with positions reversed, she slammed a hand down around his neck, threatening to cut off his air supply. Then he saw her raise her right hand and saw that ever gaping wound open up again and the tentacle emerge. He knew that this time it would be thrust down his throat. He tried to buck her off with his hips, throwing her the most furious fuck he could muster but she dug in deeper with her knees, crushing his liver. He had no idea where her strength was coming from. Still fighting, he resigned himself to this death and knew it was worth it if Alessia survived and was able to tell their tale. Fuck it. He'd done enough shit and had lived long enough.

He watched as the snarling creature thrust its hand towards his mouth and saw the flickering of shadow across the dimly lit wall. Alessia hadn't escaped after all and was trying to save him. In a last-ditch effort, he yelled with as much force from his choked off airway that he could muster.

"Alessia. NO!!!"

Alessia crawled as far as the plastic sheets before turning back. She saw the struggle that Simon was in and knew it was to the death. While she subconsciously appreciated the gesture, she couldn't let it stand. She had to help as best she could. *Besides*, her brain spoke to her, *if she kills him, she's gonna be able to easily catch up and murder you too. You're down a leg. The strength lies in numbers.* She agreed one-hundred percent and so, began looking around the room for helpful tools. Her eyes fell on the brick that Simon had used to smash in the door. She slithered over and grabbed it. Then, she began to make her way back towards where the struggle was happening, wriggling along on one knee and both elbows. She wasn't trying to be stealthy, but assumed she must have been when she was able to creep up behind the woman without her turning around.

When Alessia was within striking distance, she got up on her remaining knee and stump, ignoring the excruciating pain that screamed from the fresh wound, and raised the brick above her head. She caught Simon's eye as he screamed out.

Alessia didn't pay attention to the words, nor did she care about the reaction from the woman. All her rage and fear came bolting into her arms as she brought the brick down upon the creature's head. There was a sharp, sickly snapping sound, and then the creature collapsed to the left of Simon. Once she saw the body collapse, she waddled over until she sat astride it and began smashing the brick down upon its skull until little more than paste and pulp existed. She felt an arm grasp her bicep and found more energy from fear to continue mashing the head in front of her with the brick. Her face was streaked with gore but she didn't mind. She uttered guttural growls and brought the brick down with such force that it smashed through the remaining bits of skull and thudded upon the concrete floor. The reverberation was deadly, numbing her right arm instantly. It was only then that she felt the soft touch on her left bicep. It was Simon.

"Holy fuck! I - I - I think she's dead," he stammered.

Alessia looked down at him and for a moment saw red. She raised the brick above with a numb arm, but it never descended. When it hit its zenith she paused, and her conscious brain took over. It knew, and told her that it was Simon below her. Her hand trembled, and she dropped the brick. It clattered upon the floor with an anticlimactic *clump*. She collapsed off to the side of Simon, ending up in a puddle of blood but not caring in the least.

Simon lay there, understanding how close to an unspeakable death he'd come. He wanted to reach out a comforting hand to Alessia but didn't trust his reflexes.

"What the fuck?" he finally muttered.

There was no reaction from Alessia. She stayed in the puddle of blood that was slowly seeping beyond her hair. Simon gently pushed himself into a sitting position and surveyed the scene. He saw the inner door, still shut, as the most optimal area for a second attack, if one was going to happen. He reached out and grasped the brick Alessia had used to brain the creature to death. He held it in an upraised hand, willing something else to come through that door. When nothing did, he slowly got to his feet. He looked down at Alessia who was breathing more blood than oxygen, if he was any judge. She looked up at him with a sick inflection, her smile extended almost to her ears with the blood smears.

Simon patted her arm. He kept his eyes on the door and offered a simplistic, placating sentiment to her.

"Stay here. I'm gonna go check what's behind door number two."

He thought she shook her head but couldn't be sure. Either way, it didn't matter. His mind, being made up to save her before she'd saved him, was fully engrossed in ensuring that if one of them had to survive, it would be her.

Simon stepped toward the door, the brick dripping blood and brains poised high above his head, ready for anything that could pop out.

He swung it open. Nothing moved. Nothing stirred. It was a simplistic room that had a surgeon's table, a desk, metal table, and a mattress stashed in the corner. Simon spied a metal rolling table that was dashed with blood. He assumed there were surgical instruments upon it because the dull light from the two corner lamps reflected off the table with winks and flashes. He also noticed a large wooden bookcase, peppered with thick books, at the back of the room. He saw semi-circle scuff marks at the base of it.

Simon slowly stepped into the room, keeping his eyes, ears, and focus on anything that might pop out and accost him. Nothing came. He chanced a glance back to Alessia and saw her still lying prone in the puddle of blood. He turned back to the room and made his way inside. He saw the box of biomedical waste beside the surgical table. He lifted the lid and was greeted by the wet stump of a leg. He dropped the lid immediately and for the second time in the last fifteen minutes, struggled with his gorge. He won again. Next, he went over to the table and saw a pile of homemade notes. Some of them were on napkins, others on loose-leaf, but none were legible. He pushed them off the desk and scattered them onto the floor in a petty, childish manner. He smirked to himself and looked around the room one last time. There was nothing to gain from it, he knew.

Simon went back into the other room and over to Alessia. She seemed to be sleeping soundly, but as he approached she turned a blood-streaked face up to him and spoke in a clear, resounding voice.

"Is it over?"

He felt tears sting his eyes for the second time and spoke, choking back his emotion the best he could, which wasn't well.

"Yes."

Simon

1

Simon looked at himself in the two-way mirror. He was dressed in his street clothes, his work uniform having been taken and bagged up as evidence. Despite the crispness of his clothing, he felt anything but. It had been a long few hours since Alessia and he had emerged from the dark tunnel and back into the light. They'd gotten lost twice, and he'd felt the panic thrumming through Alessia's body. He couldn't blame her. His body had been on knife edges as well, conjuring up images of them escaping some crazy, un-fucking-believable situation just to get lost in the catacombs, slowly succumbing to hunger and thirst as they died many days later.

As it turns out, they'd been worried for nothing.

Once they were back in the hallway to The Women's Pavilion, Simon had left Alessia sitting propped up against a wall and sprinted until he found a wheelchair. Then, he'd loaded her in and took as quick a route as possible to the Emergency Department.

Simon was prepared to turn into a bull at the triage area, begging, pleading, threatening, and fighting for Alessia to be put to the front. He didn't have to worry. The nurse took one look at her face, saw the gore and vacant eyes, and took her immediately; those waiting for hours be damned.

Simon wanted to bounce while they put her on the bed but didn't have the heart to leave her alone. When the first nurse began trying to administer the I.V., she freaked out and started crying and screaming. After a few fruitless tries, the nurse told Alessia that they'd have to restrain her if she didn't stop. She cried and struggled harder. Simon went to her then and reached out to hold her hand; she grabbed it in a death grip.

With a calm, quiet voice, Simon told the nurse the bare basics of what had happened to Alessia. He made it clear that if restraints were put on her, he'd lose his job by punching the nurse out. With hard eyes, she relented. Because he was holding Alessia's hand and speaking calmly to her, it was easier for the nurse to find a vein and attach the I.V. When that was done, Simon mentioned that maybe the nurse should go and get a security guard.

Two minutes later, the same nurse came back into the room, escorted by two doctors, a P.A.B. and a security guard. While the doctors dealt with Alessia, Simon took the security guard aside, staying in Alessia's field of vision, and informed him that he should call the police.

He didn't know what the security guard had told the police on the phone, but they'd showed up less than fifteen minutes later. He gave them a quick run-down of what happened and then they asked him for his clothes.

They escorted up to his locker and made him change in front of them. It wasn't that big a deal. The finished bagging up his clothes as he did up the top button of his shirt. Then, they asked him if he wouldn't mind taking a trip down to the station to sort things out.

He said he wouldn't mind.

That was an hour and a half ago. He'd been visited twice by random beat cops since. One had taken his order for something to eat. He was surprised to find he wanted a cheeseburger and a coke. The other had dropped it off. Neither cops said anything to him, despite his insistence that he wanted to know what was going on.

Now, while checking himself out in the mirror for the umpteenth time, the door opened and two plainclothes cops came in. Detectives, he figured. Simon sat down and one took a seat opposite him at the boring metal table. The other stood off in the corner, leaning against the wall with his arms crossed.

The dick at the table reached into his suit jacket pocket and produced a notepad, flipped it open to a blank page, and rested a pen beside it.

"Hey, Simon," the seated dick started, "thanks for coming in. We appreciate it. We just have some follow up questions to your initial statement that you made at the hospital."

"No doubt," Simon said without much good humour in his voice.

"Yeah, no doubt," the leaning dick said. He was the taller of the two, and used his height as a standing advantage, trying to look grave and looming over those seated around the table. Simon couldn't help but hate him at first glance.

"So, why don't we go over your story once again, this time for fresh ears."

"I already told the two cops at the hospital what went down," Simon said, hating the defensiveness in his voice but not being able to help it.

"I know. I know," the seated dick said. "I just wanna make sure we dot all the 't's' and cross all our 'i's'." He spoke the last with a sideways smile, like he was saying, 'oops. I fucked up. Silly me.'

449

It was a set-up, Simon knew. They didn't quite believe his story, and wanted to catch him in a lie. He knew he shouldn't be mad. It was their job, after all, to figure out what had happened to Alessia, but that didn't help him from hating them all the same.

"Well, I found Alessia, the woman in the hospital, tied to a bed, way back in the catacombs of the hospital. I freed her. Some chick came outta nowhere and attacked us. I fought her as best I could, but she got the upper hand until Alessia smashed her head in with a brick. Then, I helped Alessia get out of there."

"Uh huh," the seated dick said, scribbling away on his pad. "And was she already missing a leg when you showed up?"

Simon looked across the table, dumbfounded. "Of fucking course she was," he said. "What, you think I chopped it off on the way outta that hellhole?"

"No need to raise your voice," the standing dick said. "We just wanna be sure."

Simon was astonished to find himself halfway out of his seat. He slumped back down and sighed, rubbing a hand over his face.

"Sure. Sure. No. Her leg was already missing when I found her."

"Okay," the seated dick said. "And what was this other woman doing there?"

450

"I don't know. She was just *there*. She came from an outer room and then tried to strangle me with--" he cut himself off. He didn't think adding the words *with a tentacle that came out of her mouth* would do him any good. They'd probably lock him up in The House That Renton Built. Better to let them discover that little factoid on their own.

"With what?" the seated dick probed.

"With her hands. What else you think she had? I thought she was gonna start punching my lights out when Alessia saved me."

"You're telling me that a one-legged girl was able to save *you*?" the standing dick asked.

Simon shot him daggers in a glance. He felt his pride shrivel up but knew it was stupid to argue. He wanted to get out of this mess clean. The less they knew, the better. While he felt terrible for Alessia, he didn't want The Doctor getting caught, because if *he* got caught, then Simon was hung too.

"Yes. That's exactly what I'm saying," he said levelly.

"What were you doing down there, Simon?" the seated dick asked. This was a question Simon had prepared for on his way down to the station.

"I was exploring."

"Come again?"

"I was exploring. I find the history of St. Agnes fascinating. There are a lot of old tunnels and shit that run underneath it. It's been a hobby of mine since I was able to gain access to them. For instance, there's a room in the catacombs that's filled with old toilets. Another is where they used to store the nuclear waste from back in the sixties, I guess."

"And how precisely *did* you gain access to them?" the seated dick asked without looking up. He was still scribbling away like a man possessed.

"Bribery."

Both men looked at him then. He knew this would be something they'd check out, and since he'd obtained the key through those exact means, he didn't mind telling them.

"I'm friends with a couple guys in security. A year or more ago, when I found out the hospital was gonna close, I asked one of the guys for a hookup. I gave him a nice bottle of Henny, and he cut me a key." Simon shrugged. "I felt it was a victimless crime."

"Which guy?"

"Rodgers," Simon replied promptly.

"We're gonna check that."

Simon waved a dismissive hand at them.

"And you just happened to be down there when someone was in need," the standing dick said. It wasn't a question.

"Sure," Simon replied. "I had a bit of time to kill between jobs and figured I'd take a wander. I didn't expect to find *what* I found, I'll tell you."

"And how did you even know to look in that particular room?" the standing dick asked.

"I heard noises."

"What kind of noises?" the seated dick asked, looking up from his notes.

"Noises."

"And you weren't scared? What if it had been a big rat or some homeless guy that had made camp there?"

"Then I wouldn't be talking to you two," Simon said. He could feel his anger beginning to boil up again and repressed it. "Look. I was wandering around and I heard what sounded like someone in pain beyond a door. I knocked a few times and nothing happened, except, the voice continued. I didn't know what it was, but I sure as shit wasn't gonna leave someone in that backwards assed maze to hell all by themselves. I smashed down the door and found Alessia. Then, we were attacked. That's about it."

"Okay, okay," the seated dick said. "Just a few more questions and then you can leave."

"No," Simon said at once.

"What do you mean, 'No'?" the standing dick asked.

"I mean, no. Fuck that. I got her outta there. I called yous. I've answered your questions. I ain't under arrest and I sure as shit didn't do anything wrong. Y'all have kept me here for something like two hours. I'm done. I'm going the fuck home. I want a shower and a beer. If you got anything else, come at me, but you better believe that I'm gonna get a lawyer next time. I played nice, and you're acting like *I'm* the one that did that shit to *her*."

Simon stood up and walked to the door. When neither dick made any move to stop him, he opened it and left.

2

"Think he's guilty?" the standing dick asked.

"Nope. Not of mutilating that woman, but he knows something."

"Yeah. How'd he say it? 'No doubt.' We'll have to watch him."

"Indeed."

Alessia

1

She spent the next few days in a drugged out stupor in the intensive care unit. She knew where she was, told by the first nurse who pricked her with an I.V. needle, and knew what they were trying to do, explained by the first doctor that saw her. Other than that, her first few days outside of captivity were a blur. She recognized and remembered the faces and situations that she was in, but all the details seemed to slip by her and enter the ether of the unknown consciousness. She knew that her parents had been there, that her mother had been crying almost non-stop while her father spent the majority of the time with his face in his hands. She knew that all the previous people she'd ever worked with in the hospital system had come to pay their respects to her; her drug loaded mind had made the connection that she might actually be *The* Godfather that the movie's made such a big deal about.

Her most vivid memory from that time came when she'd been picked up by a Porter, not Simon, and wheeled into the waiting area of the operating room. The doctors explained that she'd experienced some severe injuries, and that it was necessary for them to put her under and inspect the amputation site. The first time the anesthesiologist had leaned over her with the mask and skull cap on to tell her the business, she'd freaked. She began screaming in her broken, withered voice. It was the surgical outfit filling her vision that did it. She tried to explain, at least she thought she'd tried, but it never came out the way she wanted. It was an unintelligible scream that froze the anesthesiologist in her tracks. It was an unintelligible scream that froze everyone in the operating room. They all looked around, passing a 'What the fuck!?!" look between them. The original anesthesiologist tried to calm her down, but Alessia wasn't having any of it. She felt herself slipping down into the sleep of unconsciousness, for the drugs had already been added to the mixture entering her veins, and fought against it with every fiber of her being. She was still thrashing and spitting when a well-known nurse filled her vision, grabbed her hand, and spoke to her.

"Alessia. I'm here with you. I won't let anything bad happen."

It didn't stem all her fears, but it allowed her to calm down enough to let the drugs take over and pull her under.

`Her next few days were spent in recovery. Like before, it was a giant drug haze. People came to see her and spent their break time with her. She spoke to them as best she could, and when they persisted in trying to take care of her, she let them know as easily as possible that she was fine. Those that persisted in their happy hopefulness she gave attitude to. All except her parents; they were the one duo she could never shake. They stayed at her bedside from her inception to discharge. It weighed on her because every guest that came into her room her parents treated like it was their fault. Mostly however, she was grateful that they kept the other humans away. Mostly. It wasn't until they gave the business to Henne that she got mad.

He came in, a mural of worry spray painted on his face. He glanced at her parents, and the look softened. He shifted his glance to Alessia and they caught each other's eyes. She saw his face slacken into cookie dough and remarked upon the relief that was stencilled there. He looked at her and smiled. It was a short-lived moment, because as soon as they locked eyes, her mother was up and berating him like he'd had something to do with it.

"How dare you allow my daughter to come to this. She was under your charge!"

She saw Henne step back, getting into an immediate defensive posture before looking, and actually seeing, the old Italian woman berating him. His face and body softened, and he moved to embrace her. Her mother would have none of it.

"Don't you try that with me. It's your influence that has taken her further from God. From her *family*. You led her into this mess, and now you don't have the right to show up, all willy-nilly to try and get her right. We'll do it. Lord knows we always have. Just leave her alone!"

Alessia watched as her father tried to restrain her mother, surprised at the actions he took. It was a surreal experience that she couldn't quite equate to just the drugs. She watched as Henne took her parents off to the side and spoke to them. She saw the animated expressions of her mother and the calming, influencing motions of her father. Finally, it was settled. Henne left, while her parents stayed.

Her parents were still there when Simon came up to take her to an appointment, late in the evening.

The two of them hadn't seen each other since her admittance to Emerge. He came into the room, and both her parent's stiffened. They were expecting someone from the glad-handing parade of people. They couldn't have been more wrong.

"Hey," Simon said, standing in the doorway. He was silhouetted against the light from the hallway. Alessia felt a scare gurgle up in her chest, but then Simon took another step forward and she saw him for who he was. She relaxed, sinking into the single pillow afforded to her by the hospital. If Simon was here, all would be good, she thought.

"Hey," she said, looking up at the ceiling.

"You're scheduled for an appointment and then transfer. I'm gonna take you to both."

She raised her arm in defiance and Simon scoffed.

"Nah. Don't worry about it," he said easily. "I told them that I'm your chauffeur for the night. I'm on the clock for it. Don't worry."

She tried to say something, anything, but didn't trust her voice. Instead, she allowed Simon to help her to a stretcher and then wheel her down the hall; missing the aside he said to her parents.

She was brought down to the Doppler Ultrasound, where everyone was overly nice and professional. She was glad-handed through the ranks and into the machines before being glad-handed out. Before long, she found herself upon the stretcher she'd arrived on, with Simon on the front end while the elevator lifted them to the eighth floor.

The elevator dinged and Alessia felt a belt cinch around her midsection.

"Where are we going?" she breathed out.

"Oh. No one told you?" Simon asked. "They've got a room, no sorry, a suite, set up for you in The Women's Pavilion. No expense spared for you." He pushed her out of the elevator and onto the eighth floor.

"We got you. Don't worry," he added as he steered the stretcher down the hallway.

Alessia held it together until they made it to the top of the descent. She held it together when Simon angled her bed down. It was during the slow descent that her full memory came roaring back, everything from the last two weeks bleeding into her brain. She screamed then. She saw the hallway which led to the door coming closer, faster and faster, as they picked up speed upon the decline.

That was too much.

The screams startled Simon. Before he leaned over and placed a hand on her shoulder to whisper calming words into her ear he thought, *why do I always get the loud ones.*

Afterword

I'm glad you made it this far and I want to thank you for the support of my creative endeavour, and I hope you enjoyed our journey together.

I know what you're thinking, and you're not wrong. There were some character arcs that didn't seem to go anywhere, as well as some plot threads that never saw completion. Fear not. This is only book one in a two parter, (I kicked around the idea of a trilogy, but am confident that the story doesn't need a third installment; it would be bloated for nothing).

I've already started working on the sequel, so I promise you won't be waiting 10 plus years for the follow up.

Now that the business portion is out of the way, I wanna talk about the novel you've just completed.

I first got the idea for this novel when I was working at a now closed hospital in the Montreal area. It was old, full of odd architecture and hidden areas, and especially creepy at night. It got me thinking about what kind of ghosts and monsters roamed the hallways at 3am when all the patients are asleep and the staff is plunged into their paperwork.

And so, the idea bloomed for about a year where I allowed different scenarios to dance around my dome until I set pen to paper and got things under way. During the planning process, I elected to do a mash-up of two of my favourite horror novels; can you use your deductive powers to guess which ones before I spill the beans?

Done? Cool. It was obviously "Frankenstein" by Mary Shelley, and "The Shining" by Stephen King. I feel like I did a pretty good job, but I wrote the damn thing, so of course I'm going to say that. A great way to let me know your feelings about it would be to leave a review on whichever service you purchased it from. I don't mind if you give it a single star, or five. As long as you give me good feedback, I'll know what y'all are looking for when the sequel comes out.

Alas, that's it. If you enjoyed this novel, don't forget to check out my short story collection, "14 Needles: An Unsettling Collection."

Until next time, enjoy life and the arts!